Black Widows

Cate Quinn was a travel and lifestyle journalist for *The Times*, the *Guardian* and the *Daily Telegraph*, alongside many magazines. Prior to this, Quinn's background in historical research won her prestigious postgraduate funding from the British Arts Council.

Quinn is the author of the bestselling Thief Taker series. *Black Widows* is her first modern thriller.

🐦 @CathWritesStuff

Also by Cate Quinn

The Thief Taker
Fire Catcher
Dark Stars
The Changeling Murders
The Bastille Spy
The Scarlet Code

Black Widows

CATE QUINN

ORION

First published in Great Britain in 2021 by Orion Fiction,
an imprint of The Orion Publishing Group Ltd.,
Carmelite House, 50 Victoria Embankment
London EC4Y 0DZ

An Hachette UK Company

1 3 5 7 9 10 8 6 4 2

A CIP catalogue record for this book is
available from the British Library.

ISBN (Hardback) 978 1 4091 9695 2
ISBN (Trade Paperback) 978 1 4091 9696 9
ISBN (eBook) 978 1 4091 9698 3
ISBN (Export eBook) 978 1 3987 0353 7

Typeset by Input Data Services Ltd, Somerset

Printed and bound in Great Britain by Clays Ltd, Elcograf S.p.A.

www.orionbooks.co.uk

To Ben and Natalie

I

Rachel, first wife

Lord forgive me, I lied to a policeman today. I told him Blake had never raised a hand to me. I'd like to say I was protecting his memory, but that would be another lie. The truth is, I simply couldn't stand another judgment from an outsider about our way of life.

I was at the ranch when the officers came. I'd laid out my jars, neat and clean, and was filling them with cut salted potatoes. We had a big rain this year and more crop than average, so there was plenty to can.

The routine always did soothe me. It reminds me of being a little girl canning food for winter, my brothers and sisters all barefoot in the kitchen. I was humming a little tune, wiping the rims, screwing the lids. My pantry had grown steadily full, with brightly colored vegetables and corned beef. Never could get the meat to look pretty, but it sure tastes good.

I guess the Nelson ranch looks plain to city folk. It's an old smallholding of a few acres, which held a handful of cattle in the fifties. Blake fitted out the dilapidated farmhouse with a stove and basic plumbing five years back. Nothing out here for one hundred miles but the desert and some big old turkey-vultures. To me, it's a paradise on earth.

The weather was still warm for fall, so all the doors were wide open. I could already feel the beginning of change in the air. That sudden slip in heat that brings the storms and sends fat white clouds scudding into the deep desert sky. I'd closed my eyes, letting the sun beat down on my face through the little kitchen window. When I opened them again, a pack of police was standing at the farmhouse door.

'Mrs Nelson?'

I looked up, knife in hand. I must have looked quite the picture to those city officers, in a shapeless prairie dress with long wing-shouldered sleeves, buttoned neck to ankle, my blond hair plaited down my back. I wiped the white potato starch from the blade. Set it down.

'Which Mrs Nelson do you want, sir?' I looked at them each in turn.

A few of them were openly taking in the ranch. Outside is a little shambolic, with our decrepit outbuildings, dry-goods storehouse, and half-finished vegetable beds. Inside it's neat and cozy, with a good deal of home-crocheted items. There's a little couch, with two cushions I made myself, with 'Home is Where the Heart is,' and 'God is Love,' in big bright colors. Our kitchen is a basic worktop and sink. There's a shelf with a little gas stove for when we heat our food and some food-preserving equipment that Blake bought me for our second wedding anniversary.

To the back is the old hayloft, where we've put our beds. Two singles for two wives. A master, for Blake and whomever is favored that night.

One of the officers picked up a family portrait. A photograph taken shortly after Blake married Tina. The three of us stand behind our husband. Me, the oldest, my blond hair blow-dried for the occasion, pink lipstick, a flowery blouse that skims my broad hips. Emily, slender, looking even younger than her nineteen years, green eyes wide like a rabbit in the headlights, wispy pale hair curled for the photo. Then Tina, cat-that-got-the-cream smile. Straight black hair, tight dress showing cleavage, heavy makeup.

A police officer at the back pushed through at that point. A lady officer in tight pants. She had that kind of wholesome outdoorsy look some Salt Lake City gals get, if they're not the religious type and spend their weekends doing sports and what-not. Shiny brunette ponytail. Very striking light-brown eyes. Right away, I knew she wasn't in the Church.

'I'm Officer Brewer,' said the lady officer. She extended a tanned hand.

I shook it. She had a warm, firm grip.

'Are you telling us that there's more than one Mrs Nelson here?' she asked.

'Um. No, Ma'am.' For some reason, I glanced at the knife.

Brewer narrowed her eyes slightly, as if she'd caught me out in a lie.

'I mean,' I continued, 'the others aren't here right now.'

She cleared her throat.

'Are you Mrs Rachel Nelson, married to Blake Nelson?'

'Yes, Ma'am, six years Tuesday.' I smiled. 'It was our wedding anniversary yesterday, as a matter of fact.'

This seemed to wrong-foot her. She glanced at the wedding picture.

'You folk are Mormons?' she asked.

'We prefer the term Latter-day Saints,' I agreed tightly. 'May I ask what your business is here?'

'Mrs Nelson,' she said, taking a breath, 'I'm afraid we have some bad news, regarding your husband.'

It isn't the words but her tone that rushes up to meet me like a slap.

3

'Is he under arrest?' I feel my face grow hot.

She shakes her head. 'No.'

'Am I under arrest?'

'It's better if you sit down.'

2

Tina, sister-wife

I gotta hand it to her. The Wicked Witch of the West came into her own that morning. Rachel was the only one of us with the guts to go inside the morgue and identify him. You see that shit on the police shows. TV dramas. Relatives all cryin' and sayin', 'That's it, that's him.' You never see anyone sayin', 'I can't do it.'

The cops pulled me in, as I was about to get my first fix in a year and a half. Like a junkie homing pigeon, I'd found my way to Rio Grande, Salt Lake City's two-block drug district. Which is actually pretty funny, to someone like me from Vegas. Where I grew up, the whole damn *town* is dedicated to this shit. An' here everyone gets all uptight about a couple a roads with some hobos.

Anyways, when the cops took me in, I assumed they were bustin' us all for bigamy. So we get to the station. To one of the rooms they take you to before you're officially in trouble. Where they're being all nicey nice and nothing's on tape.

So here I am in this Salt Lake City police department, thinkin' not much has changed, apart from the charge. Which is some joke, right? In Vegas, I got busted for soliciting. Here they're bustin' me for being married.

Then this good-looking woman comes in. Tall, well put together. She got brown hair, in a plain ponytail, but very glossy, like her body can't help but tell everyone about her good health. Hardly any makeup, mountain-hiker suntan, sorta amber eyes. Golden, almost.

She reminded me of the tourist pictures Blake used to send me. Clean-living people in sportswear, advertising Utah's outdoor lifestyle – snowboard in winter, mountain bike in summer.

She introduces herself as Officer Brewer. I don't like women like her, as a rule. They think they understand what it's like to grow up poor, but they don't.

'You're Mrs Tina Nelson?'

I shake my head. 'I'm Tina Keidis.' I give her a mean glare, so she knows she can't fool me into sayin' I am Blake's wife, 'cause that's against the law. I lean back in my seat. 'You cops get these tables and plastic chairs wholesale?' I ask. 'They got the same ones in Vegas.'

I was making a point. I've been downtown a million times, so there's no sense tryin' to intimidate me.

'Miss Keidis,' a cop says. 'A body has been found out in the desert. We believe it to be your husband.'

That shuts me up.

That's when Brewer tells me what went down. How some soul-searching' city-type was driving out in the middle a nowhere, saw vultures circling near the river where Blake liked to fish. Then she explains about the body. How it could be suspicious. Despite how it appeared, Blake sustained injuries they're not certain he could have done to himself.

When she told me the details, I felt real sorry for the guy who found him.

'I hear the officers picked you up in Rio Grande,' Brewer added, 'You don't see many Mormons on that block. You get lost?'

I mumbled some shit about not knowing the city well. But they're not stupid. Most likely they've already pulled my inch-thick record from Nevada.

The truth? After the night of the wedding anniversary . . . I just cracked, I guess. Went downtown looking for trouble. Blake warned me it would be hard. Sharing him with other women. But I don't think he really thought it through. The other two, they were raised to it. Brought up godly, to this man-is-head-of-household stuff. To me it's new. I never even had a household. I was dragged up halfway between foster carers and my mom, if she was in town.

So I can ask Lord Jesus for strength and God for forgiveness, but every day at the ranch felt like someone was treading on my heart. I swear I could actually *feel* it, this bruised, pulpy mess in my chest.

Rachel told me it gets easier, but I don't believe she ever had that kind of love in the first place. Her and Blake were college sweethearts. Two wholesome Mormon kids, doing the right thing. She likes to do what's expected of her. And to win. She hides that part. But Mrs Mormon bed-corners has a competitive streak a mile wide.

That's why she allowed her husband to take more wives, I guess. It wasn't enough for her to be a good Mormon. She had to be the best.

So Rachel doesn't understand how it was, for me and Blakey. How he used to look out for me, in the rehab center. Try and save my soul. We'd joke about it, in actual fact. I'd tease him. What's a handsome young guy doing with a load of meth heads? That kinda thing. He told me he'd never completed his mission and wanted to make amends by volunteering at rehab centers. I ripped him on that too, how us recovering addicts were low-rent converts, so desperate for a new life we'd believe anything. He laughed at that, and said I wasn't all wrong. We laughed a lot, me and him.

The plain truth is, Blake saved me, in every sense. And that first time we danced, at that lame rehab Christmas party, my head against his warm chest, Blake had whispered into my ear that he never felt about anyone the way he felt about me.

I cling to that, in the darker times, when I'm sleeping alone, and Blake is with another wife.

Truth is, the worst time is at sunset, when Rachel starts preparing one of her God-awful Mormon canned dinners. The atmosphere sorta . . . smolders. I swear that double bed has an electric current. You see Rachel, looking everywhere but the hayloft. Emily would go even more quiet than usual. Me, I'd get antsy. Twitchy. Say mean things. Same as when I was high all the time and couldn't get my fix.

Sunset was always when we wives had our worst fights. The gardening and the cleaning and the other chores had been done. There wasn't much lighting in the ranch, no TV besides a little portable that Emily swore blind she never watched but somehow ran down the batteries on daily. Blake liked us to read the Bible together, but he wasn't always home. So I suppose we should have all seen it coming. The anniversary.

Blake had picked me three nights in a row. Things were simmering. I have this image, of us three wives, sittin' on the couch, waiting to see who would be asked. Rachel, with this weird Mona Lisa smile, tryin' to seem like she didn't care. Me doin' that thing I learned on the streets, where you make it look like you're thinkin' of somethin' real dirty. Wispy little Emily, terrified.

Funny, now I think of it, the more frightened Emily seemed, the more often she got chose.

3

Emily, sister-wife

He's dead, he's dead, he's dead, he's dead.

You know that thing people say? You don't know whether to laugh or cry? That's how I feel, sitting in the back of the police car, watching the desert road bump along.

'How do you ladies get back home after a shopping trip?' asks the policeman driving the car. 'We could barely find the place, even with the satellite picture.'

I shrug rather than answer. I'm more interested in staring out the window.

The ranch was supposed to be a place we could all feel safe. Be ourselves. On account of the Utah law against adultery.

'One husband, three wives, right?' tries the male officer. 'You were the youngest?'

I don't say much, so they stop eventually. I figure they would have already seen the wedding pictures in any case. The first shows Rachel with her blond hair flicked out at the bottom, arm in arm with Blake like she's won a prize. She was skinnier then, but not by much. Then Blake a few years later, his red hair a few shades darker, grinning down at me, like he knew something I didn't. Rachel hovering behind us with a possessive hand on the cream jacket Blake wore to all three of his weddings. Then the last picture, of all three of us. Tina, face made-up like she's ready to shoot for *Playboy*. Rachel with this weird dead look in her eyes. I look relieved.

On the drive back to the city, the police have been asking me all kinds of questions about Blake. About his sales job for the canning machine company. Why he's on the road so much.

The lady officer found me wandering, a mile or so from the ranch. I think I hoped to have some kind of revelation, like Jerome in the wilds of Syria. But I didn't get too far. My legs got tired.

It grows on you, the desert. I hated it at first. All those yawning miles of nothing. Having to bathe using a cup and a bucket of water. Measuring out all your heat and lights so you don't blow the generator.

After our wedding, Blake drove me out of Salt Lake City and over to the ranch. I felt as though more and more little pieces of me were falling away with every mile we rode deeper into desert.

Coming from the city, it was unbelievable to find all this land out here, just *empty*.

'There's nothing here at all,' I told Blake. 'It's deserted.'

He winked at me. 'Guess that's why they call it the desert, huh?'

I folded my arms and pressed my face to the window, watching the yellow and tan landscape flash by. If you watched it for long enough it made your eyes go funny. Everything got pixelated like on an old computer game. Nothing for your eyes to grab a hold of. Just the same huge mountains, layered rock like pumpkin pie, yellow-orange sand and fluffy tufts of pale green grass flying by, zoom, zoom, zoom.

'You can be your own person out here,' Blake told me. 'No laws to bother you. Nothing but mountain, sand and sky for a hundred miles in each direction.'

I think what he really meant was I could be *his* own person.

What made the journey worse was Blake was so proud, like he'd built it himself. Kept pointing out the lumpy red rocks, mountains, the circling birds of prey. I swear, if the car door had been unlocked I would have popped the door and run all the way back to Salt Lake City.

One of the first things I did when we arrived at the ranch was go touch one of those little poufs of grass. I figured it would be soft, like a little cushion, but it wasn't. The blades spiked my fingers.

Blake told me there was no cell-phone reception and the landline was restricted use, since it was expensive. If I wanted to make a call, he'd drive me to a nearby town called Tucknott. Or I could give him a letter to mail. Rachel sent a lot of letters, apparently, to brothers and sisters scattered all over.

'Rachel doesn't see her family,' he told me. 'But it's a great comfort to her, to write.'

I never thought to ask why Rachel didn't see her relations. Guess it was sinking in, I had no one to write to. No one to call. I'd made my bed. Now I had to lie in it. I only found out later, Rachel had been lying about who she was.

In fact, I did try to telephone my mother soon after I got married, but as soon as she heard my voice, she hung up. It was right after the wedding night. I still shudder at that. Don't laugh, OK? But at the age of nineteen I didn't know. Swear to God and hope to die. I had no idea what husbands and wives did together in bedrooms. It was quite a shock when I found out, yes siree.

But you know the second hardest thing about being wifey number two? You'll find it funny, when I tell you.

Matter of fact, the biggest adjustment was the food. Lordy, Lordy, that woman is a bad cook. I wasn't raised on Mormon cuisine. I grew up in the part of town where immigrant families live. We ate pasta and meatballs.

My first night in the ranch, Rachel served mystery can soup for starters, some mashed potato from a packet with bone-dry meat for main and a kind of green Jell-O and cream construction for afters. Jesus on high, what a mess.

It was only at the end of the meal when Blake muttered something about it being a fine feast, and he was proud she'd gone to the effort, I realized. This was her idea of a banquet.

The police car corners onto the freeway, headed to Salt Lake City. I draw a breath to see it. The green road signs, the giant mountains in the background, not flat-topped and shades of brown like the desert ones, but gray and peaked. In the winter, the city mountains are frosted white with snow, but my favorite time is the spring thaw when the dark parts show through. It looks exactly like someone tipped a pitcher of milk over the top.

I watch as pale, square-windowed buildings rise up, thicker and more crowded together as we reach the middle of the city.

There's a sports field with a neat red-and-white sign proclaiming: No Sunday Play.

We drive through a back street, near where I grew up. I catch a glimpse of Caputo's Italian deli downtown where my momma would sometimes buy cheese and tomato sauce from jumbled-up shelves of bright labels.

'You OK, Mrs Nelson?'

I notice I'm touching my fingers to the glass. Slowly I curl back my fist.

'I'm fine,' I say. 'I was raised here, is all.'

It occurs to me I would have been too nervous to eat on my wedding night, even if Rachel had been a good cook. The look she gave me, when I came home, I honestly thought she was going to kill me right there, on the beige vinyl floor, my blood soaking into her awful homespun knotty rug.

It was like she'd only just figured out what Blake and I would be doing in the bedroom.

A flashing blade of realization slices suddenly through all the other thoughts.

I will never have to do that again.

There's a strange noise and at first I think there's some animal sound coming from the police radio. A goat or a piglet. And then I realize, it's me. I'm laughing.

He's dead, he's dead, he's dead, he's dead.

4

Rachel, first wife

Tina tried to come with me to see him in the morgue, God forgive her. She really did. But she nearly passed out when we started down that dark corridor with its stench of chemicals. It wouldn't have been right to put her through it. Tina has had a tough enough life as it is.

So it fell to me. The hard stuff always does.

I'd managed to grab some regular clothes before they drove me to the station. T-shirt and jeans, a little snug around the waist nowadays, if I'm honest. I unplaited my hair, let it fall down my back. I saw them puzzling over me, the way people do. With loose hair, you can see the blond highlights, home-dyed but nicer than the kitchen-sink hairdresser a lot of Church moms resort to.

Officer Brewer stops at a small room.

'We'll take a break here,' she says. 'I'll explain what you can expect, going inside the morgue.'

She pauses, and I know what she's thinking. I still haven't asked how Blake died. The old fear of police has kicked in. I was raised never to talk to authorities. And I mean, *never.*

I swallow and take a seat. It's a hard-walled little room, not unlike the one I grew up in. There's a fake-leather couch, like someone has tried to make it look comfortable. The lighting is harsh.

'That's a nasty set of bruises you have there.' Brewer is looking at my forearm. Five dark marks.

I pull down my sleeve.

'You're college-educated?' asks Brewer.

I'm wondering how she knows that. Then I realize I'm wearing my old Brigham Young University shirt. The brand is along the arm.

'Yes, Ma'am.' My eyes keep glancing up to the door.

'You don't see a great number of graduates in polygamous marriages,' she observes.

Makes sense, I guess. They found me in a prairie dress, barefoot on the ranch with no running water. They probably think I'm one of those cult victims.

'Maybe the smart ones stay away from the police,' I say.

My voice comes out small and cold. I'm struck by how much like my mother I sound. That blank-faced woman, raising children in a cellar. I remember thinking the same thing, the first time Blake brought Emily home. We'd talked, she'd seemed so shy and humble. I'd thought I could help her. Bring her out of herself and into God's love. I had imagined us all friends together. The bedroom aspect, I had decided, would be gracefully undiscussed. River water, flowing prettily around a rock.

Then Blake and Emily came back from their wedding. I hadn't prepared myself for how he would look at her. God forgive me, I'd cooked a feast for my new sister, made her bed, put fresh flowers in her room. I'd planned to stand, hug her warmly, tell her how welcome she was, how loved I meant to make her. Then I saw Blake's eyes. Wolf eyes. And my mind froze on a single thought.

He never looked at me like that.

The husband I thought I knew so well had changed into a predator. A slavering animal thing. My embrace turned stilted, the kind words ashes in my mouth. And Emily, the second wife I'd invited into our home, had looked actively frightened at whatever she saw in my face.

I realize Officer Brewer is talking.

'Identification is a formality,' she says quietly. 'His body will be covered. I will draw back the sheet enough to see his face. Just nod when you've seen enough, and it will then be replaced.'

I want to laugh. It doesn't seem real.

'A quick look at the face is all we need. We've already made a positive ID based on the contents of Mr Nelson's wallet. Given the circumstances, if you're unable to identify him, we'll use a DNA match.'

'The circumstances?'

'Mrs Nelson, you need to be prepared for what you're about to see. I'm afraid your husband . . . There's been some damage. To the body.'

Tears well up. My Blake. So gentle and so good.

'We think your husband's death may have been suicide,' she continues, gently. 'But we're not ruling out other possibilities.'

It's like the floor beneath me has vanished, and I'm tumbling into the void. I'm seized with a sudden, animal urge to slap her face.

'My husband is a member of the Church,' I say.

Her expression doesn't change.

'Taking the life God gave you is a sin,' I add, pointedly, wondering how stupid she can be.

Brewer nods calmly.

'You don't believe he would have committed suicide?' she confirms.

I speak very clearly. 'I've never been more certain of anything in my life.'

'Would there be any reason for someone to harm Mr Nelson?'

For a full five seconds this doesn't make any sense. Then I understand.

'You think my husband could have been murdered?' My voice comes out all throaty. Like the words can't get past the grief. 'Everybody loved Blake. Who would want to hurt him?'

Brewer exchanges glances with her officers. And even as I say the words, I know they're not exactly true. Everybody loved Blake. Except his wives.

Sometimes, we hated him.

5

Rachel, first wife

'Please be prepared, Mrs Nelson. I'm afraid it isn't a pretty sight. You're certain you don't want someone with you? A relative . . .'

'Better we get it over with,' I say, and I mutter a little prayer under my breath, asking for strength. I don't scare easily, seeing the things I've seen. Though there's a first time for everything, I suppose.

'The way he died,' continues Brewer, 'has an effect on the facial features. There's some coloration, distortion. You might find the remains really look nothing like the person you remember.'

Remains. I guess police have to use language like that. Distance themselves.

I'm moving like a sleepwalker, one foot in front of the other.

You'd think I'd be reluctant. But it's actually the opposite. I'm mad to see him. It's the strangest thing. The feeling is so strong, it's almost reminiscent of our college days, when I would hope to bump into him in the corridor. That first year as a student, I get a tingle on my skin just thinking about it.

Brigham Young University was my first real encounter with the outside world – the place we'd all been warned against, growing up on the Homestead.

It was the first time I had ever seen a property more than two stories high, or technology beyond farm equipment.

These were things whispered of, or glimpsed in the contraband magazines my sisters used to smuggle home. Buildings crisp with glass. Wide paved sidewalks set with pretty flower beds.

More striking than my modern surroundings, though, was the fact I was alone. The way I was raised, we girls were never outdoors unaccompanied, not for a second.

Yet there I was, walking around, wherever I pleased, probably with my mouth open. There were beautiful snow-capped mountains in the middle distance, like a grounding force. I honestly felt, if it hadn't been for those mountains, I might have floated away.

It took me a full ten minutes to go through the sliding doors of the main building. I thought there might be a trick to making them glide apart and spent a good deal of time watching the other students as they strode confidently in and out. Eventually I snuck in, close as I dared to a girl in a long dress, and sort of folded myself amongst the beehive of students running back and forth to class.

In the wide vestibule, there were machines that vended drinks when you put coins in. I'd seen these at the police station, after the Homestead was raided, and had been told such things were evil. Devices to take your money.

Summoning my courage, I decided to take a step toward independence, and buy myself a soda.

Salt Lake City State, as part of my rehabilitation into the community, had given me a new outfit from the local thrift store, and thirty dollars, in box-fresh bills. I had them in my faux-leather purse, alongside the state sponsor papers which I carried like an amulet. As if someone might retract my scholarship at any point if I couldn't produce them on demand.

I reached inside and took out a newly minted five and approached the backlit image of a Diet Coke, with all little buttons by it. I wasn't sure what to do next. I was pretty sure the vending machine would decide what beverage I needed. That had been my experience of life so far.

Nothing happened.

Then I heard a voice.

'Not sure what soda ya want?' It was a pleasant, low voice, slightly concerned. As though my choice of what to drink that day really mattered.

'I never used one of these machines before,' I admitted, twirling hair around my finger, in a way Blake would later tell me was the reason he asked me out on our first date.

That first time I saw him, I can't say it was thunderbolts from the sky. He had nice eyes. A very deep blue, and long lashes, unusual in a man. Girlish almost. His hair was true strawberry blond. It got a little rustier with age. He had freckles too. The kind you get when your skin is too fair to be in the sun much but you've been raised outdoors.

'Oh, you're from the farm, too, huh?' He moved closer, and I could smell his laundry-fresh clothes. At first I assumed he knew about my awful past and crashing shame hit me. 'Yeah, lot of us grew up in the country and such.' He smiled then, and I saw he had dimples, in his sun-freckled face. 'You're used to the ones that only take coins. Lemme help ya there.' He moved me out of the way, and frowned at the machine. Then he looked at me. 'I think you look like a cream soda girl,' he decided.

Then he took a dollar note out of his pocket and slid it into the slot.

His self-confidence took my breath away. I felt my heart flutter as he reached down and extracted the cold can. He pressed it into my hand. It was icy, but I didn't feel it.

'Thanks,' I said.

He gave a little bow of his head and put out his hand.

'My pleasure. My name is Blake.'

'I'm Rachel.' It was the first time I'd used my new name, to introduce myself to a stranger. I liked the way it sounded.

'Well, Rachel, hope I'll be seein' ya around.' He winked. Then he was gone.

I peeled up the ringpull and drank a little. He was right, I thought. I was a cream soda girl.

Back then, I wondered if I would ever see him again.

I never thought I'd be seeing him laid out in a morgue, under a blue sheet.

'Take your time, Mrs Nelson,' says Brewer. 'Just let us know when you're ready.'

I feel a lump swell into my throat and stay there. The hump of blue-green fabric is in front of me now, with all its telltale undulations.

Oh God, oh God, oh God, oh God, oh God, oh God, oh God.

I don't want to do it. I wonder if I can change my mind. If someone else can look for me.

Then I remember Tina and Emily. I have to do this for them. Neither have the state of mind to cope. A bitterness bubbles up.

I had the right husband, and the wrong wives.

If only different people had come into the marriage. People more like me. We could have got along. Shared things.

Tina and I are so unalike. She will tell anyone anything. The way I was raised, that isn't right. You don't walk around with everything hanging out. Private things are private.

And Emily, oh my heck. Well she just straight *lies*. When I first met her in the diner where she worked, I thought Emily was just model-gorgeous. Like someone out of a movie or something, with those huge aquamarine eyes, and wispy blond hair. The glamor fades pretty fast once you get to know her. Now I think of Emily as a funny-looking kid.

I take a breath to steady myself for whatever I'm about to see and wrinkle my nose up, trying to stop the tears. Then I give a quick sharp nod.

'Sure you're ready?' Officer Brewer has a hand on the sheet, her eyes are on mine, concerned.

'Yes.' It comes out mousy, quiet.

She meets my eye, and I realize she is a kind woman. I think, if she were allowed, she'd hold my hand.

'OK.' She nods. 'I'll pull it back. Just give me the nod when you're done, and I'll cover him straight up again.'

The tears make everything blurry. But as she pulls back the sheet, the sight of him hits me like a ten-ton truck.

I lurch back, one hand on the metal gurney to steady myself. My body does an odd thing, folding at the hip. I'm gasping. My eyes seek out the body again, lying inches from where my fingers are gripped white. I yank my hand back on reflex.

'Mrs Nelson,' Brewer is saying. 'Mrs Nelson. Do you need to take a break?'

'What have you done to him?' I whisper. 'What have you done to my Blake? Where are his holy garments?'

6

Tina, sister–wife

The police station has a coffee machine that serves Postum, which is like this gross coffee substitute that Mormons favor. I never could get to like it, but Rachel drinks the stuff like it's goin' outta fashion.

One of the police officers pushes a button and fills his cup with dirt-colored froth as we wait for Rachel. He doesn't offer me a drink.

'So you cohabit?' confirms the officer, stirring his shitty coffee. 'With two other women, acting as wives to Blake Nelson?'

He's looking me up and down. My straight black hair is a little frayed at the ends, since I'm growing it long, as part of my religion. I still got a hot bod, even after all the drugs. Just lucky, I guess. My mom was the same. She kept an itty-bitty waist and C-cup chest into her forties. Her face got saggy, but big brown eyes and good cheekbones can ride out a lotta punishment. We got Indian blood, that was what she always said. 'Longside a lotta other blood, since my dad was a no-good drifter from across the border. But in any case, folk with Indian blood age real nicely.

In Vegas, looks don't get noticed the same as here. Half the casino girls would make your jaw drop. So I can see the Salt Lake City cop sorta checking me out, cogs turning like – *Did he get to have sex with them all at the same time?*

Rachel told me husband-and-wife relations is the obsession non-fundamental types have with polygamy. Like they're bent out of shape on how the bedroom stuff works. She didn't say that, of course. She said a long word like pru-rient. I used to think she did that on purpose to prove she was college-educated when Emily and I weren't. But now I think maybe not. Rachel is real smart, but not so smart when it comes to people, if you see what I mean. You'd think growin' up in a big family would make Rachel an open kinda gal. But in actual fact she is the complete opposite. I don't even know if Rachel knows what she's really feelin' half the time, so good luck gettin' her to tell ya.

That's why it's been so difficult between her and us sister-wives – Rachel thinks of herself as this hoity-toity private person. Which is why, I guess, she flipped so bad when Emily started delving into her secrets.

I twirl a strand of dark hair around my finger.

'You wonderin' what we get up to in the bedroom, officer?' I ask, innocently, batting my lashes at him. He flushes, because of course he is – I can always tell when men are thinkin' 'bout that stuff – but he can't admit it, being a nice Mormon an' all.

A flash of anger shows on his face.

'You know, people like you give Latter-day Saints a bad name,' he says. 'The LDS Church doesn't recognize sister-wives.'

'They will be your sisters.' I remember Blake sayin' that. Thinkin' how good it sounded. Because, really, what I miss the most from turnin' tricks in Vegas is the other girls. For all the shitty lows, we all looked out for each other. I saved a life more than once. That's sisterhood. Not sittin' round sewin' together. Waitin' for the Wicked Witch of the West to make some snipe atcha, 'cause you happen to like wearin' pink lipstick. Joke's on her though, right? Who did he take to bed most nights? Well, that would be me.

'Plural marriage has been illegal in our Church since 1904,' continues the cop. 'A true Mormon doesn't break the law.'

'Really? I never heard that before.' I realize I've lurched straight back to my former self. It feels good, actually. Least I know how to behave in a police station.

The officer's face reddens.

'How are we expected to bring more souls into the Church,' he demands, 'when folks like you make us look like inbred hillbillies?'

'Ah, well,' I say, 'baptisms count as souls you've saved, right? More wives mean more conversions to the faith, ain't that right?'

'I've got four children and they're raised to respect the law.'

'Good for them.' I lean back, wishing I had a cigarette. I gave up, right before Blake and I were married, since Mormons don't partake in caffeine, tobacco or alcohol. 'Blake and I weren't legally wed, officer. We had a ceremony in the Mormon Temple, downtown. You know the one? That great big white building with the pointy spires? You can't miss it.'

I'm being snarky here, because the Temple more or less *is* Salt Lake City. The town was built around it when Brigham Young decided to build a church here back in eighteen hundred-an-somethin'. It's a colossal whiter-than-white castle thing that you can see from anyplace in the city, and the ten-acre plot is so large, the whole area, all the streets and squares, are named Temple East and Temple West, and so forth.

First time I saw it, I couldn't believe they were gonna let me inside. It reminded me of the palace in *Cinderella*.

'There's no law against holding a spiritual ceremony,' I say. 'It doesn't make a legal marriage recognized by the state. Only a spiritual one. Cut my throat and hope to die,' I add, with a wink, knowing he's done all the weird rituals himself.

Of course, he's a born-in, dyed-in-the-wool Latter-day Saint.

So he'll have gone to Temple all set to absorb whatever they have to tell him.

Me, I'll be straight, it was hard not to laugh for some of it. Blake had already gifted me with my holy underwear. Garments, we call them. A very, very unsexy white long-john type thing, ending mid-thigh and mid-upper arm. When he explained I had to wear it always, to protect me from evil, I considered backing out right there and then. Maybe I shoulda, 'cause the Temple was a whole other level. Pretending to gut ourselves with imaginary knives. Holding hands through a sheet. Like somethin' you might play with your best friend in kindergarten. *Make friends, make friends, never never break friends.* That kind of thing.

What made it even harder was Blake took it so seriously. At one point, I thought I was going to straight out start laughing. The only thing that got me through was knowing I'd get out and into the arms of my new husband.

The police officer is glaring at me now. I can tell I've got to him.

Good. I allow myself a mean moment.

Born-into-Mormons like him hate that people like me are allowed into their club, that we know their secrets.

'You got an answer for everythin', doncha?' he spits back. 'Better hope you got an answer for God, when the time comes.'

'More of a question, actually. I'll ask him what the fuck he's doin' with my husband.'

7

Rachel, first wife

Blake's dreadful, puffed-up face seems to float on its metal trolley. Brewer was right. It doesn't look like him. It doesn't look like anyone. His head and shoulders peek above the blue-green sheet. The chemical smell of the mortuary is getting to me.

'He isn't wearing his garments,' I say, looking accusingly at the mortician. 'Where are Blake's garments?' I'm trying to keep calm, but something in my tone causes both of them to flinch.

'We have to unclothe the bodies,' explains Officer Brewer. 'It's part of the process . . .'

'I'm not talking about his *clothes*,' I say, and hear my voice come out at volume.

I'm searching for how to explain, when, to my relief, the mortician intercedes.

'Latter-day Saints wear sacred garments, given them in the Temple,' he explains to Brewer. 'They're not supposed to take them off.'

He shoots me a little sympathetic glance. I can tell he's part of the Church, 'cause he says Latter-day Saints, rather than Mormons. Some folk get sniffy about that term – it's more often used by those of us who believe in plural marriage, some of the others like to distance themselves.

'I've lived in Utah for ten years,' snaps Brewer, 'I'm well aware of religious underwear, thank you, Mr Docherty.' I'm surprised to see her annoyance. In my world, women almost never show anger. I find myself looking at her with a little awe, like she's an exotic animal.

She turns back to me.

'Mrs Nelson, I understand this is very difficult for you. I'm afraid our protocol is to undress the bodies that come to us. That includes Temple-wear. As you might imagine, in Salt Lake City, this is not the first body to arrive in our morgue wearing holy garments. I appreciate they have great significance and meaning to you, but we have to do our job. We remove all clothing, so we might better ascertain cause of death.'

'You took his garments *off*?' I realize my fists are clenched. I have an awful image of the mortician's pale hands yanking at Blake's ordained things.

Disrespectful. The word hisses like a snake in my brain.

Stay sweet, Rachel, I remind myself. *Stay sweet.*

I'm suddenly reeling. This means Blake's body is exposed beneath this sheet. Vulnerable to dark forces.

Blake was endowed in his garments aged eighteen, shortly before his mission – a staple of pre-college Mormon boys. A two-year trip abroad to save souls. Girls get their garments when they marry.

A lot of the women I grew up with never took their garments off, and I mean not ever. When they came to bathe – they'd do it one limb at a time, dangling over a bathtub, and clean their other parts very carefully with a washcloth. I grew up with tales of how garments could repel fire and stop bullets.

Mine were bought six years ago from Beehive clothing, a strangely washed-out-looking store to the west of town, where Blake assured me I'd get the best price. I remember crying right before I was endowed. When I saw the huddles of family members in Temple, waiting for their relatives, a sickening lone-liness struck. I guess I hadn't truly realized how much I missed my own people until that moment.

'It's not good to cry here,' I remember Blake advising, in an earnest, hissed whisper. 'It looks like you're not committed. Cry after.'

Through everything that happened next – the touching of my naked places by kindly women, the miming of cutting my own throat, should I reveal the Temple secrets – through all of it, I was stunned into numbness by my husband-to-be's remark. Did he think I was stage-crying to appear girlish in front of his folks? The Blake who'd courted me seemed suddenly lost. In the sea of rituals, I had never felt so alone. When my thick nylon underwear was finally awarded me, I pulled it on gratefully, ar-moring myself.

And now here I am in an opposite world, in a dark cold room, where garments are removed, not given. Where souls are not sealed but lost.

'We have all your husband's belongings safe,' the mortician assures me. He points to a pile of clear plastic bags on a nearby gurney. Some contain clothes, neatly folded. Others are dirtied and messy, as though they've been dragged from a muddy river.

I feel my mouth fill with bile.

I recognize Blake's yellowed crop-sleeve vest-top. No matter what detergent I used, I never could get the fade of nylon out. The LDS Church is a little unclear on buying new garments. It's generally accepted to keep a set as long as you can, but Blake was frugal about such things. Neither he, nor any of us wives, had ever received new garments. Mine are six years old and fraying at the edges.

I have a sudden, humiliating flash of how this must all look to non-Church members. The saggy underwear we wear as holy.

'I appreciate this might seem strange to you,' I say, keeping my voice steady. 'But an important part of our faith is to keep them by our skin at all times. May I have them please? I need to arrange it so he can be buried in them. I feel . . . extremely uncomfortable that you have touched them. No one but his wives should even *see* them,' I add, struggling with the tight knot of feelings in my chest.

My eyes draw back to his face again. I can't help it.

'Why does he look like that?' I ask quietly.

'It happens to victims of strangulation,' says Brewer, matching my tone. 'Pressure builds in the face.'

I look down to his neck, where a livid red mark runs around the top and bottom circumference, like two train tracks. At the back of his head is a lump of black congealed blood matted in his red hair. I can tell Brewer is waiting for me to ask more about how he died, and when I don't, she seems wrong-footed, like I'm not behaving naturally.

'Mrs Nelson . . .' says Brewer, '. . . to be clear. Can you identify Blake Nelson at this time?'

This often happens to me. It's like emotions bob around, waiting to be recognized, then spring on me, when I least expect it.

'Yes,' I say. 'This is my husband.'

I start to cry.

8

Rachel, first wife

The police interview room has the same smell they all have. Old coffee and strong cleaning products. I feel like all the smells are mixing inside of me. The morgue we came from. The scuffed interior of this unloved space. My eyes glide up to the rattling old air conditioner. A fat piece of parcel tape has been used to fix a crack, but part has unstuck and trembles in the breeze from the unit like an accusing finger.

'Mrs Nelson,' says Officer Brewer. 'We appreciate your answering a few questions for us. You are here of your own free will and not under arrest. However, state law requires me to inform you that you are entitled to a lawyer at this time. This could be someone chosen by you, or a state-appointed lawyer could be found.'

'Mormons don't need lawyers,' I say. 'We've got God as our witness.'

She frowns slightly at this.

'Sorry,' I say, 'I joke when I'm nervous.'

'Oh,' she frowns deeper. 'There's nothing to be nervous about, Mrs Nelson. Just routine after a fatality. So we can dismiss you from our inquiries.'

She looks up. Flashes me a smile that doesn't reach her eyes, then opens a file. On top are a bunch of exterior images of our ranch. Sandy dirt. Ramshackle outbuildings.

I'm hit with an awful memory, of the last time I was in a police station.

'You OK, Mrs Nelson?'

I nod, my heart thumping.

'Only you look a little pale. Can I get you something? Water?'

I shake my head.

'You sure you alright to answer my questions?'

'Yes.'

'Good.' She smiles again. This time it's tinged with sympathy which looks real.

I look back to the police pictures of the ranch, which even to my eyes looks a little backwoods, with Blake's broken machinery projects and such strewn around.

'I gotta tell you,' says Brewer. 'In all my years of police work, I thought I'd seen every kind of domicile. Utah always throws up something different.' She does a kind of eyebrows raised head shake. 'Your place was a disused farm?'

'It was a ranch. A cattle ranch.'

'But you didn't use it for that, I mean to say,' she flips through a few pictures. 'Cattle ranches don't generally come with . . . what is that? An old lifeguard tower?'

'Blake thought we might need a lookout post,' I explain. 'End of Days comes, and you want to be sure anyone approaching is friendly.'

She gives me a long look. 'Right.'

'Just you four out there?' she confirms. 'No kids?'

There's a pause.

'Not yet!' It's such an ingrained response, I say it unthinkingly, and it comes out louder than I mean.

Brewer's amber eyes sweep my face in puzzlement and I realize how peculiar I've made myself sound, using a future phrase after what's just happened.

Brewer turns over more pictures. 'This small wooden house thing here would be . . . where you all live and sleep. With an outhouse a little behind it.'

I nod.

'Cozy. And this?' her finger tracks across to a rusted old cattle barn of corrugated steel.

'Blake used to keep a lot of things there. We weren't really allowed inside.'

'Then I guess we should consider ourselves privileged,' she deadpans, raising a picture showing a dark interior. Messy junk Blake used to collect for his projects. Wheels and machinery parts from scrapyards. 'Man cave, huh?' she suggests.

'That's about the size of it.'

'Then . . . we've got this funny-looking barn, maybe fifty feet from the house. This is where you can your food, right?' She holds up more pictures. Neat floor-to-ceiling shelves of pickles and preserves in rainbow colors. The Survive Well 5000 canning machine is sitting squat, like it's landed from outer space. 'This isn't a professional food-storing operation, right?' she confirms. 'It's just for domestic purposes?'

I nod.

She whistles. 'Well, you sure were prepared,' she says finally, returning the pictures to the file. 'So . . .' Brewer does that not-quite smile again. 'You say your husband went out fishing yesterday?'

'That's correct.' My mouth feels dry. I swallow. 'He fished every Friday.'

'But this time he didn't come back. That didn't concern you?'

'Um. Well, he would sometimes be out late. That was when he made his biggest catches. If he didn't get anything during the day.'

'So it was usual for him to stay out all night?'

'Not all night. But after dark, maybe. He'd come home after we were all asleep.'

Something passes across her face and is gone.

'And this fishing spot,' she continues. 'That's what . . . a five-minute walk from the house?' She shuffles pictures and selects the wooden farm building. 'This place?'

'About five minutes from there, yes.'

I picture the low-lying land where the river widens, the olive-hued water cutting through dusty dirt, and wiry daubs of shrub. Opposite our bank is a wall of tan rock, weathered to a sheer vertical slab, and seeping with rivulets of moisture, like whey squeezing from curds.

Near the bank is a juniper tree, all gnarled up like an old lady's hand. Folk don't tend to appreciate junipers, on account of them being so ugly and stark, but I've always liked them. They can grow in the thinnest soil, under blazing sun, or a cap of snow, and they're much stronger than they look.

'You wives ever go down to that part of the river?' asks Brewer.

'Not often. Once a year, Blake would baptize Tina and me in the water.'

'Not Emily?' She says it a little too fast.

'She can't swim. The current frightens her, so she would be baptized on the shore.'

Brewer does that little eyebrow lift and drop again.

'So, talk me through this,' says Brewer. 'Your husband goes out. Doesn't come home. Had there been any cross words?'

'We had a fight,' I admit. My chest pulls in on itself at the memory, making my breath tight. 'But we'd resolved it.'

'Mind my asking you what that fight was about, Mrs Nelson?'

She's looking at my arm again, and I tug at the sleeve, even though the bruises are now covered.

'Um. Blake had spoken with one of my relatives. I wasn't real comfortable about it.'

'OK.' Brewer folds her hands, leans forward.

'My relationship with my family is complicated, Officer Brewer, we don't get along so good.'

'And Blake was interfering? That's what made you so mad at him?'

I meet her eyes. 'I wasn't *so* mad, officer,' I say quietly. 'But yes, I had a grievance with Blake. I thought he should have asked me. We talked about it. He apologized.'

Brewer's eyebrows lift.

'Simple as that, huh? Sure wish my husband was so reasonable,' she says. 'Maybe we'd have stayed together. OK. So then what? Blake goes out, doesn't come home. You assume, what? He's stayin' out on his lonesome, in the desert?'

Her expression makes it clear how unlikely she thinks this sounds.

'I . . . I assumed he had stayed out late, fishing, then come back after I was asleep.'

'How about when you woke in the morning and he wasn't there?'

'Well, it wasn't unknown for him to stay out all night. If he was deep in thoughtful prayer, maybe. But I, um . . . I wasn't in that bed. The . . . the, uh, wedding bed.' I can feel my face turning beet red.

'This would be the bed you designate for relations with your husband?'

I nod.

'Right.' Brewer frowns. 'Who was in that bed?'

'He had chosen Emily that night.' I try to keep my voice neutral.

A twist of pain flickers in her face.

'So you assumed he'd stayed out late, then gotten into bed with another wife?' clarifies Brewer.

'Yes.'

She tilts her head slightly, that frown again.

'That don't bother you, Mrs Nelson? I mean, I hate to ask. But if that were me, and my husband was in bed with another woman . . .' She makes a face to show how badly this would sit with her.

'It does sometimes,' I say carefully. 'It's something we all work on as part of our belief. We love as Jesus loves. We learn to manage our jealousy. It's an ongoing process.'

Compartmentalize.

My state-appointed therapist's words.

Putting things into boxes in your mind, Rachel. We call it compartmentalizing. It kept you safe.

Brewer hesitates, unconvinced, then decides to move on.

'So, to clarify, you're saying you had a fight with your husband, but it was all resolved. No bad blood between you,' she confirms. 'He goes out fishing, stays out late, which is regular enough. When he didn't come home, you didn't notice, 'cause you assumed he'd gotten into bed with a different wife. That about it?'

'Yes.' I lick my lips.

Brewer looks at her notepad, thumbs some pages.

'According to you, Emily Martinelli went out walking by herself around about the same time Blake went fishing. But in the opposite direction, right? Up away from the river.'

I nod. She thumbs her notes.

'And Tina Keidis, so far as you're aware, was in the farmhouse the whole time. You believe you would have seen her if she went down to the river, since the route passes by the barn where you were canning food. Right?'

'I've told you all this already and it's in your notes,' I say, snarky.

'Uh-huh. That's interesting,' says Brewer. 'I have to tell you, that story doesn't exactly fit with what the other wives are saying.'

9

Tina, sister-wife

They've set up for questioning now. I'm in a little room with a table and chairs. Still no tape. Officer Brewer seems smart, so I figure she's also got Rachel and Emily too, sitting apart in different rooms. So she can corroborate our stories without us knowing what the others are sayin'.

I tell the cops how things are. She's got no vices, Rachel. Apart from sugar, of course, with her Mormon fat ass. All those God-awful cookies she bakes that taste stale even when they're still warm from the oven. Emily is batshit crazy, but in that eyes-down, timid way. I guess she's too young to have acquired much in the way of bad habits. They *believe*, you know, they'll see Blake again. Me, I'm not so sure of things I can't see with my own eyes. I'm the cuckoo in the nest.

It's obvious the cops have an agenda. They're tryin' to be all understanding and all. Ask if I need to see a grief counselor. But I know the score. Police only care about you when they're worried your statement will be *inadmissible*. I'm guessing the other girls will be fooled by this, but I know how it goes. What it means is they think we must have something pretty damn important to say, and they don't want to risk some hotshot lawyer proving they bullied it out of us, whilst we were all eaten up with grief, for our dead Blakey.

So they pass me hankies, and nod and frown and offer water. Tell me how hard it must be. But not a single fuckin' one of them knows how it feels, to go to bed married to the love of your life and wake up to find he's gone. Just gone.

Language. I can still hear Blake, frowning at my curse words.

In between cryin' and gasping for breath, I notice the cops looking at me kinda funny. What they don't know is I can lip-read pretty good – learned it in the Vegas casinos so I could tell if security was about to make a pull. So I can see quite clearly Brewer ask her chubby New Yorker cop friend, 'Think she's for real?'

I'm weighing up what this means, when Brewer slides into the seat opposite me.

'As you know,' she says, 'Mrs Nelson was able to identify the body. There's no doubt it is Blake Nelson.'

This starts me up all over again.

Brewer sits back, shiny ponytail swaying.

'At this point, we have two possibilities,' she continues. 'We're not ruling either out. The first possibility is your husband took his own life.'

Her amber eyes fix on me.

'No,' I shake my head. 'I'm not sayin' things were perfect, but that's not in his nature.'

'No causes of stress?' presses Brewer. 'Nothing at work?'

I think about my answer.

'Well, he was on the road a lot,' I say, finally. 'Blake was in sales. He sold those big canning machines. The Survive Well.'

'Oh, like in the advert?' Brewer hums the jingle. I instantly picture the lipsticked ad-lady, gesturing to her big-ol' pantry of colorful preserves, the enormous Survive Well, with its pressure dials and gauges, sitting in front.

I have a sudden image of Blake, loading boxes into his beat-up truck. My throat swells tight.

'Take your time, Miss Keidis.'

I nod, but I still can't speak.

'A lot of LDS folk preserve their own food, is that right?' Brewer is trying to move the conversation to lighter things. Like we're old buddies, shootin' the breeze. It's a cop trick I'm familiar with.

'It's part of the religion,' I say, swallowing. 'At least a year's supply in storage, minimum. And now the company Blake works for are selling pre-packed,' I sniff. 'Food enough for 365 days, ready-boxed. Macaroni, rice, things like that.' It's a relief to talk about things that don't make my throat tight.

'So business was good,' clarifies Brewer.

'As far as I know.'

'What about stresses at home? Three women must be a lot to manage.' She tries for a smile.

I pick at the edges of my pink nail varnish. It's hard to keep my usual guard up when I feel my heart might cave in.

'Us wives had a big fight,' I admit. 'On the wedding anniversary.'

'"*The*" wedding anniversary?'

'Right.' I'm sneering a little. '*Rachel's* wedding anniversary. See, since she is the *first* wife, it's "The" wedding anniversary.'

Brewer's eyes widen a little. No one ever thinks this about Rachel when they first meet her. She comes off like she has all her shit together, but a lotta the time she has the maturity of a nine-year-old.

'I can see how that would cause tension,' says Brewer.

'Damn straight. Blake found us all fixin' to kill one another.'

I instantly regret my choice of words.

'It turned violent?' confirms Brewer.

'No,' I lie. 'Nothing like that.'

'But things became heated because Rachel's anniversary was considered the most significant?'

I shake my head. 'No. I mean to say, that didn't help. But it was just domestic stuff, you know. Rachel has particular ways of doin' things. And she's very private. That doesn't work so good when you're sharin' a house with two other women.'

From the way she's looking at me, I think Brewer might know I'm not telling the truth. I wonder if she'll check up at the hospital. Find out what Rachel did to Emily. They registered under a false name, but Brewer seems pretty smart.

'Rachel felt her privacy had been invaded?'

She's sharp, I'll give her that.

'You'll have to ask Rachel.' I fix her with a long look.

'What about the fight between Blake and Rachel? Can you tell me about that?'

'Well, if they fought, I didn't hear it.'

Brewer drums her fingers on the table.

'Rachel Nelson never mentioned any trouble between the three of you gals.'

I laugh. It sounds hard, even to me.

'Yeah, well, Rachel never does tell the whole story. It's her way of lyin' without endangerin' her spot in heaven, you know?'

It's actually nice, to be able to let it all out.

'So Mrs Nelson is lying?'

'No. Like I said. She doesn't lie. She just . . . misses things out.'

'OK. Well, Miss Keidis, can you tell us what Rachel might have neglected to tell us?' Brewer adjusts her shiny ponytail.

'Oh, you want me to snitch? Are you kiddin' me? You're the detective. Find it out from Rachel.'

'You gave up smoking recently?' asks Brewer.

I realize my hands are dancing all over the table.

'Uh-huh. Part of my conversion to the Church.'

'I gave up myself a while back,' she says. 'Funny thing, you can go months without thinking about it. Then something'll just trigger you.' She snaps her fingers with an impressively loud click. 'You want a cigarette?' she adds. 'Couple of the older guys smoke, I'm sure I can get you one.'

Aha. So she's doin' the good cop. I was wondering which side she'd fall to.

I move my hands off the table.

'No thank you, officer. I'm a good Mormon, nowadays.'

'If there's something you want to tell us, Miss Keidis, you don't need to be afraid.'

'I don't follow you.'

She looks at me, hard. 'Your sister-wife out there? Emily? She's got some bruising to her ear. Couldn't say for sure, but it looks like someone might have hit her head against something. And your other wife, Rachel, has five little bruises on her right forearm, I'd say about the exact size of fingerprints. Like somebody grabbed her.' She mimes, putting her own hand over her lower arm. 'Was your Blake Nelson ever violent, Miss Keidis? Lose his temper?'

There's a long pause, and I kinda figure what she's getting at. 'You don't . . . I mean you don't really think we all got together and killed our husband, right? Or, like, *covered* for someone?' Despite everything, I'm laughing, bordering on hysterical. 'To do that we would have all needed to like each other.'

'You didn't get along?'

This sobers me right up.

'You haven't figured that part out yet? No, officer, we don't get along. Not even a little bit. Which, since we're spending all eternity together, kinda sucks.'

Brewer drums her fingers on the desk.

'It would almost seem,' she says, 'as though your husband went out shopping for wives. A maid in the parlor, cook in the kitchen, whore in the bedroom.'

I laugh. 'Which one was the cook?'

IO

Emily, sister-wife

The police officer heats me a meal whilst I wait. Apparently, they want to ask us some questions about Blake, who has now been formally identified. The lady called Brewer kept trying to tell me things I didn't want to hear. Like Blake was found hanging by his own belt from the gnarled juniper tree he liked to sit under whilst he fished. Also, how he had other injuries that made no sense. Then she used a bunch of other long words, like abrasions and perineum and nasty things I didn't fully understand.

If you ask me, it's just plain rude to keep telling someone things when they've made it clear they don't want to hear them, but Officer Brewer doesn't think that way, I guess.

The police officer is sliding two white plastic packages from a cupboard. He waves them at me. 'Macaroni cheese or lasagne?' I choose lasagne.

My mouth is actually watering at the smell of it. I've been married four years now, so I guess that's four years of food so bland you have to chew extra hard to remember you're eating.

Needless to say, there was no Caputo's deli for Mrs Rachel Nelson, no siree. When we needed groceries, she and I would ride out to Deseret Holdings. A huge Mormon store, with aisles and aisles of everything canned and packed in drab containers to last a lifetime. It was like the End of Days. No kidding. The spice section contained three products: salt, pepper, and ketch-up, all in bulk-buy canisters, naturally. Rachel cooks like she's been awarded a catering contract for a prison and is looking to reduce overheads.

The lasagne is set before me, in its little white plastic tray, sagging at the sides from the heat of the microwave.

I close my mouth as I take the first mouthful. I'm not even hungry, but I don't think anything has ever tasted so delicious.

The officer in charge is watching me, fascinated. 'Food's good?' he deadpans.

I nod, rapidly.

'Well, you're a first,' he says. 'Most of 'em complain.'

He's looking at the side of my head.

'You hurt your ear?' he asks, touching the top of his own.

My hand moves up automatically. It's not so sore anymore, but the tip is dark purple.

'It's nothing. Just . . . I bumped it.'

He slides across a plastic chair and sits opposite.

'Is there anyone you can call?' he asks. 'You got family?'

'They don't talk to me since the wedding,' I say.

He nods, his face sad.

'You want us to telephone someone anyway?' he suggests. 'Maybe your mom. In my experience, something like this can overcome old resentments . . . Perhaps she'll feel different to what you think.'

I shake my head. 'She won't.'

I'm thinking of my wedding night, when I was crying so hard I could barely get my words out. If Momma wouldn't speak to me then, she's not gonna change her mind over this. Whatever this is.

Remembering that phone call brings a lot of things back I'd rather forget. Like my wedding day. How, at that awful 'welcome to-the-Nelson family' dinner, Blake sorta *nodded* at Rachel, after we finished our desserts, and she got up and left.

Blake smiled at me and suggested we go upstairs. He had a funny look I'd never seen before. My palms broke out in a cold sweat. Everything was different now. I was a married woman. I was allowed to be alone with a man.

Almost as soon as we got to the bedroom, Blake started to take my clothes off, which just *freaked* me out.

'Are we going to sleep, right now?' I asked. He smiled.

I was wearing the special thick underwear they give you in the marriage Temple. To stay pure. He began to take those off too and I panicked, because I wasn't even sure if that was allowed, but he kind of pulled the bottoms and they came off. Well, that made me even more nervous, hysterical even. I think I was crying. I'd never been naked in front of anyone since I was a little girl, and especially not a full-grown man. And then he took some of his clothes off and I saw his Thing, poking through his garments, and I felt as though I was having a heart attack. No kidding. Like my heart was beating out of my chest and I couldn't hardly breathe.

Blake still wasn't saying anything at all, and he moved me onto the bed. Lordy, Lordy. I thought I was going to die, right there on those scratchy sheets, stinking of whatever strong detergent Rachel uses to get them whiter than white.

My knees were tight together, and Blake sort of arranged my legs with his hands. I felt his Thing touch the inside of my leg, and a surge of nausea hit me. He was positioning himself . . . trying to put his Thing *down there*.

I just froze. I didn't know what to do. I lay on the bed, every muscle tight, figuring this couldn't be happening.

Blake's face was all frowny, like there was something wrong with me. Then he moves my knees further out, and I feel a rush of air between my legs, and I realize he's *looking* at it. I started crying again, little snuffling sobs. I was literally dying of embarrassment. Like I felt my whole body was about to turn inside out.

The nausea was pounding away and suddenly it rose up and all Rachel's green Jell-O and creamed potatoes and God-awful soup comes up part-digested all over the sheets.

Blake jerked back, horrified.

I managed to say I was sorry and then I was sick again. I was racked with it, like my stomach had a mind of its own. I heaved and wretched and made these gross, embarrassing sounds. And I was so ashamed to be crying and then the tears were mixing with snot.

Blake put his arm around my shoulders. His Thing wasn't big anymore. It looked all wilty, like a drooping flower. My pulse slowed a little. And then I'm looking around the room. My room now, filled with all Rachel's ornaments. My heart started racing again.

'I'll ask Rachel to talk to you,' Blake was saying.

I heaved, but there was nothing left to come up.

All I could think was, I want my momma. I want to go home. But it was too late for that. Turns out Catholics aren't real good at forgiveness, despite what you might have heard.

Blake got up and opened the door to the bedroom. 'Rachel honey!' he shouted. 'Can you come clear this up?' He glanced at me. 'Put your garments back on,' he said, and there was a little ice in his voice that broke my heart. 'You're not really supposed to take them off.'

There's a snapping sound, and I realize I've broken a prong off my little plastic fork. It's half-buried in the lasagne, which is three-quarters gone. I pout a little, wishing the meal back again.

The police officer is staring at me.

'You sure you're OK?' he says finally.

I nod, wondering if I was eating horribly. Rachel always scolds me on my table manners.

'You don't need to speak with a grief counselor?' he suggests.

My husband's died. They're expecting me to be like Rachel likely is. Distraught. Crying.

'I think I'm in shock.' I heard that on the TV and always thought it had a nice sound to it. Like an illness that doesn't hurt.

He nods, but looks uncertain all the same.

I tilt my broken fork and scrape out every last bit of food from the plastic container.

II

Rachel, first wife

It's taken me a while to notice, but I think Officer Brewer is making trips between the three of us. Going back and forth asking questions.

The idea of what Emily might say is eating away at me.

'Your storehouse, out at the ranch,' says Officer Brewer. 'Some fairly substantial equipment you had out there.'

I smile. 'You can blame my husband for that,' I say, realizing she's referring to my industrial-grade canning machine. 'He never would get domestic if something more powerful was available,' I tell her, remembering Blake's store of outrageously modified petrol tools. 'And he worked for the company, so . . .' I shrug my shoulders, letting her figure the rest.

I can still remember Blake's pride as he heaved the grossly outsized Survive Well 5000 from his Chevy.

'Faulty,' he'd explained. 'One of the geniuses down at the factory wired it to have sixty amps 'stead of thirty.' He shook his head and chuckled. 'Coulda taken a customer's head straight off. Can you imagine the news stories?'

'Why do we have it?'

He'd looked at me like I was a moron.

'You're gonna use it, honey,' he said. 'When End of Days

comes, we'll need a lotta stored food. Not just dry goods. Meat and other things too.'

'But you just said it was dangerous.'

'I'm gonna fix it up for you,' he assured me. 'Beauty part is, our storehouse battery holds a lot more power than a domestic setup. I just need to disable the cutoff and fix a transformer, and it will work like a charm. Just be real careful you don't let the pressure get to maximum, OK? I need to take a few safety features away to build enough steam.'

He had dismissed my fears of catching an explosion of boiling water to the head in his usual gung-ho fashion.

'Angels would never spoil that pretty face,' he said, grinning.

'Well, you sure put that machine to good use,' observes Brewer, cutting into my memories. 'Enough food out there to feed you all for a year, I should imagine.'

'Three years,' I tell her.

'Not every household is so organized,' says Brewer with a small smile on her face.

'Well, that's why I keep a little extra,' I say. 'For those who haven't gotten around to keeping proper provisions.'

'So you live all alone out there, the four of you? With your storehouse and vegetable garden. Just kinda living off the land?'

'Well, we still buy a lot of things from the store.'

Brewer sits back, considers.

'A few folk from your husband's place of work gave me the impression Blake Nelson was on the enthusiastic side when it came to survivalism. And that's coming from religious employees at a food-storage company. A colleague mentioned Blake had some master plan to bury a huge tank of water somewhere in the desert, because soon there'll be no rainfall. That sound like the kind of thing your husband would suggest?'

'He just wanted us to be prepared.'

It's the first time I've been confronted with how screwy this plan sounds to a regular person. Truth was, I *did* think Blake could be a little intense on the subject of the world ending.

'And you helped him prepare? With your store? You must have canned, what, a couple of thousand jars of preserves?'

'It's what a good wife and a good Latter-day Saint does.'

I'm remembering how, the first time Blake drove me out to the ranch, I thought it was just like heaven. I thought I had gotten used to the noise of the city. But I slid straight back to that wilderness as if I had never left.

That night, the roof was not in good shape. So we lay in bed looking at the thousands of stars.

In the city, stars hang in the sky, like lights that get turned on at night. Out in the desert, they're *alive*; a shimmering body of white, red, green, orange and blue, blinking on and off. Swirling. Shooting.

Blake had brought his binoculars. 'Look this way, honey.' He passed them to me. 'The skies out in these parts are so clear, you can see the rings on Saturn. No light pollution. Not for a hundred miles.'

I took the binoculars, but I couldn't make out what he was talking about.

'When the end of humanity comes,' he said, 'it will be just us. Our wives and children. These stars.'

It was the first time Blake had mentioned the End of Days as anything more than a distant possibility. The first time he'd mentioned multiple spouses. I was so sure of him back then, the first bothered me more than the second.

Faced with Brewer's reaction to the buried-water idea, I'm viewing Blake's behavior less unquestioningly.

'Are you on any medication, Mrs Nelson?' Brewer asks, breaking into my thoughts.

'Nothing out of the common way.'

'Oh.' She makes a pretend surprised expression. 'Only I saw at the ranch some medications on a shelf. At a glance, they looked to have your name on the packages.'

'I get migraines. I take pills for that.'

'Prescription?'

'Yes.'

'Powerful?'

'Sure,' I shrug. 'I mean, they fix the headaches, most of the time.'

'An antidepressant?' she asks. 'I noticed those packages too.'

'You sure do ask a lotta questions you know the answers to.'

She looks a little taken aback. I'm sounding more like my mother by the minute, I realize. That cold, snippy tone came right from her.

'Is it usual to go looking around a person's kitchen without their permission?' I ask.

'I only noticed it in passing,' she says smoothly. 'Prozac, right?'

'Same as half the women in this state.' I try and sound jocular, but it doesn't come out right.

'Forgive me,' says Brewer. 'I'm not from Utah, originally. It seems strange to us out-of-towners that so many women and children here are medicated. Antidepressants twice the national average, right?' She makes a little pretend smile.

I don't smile back.

'You also take sleeping pills? Something keeping you awake at night?'

'I have vivid dreams. They help.'

'Dreams, as in nightmares?'

I tilt my head. 'You might term them that way, I guess.'

In actual fact, it always feels more like a memory. An image that had been swept into some dark recess of my brain. I'm in a graveyard at night, shovel in my hand, standing over a grave. When I look down into the coffin, I see I'm tossing dirt onto my own dead face. I wake up just as the lid closes. Since the night of the anniversary that dream in particular won't leave me alone.

'OK,' says Brewer. 'Did you take a sleeping pill the night your husband died?'

'I . . .' I think for a moment. 'I can't say for certain,' I admit.

'You're not sure if you took a sleeping pill?'

'I was . . . agitated,' I say. 'Had a lot on my mind.'

'On account of the fight between you and your husband?' Brewer clarifies.

I hesitate. 'Yes.'

'The fight that was peaceably resolved?' Her eyes are searching my face.

I give her a hard stare. 'Right.'

12

Emily, sister–wife

I must have been staring at the policeman's pack of gum 'cause he looked at me kinda funny and offered it to me. I took a stick real fast before he could change his mind, stripped off the paper and crammed it straight into my mouth. It was only when I was a few chews in I remembered to say thank you.

'You not had gum in a while?' he asks.

'Oh, sure. We were allowed candy,' I say.

They kinda glance at one another, like I've said something strange. I'd forgotten that, about people on the outside.

'Rachel only stopped at the big wholesale store,' I clarify. 'I forgot gum even existed until now.'

I give him a big grin. He smiles back but looks a little un-nerved too.

Now Brewer is talking to me, but I'm only half paying attention. Most of my mind is on the gum. I'm rolling it around my mouth, listening to the click and the pop.

'So, to confirm,' says Brewer. 'You woke up in the marriage bed. Your husband wasn't there. You didn't think anything of it?'

'Uh-huh.' I twirl the gum in my mouth. I feel like they want me to say more, so I shrug. 'Sometimes he stayed out in the fishing spot,' I tell them.

'And the evening before, Rachel was out in her storehouse, Tina was in the house, so far as you know, and you went for a walk?'

'Right.'

'In the opposite direction to the fishing spot?'

'Uh-huh. Out in the wilderness.'

'Then . . . how can you be so sure Rachel was in her storehouse?'

'I could hear the canning machine. It's pretty loud. Not much noise in the desert.'

'Think you could hear it all the way down at his fishing spot too?'

'Maybe.'

Brewer opens a file and pushes some pictures my way. I stare and stare.

One image is a close-up of a man's palm, with three stumps where the fingers were, cut down at the knuckle, or just below. The skin is bloody, and dusted with a little sprinkle of red hair. I remember hating that hair.

'What happened to his hand?' I say finally.

Brewer's lips draw tight together, like this isn't the right answer.

'We've got a couple a theories,' she says. 'One idea is a desert animal got to the body.'

'A desert animal?'

'A coyote. Or a bobcat.'

'Don't those animals usually start with the innards?' I'm trying to be helpful, but I get the feeling Officer Brewer doesn't appreciate my playing detective.

'It is unusual for predators to attack extremities,' she concedes. 'But not unknown. We had it checked out with a wildlife expert at Utah State Park. He confirmed that a little prey animal might attempt to carry off some smaller body parts. Particularly if

55

there were larger animals nearby. The autopsy documented several fingers on one hand were missing, and part of the left ear. There were also a few teeth marks in the nose, consistent with some kind of wild cat.'

I feel my eyes widen.

'You think a cat, like, *chewed* on him?'

'It's one theory,' says Brewer. 'If your husband died early or late evening, there would have been time in the night for wild animals to maul the body. We're still waiting on forensics.'

'What's the other theory?' I chew the gum, opening my mouth wide, and shutting it so my jaw clicks.

Open, shut, open, shut.

I look up at the ceiling so as to fully concentrate on the sensation.

When I look back at Brewer, she seems annoyed.

'If you notice,' she says, pointing to the picture, 'fingers are missing. But if I was using forensic speak, I would say he is missing parts of his index and middle finger. Only one finger is completely absent. His wedding finger, to be exact.'

Her eyes lift to mine.

'The second theory is that someone killed him, and attacked that finger in some symbolic way.' She points at the picture. 'See these straight marks? These could be the result of some kind of implement being struck at the hand repeatedly with some force but not a lot of accuracy. Someone is aiming at the wedding finger. The others are collateral damage.'

She mimes cutting across her hand, with her palm as the blade.

'Oh. Like they couldn't stand being married to him? And the ring finger represented the marriage?'

Brewer pauses. 'Something like that,' she says. 'A moment of passion.'

I lean forward on my elbows, rapt, chewing gum.

'Or,' her eyes fix on mine, 'someone who wasn't in their right mind.'

I nod, knitting my brows together.

'Did you ever see *Cagney & Lacey*?' I ask her.

She's taken aback, though I can't see why. People must ask her this all the time.

'Um. You mean that old 1980s police drama, with the two women cops?'

I nod, remembering the first time I saw those lady cops, guns in hand, hair all bouffant, with glossy pale lipstick and brick-red blush on their cheeks.

'Sure,' says Brewer. 'As a kid. I think. Reruns.'

'I love that show. I've watched every single episode, a million times over.'

She frowns, like she can't understand why someone my age would be watching that show.

'Miss Martinelli, could we return to the questioning please?'

I curl my lip. 'Just trying to be friendly.'

I'm secretly wondering how good a police lady she can really be if she doesn't like that show. There's one where Cagney goes undercover in a wheelchair, for example, that makes me laugh out loud every time.

'You don't seem particularly distressed at your husband's passing,' she says, 'if you don't mind my making the observation.'

'I don't mind at all.' She seems to be expecting me to say something else, but I'm not sure what. 'It wasn't a happy marriage,' I fill in.

I giggle, and realize they're looking at me funny.

I'm feeling a little lightheaded, like I don't care about anything.

'It's like that song, isn't it?' I say. 'Lizzie Borden took an axe,

57

gave her mother forty whacks. Only the daughter is a wife, and the mother is the husband.'

Officer Brewer straightens up, quite suddenly, as though I've said something very shocking.

'I never did have a good relationship with my momma,' I say, by way of explanation.

'Miss Martinelli.' Officer Brewer leans forward slowly. 'Why would you assume an axe was involved?'

I shrug. 'Wild guess.'

'You say you heard Blake and Rachel fighting?' she says.

I cough, putting my hand in front of my mouth, ladylike. It hurts my ribs.

'Yeah,' I say. 'You could hardly miss it. They were both kinda loud.'

This isn't exactly true. I was listening at the door. A bad habit. I tap my fingertips at my collarbone.

Our Father, hail Mary, hail Mary, hail Mary.

'And what would you say the fight was about?' prompts Brewer, staring at my fingers.

'I don't need to *say*, officer. I *know*. Heard every word.'

I pause for effect.

'Care to enlighten us?' Brewer has an eyebrow raised.

'Same thing they always fought about. Me. Rachel was real jealous of me. 'Cause Blake was always sayin' how beautiful I was. Buyin' me flowers. Pretty dresses. Stuff like that.'

'He used to buy you gifts, and not the others?'

'Yes, Ma'am. Every Friday he'd go to the big store in Salt Lake City and get me a new dress. Brand new. Always full price too. Didn't even like to find things in the sales, 'cause he thought I deserved the best.'

'Only for you?'

'That's right. And a big bunch of roses. That's what used to make Rachel so mad. She'd shout about how I was the favorite wife.'

Brewer nods. 'That how you get the bruise on your ear?'

My hand moves to my ear.

'You know,' she says, when I don't answer, 'when we came to the ranch, I didn't notice any clothing that looked new. No plastic bags from the store. No flowers either. Matter of fact, I didn't even see a vase.'

I chew the gum harder. I don't like Officer Brewer anymore.

'Thing is,' I say breezily, 'I liked to tidy them away, so the other wives wouldn't see and get jealous.'

I work the gum around my mouth. *Pop snap, pop snap.*

'You crack a rib, Miss Martinelli?'

'What?' The gum is a hard ball.

'Your ribs. You're kinda supportin' your right side there. When you coughed earlier, it looked painful. Reason I notice is my brother cracked his ribs one time. Skiing accident. He made the same expression as you do. Moved a similar way.'

'Oh, well, I've never skied.'

'So if we were to check with the hospital, we wouldn't find any record of your being treated?'

I don't answer that. Instead I concentrate on the sensation of gum in my mouth.

'You know,' she continues, 'Miss Keidis, Tina, she mentioned you wives had a fight. Domestic issues, she said. Is that how your ribs got hurt? Things turn violent?'

'No, Ma'am.' I shake my head real slowly. 'We love each other.'

'So there'd be no problem with the three of you going back home together? That wouldn't make you nervous at all?'

I shake my head. Brewer's eyes are fixed on my hand. I look down at it and see my fingers are doing a little dance. Carefully, I curl each one back in on itself.

'Miss Martinelli, are you sure you don't need a lawyer?' the blond man interjects. 'We can fix one up for you, no problem. No charge.'

'Um. No thank you. Could I get another one of those lasagnes?'

13

Rachel, first wife

'I'm wondering if there's some more information you'd like to share with us, 'bout what happened that night?'

'I've told you everything I know, officer.'

'Nothing springs to mind? Only, your sister-wife, Emily, she seems in pretty bad shape. I'm not a doctor, but it looks to me as though she's broken a rib or two. Side of her face has some injuries too, her ear.' Brewer taps her own. 'I noticed you had some bruises yourself, that seemed to me out of the common way.' Brewer mimes with her hand, 'Like someone grabbed you, here.'

She thinks, looking at me.

'I've seen a lot of domestic scenarios, abusive husbands,' she says. 'Matter of fact, that was my department for a number of years. Saw more than I ever expected to see in Salt Lake City. Somethin' in the water.' She smiles. 'If I were to take a guess, I'd say you and Emily had some kind of fight. She grabbed you and you pushed her away. She hit her head, maybe fell on top of something sharp-cornered, something like that, cracked a couple of ribs. Is that how it happened, Mrs Nelson?'

'No.' I've reverted to my childhood training, I realize. Retracted into myself.

Where the bad people can't get you.

Brewer looks very tired suddenly.

'Mrs Nelson,' she says. 'I'm going to be very honest with you. There were some unexplained injuries to your husband's body. Something you weren't shown in the mortuary, because it wasn't related to identifying Mr Nelson and it most likely would have upset you.'

The image of those plastic clothing bags comes back. The ones dirtied, muddy-looking. I feel my stomach turn.

'What kind of injuries?' I say weakly. It's hard to imagine he looked worse under that sheet than the parts I saw above it.

'Injuries the forensic team have now confirmed it is highly improbable he did to himself. To the groin area.'

Just like that, a horrible picture is in my mind. So real it's like I'm watching it on TV.

Blake, without his garments. Naked women writhing together on a white bed.

It takes me so completely by surprise, I just freeze. I shake my head and the image wings away.

'Um.' I'm fighting for the words. 'Why would you ever think he would injure his own . . . that part of himself?'

'We were working on the possibility of suicide, Mrs Nelson. We couldn't rule out self-harm.'

'What possibility are you working on now?' I get the strong impression she isn't telling me everything about this groin injury thing. But I'm not about to ask.

'First thing, we'll get more information from forensics, since we've only had a preliminary report.' She watches my face, waiting for a reaction. 'OK.' Brewer rubs at her forehead. Guess it's been a long day for her too. 'Well, I'm gonna run ya through what happens next. We're going to send Blake's body for official autopsy.'

Her eyes raise to mine, checking I understand what this means.

'You're going to cut him up?'

She pauses before answering. 'We have experts who are very sensitive to the fact this is someone's relative. There will be cuts made, here to here.' She mimes right across the sternum and down to the top of the pubic bone. 'It will be done as neatly as possible. Certainly nothing you'd see if you choose an open casket.'

'Will someone fix up his face?'

She hesitates. 'I believe that's something a funeral home can arrange, yes.'

I start to frown and consciously stop myself.

'I've got a lot to organize,' I say, running it all through my mind, and remembering the shredded remains of Blake's garments after they'd been cut from his body. 'Would it be possible, if I were to buy some new garments and drove them here, could they be put back on him?'

'That would be a question for the mortician,' says Brewer. 'You want us to help you with that? We have a list of recommended people, in cases like this.'

Cases like this.

'No. Thank you. Our Bishop will give us some recommendations. You're sure . . .' Tears bubble up. 'I don't like the thought of him being out of his garments. Couldn't I come by with a set for him? Please?'

Brewer sighs.

'Bring them along as soon as you can, Mrs Nelson,' she says. 'I can't promise anything. I'll see what I can do.'

I let out a long sigh.

'Thank you. God bless you.'

'Well, I guess that's all,' says Brewer. 'We'll be in touch, straight after the autopsy. You'll need to leave details.'

'You're letting me go?'

'You weren't expecting me to?'

'The police never let you out, once . . .' I stop myself. 'You're letting us *all* go?' I confirm.

Something flickers on Brewer's face. Her lips part.

'No formal reason to hold you here, but when we get the autopsy results, we'll likely have some more questions. We're releasing all three of you under what's known as a suspended bail. That means you're not under any charge at this time, but neither are you free to go someplace we can't reach you, understand? No last-minute trips to Mexico, OK?'

I smile, relieved she's making a joke of it.

'So we'll be sending you all home. Together.' She lets this sink in. 'Unless you have some other place to go?'

I shake my head. For some reason, I'm picturing all the sharp-edged equipment and power tools back at the ranch.

'Usually we'd expect you to reside at the address we have listed for you . . .' she pauses, searching for the words. 'However, since your ranch is nowhere on a map of nowhere, with no phone line, we've made temporary arrangements in the city. You're certain that's OK with you, Mrs Nelson? All three of you girls living in the same place?'

'Yes.'

Brewer blinks as though I've answered too quickly. It's ingrained, I think, not to trust police. No matter what the therapist told me, I always cross over the road.

'I mean,' I raise my eyebrows to stop myself frowning, 'why wouldn't it be?'

14

Tina, sister-wife

You know that feeling you get, right before a thunderstorm? Like you're just *waiting* for something to happen?

Yesterday, the cops drove us to this house on the edge of town, with a bunch of leaflets on how to make funeral arrangements.

My first thought was that Rachel doesn't understand. The way Blake died, the belt around his neck, pants around his ankles. That's choky stroky, as we call it on the block. Cuttin' off your air supply, whilst you jerk off. Poor Rachel hasn't got a clue about stuff like that. Emily neither.

The cops can't charge anyone before the autopsy comes back, but we all know the truth. If they decide Blake didn't kill himself, then someone must have murdered him. Which kinda narrows the suspect pool. 'Cause no one knew about the ranch, and I mean *no one*. Blake wanted it secret so we could relax and be ourselves without livin' in fear of the law. So unless you count the realtor who sold Blake the plot, there's not another soul who even knew there was a domicile in those parts.

Since the only people within a hundred miles were us three wives, it's only a matter of time till they realize one of us did it.

When they let us go, I could hardly believe it. My first thought, honestly, was *jackasses*. Like, how can they not figure this out? I guess, since someone was driving in the vicinity, saw the vultures and came to take a look, they haven't realized how remote the ranch really is – how freaky-deaky unlikely it was, in fact, that anyone other than us found him first. It's hand-of-God sorta thing.

My second thought was I am *not* goin' home with Rachel.

Brewer offered me some temporary accommodation – a motel-apartment thing. That was when I knew. Me and four walls and all this *stuff* in my head. *No, no, no.* I wouldn't stay clean two seconds. Since I don't know another soul in Utah, that means I'm trapped with the Wicked Witch of the West and Emily, the craziest little liar you ever did meet.

I've kinda made my peace with it as a temporary solution. Just until after the funeral. The big decisions can wait. Until then, I'll sleep with my bed pressed up against the door.

The house they found for us is regular. And when I say regular, I mean regular. Like, you might put a sign above the door, stating 'Example of normal American house'.

I snuck a look at Rachel, and I could tell she was pleased. Holy Grail for Miss Rachel is Look Normal At All Times. Despite, you know, the kinda freaky marriage setup – or maybe because of it.

So, we arrive at the new house. I'm expectin' . . . I don't know. Someone to erupt or go crazy. But lemme tell you the weirdest part. Rachel is *great* at this. Pretending everything is fine. It's like her superpower. Acting like her husband hasn't been killed by his own wife is nothing to her.

Even weirder than that, she kinda sucks you into it. She's like a repression tornado, scooping up any feelings in her path.

Rachel walked straight into the kitchen and started moseying about, clucking about fixing dinner and how we all must be hungry.

And Emily and me? We went along with it, like we always

do. Perched on the mulberry-colored love seats, pretendin' like nothing happened. Emily was so white, I thought she might puke, and she's workin' a little patch of the couch with her thumb, pushing the velvety pile through the mesh.

Then a smell of canned soup wafts from the kitchen, shortly followed by Rachel. She stands in the doorway.

'They left us a little store cupboard of things,' she says. 'Nothing fancy, but I made Campbell's mushroom and noodles.' She tucks a strand of blond hair behind her ear. 'I figure we could all use some comfort food.'

She waits like that for a moment, her eyes twitching back and forth to both of us, like she's got something important to say. Then she frowns.

'Emily, I owe you an apology,' says Rachel, in this strange tight voice. 'I shouldn't have done that to you on the night of the wedding anniversary. I lost my temper, and I'm real sorry for it. I hope you can receive this with Christ's forgiveness.'

I can't see Emily's face, but I can guess what she's thinkin'. Any apology Rachel makes is always put alongside some religious instruction. Like you *have* to accept it, or you're not godly.

Emily says nothing. She doesn't even look up.

Something flashes across Rachel's face, like she's boiling with anger.

'Emily!' she snaps. Emily's round blue eyes flick up, frightened. 'Stop worrying the couch,' says Rachel, glaring at where a bald patch is growin' in the fabric from Emily's rubbing the velvet. 'This isn't even our home.'

That does it. I can't keep it in.

'How can you act like nothing happened?' I demand.

Rachel's face kinda freezes. She's scared I'm gonna mention Blake.

'You put her in the hospital,' I say, pointing to Emily, who's sitting like a rabbit in the headlights now. Not knowing where to look. 'You *lied* to us.'

Rachel blinks a little, like she's been slapped. There's a pause. An angry bubbling sound can be heard from the kitchen.

'The soup is boiling,' she says, turning and walking straight back out.

Emily and I sit there for a moment, not moving. Then Emily turns to me.

'Thanks,' she whispers, a strange little smile on her face.

Unexpectedly, Rachel's head pops back through the doorway.

'Um, did either of you by any chance see a cooking knife anyplace?' She says it just a shade too casual.

Emily and I shake our heads.

'Darnedest thing,' says Rachel, with a little puzzled smile, all sweet and confused. 'I can't find one in the kitchen.'

'Maybe police safe houses don't come with them,' suggests Emily.

'What would you need a knife for?' I ask. 'You're fixing soup, right?'

Her expression darkens just a fraction.

'I always add a few vegetables. I like to cut up the tinned corn.'

'Ah well,' I shrug, meet her eye. 'Guess we'll have to eat corn whole.'

I can see she's mad, but, of course, there's no Blake to tell. Rachel's lips compress. 'Well, dinner's almost ready,' she says. 'Would you mind setting the table?'

We stand and shuffle through into our little dining room. Emily lays out cutlery and napkins, in the way Rachel likes.

Rachel brings in a casserole dish and we all sit. She lifts the lid to reveal gray mushroom soup, swirling around three nests of instant noodles.

Rachel seats herself, and begins saying grace. When she's finished, she looks up at both of us.

'I never lied to you,' she says quietly. 'I just didn't tell you *everything*.'

She says everything as though it's a dirty word. This is directed at me.

Rachel thinks my lack of personal barriers makes me vulgar, indiscreet. In actual fact, she's jealous I can tell Blake things she can't.

'We should discuss funeral arrangements,' says Rachel, chewing.

The funeral. Oh boy. I can almost feel the fight surging toward us, like a physical being.

There's a thud of a spoon hitting the table. I turn to look at Emily. She's wearing an expression, like she's just figured something out. I can see her mouth working, but no words come out. Then she whispers, to no one in particular, 'I'd like to choose the funeral home.'

Rachel looks like she's been punched in the gut.

'I don't think . . . I mean, I've looked into it already,' Rachel begins.

'Even so,' says Emily, looking into her soup, 'I'd like to decide. My ribs hurt,' she adds meaningfully. She lifts her spoon and chews a noodle.

Rachel's blue eyes track to mine. I don't meet them. Actually, I'm tryin' not to laugh. This is sorta brilliant.

'If it's important to you,' says Rachel, crushed, 'then of course.'

Emily twirls her fork victoriously. We finish our meal in silence.

15

Rachel, first wife

When I was a little girl, my mother told me your head is a bunch of boxes. The way to get through hardship is to stay in one box.

I remember her as a gray lady, my mother. As though she'd been in the wash too many times and was limp and colorless with overwear. She died when I was seventeen. Placental hemorrhage. Occupational hazard when you give birth a lot.

'Some people try to live in all their boxes at once,' she told me, 'that's how you go crazy. When something bad happens, you dive into one of your boxes and stay there. Cooking, cleaning, prayers, don't matter what, just keep busy.'

Aged thirty-three, she was pregnant with her ninth baby. Twelve, if you count the stillbirths. Guess that's how she must have gotten through it. Pick the next box, hop across and don't look up.

That's how I feel at the moment. I'm staying inside that one box, because if I peek out, all the walls will fall down.

I felt that way the day I fought with Emily. She'd found my documents. I was so mad, I honestly can't even say for sure what happened.

Truth is, since Emily discovered those papers, I'm remembering things. Some of those old boxes are opening.

Compartmentalize.

You learned to compartmentalize, Rachel. It kept you safe.

When we got to the little house, I got right on with taking care of everyone, and didn't allow any stray thoughts to get in the way. Feels funny to be back on a crowded-in street again, being looked in on. Out in the desert, there's so much land and mountain, no one knows you're there.

There was a little to-do over who got which bedroom. Tina and I both wanted the one nearest the front door. Emily wanted the room at the back, which had a strange smell to it. It was only afterwards I realized she got the one with a big window that drops directly onto the street.

It's a nice little place even so, not Tina's style, I guess – a little too regular for her. One of the things we butted heads over is how she would try and impose her wild decor. She dressed pretty wild too. Though Blake seemed to like that.

A memory floats back.

The black dress with ivy-leaf patterned neckline I bought half-price at the dollar sale at Macy's. Blake had sorta pursed his lips and stared.

'Can you return it?'

'Um . . .' Tears welled in my eyes. Blake stepped forward and took me in his arms.

'Hey, don't cry.' He wiped the tears. 'Why don't you pick yourself up a pair of new jeans? You always look great in those.'

A few weeks later, Blake took Emily and me to meet Tina. We'd been on our best behavior, trying to be friendly. In those early days, I think Emily hoped they would be friends. That was before we both realized that Tina's only friend is Tina.

Blake took us all to Kirker's Diner on the outside of town. He doesn't like fancy places. Always said what he liked best about me was I was a real simple gal. Homely. I had never even been to a restaurant before I met Blake.

Tina had arrived with a whole lotta makeup and this inappropriate tight black ensemble, *especially* for a single lady out with a married man.

It took me until the menus were handed around to realize – it was the same ivy-leaf pattern neckline on the dress I had returned, though I have to admit it looked very different on Tina. Exact identical dress though. No mistaking.

'Nice outfit,' I said, more coldly than I meant to, when Blake excused himself to go to the bathroom.

'Yeah,' she smoothed the front, looking down at where her cleavage was pushing up for attention. 'I was so worked up 'bout what to wear for this dinner, that Blake bought me this. You know how he is about modesty.'

'Oh my heck, you think that is *modest*?' It came out far quicker and more spiteful than I ever intended it. Even Emily winced. I saw Tina take stock, like she was drawing battle lines.

'Yeah,' she said. 'Well, I guess Nevada is a lot different to Utah.'

She looked pointedly at her menu.

'You should try the meatloaf or the chicken fried steak,' I said, trying to sound friendly.

Blake returned, sliding in between us, but he was only looking at Tina.

'Everything OK?' his eyes were searching her face, concerned. I felt a stab of pain. It had been a long time since he'd looked out for my feelings like that.

'I was recommending the fry steak.' My voice came out all bright and brittle. 'It's Blake's favorite, isn't it, honey?'

'Is it deep-fried?' asked Tina. 'That's bad for cholesterol.'

'Tina's not from Utah,' said Blake, not taking his eyes from her. 'She's a little more sophisticated than you, Rachel, but don't worry, she'll learn you.'

Tina had ordered a Cobb salad.

I hated her then.

You know, I can't well recall what we did for her wedding. I do remember there was a stack of cupcakes. Usually I would have thought that was *for cute*, as the saying goes in Utah, but the frosting was so bright, I thought it was just the kind of tacky thing she would do.

16

Emily, sister-wife

When Officer Brewer said we were going home, I had this fantasy. I'd come out the front, and my mom would be there, waiting for me. I'd run into her arms, and she'd say 'I forgive you.'

She wasn't there, of course. The police said they hadn't been able to find her. Like maybe she'd moved. I knew that wasn't true. They were just being nice.

In the days we had a phone line, I'd call my mom, like ten times. I think she knew it was me. I wouldn't say anything. Just ring, ring. Hear her voice. At first she'd demand who was calling. Then I took to breathing real quiet, hoping she'd know it was me. After that she'd listen for a time. Maybe a few minutes. Then she'd whisper, 'God forgive you,' and replace the receiver, very gently, like a blessing.

I did that for a few months, right after my wedding, but when Blake saw the bill, he had the phone disconnected. Sometimes I'd steal a dime from Rachel's pocketbook, and sneak to a payphone if we were making a trip to the store. I didn't call my mom the day of the wedding anniversary, because I was in hospital.

After Rachel and I fought on the wedding anniversary, I broke a rib and the nurses thought I might have kidney damage, but in the end it turned out I didn't. It was something else, they said, to do with my waterworks. I think they maybe hinted it was involved in the Wifely Act but were too embarrassed to say more, only told me to visit the women's clinic out of town.

I couldn't exactly tell them I'd been going to that women's clinic each and every week for the longest time, only now I couldn't go back. Because Blake lost his temper with the folks there and told me we couldn't make regular visits anymore.

In any case, the hospital nurses took a good long look down below too and I saw a nurse writing something down about my scars.

Blake drove me back home. Didn't say much. Only that Rachel was under a lot of pressure and he hoped I could forgive her.

The best thing about all this happening is Rachel trying to be nice. She knows I could likely go to the police. Turns out that's what scares Rachel most – authorities, paperwork.

So, when the big fight came, about which funeral home to use, I got my way for once. Rachel wanted a place with experience of polygamist Mormons. She said she didn't want us exposed to judgment when we were burying our husband. I wanted the place I'd seen downtown. A cute little place with pink flowers in the window, run by a caring lady funeral director. That was what the sign said. I thought it sounded nice; a lady being kind to you.

Now we're actually at the pink flowers place, the funeral home lady is looking at us kinda funny. I'm secretly thinking Rachel might have been right.

The funeral director reminds me a little of the women I knew growing up in the Italian quarter. She's maybe fifty, smelling of strong perfume, with loud pink lipstick on thin lips. I guess you gotta look a bit bright, when you spend your days tendin' to dead folk.

'You were *all* his wives?' she confirms.

Rachel rolls her eyes at me, *I told you so.*

The lady starts fiddling with her necklace. Regular Mormons

get all nervous around plural types like us, on account of the fact we're fornicating and going straight to hell.

'Yes, Ma'am,' I say. 'Blake was a husband, a lover and a friend to all of us. We know that plural marriage isn't for everyone, but it worked for us.' I give her a winning smile. Tina and Rachel exchange glances. They never like it when I tell what Rachel calls *my stories,* in public.

'I'm not sure this is the best place for you ladies,' says the funeral lady. 'We don't generally serve . . . I mean we have a moral duty to our customers . . .' she swallows, choosing her words. 'There's a place over town, I can give you a card. They handle funerals for folk with no religion at all, so I don't suppose they would have an objection to,' she waves a manicured hand, 'whatever it is you people need.'

Rachel wears a pained expression now. Tina just looks mad.

'We'll be needing a very special headstone,' I say. 'And a whole mess of flowers.'

The funeral lady shakes her head firmly.

'Plural marriage is forbidden by the Church,' she says. 'If you had any respect for religion, you'd know that. I won't serve a pack of adulterers, plain and simple. If it gets found out I helped you, they'll all come here.' Something passes through her eyes. Like she's imagining hordes of buck-toothed inbreds winding up outside her nice pink-curtained funeral home. She starts walking toward the door. 'I really would rather you all just leave.'

Silently, we troop out of the door, me burning up with embarrassment, Tina sort of introspectively glowering.

I glance at Rachel. She looks thoughtful. Guess this kind of thing has happened to her before. Since I know all about her now, and her name isn't really Rachel.

Rayne Ambrosine.

That's her real name. I wanted to shout it right from the roof-tops when I found it out.

Whaddya know, folks!? Rachel Nelson has a *different name. And* she was even born somewhere else to what she likes people to think.

Truth is, I turned into something of a snoop. Cooped up all alone in the ranch, I got bored. I used to pretend I was Cagney from the old detective stories I'd seen on TV. I'd poke around in the bedrooms, behind pictures, acting like I'd found something incriminating. Then one day I actually did. A pile of papers in Blake's suitcase.

Most of 'em I couldn't really understand. They looked like property, or deeds or something. But right at the bottom was a birth certificate. A birth certificate for a person I'd never heard of.

A girl named Rayne Ambrosine. I thought about this for a good while. Then it occurred to me to check the date of birth. It was Rachel's.

I kinda sat on the information, like this secret present, for months, not sure what to do with it. I wondered what would happen if I put the certificate name into the internet.

I thought and thought about it. It bothered me. We don't have a computer or anything like that, so I couldn't actually act on the impulse. Blake had a phone with internet, but I could hardly ask to use it. Firstly, I'd have to tell Blake I'd been snooping, and I'd get a scolding, or worse. Second, he doesn't like us to have anything to do with computers. So he'd likely say no in any case.

Then, one day, Blake drove me downtown for what wound up being my final appointment at the women's clinic. When they said my condition for sure wasn't physical and suggested a psychologist and Blake started talking so loudly about government mind-control that they asked us both to leave.

Blake must have known I was upset, since he let us stop off at McDonald's on the way back, and even bought me the meal that came with a heart-shaped lip-gloss.

When Blake went to the bathroom, I noticed that Mc-Donald's have internet consoles. I waited there for the longest time, wondering if I'd be brave enough to actually do it. Then I got up, walked quickly across the room and sat down in front of one.

There were some teenage boys next to me, and I saw them nudge each other as I punched in the letters one by one, my mouth working to sound them out. But I managed to enter in the name: Rayne Ambrosine.

That's when I saw Rachel was *all over the newspapers*.

That was how the fight began, on the night of the wedding anniversary a few days later. I told her I knew. I was still mad at her, I guess, 'cause she was clearly so pleased about the doctor saying there was nothing wrong with my hoohah. So I just came right out and said it.

I know what you really are, Rayne Ambrosine.

And she pushed me, right down the stairs.

17

Tina, sister–wife

The way things are with me at the moment, I can't handle keeping any amount of forward-thinking in my head. That's why it's easier to let Rachel take charge with all the funeral arrangements. Things like that always were her department anyhow.

If I start thinkin' about the burial, I'll relapse. If I start thinkin' about how Blake died, *why* Blake died . . .

My counselor used to say one day at a time – but sometimes you have to take that down to one hour, or even one minute. Like I'm on a tightrope and you have to stay fixed on puttin' one foot in front of the other.

I remember asking him when you get to the end of the tight-rope, and he said you might not. But the tightrope is a better place than the floor.

Rachel has driven us all out to her favorite place in the whole world – Deseret Stores – where food is packaged in bins, buckets or ten-kilo sacks and generic root beer comes in seven-liter bot-tles. She wants to load up for the funeral.

'No such thing as fun-sized here, huh, in more ways than one,' I whisper to Emily as we follow Rachel, with her enormous shopping cart, along the towering aisles of bland packaging.

She giggles, then covers her mouth.

'The fun is in the discount, right?' she grins, putting on a pretty good impression of Blake. 'So long as you don't like having fun,' she adds in her regular voice.

We exchange smiles. Blakey took frugality to the next level. I've never heard Emily rip on him before. Emily and I never talked a whole lot, on account of everything coming out of her mouth being a lie. It's nice to see she has a sense of humor. Guess she hid it.

'Sure wish Blake was here now,' I say. 'Even if he woulda made us skimp on his own funeral supper.'

Emily looks away. 'Hey,' she says, eyeing a shelf. 'We could use some Draino, right?'

'Um . . . No?'

Emily starts loading bottle after bottle. 'Sure we do. Can't have too much. Like the lady on the commercial says.'

'Gosh, darn it!' Rachel's voice floats down the aisle. She's struggling with a paper sack of something bigger than she is.

'Come on,' I say to Emily as she tosses another bottle into the cart. 'We'd better go help her before she kills herself.'

It's a bad choice of phrase, but Emily doesn't seem to notice.

We reach Rachel just in time to manhandle an outsized bag of chocolate-sheet-cake mixture into the shopping cart before it falls and splits.

'Jiminy cricket,' she makes a comedy pretend-wipe of her brow. 'I really thought it was gonna fall. Good work, team.' She doesn't smile though. Hasn't since we heard the news. Instead she glances in the cart. 'What's with all the Draino?'

I shrug.

Emily ignores the question and starts reading one of Rachel's large packages.

'Choc-olate cake,' she says slowly, her finger following the words. 'You got a premix?'

'Blake liked this brand. No need for eggs or milk. No need to rely . . .'

'On provisions that can't be stored long term. I heard that a million times already. But Blake's not here.' There's a strangely determined look on Emily's face. A little steel behind the bug eyes I've never seen before. 'I'd like to bake a real cake,' says Emily, quietly.

Rachel is taken unawares by this new version of Emily. She looks at me, like she was expecting me to step in. Assert her position as head baker.

'We'll both bake,' Rachel decides. Judging from how she's looking into the shopping cart, I think part of her decision is she doesn't want to unload the mega-sack.

'No,' says Emily. 'I'll do it.' She looks at Rachel, then to me. 'Blake always said I wasn't a homemaker,' she says. 'Well, I want to prove him wrong.' She has a real funny expression. Like she's getting her own back for something.

'I don't recollect Blake saying that,' says Rachel.

'Well he did,' says Emily. 'Maybe you only listened to the things he said about you.'

A thought bubbles up.

We don't have to kowtow to Rachel as head wife. There's no Blake to step in. Guess Emily has already realized it. But, in actual fact, I find myself feeling sorry for Rachel. She looks real hurt.

'It's not fair for you to do everything, Rachel,' I say. 'Let us help.' I shoot a look to Emily. A look that says, 'If you make the cake, there's a fighting chance we'll have something edible.'

She smiles, then hides it with her hand, looking away.

'You can do the funeral potatoes,' I assure Rachel. 'That's the most important part, ain't it?'

A word on funeral potatoes. They're legendary in Utah, and

absolutely nowhere else. Potatoes baked in canned soup, cheese and cream, topped off with crunched-up buttered cornflakes, or some other crunchy sprinkle. A dish for when men did manual labor, and the women stayed home with twenty kids tugging at their skirts, and a Valium prescription. Welcome to Utah. Set your watch back fifty years.

'I'll make the special kind, with Ritz biscuit sprinkles,' says Rachel, taking a determined grip on the shopping cart. 'I'll have to pay a visit to the city, to pick some up. And I'll need to ask the minister if I can borrow his wife's big dish. She's got a three-gallon casserole. We'll need a big drum of margarine, and those three-quart cans of chicken soup are economical.'

She nods, reassured, but still slightly confused. She's still trying to work out her place, I think, now Blake has gone. Guess we all are.

Emily and I exchange another meaningful glance. Rachel is back in full Rachel mode. If she's cooking the most Mormon of Mormon dishes for her own husband's funeral, they're gonna be the holiest potatoes anyone ever ate.

I kinda love Rachel a little for that. She can't help but do her level best.

Emily turns around and strolls off, humming a funny little tune.

I guess she's going to get cake ingredients.

'Maybe I'll get the mushroom soup instead,' says Rachel, half to herself, half to me. 'Blake didn't like potatoes that way, but I always thought they were better.'

She looks at me for reassurance. Something passes between us. Like we both got an inkling that we didn't have to be those women who Blake made. We could be whoever we wanted.

'You know what Blake would say 'bout that,' I say, wagging a finger, 'he'd say a loving wife would fix potatoes the way her husband liked them.'

I said it as a joke, but I've pitched it wrong, 'cause Rachel's eyes are suddenly alive with pain.

'Just because I don't get all emotional,' she says, her voice all choked. 'Just because I don't scream and cry, doesn't mean I didn't love him.'

And she pushes on the shopping cart and walks very straight-backed toward the margarine in three-pound buckets.

I watch her go, thinking it's something we always fought over. Who loved him the most. And the strangest thought slides into my head. Blake liked us to fight about it.

We join Rachel at the checkout, to help her heave her outsized purchases onto the counter. I notice Emily's bulk purchase of Draino is mysteriously missing. Rachel must have dumped it out of the cart whilst no one was looking.

'You ladies sisters?' asks the checkout girl cheerily, as she heaves a full shrink-wrapped case of Hawaiian juice cartons through.

There's an awkward pause. The checkout girl's cheeks get a little redder, her eyes switching back and forth between us.

This was part of the life Blake never told me about. I always figured Utah had no problem with polygamy. Never realized sayin' the wrong thing could have us all arrested. I'm a worse criminal here than I was in Vegas.

'Yeah,' I tell her casually, stuffing some of the smaller items into a bag. 'We're sisters.'

The checkout girl sorta sags in relief.

'Thought for a moment you were some of them freaky polygamists,' she says with a slightly hysterical laugh. 'Boy,' she adds, pushing more groceries across, 'we had some of 'em in a few months back. Those ones that hide out in the desert where the law can't get 'em.' She adjusts the sleeve of her uniform to cover her garment line. 'If you ask me, the manager shoulda called the cops,' she concludes with a spiteful expression. 'Throw the lot of them in jail.'

18

Rachel, first wife

In the run-up to the funeral, it's like there's this awful deadline looming. The police haven't yet been in touch with the autopsy results. We've driven out to an industrial-looking place on the edge of the city, where you can get coffins and urns and whatnot at good prices. It's the only place willing to do business with polygamists, and reminds me a little of a movie I saw once where some Italian mobsters went to a warehouse to buy illegal guns.

A man in a shiny suit, young enough to have acne, directs us to view caskets. Just like we're in a department store, shopping for household goods. You can tell he's nervous about the plural-marriage thing. He keeps snatching little glances at us, like he's imagining us all in bed together.

He gets a little absorbed in explaining his products though. Brass handles and so forth.

It's the darnedest thing. Something about being in this funeral place. I keep *seeing* a box opening. I just know there's something inside that shouldn't be let out. Something to do with why Blake is dead.

Keep sweet, Rachel, I remind myself.

But things are spiraling out, like octopus tentacles. Like Blake had a role for each of us, and now he's gone, it's hard to know who I'm trying to be.

The funeral place has a big mirror taking up an entire wall, and I can see all our faces in the glass. Tina has a weird smirk, Emily looks guilty. And there's another woman, round-faced, in her thirties. It's me, I realize. I have this real strange stony look on my face. Never knew I did that. Sure does make me look older. I pull my mouth into a smile.

Tina leans closer to me.

'Creepy, huh?' she whispers.

I feel suddenly warm toward her. I glance over to Emily, thinking she's gonna fall to pieces anytime soon, but she's right next to the funeral boy, nodding earnestly at the list of casket accessories.

She has a glow, like she's planning a wedding. Maybe she's making up for her own one. I'll bet it was a big letdown compared to what Emily was raised to. After she married Blake, I saw a Catholic marriage party spill out of a downtown church. The bride wore a huge poufy white meringue and had a bouquet bigger than her head. It clicked then how disappointed Emily must have been.

There were wedding arrangements, of course. Modest ones.

After, during those first months, Blake would take Emily out for dinner, to places he never took me. He wanted to try and work on her timidity, he said. I would get into a cold sweat, trying to decide the right way to be when they returned. Him with those awful hungry eyes, her meek and silent at his side.

Then things changed. Blake announced he was taking Emily to the women's clinic. When he wouldn't say why, I knew. I just knew. And I couldn't stop the smile creeping onto my face.

She can't do it.

In the very early days, Emily had talked to me about her problems, but she'd never gone into great detail. If a doctor was involved, I had to assume things weren't working at all. Not even a little bit.

'This way please.' The adolescent funeral director leads us into a room of coffins. Tens of them, all laid out in rows. My feet feel as though they're made of glue. Something is hitting me hard, right below the solar plexus. Seeing those coffins laid out. It's like the dream I keep having. Where the lid slowly opens and there's a smell of bleach and a bloody *something* inside.

But now that image is overlaid with something else too. Something like . . . *a white room.*

I'm seized by nausea, as though someone has socked me right in the gut. If I don't get out, I'm going to vomit straight onto the funeral carpet.

Keep it together, I tell myself. *Don't make a scene.*

My head is hurting. I put a hand up to my forehead.

A white room. A blood spot on a green dress.

The funeral man is walking up to the first one, explaining something to Emily, who is nodding earnestly.

'Wait . . .' My mouth is dry. Like the words won't come.

Tina turns to me, and I see shock.

A room where everything is white. Carpets, walls. There's a snowy bed, like in a fancy hotel, all plush linen and starched sheets. Naked women stand all around the white bed. Blake is choosing which one he wants.

I feel as though I've been dropped in a cold bath.

The funeral man is resting a hand on the polished coffin lid. He hooks his fingers on the handle.

'Wait,' I whisper, 'don't . . .'

He isn't listening.

I'm seized with an urge I can't explain. Something primal. All I know is I have to stop him raising that lid.

I know if he does, something absolutely awful will happen.

A terrible memory is clawing at me. I'm a little girl again, back on the Homestead, helpless terror swelling. A scratchy voice in my brain whispers. A child's voice.

You've been a bad girl.

Then everything goes black.

19

Emily, sister–wife

It was such a funny feeling, getting into that black hearse car. Like being a famous person. Then climbing out the other side, at the chapel. Everyone nodding and smiling. It felt like it should be someone else up the front. Like his actual family, or something.

Rachel didn't ride with us. She drove our beat-up Chevy with a trunk full of extra food. Tina thinks she was making a point to Bishop Young about how she is the most important wife. I don't believe it though. Rachel decided to drive herself when she saw the white casket in the back of the hearse.

In the end, *I* had picked out the coffin and the flowers, because Rachel had lost it at the funeral store.

We'd driven to some big warehouse out of the city, which I wasn't happy about *at all*, because it didn't seem like a nice place. More like a bargain basement for coffins. But Rachel told the man we were all three of us married to Blake, and I noticed right away, he started to treat us different. Adding tax to some of the prices. The secretary out back kept shooting us nasty looks too.

Funeral man changed his tune when Rachel began screaming the place down, though. It was hard to hear exact words, 'cause she was speaking all funny. Like the thing they do in some churches when people speak in tongues.

Tina thought she said: 'Don't open the box!'

But I thought she said something different. For sure, at the end, Rachel said something that sounded like a prayer. Like a protection invocation. In the name of Jesus Christ, something like that. I recognized it, 'cause my momma did something like that when I was little, to stop the devil putting lies in my mouth.

I was pretty certain Rachel was experiencing some kind of sacred visitation, and that's what I told the funeral man too, being as he looked about ready to call the police.

'We're real holy folk,' I said, 'and Rachel here is visited by the spirit. She has revelations and things of that nature.'

It seemed to do the trick, though you could tell he couldn't get us out fast enough after that. I even managed to get him to discount the white-and-gold open casket with the cream satin lining.

Mr and Mrs Nelson senior didn't ride in the funeral car with Tina and me either. We don't get along, on account of Blake's folks doing the regular LDS worship and us practicing an advanced form, where you get into a better sort of heaven.

Right before Blake and I got married, he took me to his parents' house, in some little dirt town above a general store. I was all dressed up, in my favorite pink sweater and ballet pumps. Only while I was sitting on the couch, waiting to meet with his mom and dad, Blake's whole family apparently trapped him in an upstairs bedroom, and read him a bunch of scripture. The plan was to change his mind. Make him recognize polygamy as a real bad sin.

Tina told me later what they did is called an 'intervention'. Getting the whole family involved, trying to explain to Blake how God would judge him as fornicating. Blake and I left straight afterwards, so the first time I actually met Blake's mom was on my wedding day, when she came to try and stop the marriage going ahead.

Our shiny black car pulls up real silently outside the local church. It's a modern building, made of white brick with a sloping red roof and a small white steeple for effect, and I remember being disappointed the first time I saw it. I'd expected all Mormon churches to be like the Temple, all white stone and spires to the clouds.

The funeral men carry the discounted coffin inside. There's to be an open-casket viewing. Just members of close family, which in Blake's case is a whole lotta people. I mean, everyone thinks Catholics have plenty kids, but they got nothing on Mormons, no siree.

Blake has two brothers, who look a lot like him, and two sisters, who don't. They got about four babies apiece already, even though the youngest brother is only a year older than I am.

Rachel is already somewhere inside, organizing the food most likely. There'll be a big buffet tomorrow, but she can't help but feed everyone up.

Tina comes to stand next to me.

'Listen,' she says. 'We need to figure everything out ahead of time.'

'Figure what out?'

'Well,' Tina shifts a little on her high-heeled shoes. 'Rachel's losin' it, right? I mean, you saw her in the funeral place.'

'Guess Blake's death is hitting her hard,' I offer.

Tina's eyes kinda bulge.

'Emily,' she says, 'I've been sleeping with my bed pushed against the door. You do realize our desert ranch is an hour from nowhere in every direction?'

'What do you mean?'

'Back at the police station, Brewer was askin' me all kinds of things about Rachel's medication.'

'Me too. So what?'

'Brewer thinks Rachel must have . . . I don't know. Lost her mind. Like temporary insanity.'

My mouth is moving, trying to work out what she means.

'I'm not sayin' she meant to do it,' adds Tina. 'But she needs help.'

'You think *Rachel* killed Blake?' The idea gives me a fit of the giggles.

'Well, she and Blake had some kind of falling-out,' says Tina, 'right before he went out fishing. You heard it, I know you did.'

I chew my fingernail. I guess Blake isn't around anymore to hand out punishments for bad behavior.

'I didn't hear everything,' I say. 'But I heard enough. Never known Rachel get so angry before,' I conclude, 'but, holy moly, she sure did lose it.'

'She was angry?' I can tell Tina isn't sure whether to believe me. Downside of having a colorful imagination, I suppose. Rachel *never* gets angry in a shouty way. The way she does it is kinda worse.

'Like *real* angry,' I say, laying it on thick. 'Fixin'-to-kill-some-one angry.' I'm enjoying painting the picture.

There's a pause.

'So . . .' says Tina, sounding annoyed. 'Why was she angry?'

'Be. Cause,' I say, drawing it out, 'Blake had done something real bad, without telling her.' I pause for effect, opening my eyes wide. 'Blake had gone shopping for another wife.'

20

Rachel, first wife

Blake's church is in the small town of Tucknott, a mom-and-pop-store place, where Blake's parents were the real-life mom and pop. His father's store has been in business since the 1800s, selling sodas and sundries and farming supplies. Since his great-great grandparents emigrated to America from Denmark. Shortly after we met, Blake told me one of his earliest memories was sneaking root-beer syrup direct from the dispenser with his sister. I remember thinking Blake was too All-American to be true. Like an actual Godsend. I'd asked for a regular husband, and there he was, the most regular of boys you ever did meet.

That was until I met Blake's mom. Never really knew what it felt like to be trash until I encountered Adelaide Nelson. Six generations of respectable Mormons, and no room for people like me, who drag their teeth on their fork when they eat.

Bishop Young is standing to greet guests and forming a barrier between us wives and the rest of the Nelson family. They're milling around at the back.

We're not really allowed to mingle with regular churchgoers, on account of our corrupting influence. Regular Mormons figure the slightest whiff of polygamy will tempt their members into adultery.

I stop dead when I see Blake's mom. Adelaide Nelson is dressed in a black Jackie-O-style suit, pillbox hat atop her teased-up highlighted hair, and a black veil, beneath which snatches of pink lipstick and spidery eyelashes can be seen. Naturally, Mrs Adelaide Nelson hates me. So far as she's concerned, I corrupted her angel son. She leans on her husband's arm, weak with grief.

I realize I'm actually grinding my teeth.

She has to make it so clear that she's the one grieving the hardest.

Hunter Nelson conveys his wife rigidly, looking neither right or left. He's a sinewy-faced man with a permanent expression of disapproval.

The food is all laid out ready. My funeral potatoes right in the center, and a lot of kind people have brought things. Emily's cake is there too, and I have to admit, it looks good. I didn't know she had it in her.

Braxton's wife, Sukie, arrives, holding a baby, a toddler in hand, with a casserole dish wedged awkwardly under her arm. Braxton is Blake's younger brother, so in some people's eyes we would be sisters-in-law. But since our family is damned for adultery, they don't really like to use that term.

Her two other kids are causing merry hell somewhere at the back of the room, running around like wild things. But they're pin-smart in little suits, with their hair combed and gelled.

For a long moment, I can't stop looking at her baby. A familiar desperate feeling of unworthiness rises up in my throat. I prayed so hard, for so long.

I remember rehearsing how I would tell Blake, when it finally happened for me. The extra line on the testing stick. Maybe I'd come home with a pair of cute little booties I'd picked up in the mall.

Looks like we'll be needing some of these . . .

I realize I'm staring and drag my eyes away from the little girl.

'She looks just like you,' I say, smiling. 'Here, lemme help you with that.' I wrestle free the container.

'Thanks.' Sukie shifts the baby to the opposite hip. 'I'm real sorry for your loss. How you holding up?'

'I'm OK.'

The baby makes a strange noise and Sukie jiggles it automatically.

'He was a good man,' Sukie says in a whisper, tears welling. 'I always meant to tell him . . . To apologize for what I did to him . . .' Her voice breaks.

I never did learn how to process oversharing. I was always taught to keep difficult things to yourself, and not to dump them on other people.

'Well,' I say in a high voice that signals I'd rather she stuck with the usual condolences, 'I'm sure whatever you would have told him, he knows it now.'

Sukie leans in and takes my arm.

'I was under a lot of pressure from my family to break the engagement, you know?' she says. 'To marry a perfect Mormon boy. When Blake came home early from his mission, they never could quite reconcile it.'

I remember Blake, crying in my arms, telling me how awful his mission was. Working fourteen hours a day to convert people who didn't want to be converted.

Sukie glances in the direction of the open casket. She looks so sad. I send up a little prayer to give me better thoughts.

'You'll tell him for me, won't you? When you see him up there?'

'Yes, yes, of course I'll do that.'

Sukie hesitates, then her next words come out in a rush. 'I want you to know, what everyone is saying, I don't believe it. Not for a second.'

I feel completely blindsided.

'What . . . um. What is everyone saying?'

She blinks really fast, birdlike, toys with a strand of hair, then looks down to address the little boy holding her hand.

'Go play with your sisters, honey,' she says, releasing her grip. He runs off to the far side of the church. 'I'm so sorry . . .' She begins. Her voice breaks and she swallows. 'Listen. They're all such gossips. People are working up theories about the mystery blond Blake had lunch with.'

'They're still on about that, huh?' I keep my voice perfectly neutral. Tucknott's worst gossip had made a trip to Salt Lake City for a skein of rayon sewing thread and *just happened* to see Blake through the window.

Sukie jiggles the baby some more. 'Some people got nothing better to do,' she says. 'You gotta ignore 'em.'

'Most likely it was a work meeting, or something of that nature. Plenty women got careers, nowadays,' I say.

Yeah right. A work meeting in Kirker's Diner. Blake's courting eatery of choice.

Sukie nods emphatically. I look around. People seem to be swerving my gaze.

'Folk here think Blake was courting some blond?' I deduce.

'Well, not *everybody*. But people leap to conclusions, you know. Leastways, they do in Tucknott.'

It has suddenly dawned on me that Sukie is the only person to come within ten feet of me at this community gathering. Even as a plurally-married pariah, I would have expected a little sympathy. A few words. People here *know* me, after all – I'm the first wife. Guess it doesn't take a genius to work out what people have concluded.

I've been deliberately not paying any mind to the rumors about Blake and his mysterious lunch. Best to act like it's all beneath my notice. But I allow it the tiniest corner – just a flash of daylight – in my mind. And just like that, there she is. A picture of the blond lady at Kirker's Diner, who, of course, I never met, or saw.

Her hair is styled like very devout girls have it, brushed up high into a towering quiff, and very long down her back, almost to her waist. She wears a green prairie dress, buttoned to the neck and falling to her ankles. Somehow, I also know what she looks like with no clothes on.

The strangest thing isn't that I have an image of the mysterious blond. It's *where* I remember her. Because it's not a memory. She's from the dream I have.

I'm in a grave. Blake and the blond woman are standing over me. They're burying me.

21

Tina, sister-wife

I knew, of course. About the fourth wife.

I mean to say, I didn't *know*. Like, Blake hadn't told me. But I think deep down I'd figured it out. He always talked about this vision, 'bout a farm and four wives. I just didn't think it would all happen so quickly.

That's why I've locked myself away in the room with all the chairs, to cry my eyes out.

There's a soft knock at the door, and I'm praying to God it's not weird old Bishop Young, when Braxton Nelson walks in. I kinda sag with relief.

'Hey,' he closes the door behind him. 'My sisters said you could probably use some help. How's it goin' back here?'

'I've been better.' I smile at him.

The Nelson boys all look alike. Braxton is like a younger version of Blake. Red hair, freckles. His face isn't as classically handsome as his older brother. It's a little narrower, quirkier maybe. In some ways more attractive. He has the same blond eyelashes, and pretty blue eyes. His top lip has a twisted scar running right the way through it, that always made me think of him as kind of a pirate.

I've always liked Braxton and his wife Sukie. I met 'em a

couple of times at barbecues. They were the only ones from Blake's family who didn't shun us.

'You shouldn't worry about what people are saying,' he says.

I smile at that, because I never do.

'Why, what are they sayin'?'

'Oh, you know, there's that rumor goin' around that Blake was seen out with a woman. I don't believe it personally. My brother might have interpreted the Book of Mormon different to the rest of us, but he would never have committed adultery. That's a straight ticket to hell.'

'Bishop Young told you that?' I remember I saw Bishop Young deep in conversation with Braxton, all serious, like he was tellin' him something real important.

Braxton pushes a hand through his red hair, embarrassed.

'Not exactly.' His eyes lift to mine. 'He's more concerned about my soul, you know, on account of it being traditional in polygamy, if a man dies, the brother marries his wives.'

He has cute dimples when he smiles. It's the first time I noticed it.

'How is your dad taking things?' I ask.

'Oh, you know.' Braxton has a distant look. 'He's a strange old bird. Thinks the only way to God's grace is to work your fingers to the bone and frown a lot while you're doin' it.'

He manages a smile, but only just.

'I think Dad's heart is broken, but he can't show it,' he adds. 'Blake and he never really patched things up after the failed mission. Then Blake joined in with that touchy-feely church at college, and you know how Dad is about any suggestion a husband and wife might have fun.'

I nod, though the truth is, I don't know, because Mr Nelson and I have never spoken. All I really know is he keeps a calendar all filled out in tiny writing, allocating slots for everything, including his children and wife. According to Blake, the only time Mr Nelson ever broke his schedule was to drive to Salt Lake City after his decade-old hobnail boots had finally worn out. The only store still carrying his brand was a vintage store selling to hipster kids, and Blake painted a real funny picture of Mr Nelson in his scratchy overalls, glaring at the espresso-sipping young-uns. At the time, he was laughing about it, but now I think on, I guess it must have been hurtful too, that Papa Nelson wouldn't take five minutes for a root beer with his sons but threw out the timetable for footwear.

'What about you?' I ask Braxton. 'You OK?'

'Well, I'll miss him for sure, until I join him up there, God willing,' he says. 'Never met anyone more committed to God's word. You know he used to beat up on me a lot, when we were kids, for not singin' the hymns right?'

Braxton smiles. His teeth are a little crooked, but in a nice way. Guess only Blake qualified for braces in their family.

'No he didn't!' Though I can well imagine Blake rough and tumbling, keeping his kid brothers in line. I recollect him telling me once how hard it was for his mom with all the children. How he tried to help out.

'Yeah,' Braxton nods at the memory. 'We worked it out though. Mainly, I got bigger.' He shows the crooked teeth again. ''Course, he had his own beliefs, when he married Rachel.' An uncomfortable look flits across his face. 'Blake always was a maverick. More open to a joyful interpretation of God's will than he was raised to. We all admired his bravery. Imagine we'll have some long conversations 'bout that when we meet up again.'

His conviction floors me. I thought maybe he didn't like Blake so much. Now I realize, he believes with all his heart he'll see him again.

'You know,' I toss a little dark hair over my shoulder, 'I don't even know what to wear in front of your family. I wore something Blake woulda liked. Likely it's not modest enough.' I toy with a bra strap, smiling up at him.

He takes in my tight black dress, low-cut at the front.

'I like it,' he smiles.

The way he says it, I *know*. Same as I always know with men.

'It's hard,' I say. 'I miss him so much. I know everyone here thinks I'll see him again, but I wasn't brought up like that, you know? It's harder for me to see it.'

I start to cry. Braxton puts his arms around me and I sob onto his shoulder. It's strange. He doesn't smell like Blake, or feel like Blake. Something about that is really wrong, and really right too.

I take a shuddery kinda breath. Wipe my eyes again. 'You look like him,' I say. 'Shame I didn't meet you before.'

A rush of grief hits me, like a wall. All I can think is, I can't handle it. I have to put it somewhere else. I look into Braxton's eyes. I never realized how much alike they were to Blake's. I tilt my head up, just a little, like a question.

Could we?

Braxton doesn't say anything, but he's looking right back at me, and his chest is rising and falling, as though he's breathing a little harder than usual. I feel like I'm on a ledge, and staying balanced is this difficult endless thing, and I'm so freakin' *tired* of it.

I could just let myself drop.

Before I really know what's happening, I'm pulling Braxton toward me and we're kissing.

22

Rachel, first wife

The coffin is at the back. I guess Emily must have chosen all the fixtures and fittings. I would have thought, left to her own devices, she'd choose something unsuitable. All shining brass and huge flower sprays. But in actual fact, it's far less gaudy than I might have expected. Tasteful, even.

My phone rings for the third time since I got to church. Withheld number. I silence it and put it back in my purse. Safest to ignore the call. I have a bad feeling it's the police with news of the forensics.

I look across to check Blake's folks are still huddled near the coffin. I notice Blake's mom, working her way up the aisle, fancy funeral clothes accentuating how she's bird-thin, from regular fasting and a diet of Graham crackers and Mountain Dew. That part of Mormonism skipped us Homestead folk by. I guess our mothers thought we were all hungry enough, without adding religious starvation to the brew-ha-ha.

When I first met Blake's mom, she just took my breath away. The mothers I knew growing up were sad, and hard-faced, in long dresses and hair whipped into crown shapes. Adelaide Nelson was this perfect housewife, like something out of a movie, all hairspray highlights, snow-white slacks and capri sandals, despite five grown-up children. Blake had painted a picture of her as real strict, so she wasn't at all what I was expecting. I guess Blake's idea of strict and mine were worlds apart.

I remember thinking how lucky Blake's dad was. Mr Hunter Nelson was a peculiar man, ten years older than his wife, and wedded to the workings of his store cash register. The kind of man who always knows how much change is in his pocket, right down to nickels, dimes and cents. I only ever heard him make one joke, so well-worn none of his family even reacted. About how Adelaide's family had virtually sold her to him, and if he'd have known how much she was going to cost, he'd have kept his pickup truck. Blake talked about their marriage like it was an eternal tight-lipped tug-of-war over a single dollar bill.

At first I thought it was strange that Mr Nelson barely seemed to notice Adelaide. After getting to know her better, I understood why. Being in her radar meant being in the firing line. Blake's mom had planned his life out for him the day he was born. And she was darned if he was going to mess with her plans. Guess now Blake's gone, poor Braxton is next in line.

Blake's mom flips her veil back as she nears. Everything on her face is small and neat – chin, eyes, forehead. None of her children have inherited her features. They take after Blake's silent dad, with his horsey face, even the girls. She walks very erect, head held high.

My phone starts ringing again. It's on silent now, but I can feel the buzz in my purse.

Leave me alone!

I leave it to ring out and try to stay composed for Mrs Nelson, who is almost on me now.

'I'm sorry for your loss, Mrs Nelson.' I try for a smile, but it won't come. 'We all loved Blake very much.'

She keeps right on walking, and for a moment, I think she

means to pass me by without a word. Then she comes in very close.

'I won't shed tears,' she says. 'I know he is in Heaven. God wouldn't want me to be ungrateful. I . . . I have prayed and prayed for God to take this *anger* out of my heart. Anger at the person who did this. Who harmed my Blake.'

Her hand closes on my forearm.

'I want them to *burn in hell*,' she says. Her eyes seem to be searching mine, like she's looking for something. Her fingers tighten, hard enough to hurt.

I'm so surprised, I step back slightly, but her grip locks, pinching the skin.

There's a horrible smile on her face, made ghastly by the lipstick.

She leans in very close, and the loud floral of her perfume makes my eyes swim.

'I *know* . . .' she hisses. Her voice breaks, and she pulls back, looking around to see if anyone has witnessed her display of emotion. '*I know you did it.*'

23

Emily, sister-wife

My job is to give out pineapple sugar cookies. Three per guest. But it's hard because everyone is trying to pretend I don't exist. That's the problem with plural marriages. No one really knows how to greet you or anything.

My eyes drift over to Blake's mom, in her smart funeral outfit. Blake once told me Mrs Nelson never, ever asked for anything, but you always knew what she wanted just the same. I always hoped to learn how to do that. You caught a glance of Mr Nelson sometimes, sort of surprised and thoughtful, like he knew he'd been tricked but couldn't figure out how.

Mrs Nelson always looks real lovely, like she knows just what to wear at any occasion. I think Blake wished his wives could be that glamorous. Closest he got was Tina, who is kinda slutty-glamor, despite her exotic dark hair and tan skin. Adelaide wrote us off after Tina. Guess she was the final straw. She and Mr Nelson never visited the ranch. Adelaide and Blake had this weirdly formal lunch together a few times a year, on neutral territory in a pancake house just outside Tucknott – like there'd been a divorce with access meets.

Adelaide Nelson is corralling Blake's brothers and sisters now – two of each – and I catch snatches of what she's saying.

'. . . Brigham, you always did dress the nicest. Can't you teach

Braxton a thing or two 'bout smartening up his act? Lordy, Braxton. A check shirt to your own brother's funeral – people will think I raised you that way . . .'

I let my eyes settle on the two brothers, neither of whom have looked at me.

Adelaide's attention is now on the sisters and she's praising one for her food, exclaiming loudly how she always was the best cook and her older sister never could match it.

I'm hit by the strangest feeling. I don't know how I couldn't have seen it before.

That's what Blake used to do. With us.

I pick a cookie off my napkin and crunch it between my teeth.

Bishop Young arrives next to Adelaide, his face all nodding in sympathy. He kinda looks as though he's been pumped full of air, all puffy cheeks and neck, and fingers, topped with a swish of clean white hair, like the snowy cap of a mountain. I'm trying to avoid him, 'cause he does his creepy double-hand shake, like he owns you or something. Blake and I visited with him for marriage counseling, and I have outright hated Bishop Young's guts ever since.

Adelaide passes Bishop Young some handwritten pages, which I guess must be the funeral speech. Mr Nelson spoke to Rachel on the telephone about it. I didn't hear what was said, only Rachel hung up looking all white-faced, and said Blake's dad didn't want us to contribute. Didn't think it would be appropriate. Tina looked kinda mad, like maybe she thought Rachel shoulda stood up for herself.

I head for the food table at the back, where a lot of unfamiliar people are putting dishes down. Food you would never see at a Catholic funeral, like cold mac and cheese with cubed spam in it, potato salad sculpted into a beehive shape, this pretend dessert which is actually round pasta mixed with cream.

Also about a million square feet of tray-baked cake.

Back when I was a waitress at the diner, Blake took me to a few church functions. One of the jokes I made was: *What's with all the sheet cake?* Catholic cakes I grew up with being towering tiers and multilayers and all. I told Blake right out, I didn't understand why anyone would make a flat cake.

Blake had taken a knife right there and then and cut three big pieces of frosted sheet-cake, then layered them up to make one giant piece.

Big enough for ya? I remember thinking Blake could solve any problem. You didn't get men like him in Salt Lake City. One time, our generator broke down and Blake climbed right on top and fixed it with these oily spare parts that had been lying around on the ground. He was that kind of person. You just knew he could take care of you.

I used to like hearing Blake's stories too. How fire would sweep the earth and we'd be lifted up. Though you never knew which way it would go, since sometimes he'd just talk on and on about Bible things until your ears hurt.

I pick up the cake knife. There's a big bowl of brightly colored punch, with cartons of premix Juicy Hawaiian Punch stacked behind in case it runs low. Someone has arranged them in neat rows. Rachel, most likely.

I stab the blade into the foil top of a carton. Red liquid spills out, like blood.

That's when I hear Rachel talking in this weird polite voice. I turn to see Mrs Nelson has crossed the room and is holding Rachel's arm.

'I'm so sorry for your loss, Mrs Nelson,' Rachel says. 'We all loved Blake very much.'

Rachel used to use that voice with Blake too. Never with us though.

Mrs Nelson's face is pale, washed out, eyes dull. I feel really, really bad for her.

She mutters something to Rachel that I don't hear, and walks off all proud and stately, but she has this weird expression on her face that ruins it. Like a sneer.

I lick my wrist, where red juice has run down it.

I'm wondering about that, when I notice Rachel is walking toward the coffin with this really strange look on her face.

Like she's remembering something.

24

Tina, sister–wife

Braxton. I kissed Braxton.

I can't quite believe it.

He pulls back, but doesn't look embarrassed or awkward.

'Let's forget that happened,' he says in a kind voice.

'Yeah,' I whisper. 'I'm sorry, I . . .'

'You're grieving. I know.' He smiles. His arms are still on my shoulders. 'It's not easy for you, and I know my family makes it harder. 'Specially my mom,' he says, looking very sincere. 'You gotta ignore that, OK? She's going through a process.'

I wipe the edges of my eyes where makeup is probably running.

'Is your mom being meaner that usual? I hadn't noticed.'

Truth is, I don't really mind Blake's mom. It's Rachel whose skin she gets under. Rachel thinks Adelaide is always tryin' to outdo her. But I don't think that's true. Rachel has a lot of rage she doesn't let out.

Blake once let it slip his mom was dirt-poor growing up. If you ask me, Adelaide joined the Nelsons' all-American family and tried to edit out her past. Hence showing up to every event like one of those dress-up dolls. Barbie does home-maker, Barbie does church, Barbie does funeral. I get that. The need to fit in somewhere you don't belong. You see *a lot* of it in Vegas.

Braxton laughs softly.

'Far as Mom's concerned, she spent her whole life raisin' Blake and now he might not be at her side in heaven. She'll come around. It's somethin' she's goin' through. We're all going to the celestials together, right?'

Tears come, I wipe my eyes with the back of my hand.

'Also, I think she's very concerned right now, that one of us brothers is gonna be seduced into the plural lifestyle, what with all you gorgeous widows.' He smiles. Braxton has a nice mouth, despite the scar.

Hope beats in my heart.

'So you're not planning on converting, and marryin' your brother's wives,' I say, tilting my head.

Something passes over Braxton's face now. Something I can't quite read.

'Not in my style of the religion.' He tries to say it casual, like a throwaway remark. But his voice comes out all throaty. 'Blake was the rule-breaker.'

'You sound sad about it.'

He smiles.

'Well. Maybe. Maybe I'll get a sign from God one day. Maybe Sukie will.'

'Is this a sign? Us? Here?'

Something in Braxton sorta shifts. Like he's teetering.

'You know,' I say, in a low voice. 'If Blake used to beat up on you, this is your chance to get your own back.'

I kinda mean it as a joke. But then Braxton's lips hit mine, and it's like *whoooaaa*.

Everything seems to come alight. Before I really know what's happening, my hands are all over him.

'Wait,' whispers Braxton, but he's saying it into my mouth as we're kissing.

'It's not adultery if we're planning on marrying,' I say. 'We're not doin' anything that counts.'

Blake told me that, once upon a time.

'Stop.' Braxton tries to move me gently away.

'No,' I pull him close. 'I miss him so much. Just give me this one moment. Please. Lemme pretend he's still here. If there is a God, he wouldn't say "no" to that.'

Braxton is tryin' to steady his breathing.

'You're grieving,' he says. 'We both are. This is ... It's a temptation.'

I take his hands and put them on my throat.

'Squeeze your hands around my neck,' I say, tugging at his clothes. 'Pretend like you're choking me.'

25

Rachel, first wife

Everything is reverberating around my brain. I can still feel the pinch on my arm where Mrs Nelson gripped it.

A memory is clawing at me. I'm back on the Homestead in a long dress and heavy boots, helpless terror swelling. The earth beneath my feet is yellow. Flat scree rock, like an old riverbed.

It was a game of dare we played. Something scary was on the other side, on the toffee-color ground.

'That's the part we're never allowed to go.' It's a child's voice, scratchy, but familiar. I don't want to think about who that voice belonged to.

I notice that somehow I've walked myself right up to the coffin, without meaning to at all. I can make out the reddish top of Blake's hair. Part of his face. It's been heavily made up and doesn't look anything like him.

The funeral director moves forward to close the coffin. Blake's face vanishes. Then, just in the moment, a terrible scene rushes up from nowhere.

A dark-haired girl lies on a white bed, moaning, head tilted back in abandon. Blake is removing her panties, kissing her stomach, running a finger along her belly. The other naked women crowd in, watching, touching one another.

One is different to the rest. Older, my age maybe, very long blond hair. She turns to look at me, and fear hits me square on. The blond lady whispers in Blake's ear, looking in my direction.

'You need to get her out of here,' she hisses, her face twisted in contempt.

I'm so shocked by the force of the image, I feel unsteady on my feet.

'By the power of Jesus Christ,' I mutter. 'By the power of Jesus Christ, *I command you to leave me alone!*'

The image slips away. My eyes are screwed tight, and my breath is coming fast. It's as though I'm in a kind of bubble. My skin is cold, and my heart is beating out of my chest. I feel like I'm going to die.

You're not going to die.

For a euphoric moment, I think God is reassuring me. Then I realize someone is speaking to me. A soft little voice.

'Rachel?' I open my eyes to see Emily standing next to me, a plate of my home-baked sugar cookies in her hand. 'You need to let go of the casket,' she whispers. 'They're all looking at you funny. You were saying some strange things.'

I look down to see my fingers are grasped tight on the closed white-gold lid. All around, Blake's relatives are staring. I have a sudden picture of how I must have looked, the widow of a murdered husband, muttering incantations over her husband's remains.

I must have looked guilty.

'I say things without meaning too, sometimes,' Emily says, conspiratorially. 'My momma always said it was the spirit visiting.'

I nod, tears rising.

What did I remember?

'I really am sorry,' I manage, 'for pushing you. I just got so mad. Seeing that birth certificate . . . It reminded me of things I wanted to forget.'

'It's OK,' says Emily. 'Ribs heal real fast. I can hardly feel it anymore.'

It's been barely a week since the anniversary night, so I don't believe her, but I can't bring myself to say anything else. The terror I felt in that white bedroom still spikes at me. A dark place, swirling evil.

The images are gone, but the feeling of it remains like an aftershock, lurking at the edge of my conscience.

Blake in that white bed.

I'm dimly aware Blake's mom is looking toward me, but my body has broken free of my control.

My fingers are tingling and my chest hurts. I feel as though I'm losing my mind.

This has happened to you before, says a strange voice in my head. *Don't you remember?*

A ripple of consternation passes through the congregation, like a wave. The air is filled with whispers. At first I think I must have said something just awful. Then I notice heads begin to turn, one by one, toward the door.

'Rachel,' Emily hisses. 'The police are here.'

I follow her gaze. Officer Brewer and several other policemen I don't recognize are gathered at the back. Sweat prickles at my hairline. Something about the public setting, the children all over . . .

What happens next is in slow motion. I see them walk into the building. They only look around momentarily, before Brewer's eyes land on me. She points, says something to her colleague. Then they both stride in my direction.

Oftentimes I have wondered how I might respond to being arrested. It was the specter that haunted first my childhood, then my marriage.

'Mrs Nelson,' Brewer's eyes are alive with sympathy as she reaches me. 'We tried to call.'

'Is it about the autopsy?' I whisper, even though I know it isn't.

'I'm very sorry to show up here. We wanted you to come in of your own accord.' She takes a breath. 'Rachel Nelson, we're arresting you on suspicion of murder.'

She explains she needs to use the handcuffs. It's part of the procedure. I see Emily with a look of pure fear on her face. Everything hits me in a rush.

'Wait,' I mumble, as Brewer begins leading me slowly out of the building, a gentle hand on my lower back. 'Who will take care of Emily and Tina?'

'I really didn't want to have to arrest you here, Mrs Nelson,' says Brewer. 'Truly, I am very regretful. Let's hope we can get this all fixed up and get you home soon.' But I notice the pressure on the small of my back increases.

As I'm led handcuffed from the building, I see Adelaide Nelson standing at the front, watching me, a victorious look on her face.

26

Emily, sister–wife

The police lead Rachel out, and I sit there with my mouth hanging open.

I look around for Tina, thinking she would know what to do, but I can't see her anywhere. Everyone is muttering to one another and looking over in the direction Rachel left.

Bishop Young is frozen to the spot halfway to the pulpit, like he doesn't know whether he can go ahead without the deceased's wife.

Then Mrs Nelson walks real quietly toward the lectern and slips the handwritten speech from Bishop Young's hand as she goes. She lifts her veil over the black pillbox hat and begins reading.

I kinda want to laugh. I mean to say, it reminds me of a movie or something. Mrs Nelson all dressed like President Kennedy's wife, and Bishop Young too frightened to make a scene and stop her. Grief is like that. You're not allowed to interrupt.

Looks as though Mrs Nelson overestimated her ability to do public speaking though, because the words all come out in this thin reedy voice, and her eyes are, like, *glued* to the page, like she's scared to look up. She gets stuck a couple of times and has to revisit the page, her hands shaking.

I get the impression Mrs Nelson was thinking she'd give this big moving speech on account of being so heartbroken, but it isn't working out how she wanted.

'As a young boy, Blake was a keen Boy Scout,' she quavers. 'Then, during his mission to Mexico, Blake broke the record for converting souls.'

I'm staring at her. Because it isn't *right*. Blake never even completed his missionary trip. Rachel let slip the last straw was when his bunkmate started rubbing his thingy all the time when he thought everyone was asleep.

I hear a door open at the side of the chapel and see Tina and Braxton sort of spill out of the room where they keep the spare chairs, looking all red-faced. I guess they must have lost track of time in there and not realized the speeches had started. They both look very flustered.

Braxton goes to sit with Sukie, but she twists away from him, like she's real mad.

Tina slides in beside me.

'We can leave after this speech, right?' She's breathing fast, and smooths her hair away from her face.

Maybe she doesn't know Rachel has been arrested.

'Mrs Nelson is telling straight *lies*,' I hiss. 'And she hasn't even mentioned us. Your lipstick is smudged,' I add.

'Thanks.' She wipes her mouth. 'Well, that's to be expected from Momma Nelson, right? She never did like us.'

Tina settles back on her hard chair and swivels her head toward the pulpit, but I kind of get the impression her attention is elsewhere. Every so often she sneaks a glance in Braxton's direction. He isn't looking at her though. He's staring straight ahead, like his head is clamped in place, turning the wedding ring on his finger.

'His proudest accomplishment was working as a custodian in the Holy Temple,' Adelaide Nelson continues.

I'm squirming about in my chair now. I can hardly stand it. Blake worked as a canning-machine salesman. And he was so bad at getting his commission, he even had to take a second job as a janitor, for Pete's sake. At least half of the family money came from Tina, since she worked freelance for a realtor firm in the city.

'He had two jobs,' she adds, 'despite his other commitments.'

Her eyes seek me out. Mrs Nelson never did agree with Blake's fundamentalist choices.

You're the reason why my boy might not get to heaven.

'But he was always smiling, always upbeat.'

My mouth drops open. Because this just isn't Blake. She's painting our husband like some smiling Boy Scout, when he wasn't like that at all. I mean to say, Blake was a lot of fun, and he did things that made us laugh. Crazy things too, like the time he hired a tractor he could barely even drive, and craned our new roof into place. But there were also times he wouldn't even get off the couch. Like life had just paralysed him.

'He never let anything get him down,' continues Mrs Nelson.

I turn to Tina. 'This isn't right,' I hiss.

A few people turn around to look at me. Tina pats my hand like I'm a dog.

'He wasn't like that,' I tell Tina, not bothering to keep my voice down now.

From her position up front, Mrs Nelson shoots me a look, like I need to pipe down, then goes right on talking about her perfect boy.

'No!' I stand up. The plate of sugar cookies falls onto the ribbed carpet. I can feel Tina pulling at my arm, trying to get me to sit down, but I tug out of her grip.

Mrs Nelson is glaring at me again, her hands gripping at the podium like claws.

Most people have turned to look in my direction now, but I don't care.

'That's not right,' I say.

27

Rachel, first wife

Brewer has brought me into a different room this time. It has a machine that I guess is for recording, and she unwraps a silver DVD and pushes it in.

The door behind her opens and a chubby young man enters, balancing a messy stack of papers wedged under his arm and a tray of drinks – two that look to be coffee and one filled with some kind of chocolate drink and topped with whipped cream. I think he could perhaps be good-looking in the right circumstances, though not handsome. He's broad-shouldered and tall, but his light blond hair almost blends into the unhealthy pallor of his yellow-tinged skin. The extra weight hangs on his large frame like uncooked dough and there's a sheen of sweat to his forehead, as though he's run here.

Brewer looks up in slight annoyance.

'Sorry I'm late,' the young man places the cardboard tray of cups jerkily on the table, and dark liquid splashes from the top of one. 'Thought we could all use coffee.' As he extracts the files from under his arm, several loose papers fall free and he bends to pick them up.

By the time he retrieves them, and pushes them untidily back into the pile, Brewer is shaking her head in amazement.

'Would your time have been better spent ordering your papers?' she suggests.

The man grins, pulls out the chocolate cream drink, and slurps a loud tug on the thick straw.

'Nope,' he says, seating himself, chunky limbs sprawled.

'This is Officer Malone,' says Brewer wearily, waving a hand toward her blond companion and working a paper cup from the tray. 'He's from New York,' she adds, as if this explains everything.

Malone sits, gives me a disarming smile and lifts a drink free to pass it to me.

'I don't drink . . .' I begin.

'It's the chicory kind,' he interrupts good-naturedly, pushing it toward me. 'I noticed you had a can at your ranch, and we had the same brand in the back of the cupboard, so . . .'

My heart picks up. *They searched the ranch?*

Out loud, I say: 'Thank you,' in a quiet voice, and take the coffee.

Officer Brewer shoots him an outright glower, but it seems to bounce right off him. She coughs again and shuffles papers.

'I imagine you want to know why police were at your home,' she begins.

I feel my mouth twist.

'Most likely,' I say slowly, 'you were taking DNA and finger-prints, to match the body you found.'

Brewer hesitates.

'No,' she says. 'Identification of the victim was really very straightforward. There was no reason to suggest the body be-longed to anyone other than your husband. And you were able to identify him.'

'I couldn't be one hundred percent certain from the face,' I stammer. 'It was so swollen . . .'

I swallow, the image rushing back up at me. The deep purple lips, and protruding tongue.

Brewer nods in sympathy, closing her eyes for just a little too long.

'You're a smart lady, Rachel,' she says. She regards her papers. 'You won a college scholarship. Always top of the class. We've asked around and teachers said you were a model student. They tell us your local bishop had so much faith in your abilities, he paid part of your living costs from his own checkbook. So I guess you're smart enough to know that no one could have got out in that desert, dressed a dead body in your husband's clothes and put his wallet and ID in his pocket, right?'

I feel the wind knocked out of me. I'd been nurturing a small stupid hope, that somehow it wasn't him. But, deep down, I knew the truth. I notice Brewer is still speaking.

'So-o,' she lays out documents. 'We have the results of the autopsy back.' She looks down at the papers. 'The official verdict is now murder.'

A cold feeling washes through me.

'Best guess from forensics,' she continues, 'is someone came up behind Blake, struck him on the head with something, then throttled him with his belt.'

She says it so matter-of-fact, I want to hit her.

'Mystery part,' she continues, 'is how could he not hear someone sneak up behind him? He's out in the wilderness. Nothing but June bugs and crickets. Blake must have heard his attacker crunching across that sandy desert long before they got close enough to take him unawares. So how does that person manage to land a blow that fractures his skull?'

I don't answer.

'No evidence he put up much of a fight. No chips to the fingernails, bruising to the legs, which you'd expect if he'd clawed at someone, kicked out at 'em. Our guys in the lab hypothesize the killer was likely known to the victim, which I guess we all knew already.'

Her eyes meet mine again.

'Officers have combed the immediate area,' she concludes, 'but been unable to find the weapon, or the missing body parts. However, the river has a strong current. We're searching further downstream. Maybe something washed up.'

I sit, stony silent.

'Why don't we find out a little more about you?' suggests Brewer. 'By my understanding, you undertook missionary work after college. That usual for a female? Banging on doors, preachin' Jesus?'

'More so nowadays,' I say, 'but women only serve for a year.'

'You were particularly good, right?' Malone is speaking now, shuffling his long body forward slightly. 'The best, so say your fellow missionaries. Over twenty baptisms, when most kids get none in two years. What was your secret?'

I have no idea why they're asking me this, but there seems no harm in telling them.

'Um,' I roll the coffee cup in my hands. 'Well, I got an easy assignment. I was working in a New York community with a lot of single moms. I just did things for them, I guess. I was always raised to be helpful. I did the laundry, dishes, cleaning. Sometimes caring for the children. If something was broken, I'd try to get it fixed.'

I'm enjoying the memory. If Blake hadn't insisted I give the work up, I would have carried on. But my husband didn't want a wife who was out of doors all day.

'You didn't preach the Book of Mormon?' confirms Brewer, breaking into my thoughts.

I shake my head. 'No, Ma'am. Not unless you want to get

turned right outta the door. People say that the way to a man's heart is through his stomach. Well, I can tell you, when a woman has a family, the way to her heart is through her dirty dishes. It's not easy to let God in when you've a clutch of rug rats need feeding and a trash can full of diapers.'

Malone beams, enjoying the soundbite.

'Mrs Nelson,' says Brewer, 'we went to the ranch, because we wanted to be sure there were no other wives there.'

I don't like the way she says wives. I fold my hands around the coffee cup, drawing it against my body.

'There are some large outhouses and so forth,' she adds. 'It was important to assure ourselves no one was being held against their will.'

My body flashes hot then cold.

'Why would you think that?' I sip the Postum, but the taste doesn't register.

Brewer only gives me a long look.

'I think you know the answer to that, Mrs Nelson.'

Brewer looks me in the eye.

'You know,' she says softly, 'I thought there was something familiar about you. It was a long time ago, I only saw pictures. This isn't the first time you've been in this police station, is it?'

'No . . . But . . .'

'Mrs Nelson. Why didn't you tell us you were raised in a cult?'

28

Tina, sister–wife

Whoa. I mean. *Whoaaaa!*

Can you believe it? Little crazy Emily gets up during Momma Nelson's big bullshit speech, 'bout what a perfect guy her boy was.

Adelaide Nelson is droning on about her great son Blake, and this little voice cuts through all of it.

'*That didn't happen*,' Emily says, just like that. A ripple of shock travels around the church.

I try to pull her back down, but she pulls free of my grip with a lot more strength than I would have credited her with.

Emily stands, tiny in her little black funeral dress, and turns to face the audience.

'*First* of all,' she says, 'Blake wasn't a *custodian* at Temple. He was a janitor. And it wasn't some holy calling. He took a second job 'cause we were real bad in debt. Blake wasn't making enough sales at Survive Well.'

Shocked murmurs pass around the rows of seated mourners. Mrs Nelson's face is all hard-looking.

'Secondly, she hasn't even mentioned us,' says Emily, looking around at all the faces which have turned to look at her. 'We were his *wives*. We had to go to *bed* with him.'

I glance at Mrs Nelson senior. She's white with shock. Pity bubbles up.

'Emily,' I hiss out of the corner of my mouth. 'Sit *down*.'

'But why should she say stuff that isn't right?' hisses Emily, looking at me. 'I mean, he was *our* husband!'

My eyes travel back to Mrs Nelson. Tears of grief and humiliation are brimming in her eyes now. Sympathy for her gains the upper ground. I take Emily's arm. I sigh.

'Why is *she* allowed to lie?' Emily insists.

'Because she's a straight-up crazy bitch, Emily,' I say quietly. 'But she's his mom, and she can say what she likes at her son's funeral. So sit your ass down and show some respect.'

Emily flops down like a puppet with her strings cut.

Mrs Nelson tries to carry on, but you can see she's mentally editing out a lot of material. I guess anything else she feels might not pass Emily's truth radar. Which by the short length of her speech is a fair amount.

The other mourners are all facing firmly forwards now. Like they don't dare sneak a glance back, 'cause it will confirm what just happened.

After she's finished, Adelaide goes back to sit with Mr Nelson. He puts a hand on her arm, half sympathy, half restraining. Like he's frightened she'll embarrass everyone a second time with another awful lurching funeral speech. Some awkward clapping starts up in one part of the church, then stops.

Bishop Young is taking the pulpit now. I lean back, ready to be bored out of my mind for the next hour. But it doesn't turn out that way.

Someone I don't recognize sorta scuttles up to Bishop Young and whispers in his ear, stealing glances at me.

He looks at me, with shock, at first, then rage. I feel myself growing hotter. Like I want to shrink into my chair. All I can think is, *he knows*. He knows what happened between me and Braxton in that back room. I didn't think about it at the time, but maybe sound travels in that little room. It's connected onto a little kitchen part at the back, which I assumed was empty.

Bishop Young walks toward me, far more quickly than I might have thought possible for a fat man. He closes in, kinda *shaking* with anger. A few people turn to watch him, confused, like maybe this is part of the show.

'Miss Keidis,' he says, low enough that only I can hear, 'you are no longer welcome in this community.'

'What?' I try to pull an innocent smile.

Emily is looking back and forth between us, like she's at a soccer game where she doesn't understand the rules.

'I know what you did in that back room,' he says, furious. 'You were overheard. I'm not about to shout about it in a house of God. But I'd like you to leave. Leave and don't come back.'

29

Rachel, first wife

Brewer nods at Malone, and he pulls out a brown file from a stack of other papers. Considering the size and nature of his document pile, it strikes me as impressive he's laid a hold of it so fast. Brewer's expression suggests she's thinking likewise.

Brewer opens the file to reveal a yellow cover page I haven't seen in ten years. Longer. Even now, the sight of it brings me out in a cold sweat.

Brewer is looking at me carefully.

'As you know, we're now treating this as a murder inquiry,' she says.

Malone takes another loud slurp of his cream drink. 'Should we call you a lawyer?'

I shake my head.

'No,' I say firmly. 'I've got nothing to hide.'

Brewer and Malone exchange glances.

'You didn't think it relevant to tell us,' continues Brewer. 'About your being raised in a cult?'

My lower lip is quivering.

'It wasn't a cult.' I say it very quietly. 'It was a religious community.'

'The Sunshine Homestead,' Brewer says. 'They were raided and the founder prosecuted. Lemme see here.' She licks a thumb, flicks. 'Underage marriage, rape of minors, child abuse, child neglect. Seventeen counts and twelve indictments. Seems your daddy was a very bad man.'

I'm hit by a lurching sense of shame. My father was known to his followers as 'The Prophet', and had over sixty wives at the time of his arrest. His favorite few lived in luxury in a big house, whilst the rest of us scraped and starved, crammed ten to a mouse-infested bed.

'They told us it would be a fresh start,' I say miserably. 'No one was to know. Not even police.' I make a strange choking sob.

Brewer lifts a box of Kleenex from the table and proffers it. I draw one out and she leans back after I take one, her glossy ponytail swinging.

'Yeah, well.' She taps the page with a neatly cut fingernail. 'Some things are always kept on record. Even if they're no longer on your official file.'

'You ran away, is that right?' asks Malone.

I nod, feeling my face redden with the shame of it all. I've been hiding out as normal for so long, I almost convinced myself my past didn't matter. But of course it would come chasing after me. Isn't that what my father told me all along?

God will find you out. There's no running from family.

'The police report says you were found aged fifteen, wandering Salt Lake City late at night, with injuries to your face. Told them you were running from an arranged marriage?'

There's a long pause. I realize I've been shredding the tissue they gave me, and ball the ragged pieces into my fist.

No hiding it now, I guess. Might as well tell them what they already know.

'My father had promised me to one of the leaders,' I say, taking a breath. 'This,' I wince at the memory, 'disgusting old man with bad breath. All the girls were terrified we'd end up as his wife.'

Brewer nods, listening.

'I said I didn't care to marry him. That wasn't very common, at the Homestead.'

Brewer returns my smile.

'So,' I begin shredding the tissue again, looking down. 'My uncle drove me out to a barn on the edge of town. He hit me with a belt and punched me. I lost count how many times. Broke my nose,' I say, 'split my lip. I knew it wasn't right. I knew that God was a kind father. It wasn't right to do that to girls. In the face.'

Malone's eyes widen almost imperceptibly. I realize my phrasing is strange to him. I guess where he grew up, it wasn't right to hit women at all.

'So you ran away?'

'I let him drive me home,' I say. 'My mother received me as if nothing at all was wrong. Promised my uncle I would behave as God willed. She put me to bed as though I was sick, and tucked the covers right up to my chin.'

'Women stay sweet,' she urged me, in a whisper, as my brothers and sisters slept on, in nearby beds. 'It's part of God's plan. No more sassiness. You may not understand it all now, but you will do.' She kissed my head. 'I'll have your father give you a blessing tomorrow,' she reassured me.

I remember her as colorless. And never more so than that evening, promising Godly intervention, from the husband who kept her as a twentieth wife in a damp cellar. Perhaps it was that realization, more than anything, that made me get up quietly, slip on my hand-me-down shoes and walk all the way to the nearest asphalt road.

'I went looking for a church,' I say. 'Two policemen found me, wandering the streets, with my face all busted. They took me in.'

Officer Brewer is watching my face.

'The police sent you back home,' she says, quietly. 'Is that right?'

I nod slowly. 'They took me to hospital, fixed me up. Asked me a lot of questions. Drove me back to my family.'

Brewer looks pained.

'That must have been hard. You were very courageous. And you must know that your contact with the police drew attention to the Homestead. You were part of the reason it was eventually raided.'

I nod. The familiar shame flares in my belly.

They hate me now.

'Are we to assume, Mrs Nelson,' inquires Malone, 'that the relatives you fought with your husband about, the night of his death, are the same people you lived with at the Homestead?'

'Yes.' I can barely hear my own voice.

'You ever meet with your relatives?' asks Brewer. 'Bump into 'em at weddings? Special occasions?'

'Not since I went to college. They didn't agree with . . . my lifestyle choices.'

'They didn't like your choice of husband?'

'They didn't want me educated.'

'Your folks live out at Waynard's Creek nowadays?'

'Some of them. The Homestead was seized after the raid,' I explain.

'A lotta those folk set up another community, that right? Refused to accept the so-called Prophet's incarceration was lawful?'

'It's more complicated than that,' I say, bristling at her use of language. 'These are people with no social security, no education. People with strong beliefs. They can't just slot back into society.'

'The thing that strikes me,' says Brewer, 'is this puts our earlier conversation in a different light, doesn't it, Mrs Nelson? Do you recall telling us how you and Blake fought because he'd been in contact with your relatives? Your husband tell you why that was?'

Pain sears into my palms. I realize I'm bunching my fists.

'Blake wasn't in the habit of explaining himself to me.'

'But you had some ideas, right?' Brewer pauses, taps her fingers. 'Ever take a glance at your husband's GPS, Mrs Nelson? I noticed he had one in his car.'

I shake my head. 'I'm not sure what that is.'

'It's an electronic mapping system,' she says, 'shows you how to get to where you want to go. Some companies give 'em to employees. Even Utah ones.' She smiles at her own joke. 'Your husband had one. Nature of his job, on the road a lot. We took a look at Blake's journeys. Guess what? He drove out to Waynard's Creek recently.'

My stomach lurches.

'Mrs Nelson, did your husband go out visiting with your relatives because he was shopping for a fourth wife?'

30

Tina, sister–wife

I walk right out to the parking lot fast. At the very back is our car, sitting in its regular spot. It's a beat-up Chevy that Blake bought for a discount from some friend out of town.

God bless Rachel.

If she hadn't been playing Super-Wife, I'd be stranded out here with these freaks.

My heart is pumping with what feels like relief. At last I'm taking a decision. I need one little fix, is all. I can almost feel it now. That white cold energy, clearing out my brain, making everything OK. If I can get out of my own head, just for now, I'll deal with the rest later.

Just as I near the car, in comes a memory of Blake, crashing, uninvited, like I'm having a physical fight with it. The good old days. That fluttery feeling when he showed up at the rehab meetings to read scripture.

Even though he was godly, you could tell Blake wasn't the least frightened of the nasty junkie guys who only showed up under court order. He reminded me of a cowboy in those Wild West films, all rugged and fearless and muscled under his plaid shirt. In any case, after a few meetings I just had this sneaking suspicion he had come back for me. When we broke for the warm soda in red cups, Blake always poured mine for me, clasping my hands as he passed it, like not spilling that root beer was the most important thing in the world to him. Confusingly, he wore a wedding band. But confusing in a good way.

One day I looked him right in the eye and said: 'What *exactly* is a guy like you doin' here anyway? Are you making up for being a bad boy?'

I was testing him, and just like I thought, there was a glimmer there. He smiled this truly sexy smile, and was like: 'Maybe I was hoping to meet someone like you.' I swear, it was like someone had passed a bolt of electricity right through me.

I kinda laughed it off, and was like, 'What does your wife think about that?'

He smiled again, and his red eyebrows did this cute little waggle.

'Actually, it's my *wives*,' he said. 'And I think they'd like you a lot.'

Now I was plain perplexed. I actually thought maybe he was messing with me. Or my brain was rewiring after the withdrawal, 'cause they said that was a thing.

He stepped a little closer. 'Tina. What me and my wives have is a holy thing. We try and love as Jesus would love. And we listen real hard, for God to tell us who will join our family next.'

He gave me this long deep look, right into my eyes, then took a step back. I felt as if I'd been severed. Honest to God, my body flushed cold, like all the light had gone out of the world. And I got to thinking, This is it. This is what a sign feels like. Because this sure as hell wasn't normal, the way I felt about this man. It was like being high without the drugs. My fingertips were tingling.

Now he's gone, I'm just *empty*. Like I have to kick at something to feel anything at all.

I reach the car and pull the spare set of keys from my purse. That's when I hear a little voice singin' out behind me.

'Hey!'

I turn to see Emily is running toward me. I never saw her run before. She's fast. By the time I've started to unlock the car, she's next to me, her hand on the handle.

'Wait.' She's panting. 'Wait.'

'I'm takin' a drive around,' I say, sliding back into my convincing junkie lying easy as breathing. 'Clear my head. I'll be back before you know it.'

Emily just shakes her head. Liars know liars, I guess. 'Cause I know Rachel woulda believed me. Blake too.

In that moment, I think if Emily had said anything about my habit, or talking me around, or anything like that, I woulda shoved her aside and got in the car. But she doesn't. She blows some wispy hair out of her face and keeps her hand right on the battered Chevy door.

'It won't feel like you think,' she says.

She looks up at the sky.

'It won't help you feel better.'

I swallow.

'How would you know?' I say it all sarcastic, but Emily takes it all earnest, like a real question.

'I hurt myself too,' she says simply. 'It changes how I feel for a little while. Then I feel worse.'

In all my time of counseling and the programs the cops make you do, I never heard it put that way.

I hurt myself.

I always thought of the drugs as something I was giving myself. Like a little treat, a reward, a release. Something to make me feel better.

'What do you mean, you hurt yourself?' I ask Emily.

'I do it with a pair of scissors.'

I sniff. Take my hand from the car. 'You still do it now?'

She shrugs as if it doesn't matter.

'Good days and bad days,' she says.

The need to get downtown is draining away. If it gets too bad later on, I promise myself, I'll go. I mean, if you can't relapse when your husband's been murdered, when can ya?

Just put one foot in front of the other.

'We need to go see Rachel,' I say. 'Get her a lawyer. She has no clue how cops operate. I'll bet she's sitting there now, like she's at a coffee mornin', tellin' 'em all about herself, without the faintest notion they're mining her for incriminating dirt.'

Emily's mouth twists.

'I've got a better idea,' she says.

'You do?' It's still a novelty to hear Emily express any opinion about anything.

'You know,' says Emily, 'Blake went out to Waynard's Creek, without telling Rachel.'

'What's at Waynard's Creek?'

She kinda rolls her big bug eyes. 'Rachel's relatives live there, dummy, the ones she's not allowed to visit.'

I'm not catching her point. 'I don't get it. Why would Blake go there?'

31

Rachel, first wife

The police station feels uncomfortably hot. Brewer is looking at me, waiting for an answer.

I rub my forehead. 'I had an idea,' I agree. 'I thought . . .' I sigh. 'I thought Blake might have been looking for a wife. Down at Waynard's Creek.'

Malone's face registers shock. Brewer's expression doesn't change.

'OK. So let me check I'm clear on this. You believe your husband was dating another woman, with a view to marriage.'

'Yes.'

Brewer rubs her forehead. 'And that wasn't OK with you? I mean to say, he'd already done it twice before, right?'

I don't like her tone one little bit. I can feel a headache starting, pulsing in the side of my temples.

'It's hard for folk outside our faith to understand,' I say tightly. 'Religious polygamy is a respectful arrangement. All the parties are honored for their different positions. I would expect to be consulted before Blake began courting another wife.'

'Gotcha. So . . . your husband,' Brewer leans back, 'he ever ask Emily about getting hitched to Tina?'

I hate her a little now. 'That's not the same. I'm the first wife. The first wife is always consulted.'

'Forgive me. I thought you were all equals.'

I shake my head wearily, wondering how she can't understand something so basic. 'No, we're not equals.'

'Then what are you?'

'I told you already. We're *wives*.'

Brewer sits back in her chair, absorbing this.

'So, your husband didn't consult you about courting another wife. That was against the rules. And this had been going on for, how long?'

'A few weeks, maybe.'

Malone raises his eyebrows.

'Not long, to be fixing to marry.'

'Plural-marriage courtships are short, officer,' I say, trying to keep my voice even. 'Out of respect for the existing wives, and the newcomer. If relations aren't sanctified promptly, a woman could risk being seen to be behaving inappropriately with a married man, which could damage her standing in the community.'

'So, she would be thought of as a hussy, unless the husband legitimizes her real quick?'

'Yes.'

Malone shakes his head, as if failing to take it all in.

'Did that make you mad, Mrs Nelson?' asks Brewer.

'Yes,' I say. 'It did. I told him so.'

'How about the other women in your marriage, Mrs Nelson? Did Blake ask you if he could marry Miss Martinelli?'

'Yes.'

'Miss Keidis?'

I hesitate and see Brewer take it in.

'I think so,' I admit. 'I'm not entirely sure. It's always tricky in the early stages. There are legal considerations.'

I rub my temples, feeling suddenly exhausted. In the early days, Blake and I had been a partnership. How did it change?

'OK.' Brewer leans forward, leafs through a few papers. 'You're telling us plural marriage is illegal, so you have to keep things hush-hush, right? And that's why no one knew about your ranch.'

I nod.

'Absolutely no one?' Brewer spreads her hands. 'Help us out here, Mrs Nelson. If there's something you're holding back, now would be the time to share.'

'No one else knew,' I whisper, tears welling up. 'That was the whole entire point. It was a place where we didn't need to fear persecution.' I wipe away the falling tears. 'The only visitor we ever had was the realtor, when he gave Blake the final paperwork.'

'We've already checked out the realtor,' says Brewer. 'He moved to Sacramento three years ago, but he also confirmed what you're telling me. There'd be no reason for your little love nest to be known to anyone but yourselves.'

She looks at me, like she's waiting to be corrected.

This would be the time to lie, I tell myself. *Tell them you threw a wild party a few months back.*

But I just wasn't raised that way.

Brewer sighs. The churning unease grows.

'Here's what I think,' says Brewer. 'You're a clever woman. You bottle things up. Perhaps you put two and two together. Realized Blake was on the hunt for wife number four. It made you angry.'

I spread my hands out.

'I won't deny I was . . . put out,' I say. 'A new wife is always a hard issue, no matter how much you pray for an open heart. But it was a minor issue. My husband had already married two other women. I was the one who persuaded him to convert to the fundamentalist branch of the faith. I was the one who suggested he take other wives.'

'That so?' She looks like she doesn't really believe it. 'You went right on in and talked your husband into abandoning the faith he'd grown up with?' She raises an eyebrow like this doesn't fit with what she knows of me.

'It was . . . a dream I had,' I say. 'A revelation. Blake and me with other wives. Happy. Harmonious.'

Brewer's eyebrow stays raised. 'Was it your husband who deemed this dream of yours a revelation, by any chance?'

My palms feel itchy, remembering how Blake had seized on the dream, like he was so proud of me. 'You had a revelation, honey! The Holy Spirit was with you!' Blake's bad opinion of my upbringing had changed too. Slowly, so I barely noticed, like beans filling a sack, he'd decided my upbringing hadn't been *all* wrong.

'Did you think your husband had been lying to you, about his movements?' asks Brewer.

I feel my fists curl into balls. 'I don't believe so.'

'Do you recall telling us you had nightmares, Mrs Nelson?'

'Vivid dreams, yes.'

'Your sister-wife mentioned you have bad dreams about a clinic,' presses Brewer.

My eyes pop wide open.

'I don't see . . . Um. There was a place on the Homestead. The older kids used to make up stories to scare us.'

A blood spot. On a pastel prairie dress, at waist height. I'm lying down on a bed. The blood spot moves closer and closer. It's her. The blond lady. Only this time her hair is styled up in a quiff, plaited down the back. She snaps on green hospital gloves. Fear lurches through me.

'You've been a bad girl,' she says.

'What kind of stories?' Brewer is saying.

'Uh. Just dumb stuff. You know how boys are. They said it was where bad girls got sent.'

Brewer leaves a long pause.

'It seems to me, your husband picked vulnerable women.'

'What makes you say that?' My palms feel prickly.

'Mrs Nelson, do you have any family you can contact?'

'Not at this time, no.'

'That's what I thought. Did you know we tried to call Emily Martinelli's mother? An officer explained her husband had been murdered. You know what she said?'

I shake my head.

'She said: "I don't know anyone called Emily."'

She pauses to let this sink in.

'Pretty unusual, don't you think, for a mother? To deny she has a daughter?'

'Um. I guess so.' The truth is, I have no idea what normal is.

'Tina Keidis, Blake's third wife.' For some reason, the way she phrases this makes me wince. Brewer flips papers. 'Brought up in a halfway home, irregular contact with mother, father unknown, a bunch of half-siblings scattered across seven states. Can you see the picture I'm building, Mrs Nelson?'

'You're implying my husband deliberately chose women without families?'

'It's a very common practice in cults, sects, places where people are brainwashed.'

32

Emily, sister-wife

Tina doesn't seem to be understanding me.

'Blake went out to Waynard's Creek,' I say patiently. 'Like *went out* there. In his car.'

'So, he thought Rachel should build bridges?' suggests Tina, in her gravelly low voice.

I roll my eyes. Honestly, sometimes Tina is kinda stupid.

'It was a *girl relative.*' I study her, to make sure this has sunk in. 'One of the cousins or whatever, who live out near Waynard's Creak. Rachel's folks are all fundamentalists.'

I look at her again. She still hasn't got it.

'*Polygamists*, right?'

Tina shakes her head slowly.

I open my hands up, stare in disbelief. I'm just going to have to spell it out for her.

'If Blake was going out, *alone*, to visit one of Rachel's relatives,' I explain patiently, 'it means that was where he was courting the new wife.'

Tina sorta blinks into the distance for a while, like she's taking this in.

'So ... Blake was visitin' with religious girls?' she says finally.

I nod emphatically.

'Blake must have been looking for someone real submissive,' I say. 'Those folk believe the husband is God on earth and you have to do everything he says without question. Prayers every hour. Hair down to their butts, so they can anoint their husband's feet with oil, scraped up in that weird claw thing they have.' I gesture the sweep, folding my hand up at the forehead. You see those girls sometimes, in Salt Lake City, the real devout ones. Mostly they're homeschooled, so you never see them in regular places. But you might catch a glimpse in a truck, or on the way to the store, or whatever.

They braid their long hair in all kinds of plaits and brush up the front into the oval pillowy quiff thing above their foreheads. As a girl, I used to think they looked like angels. The mean girls at school used to call them claw-heads, on account of the quiff looking like a giant claw. Rachel told me once she was brought up to think the higher the hair, the more devout the woman, since it took forty minutes each and every morning to get all those plaits and quiffs right.

Tina has a weird look on her face.

'You think he thought I wasn't devout enough?' she says. Her voice sounds all wobbly and weird.

I shrug.

'Doesn't matter now,' I point out. 'He's dead, isn't he?'

Tina's mouth sorta flickers, like she can't tell whether I'm being funny. Finally she settles on a halfway smile.

'Guess so,' she says, real thoughtful.

I decide this is a good moment to tell her my theory.

'What if Blake was out there courting, and something went wrong?' I say. 'Like maybe Blake changed his mind . . . Or, or picked someone different, and the Waynard's Creek girl got mad? Maybe even mad enough to kill Blake.'

'How's that even likely, if those girls are raised to be submissive?'

'A relative then.' I pout. 'Like an angry father or brother or something.'

'Emily . . .' she looks pained. 'There's a million reasons why that could never have happened. How would they even know where the ranch was?'

'Did you ever watch *Cagney & Lacey*?' I ask.

'Couple of times maybe. The old cop show, right?'

I nod. 'Which would you be?'

'What?'

'Which one,' I say patiently. 'Cagney or Lacey?'

Tina is pulling the strangest face.

'I dunno, Cagney I guess. She's the blond one, right? Why in the hell does it matter?'

I pout a little.

'We can't both be Cagney,' I say.

'Emily, are you plain nuts?' She digs long pink fingernails through her long black hair, exasperated.

'I'm saying, we need to be detectives,' I explain, a little upset she's not understanding me right. 'I mean, if that show has taught me anything, it's the killer is never who you expect.'

Tina doesn't answer.

'No one at Waynard's Creek is gonna speak with the police, right?' I press. 'But they might speak to us. Don't you want to know who Blake was checking out?'

Tina's lips come apart very slightly. I guess she's thinking, maybe she'd like to know who Blake was fixing to marry.

'I say we go find out who Blake was courting,' I explain. 'It's the part that doesn't fit, right? In a plural marriage, the husband is supposed to ask the first wife's permission. But Rachel didn't even *know*.'

'No one told me Blake needed Rachel's permission.' Tina sounds like she's not really following my point.

'There could be more to the whole thing,' I press. 'Maybe we'll find the murder weapon, or something that proves this fourth-wife person killed Blake.'

Tina's mouth twists, and for a moment I think she's going to do what Rachel always did. Tell me to calm down, and not get overexcited and talk like a crazy person. But instead she nods.

'OK then,' she says. 'Let's go check it out.'

33

Rachel, first wife

'We searched your property in the desert. The ranch,' Brewer explains. 'Found some interesting things.' She looks at the desk, eyebrows raised, as though her definition of interesting is 'bad'. 'For starters, this Bible. You recognize this?'

She holds up a navy-blue leather-bound book, with *Book of Mormon* in gold writing.

I feel strangely uncomfortable that she's holding it. Like she's disrespecting God's word.

'It looks maybe like Blake's,' I say, wishing she'd put it back down. 'I couldn't be sure.'

'You can't be sure about a holy book, Mrs Nelson?'

'Well, we're part of the same ward,' I explain, 'so all our copies look kinda the same.'

'So you're saying this could be yours?'

'I always keep mine with me.' I pat my faux-leather purse. 'Force of habit after missionary service.'

'And they couldn't have been switched around? On account of the books looking similar?'

'No. I mean. I don't think so.'

'Reason I ask, is this copy has some parts underlined.' She lets it flop open. 'Fairly disturbing passages given the recent turn of events. Here, I'll read 'em.'

She settles into that strange droney voice people oftentimes use for Bible reading.

'If you found your brother in bed with your wife,' she reads 'and put a javelin through both of them, you would be justified, and they would atone for their sins, and be received into the kingdom of God.'

She looks up and, getting no reaction, licks a finger and turns one of the thin pages.

'Then, we have here . . . "It is good and right to defend your family, even using lethal-force weapons." That have any significance to you, Mrs Nelson?'

'No. I mean, other than it sounds awful violent.'

Something sparks in my mind. How Blake would get a bee in his bonnet about some part of scripture. Read Bible at us for so long, Tina and Emily would start giving one another funny looks.

Brewer puts the book down.

'Well, that wasn't the only thing we found. Tell me, Mrs Nelson, did you know your husband owned two cell phones?'

When I don't reply, Brewer slips out a plastic bag and dangles it. There's a large black phone inside. Far more expensive-looking than Blake's regular cell, though I'm not much of a judge of this kinda thing.

'Have you ever seen this phone before?'

'No.'

'You sure about that?'

'Yes.'

'You never saw Blake use it? Or another wife call from this phone?'

'None of us used phones at the ranch,' I explain. 'Blake had a work cell, but he kept it in his car. There's no reception, anyway,' I add.

'Makes it even more surprising why this would be on the property,' says Brewer. 'We found it locked away in a box. You certain you've never seen this before?'

'Yes.'

'So you wouldn't know the code to unlock it?'

'Blake never told me things like that.'

Brewer does that face again. Like she's judging my marriage.

'Just so you know, Mrs Nelson, I am in the process of applying for a warrant and tech resources to unlock this phone.'

I guess it must show in my face, that I don't know what she's talking about, because she clarifies.

'We found this phone in a locked box containing objects of a sexual nature.'

I flinch.

'It's my belief this phone contains recordings,' she adds, 'of a personal kind.'

I'm struck dumb.

'Did your husband do or say anything during the marital act that made you feel uncomfortable? Things that might be termed abusive?'

'No.' I've answered too quickly to sound convincing.

'Only we found something else in that box. This, for starters.'

She pushes a book toward me. I feel numb. The title is *Christian Domestic Discipline Marriage*.

'You recognize that?' she asks.

When I don't answer, Brewer picks it up. Flicks it.

'I've taken a look,' she says. 'Seems to advocate the use of physical violence against women. Any reason why Blake would own this book?'

'I believe Bishop Young gave it to him.' I'm flushed with the memory of this. 'Shortly after he married Emily.'

'So your bishop recommends,' she licks her finger and leafs

through a few pages, 'physically punishing wives who fail to carry out their perceived duties?'

I close my eyes tight. Brewer is talking, but all I can hear is a boiling noise. Like the ocean. When I open them again, Brewer sits silently, and Malone is holding the book. It's more of a pamphlet really, spiral-bound and eerily reminiscent of the things that were printed for our education at the Homestead.

'Have you read this?' Malone is asking me.

'No, I haven't.'

He thumbs a few more pages. 'There are *tools* recommended, for the abuse of women. Hairbrushes, switches . . .'

I realize there are tears on my face. I wipe them away.

'I knew Emily and Blake were having some difficulties. Bishop Young was counseling them,' I whisper, sobs rising up. 'I didn't know . . . Is there a reason to think Blake used that book?'

'Well, here's a funny thing,' says Brewer. 'The guys here at the station, they think your sister-wife Emily has either been groomed, or kidnapped. Maybe even both.'

My eyes snap to her in shock, affront.

'See, Mrs Nelson, we checked up at the hospital,' says Brewer. 'No one came in that night under the name of Emily Martinelli or Emily Nelson. But there was a Miss Cagney. No given name.' She pauses to arch an eyebrow. 'And the nurses remembered Emily when we showed them photos. Matter of fact, they'd already reported her admission to the police. Reason being she had a lotta old injuries, as well as that cracked rib. Scars in a fairly sensitive area.'

She closes the pamphlet.

'You know anything about that?'

34

Tina, sister-wife

I know it's a dumb idea. To go out to Waynard's Creek. Poor crazy Emily is on some mad play-pretend. Me, I'm just hurtin' real bad that Blake was looking for another wife.

I mean, like I can hardly process it. And like a scab you can't help picking, I want to *know*. I want to *know* who Blake was puttin' the moves on behind my back.

As I swing the car along that dusty road, with Emily chattering away about cops and robbers, I realize how Rachel must have felt when I came along. Knowing you weren't good enough. Your husband needed more. Maybe it even hurt twice as bad since he'd already taken a second wife. I glance at Emily, wondering if she had any of the same feelings, or was just relieved to share the load.

We're putting more miles between us and the city, entering what I privately call the badlands. Places the authorities don't even *know* about. A big old nothing stretching all the way around Salt Lake City, and down as far as Nevada. Our ranch is toward the east of these parts, where the mountains are flat-topped and tan. Out this way is more copper-colored and craggy.

I remember Blake telling me, as he drove me to our ranch, a story of a family who lived out in these parts for straight generations without anyone even knowing they existed. The way Blake talked about the land made it sound like Eden. All soft green grass and clear rivers between majestic amber mountains. That's true in spring, when the flowers are real pretty. Rest of the time, the view from our window comes in three colors: dirt, sand, and a kind of faded army-green for any grass or brush stupid enough to try its luck – like someone ordered from a paint book with a whole bunch of pages missing.

I'm used to the desert now. Maybe I even like it. But in the beginning, I remember tryin' to talk myself down. *Like chill out, Tina. You can be a country girl.*

I just wasn't prepared for the isolation. You could *feel* it, driving out from the city. Like you could get lost out here and no one would ever find you.

'Like the Wild West, huh?' I remember Blake saying with a smile, when I told him I hadn't realized there was still wilderness like this in the States. 'No one to bother us out here. Just us, a few birds of prey, maybe a couple of bobcats.'

He loved that. Bein' a cowboy. I remember coming outside, my hands over my ears, to find him firing a gun into the sky to scare off birds of prey.

'Gotta let 'em know it's our territory,' he told me, the rifle butted against the side of his face, one eye shut. 'You let the raptors in, wild cats come for the eggs.'

'What kind of wild cats?'

Blake lowered his gun, pulled me in close.

'Don't worry, honey,' he kissed me. 'I would never let anything hurt my wives. God protects the faithful.'

I had never been with a man like him before. A real-life All-American outlaw, muscled from outdoor work.

'Be careful not to actually shoot 'em,' I told him. 'Those birds are protected.'

He laughed. 'I'm real careful. If it bothers you so much, I'll buy a box of blanks.'

He did, but he never loaded them.

It takes us a good hour driving into nothing, before we get near to where we're going.

I've driven the main highway a few times, in and out of state, when Blake and I were arranging our wedding. That was back when I had my own vehicle. I'd just gotten myself clean. Picked up where I'd left off with my realtor's exams. Got my license, and put aside enough to buy an old Dodge. Don't think I've ever been so happy, driving my own car, down that long road from Vegas to Salt Lake, knowing I'd see Blake at the end of it. That Dodge has since been sold, on account of the family having financial difficulties, and you know what? Rachel never even said thank you.

I take in the rolling horizon. Never been so far out into the wilds.

'This place is somethin' else,' I mutter, taking in miles of open space. The asphalt road ran out a long way back, and we're rolling along over flame-colored ground and flat scree rocks now, blazing orange mountains in the far distance, a cloud of sand churning up behind us.

'I think I see something.' Emily points to the achingly blue sky of the horizon. In the middle distance are dark square shapes that don't belong to the empty wilderness. Shipping containers, looks like.

The ground begins rolling down to a dusty valley spiked with hard tufts of grass, like the desert is havin' a real bad hair day.

Crowded on the flattest part, there's approximately five rows of maybe ten to fifteen steel boxes. Large ones, with peeling paint announcing whatever shipping company once used 'em.

Behind is a big silo thing, like a water tower, mounted on rusted legs.

'What do we do?' I'm getting nervous now. There's a neglected, desperate air. For all its remoteness, this place feels a lot like the crack dens I knew in Vegas. Places where real dangerous people hung around. Park up too close whilst someone was bagging up and you're likely to get popped in the face by some wasted gangster. 'You're sure we should park up?'

'This is the place.'

'I mean about pullin' up on someone else's property. They're gonna be armed to the teeth out here, right?'

'Maybe,' agrees Emily. 'We'll try not to annoy them, right? I can't *see* any guns,' she adds.

'What, you think they'd lie 'em out in the dirt? This is Utah,' I say. 'Seven-year-old kids carry concealed weapons.'

I slow the car, and grind to a sandy halt near to the shipping container she pointed out.

Every instinct is telling me not to get out of the car. Especially with a pathological liar for company.

'Listen,' I say, 'if we do this, you've gotta . . . Just try to be normal, OK? No lyin'.'

At first I think she'll deny it all, but instead she says, 'Ho-kay,' in a happy little voice.

As we exit the car, I'm soaking it all in. I can't imagine Rachel anywhere like this. I mean, even her underwear is neatly folded. This place is like the apocalypse is nigh.

It looks like the shipping containers serve for homes. Little girls in sturdy boots and neck-to-ankle dresses are play-ing a game, running over the top of them. A stray horse is mooching about, looking for something to chew on. Grubby washing hangs about. Judging by the orange color of it, they have to do laundry in the nearby sandy creek. There's a stink on the air from some hole-in-the-dirt latrine.

'It's like that movie,' whispers Emily, *'Mad Max.'*

I'm about to ask her how she saw that movie, since Blake was very strict on things viewed at home, when there's a shriek of metal. One of the big sheets of iron that serves for a door is inching open.

A woman emerges who couldn't look more inbred if she tried. She has a great moon face with features kind of scattered about on it, a snaggled-up top lip, and a real noticeable slant to her wide solid-looking hips. Despite the squalor all around, her hair is glorious, brushed smartly up into a teetering quiff and plaited intricately down her back. In her long pastel-colored prairie dress, she could be anything from twenty to late thirties, but I'm guessing somewhere in between.

She waddles out toward us, and that's when I notice she's carrying a hunting rifle, which she raises in our direction.

Whoa!

'Whaddya want?' she demands, aiming the gun first at me, then Emily.

'Let's all slow down.' My hands are raised in the air, and I'm backing up.

'Excuse us, Ma'am. We're wondering if someone showed up here,' says Emily, in a polite butter-wouldn't-melt voice, as though nothing out of the ordinary is happening. 'Red hair, kinda good-looking. His name was Blake Nelson.'

The woman hitches up the gun onto her shoulder.

'None of us folk here wanna talk to you,' she says. 'Frickin' outsiders, comin' round here, tryin' to buy things them's got no right to.'

Emily and I exchange glances.

'Are you tellin' me,' I ask, 'this man came to buy a wife?'

'Get out,' she says, 'before I put a bullet in ya both and bury ya out back.'

We're backing away now. The woman's young-old face settles into triumph.

'Come on, Emily,' I say, taking her hand. 'Let's go.'

But Emily pulls back, like a toddler digging its heels.

'I'm gonna give ya til the count a three . . .' says the woman, glaring at Emily's refusal to vacate.

'Emily, come *on*,' I hiss. 'You're gonna get us both killed.'

She ignores me, dragging against my grip. For such a slight girl, she is surprisingly strong.

'Excuse me, Ma'am,' says Emily in this strange voice I've never heard before. 'Just one last question. You know someone by the name of Rayne Ambrosine?'

The woman's face changes completely. Her gun drops a little.

'Rayne?' she says. 'What about Rayne?'

'You know her personally?' asks Emily.

'Well, dern it, *yes*. Me 'n' her are cousins.'

35

Rachel, first wife

There's a man arrived I don't recognize. He has a small-town sheriff appearance – big gold-buckled belt, shaved balding head, and a contemptuous expression in his small blue eyes. I figure him to be maybe early thirties, but trying to look older and larger than he is, with his bulky gun holster and handcuffs all on show. He reminds me of the little bantam cocks we had at the Homestead, all puffed up and full of their own importance.

'This is Detective Carlson,' explains Brewer, and there's something strange in her expression, almost like an apology. 'He's taking over from Malone for the moment.'

'The department got tired of namby-pamby,' says Carlson, hitching his flashy belt a little higher. 'Think it better we get this thing closed down. Our boys just found a blood trail, leading from the river to your canned-food store. Pretty faint, but it's there, and only a matter of time before forensics confirm it belongs to your husband.'

He pauses, waiting for this to sink in. My heart is pounding a slow flat beat.

'Time you gave us some real answers, Mrs Nelson.'

He sits, scraping the chair on the floor. He's a solid man, broad-shouldered and stocky. The kind of person who would intimidate criminals.

'Officer Brewer here is new to these parts. I'm not. I dealt with you people from the Homestead before. You folk think you're above the law – that you don't have to answer to cops. Well that's not gonna fly with me, ya hear?'

He pauses to let this sink in. A wave of despair washes through me. I guess he must have been one of the police officers who busted the Homestead. They tend to bear a grudge.

'So,' he begins. 'You take a lot of prescription drugs, that right?' he leans forward, eyeballing me.

'I . . .' I'm suddenly so nervous at the aggressive line of questioning that I can barely stammer out a response.

'You tryin' to think up some clever answer, Mrs Nelson?' He puts his elbows on the desk, closing the space between us.

'No,' I whisper. My eyes track to Brewer. She seems to have retreated in on herself, like she's thinking heavily behind those amber eyes. In contrast to Carlson, she looks even prettier, with her tan skin and shiny black hair. Like she's a TV cop and he's a real one.

'Glad we've finally gotten the truth out of you.' Carlson shoots a triumphant glance to Brewer.

'Mrs Nelson has always been open and honest about her pharmaceutical use,' says Brewer in an icy voice. 'I didn't judge the consumption to be anything out of the common way.'

We exchange a look.

'Well, by my count, antidepressants, sleeping pills and a dead husband is a long way out of the common way,' says Carlson. 'We also found some . . . What do you call them, bladder pills?'

I flinch in my seat. I can feel my cheeks burning.

'Those were for urinary tract infections,' cuts in Brewer. 'It's something that affects a fair few women. I don't think we need to make Mrs Nelson uncomfortable about it.'

'An' I think you're being naive. You don't experience any side effects from the antidepressants?' he turns his attention on me. 'Fuzzy brain, memory problems?'

This brings me up with a start.

'No. I mean, aren't they just the regular kind?'

'If you count crazy-pills as regular, then sure,' he says, with a little grunting, humorless laugh. 'You don't think your medication's of note, Mrs Nelson? Given your background? Or did ya just forget you took 'em?'

He moves forward, near enough to make me uncomfortable. I press back against my seat, trying to create some distance. I just have the worst feeling. Like this man is going to make me say something I regret.

36

Rachel, first wife

I can't quite describe the emotions boiling inside of me. The idea that these strange people, not even members of the Church, can gain access to my private information. I don't think I could feel more awful if they'd made me take all my clothes off.

'Are you suggesting,' I say, teeth gritted, 'I murdered my husband, and just *forgot* about it?'

'Well,' Carlson spreads his hands, 'you'd hardly remember if you had, now would you?' He purses his lips. 'Brewer here wants to be all cuddly with ya. Not your fault, abusive husband. Me here, I look into things a little deeper. Alrighty. So you're now saying, Blake was on the hunt for wife number four?'

My throat constricts to hear him say it out loud.

'I'm not *now* saying it,' I protest. 'It was never relevant before.'

'Mrs Nelson,' he says. 'I've dealt with you Homestead people a thousand times, and I'm well aware you know the system, and you like to give us the runaround.'

'I don't live on the Homestead anymore,' I say tightly. Carlson waves this away.

'My instincts are telling me this is a smokescreen,' he continues. 'You're tryin' to deflect attention from what really happened that night. Send us all off looking for someone who doesn't exist.'

'Why would you think that?'

'Because it's the kinda stunt you people pull.' His eyes slide to Brewer. 'Their so-called Prophet claimed there were four hundred people on that land. When we raided it, there was more like two thousand, crammed into homes, twenty to a room. It was the worse squalor I've ever seen in the United States of America. Fourteen-year-old girls who were full-blown pregnant.' He glances around. 'Everyone acting like that's normal.'

Carlson's eyes are on me now.

'When we arrived, the women kept moving around, giving us false names. There were secret rooms and doors all over the place. Everyone was related, so they all sorta looked the same. Never seen anything like it.' He shakes his head. 'What Brewer here doesn't understand is you folk were raised to think of cops as devils, that right?'

'Yes, but—'

'Lying to the police is practically in your DNA.'

I open my mouth to object.

'Before you contest that, Mrs Nelson, you should know I got your therapy notes. All paid for, care of the state, naturally.' His lip curls.

My heart beats faster. I picture my therapist scribbling away, eyes lowered behind her designer glasses.

With her big city clothes, expensive-smelling perfume and gold-nibbed fountain pen, she was the most glamorous person I'd ever met. I trusted her. A powerful feeling of violation is coursing through me.

'Sessions with Madeline Overbacht,' he continues. 'Who for some reason found you so fascinating, she gave you an extra session for free, a few months back. That right?'

'It was just a phone call,' I say, flustered now. 'She contacted my old college and got a hold of Blake's number somehow. Said she wanted to check back in before closing the file.' I can feel my cheeks burning.

There's a pause.

'You were assigned to her care, shortly after the Homestead was raided, is that right?' asks Carlson.

I nod again.

Carlson shakes his head. 'The apple didn't fall far from the tree did it, Rayne? Seems you got a history of messing people around who are nice to you.' He slaps the notes on the table. The familiar handwriting is like an electric shock. I have an image of my therapist, her pen moving, then a memory.

I'm being carried over sandy earth. My private parts are hurting. I don't know where they're taking me. I am hopeless, trapped.

Carlson is flipping pages.

'You sure kept your therapist busy, didn't ya? There's a whole box file of your cock and bull.'

I feel myself vanishing into the handwritten notes. The things I told her. The things I didn't.

'Why is she making those noises?' It's Blake. He stands over my bed, frowning. Then the blond woman is at his side, green hospital gloves, hair plaited up. She hates me. Thinks I'm dirty.

'I gave her morphine,' she tells Blake. 'She doesn't know what she's doing.'

Blake's frown deepens. 'Give her some more, would ya?' He shakes his head. 'It sounds like she's . . . You know.' They exchange a look.

The blond lady moves forward, the blood spot on her waist almost touching my face. She selects a needle from a trolley next to the bed and pushes it into my arm.

Carlson's voice plays over my thoughts.

'Some *clinic* where they took evil women?' he rages incredulously. '"Cause I was *there*, Mrs Nelson. And we never found none of this stuff.'

Because you never found the basement.

'Hey, that's enough,' says Brewer. 'Mrs Nelson—'

White beds. Bloody napkins . . .

'No one did bad things in some secret clinic,' interrupts Carlson, speaking over her, 'did they?'

A tangle of naked limbs. Blake without his garments, grunting, panting.

'By the power of Jesus Christ,' I mutter. 'By the power of Jesus Christ, *I command you to leave me alone!*'

I look up to see Brewer glance at Carlson, then back to me.

'Are you quite alright, Mrs Nelson?'

I breathe out, pushing the memory back where it can't bother me.

'I'm fine.' I smile at her. For some reason she sort of recoils.

37

Tina, sister–wife

The name 'Rayne Ambrosine' works like a golden key for the gun-toting woman. She lowers the rifle and introduces herself as Marsha, shaking both our hands awkwardly in her thick-fingered, calloused palm.

'Rayne comes every month and leaves a care package,' explains Marsha. 'She knows the menfolk won't let us accept charity,' Marsha adds, 'so she leaves 'em in the bushes over there. We kinda pretend to we husbands like we found 'em, and they don't ask too many question with so many lil' mouths to feed.'

Emily and I look at one another. Rachel makes a monthly trip to the wholesale store out on the main highway. She always made out it took her so long because she liked to take her time wanderin' the aisles. Classic Rachel. Not a *lie*. Just something frickin' important not mentioned.

I look around the hovel. There are kids with clothing hanging off them. I recognize the hungry look in their eyes, like they're eyeing us for what we might be worth to 'em.

I grew up in the shittiest squat you can imagine, with pimps and junkies, and a mom who sold herself for five bucks when she could raise herself out of the drug haze. Never thought I'd find anywhere worse than the place I grew up. Guess I was wrong.

'That man you said,' says Marsha. 'Blake, you say his name was?'

I nod. I'm taking her in now, wondering if she was the chosen one. If Blake regarded this as his duty, I guess he wouldn't be takin' face and figure into account. I wonder how many children she would have been bringing with her.

'Yeah, he was here.' She picks at her back teeth with a finger. 'Same reason as all the rest of 'em. We've had men from all over. Texas, Las Vegas. Come wanting ta lay a purchase to things folk are not entitled to own.'

'They want to buy women,' asks Emily, wide-eyed, 'wives?'

Marsha's bland features maneuver into confusion.

'What? Heck no. All the women here are married. Or already promised. Them outsiders be comin' to buy the land.'

'They want your property?' I'm looking at the scrub desert, with the rusting shipping containers.

'Not *this* land,' says Marsha. 'The old place. The one we were kicked outta, when our Prophet got sent ta jail. Big old Homestead, on the state line. Rayne din't tell ya 'bout it?'

I shake my head.

'Guess it's a lotta bad memories,' she decides. 'Well, the police came. Took away all the chil'ren. Law got involved, gave 'em all back. But by then, them's had took a good look around and found the beds and whatnot. Arrested the Prophet for . . .' she frowns into the distance, trying to remember, '. . . indecency, I wanta say. Somethin' like that. Sure ta frickin' dang heck din't understand our way a life.'

'I read about that,' says Emily guilelessly, 'in the papers. He did things to underage girls. Made them hold each other down and stuff.'

I feel sick, thinking of Rachel.

'Yeah well, those newspapers say a lotta things. Sacerlijus things mostly.'

'So Blake didn't come here for a wife?' I feel kinda bad askin', but I just have to know.

'*No-o*.' She rolls her eyes. 'He came here 'bout the land. Same as they always do. Them's always want ta know 'bout the secret cemetery.'

'A secret cemetery?' I must have said it happier than I meant, 'cause she looks at me funny. Awful as it sounds, relief is coursing through me. Blake wasn't here for another woman.

Marsha leans her head, assessing me more keenly with her cow-like eyes.

'I'll tell ya same thing I told yer husband Blake. I don't frickin, *know* about any hidden burial places. None of us do. The Prophet never told us about anything like that. Not nice ta ask us things like that not-neither,' she adds, her lip curling. ''Cause we be gettin' inta trouble, talkin' 'bout secrets.'

She looks like she might close down on us, and then she rubs her big face.

'Did anyone tell you *why* they were looking for a graveyard?' I'm still trying to turn over what this might mean.

Marsha sorta snorts. 'The menfolk don't tell us nothing.' She thinks for a moment. 'You wanta find out 'bout that cemetery, you might ask Rayne. There was always stories flyin' round that she snuck out, explorin' places we weren't allowed. Some folk even said she found the clinic. Rayne was pretty wild, so meybbes it was true.'

'What clinic?'

'There was a place at the Homestead we weren't s'posed to go,' she says. 'Bad mothers went there. Some even tell it, the clinic is still in business, to be sure us ladies behave ourselves with the Prophet away. Maybe Rayne saw something she shouldn't have. Sure would explain why they did what they did to her.'

She looks at the sky.

'What did they—?'

But she interrupts me. 'Ya gals better be on the road,' she says. 'Can't be seen here when the men get home.'

There's something steely and cold about her now.

'Tell Rayne, we pray fer her,' she adds, 'but ya gals best not come back here, 'K? Y'all only end up hurtin' us an' gettin' us inta trouble.'

It's like she's switched. The kids are all heading toward the shipping containers. I guess the men come back with the food.

I rummage in my purse for something to give her, find a ten-dollar note and wish I had more. I shake out all my dimes and quarters and hold it all out in my palm.

'Here,' I say. 'Take it. Please. Buy the children something.'

She shakes her head sadly.

'I can't take that,' she says. 'If folks here knew I done took money from outsiders, my husband would lose standin' in the commun'ty. The Prophet might decide to take us wives and kids and send us to another husband.'

'But . . . he's in jail, right? Your prophet?' says Emily.

'He issues orders. We listen. We're faithful. Waitin' for Zion.' She sighs. 'Fer sure can't come soon enough,' she says, more to herself than us. 'Most of us wives wake in the morning and pray ta die.'

A hole opens up in my chest for Rachel. She's been bearing all this alone. These dumbass people with starving children who won't take help.

'Here.' Emily is passing something. 'You can take these, right?' She's holding a box of Tic-Tacs.

Marsha smiles. Shakes some out. Puts one in her mouth.

'Holy heck.' She closes her eyes and beams real wide. 'Them's ta die fer.'

Even doin' that small thing for her helps me in some way. I want to do more. Like Rachel, I guess. As we leave, I remember a package of chocolate mints I still have in the car and bring them out to her.

Marsha stares at them for a moment, like she can't quite believe what she's holding.

'Well shut the door,' she breathes, showing all of her flared teeth. 'This is the most givin' I've ever had in one single day. The kids ain't never gonna forget this.'

I smile at her and go back to the car, guilt and confusion eatin' at me in equal measure.

Marsha digs her hand in her long dress suddenly.

'Blake give me a number of some lady I should call,' she says. 'If I remembered anythin'.' Her mottled fist draws free a folded piece of paper. 'I meant ta toss it, but I guess somethin' be stoppin' me. Take it,' she says.

My hand closes around it. There's a roar on the horizon of approaching vehicles.

'Ya don't come back now!' she says loudly. 'I mean it.'

Then she turns quickly, as though regretting talking, and makes her strange slanted-hip waddle right back into her awful home.

38

Rachel, first wife

My lawyer is a young man, very cleanly shaved, in the kind of suit I can tell is laundered by a very tired wife at home. Something about the creases gives it away. I idly wonder how many children he has, and guess at two very close together. He's in his late twenties, likely married after completing his mission and graduating law school.

He tells me his name is Steven Clark, and he looks every bit as average as his name. Mousy hair, unremarkable features. His blue eyes are kindly. I think he really wants to help. But I get the impression he's wildly out of his depth.

'May I ask, when your husband proposed, did he also suggest he would be interested in pursuing a polygamous marriage with you?'

I feel the muscles in my neck tighten. Like a migraine is just on its way.

'No.'

'Yet you wound up living a polygamous lifestyle, with two other wives?'

I can tell he thinks I'm guilty. I can't explain I'm not good at being the center of attention. It makes me uncomfortable. I'm not used to answering questions about myself.

He purses his lips.

'Mrs Nelson, I'm here to get you the best deal possible,' he says.

I feel cold all over.

'What do you mean, deal?' I whisper.

'Mrs Nelson, I'm not going to lie to you,' he says. 'You're not in a good situation. The state of Utah has a lot of empty land and uninhabited mountains. Plenty of places for people to hole up and evade the law. Those people are almost impossible to police, but when the state does find them out, they come down hard. Around Salt Lake City, we got a reputation for inbreds and polygamists and such, living outside legal jurisdiction, that the state wants to stamp out for good.'

I put my hand on my forehead. 'I don't understand. We weren't doing anything illegal,' I say. 'It's not a crime to live out in the desert.'

'I've read your file,' he says. 'I know how a court would see things. You were raised in a religious "community",' he pauses to make quotation marks with his fingers, 'raided by the police twelve years ago. The leaders were indicted on thirty counts of child abuse, underage marriage, rape of minors.'

'That's in the past,' I say. 'I started a new life.'

I don't want to think about that awful bleached-out place. The children heaped up in abject poverty.

Steven taps his pen on his lips. Frowns.

'What a jury will struggle to understand,' he says, 'is why such a brave young lady, who ran away from a cult she was born into, would then willingly walk right back into similar conditions?'

'My marriage was nothing like that!' I'm so angry, it takes all my effort to stay sitting. 'I'm the *first wife*.'

He changes tack. 'Thing is, Mrs Nelson. Make no mistake here, the police have arrested you on suspicion of murder. That means, they've got enough evidence to bring you to trial.'

He folds his hands, letting the image sink in. There's a plain gold wedding band and neatly cut fingernails.

'From what I can gather, the police are on your side. But a prosecution won't be. They'll throw anything and everything at you.'

His lip twitches slightly.

'They'll try to paint you as unstable,' he says. 'Prone to violence. A physical fight with a sister-wife, the night before your husband was murdered.' He holds out his hands. 'You have to admit, it doesn't look so good.'

He spreads the therapy report on the table.

'Officer Brewer was under the impression there were things that happened in your childhood . . .' he chooses his words. 'Perhaps things that you saw, that you can't bring to mind. Things that give you nightmares. You told your therapist there was a place on the Homestead you had nightmares about? You mentioned a graveyard? And a basement where they took women?'

There's a long, horrible pause.

A blood spot. Butterscotch-hued earth. A scree of flat yellow stones like a riverbed. A coffin lid closing. Something awful inside.

I'm lying in a white hospital bed, pretending to be asleep. Through my half-closed eyes, I see the blond woman. I'm praying she'll walk past. I'm praying she'll hurt one of the other girls instead.

'What I'm suggesting is, there are a number of very powerful reasons why you might have done something you don't remember. Reasons someone like Brewer could persuade the District Attorney to sympathize with.'

I blink at him.

'I just don't know how to reply to that,' I say finally.

'You're on strong antidepressants, sleeping pills,' says Steven, 'you find out your husband is out, not having an affair, but looking for a *fourth wife*.'

I'm struck by how appalled his tone is.

'That could push someone with a background of trauma over the edge. And, luckily for you, the acting District Attorney will entertain reasoning of that nature. *Psychological* justifications.' Steven mimes a turning action, finger against his skull. '*But*,' his voice goes singsong, 'I have to tell you, it's complicated for your average jury. Folks round here see things more black and white. They're less open to factors of mental health than people might be in, say, California. Last few cases of spousal abuse I've seen, juries all sided with the husband.'

'My marriage *wasn't* abusive.'

He shakes his head sadly.

'We don't want you before a court, Mrs Nelson, do we? I'm going to come right and out say it, you risk the death penalty.'

Hot fear sweeps through me.

'Not to mention,' he says, wagging a finger, 'if you act difficult, it's within the power of the state to prosecute your sister-wives.'

'*What*?' I feel sick.

'Bigamy is a crime. Salt Lake City is tired of being associated with polygamy. Your friends broke the law, and the state will throw the book at 'em. Full sentence could be as much as five years in prison apiece.'

I feel I'm in a narrow corridor, with doors clanging shut.

'What do you suggest?' I ask, in a meek little voice.

'Let me handle things,' says Steven. 'I'll tell the DA you're prepared to consider compromises.'

Be reasonable, I think. *Stay sweet.* I have an image of the important men deciding my fate. They wouldn't like it if I started being disagreeable.

I nod my head, twisting my wedding ring. Steven beams.

'Good girl,' he says, sounding a lot like the young men on the Homestead. 'This whole thing will be a lot easier if you're reasonable.'

39

Emily, sister-wife

Tina drives a little distance away, and sits for the longest time, resting her elbows on the steering wheel, staring out the windscreen.

The phone number Marsha gave her is folded up in her hand.

We sit there for a moment, with the bugs and birds loudly chittering away outside. People never tell you that about the desert. You'd think it would be quiet and still. But between the blue jays and cicadas in the day and the bullfrogs and coyotes at night, there are lizards every ten paces that bolt and scare the life out of you, and these enormous crows that croak at about a thousand decibels with no warning.

'You know,' Tina says, finally, 'I really thought Blake had gone out there for a wife.'

She starts making these choking noises. For a moment I think maybe she's got a Tic-Tac stuck, or something. Then I realize she's crying. I pat her shoulder. I don't really know what else to do.

She wipes makeup where it's run under her eyes. Sniffs.

'Him taking another wife wouldn't have bothered you,' Tina says, 'would it?'

I shake my head. Anyone to take the heat off me was good.

'I don't think I felt the same way about him that you did,' I say, remembering how Tina and Blake would look at one another when they were first married. All lovey-dovey and adoring. 'Some marriages are more practical, I guess.'

She sniffs again. 'Did you ever love him?' she asks.

I think about this. When Blake first took me out to the Wendy's near where I worked, he made me feel like I was the most interesting person on the planet.

As a girl, I used to imagine a hero who could ride me off into the sunset, where nothing would hurt me ever again. I don't know quite how it happened, but, somewhere, Blake's face wound up in the picture.

'I was maybe a little in awe at the beginning,' I decide. 'But it wore off.'

I want Tina to call the number, but I have a feeling it wouldn't be appropriate to suggest it.

Tina frowns, then looks down at the paper in her hand.

I eye it hopefully. She sorta shakes her head when she sees that and unfolds it.

A Xerox picture of a lady's face is revealed. Blown-up and grainy, criss-crossed with grubby lines where it's been folded. She looks like the old-style Mormons. The fundamental ones. Her hair is crowned above her head, and her collar is prairie-dress style, buttoned to the neck. There's a real creepy smile on her face.

Tina turns it over. A name and number is scrawled on the back in Blake's heavy handwriting.

'Dakota Jessop,' reads Tina, flipping back to the image side. 'I guess this is her.'

We both stare at the claw-haired lady.

'She looks kinda evil,' I say. I'm feeling nervous now, but I couldn't really say why.

Tina is looking real hard at the face.

'You don't think . . . I mean . . . Blake told Marsha to call this number, right?' says Tina. 'If she remembered anything about a secret cemetery.' She puts a finger on the claw-haired lady's grainy face. 'Who d'ya think she could be?'

'Maybe someone from the Homestead looking for the burial place herself,' I suggest. 'Got a loved one buried there or something.'

This only raises more questions, and we both sit silently for a good while, thinking it over.

Tina opens her mouth to speak, shuts it again. Clears her throat.

'You don't imagine there was anything *romantic*, between Blake and this lady?' Tina sounds like she wouldn't believe it, even if someone told her it was true.

I shake my head. 'I think there's something bigger goin' on,' I say, putting on my best Cagney-detective voice. 'Something to do with that land.'

Tina looks relieved.

'Guess we should call the number,' she decides, taking out the phone the police gave her when they set us up in Salt Lake City.

I'm secretly delighted. This is *just* like a police show.

'It's a Vegas code,' says Tina, pressing buttons. 'Don't know what *that* could mean.' She eyes the claw-haired lady's face as she taps numbers. 'There's no one who looks like *her* in Vegas.'

Tina says it like a joke, but I can tell she's upset, because her hands shake a little. She presses the phone to her ear for a long while.

'No answer,' she says eventually. 'Voicemail for Vegas Real Estate. Guess Dakota works for them.' Her face twists. 'Vegas

Real Estate,' she mutters to herself. 'Why do I feel like I've heard of that firm?'

I don't answer, since I don't know.

Tina dials again. A third time. We sit waiting, but no one picks up.

Tina looks relieved. 'We can try later. Maybe she's busy.' She looks out the window and drums her fingers on the wheel. 'I really owe Rachel an apology,' she says, looking thoughtful. 'I really thought . . .' she wipes more makeup. 'Doesn't matter now, I guess.' Tina shakes her head. 'It's all so *creepy*,' she says. 'A secret cemetery. A *clinic*, for Chrissakes. What in the world was that about?'

'You're not allowed to swear,' I point out.

'Yeah well,' Tina forks a hand through her long black hair. 'I'm just lettin' off a little steam. Seems to me,' she concludes, 'it all comes down to Rachel.'

'We should go ask Rachel about the secret places,' I say. 'The clinic.'

'I don't think she would say anything about the Homestead in front of the cops,' says Tina. 'From how I understand it, her people kinda go into lockdown with authority figures.'

Tina's getting into it now. Being a detective. I knew she would.

We sit in silence for a little while. I'm enjoying being out in the big wide world, not cooped up in the little ranch with nothing to do. It feels like an adventure.

'We can't get Rachel out unless she's proved innocent,' I say. 'But the only way to prove her innocent is to get her out. That's a regular catch-22.'

Tina bangs her hands on the steering wheel suddenly, making me jump. Then she puts the car into drive.

'Where are we going?' I ask, as we speed along the highway.

'I'm goin' back to the police station,' says Tina. 'I got a plan. Kinda.' She has a real determined look about her. 'I might have a way to get Rachel out.'

40

Emily, sister–wife

Tina was not making any sense, trying to explain how she was going to help Rachel. In the end, she got frustrated and dropped me back at the safe house. So she's at the police station now, trying to do some lawyer things for Rachel. It all sounds a little crazy to me. I know Tina has her realtor's license and all, but she was talking about legal papers, and that's something different.

So. Rachel is in the police station. Tina has gone to try and get her. That just leaves me. Home all alone. For some reason, that makes me giggle. I walk around for a while, just, I don't know, humming a little tune, looking about.

I pick up the TV remote, flick through some channels. Go to the bathroom, wash my hands using Rachel's special soap. Each little thing I do, something sorta *pings* in my brain.

You can't hurt me now.

I open the medicine cabinet. The police must have brought out a few supplies from the ranch, because mixed in with our toothbrushes and hairsprays and so forth is Blake's cologne. Guess they must have mistaken it for perfume.

I pick up the bottle, pull off the stopper, raise it to my nose.

Blake wore this scent on sales trips. I always associated the smell of it with freedom. Knowing he was going to be gone for a few days at least.

I tip the glass container and pour it all down the sink. Oily liquid swirls away with a gurgle.

I catch my face in the mirror. I'm grinning, like a crazy person. I look a little scary. This makes me grin harder.

You can't hurt me now. You can't hurt me now.

I start to sing it, waltzing around the little house the police have allocated us.

I'm still holding the cologne bottle as I go to my temporary bedroom, and open the closet. A faint waft of Rachel's favorite laundry detergent rolls out. She never did get it out of her head that's she's not in a large family any longer, and likes to buy the bulk kind, in ten-kilo boxes.

Inside are my clothes. The ones *he* liked me to wear.

Long skirts. Modest shirts. A few pioneer-style dresses in pastel colors, ironed flat. Courtesy of Rachel, since Blake never did like another wife to do the laundry, not even Tina.

Right at the back is my old waitressing uniform. Short. Low-cut. I always had to put it on in the bathroom at the diner, because if Momma had seen me leave the house in it, she would have screamed fit to burst.

I don't recall when Blake took to coming in the diner, but he always took the same spot, right at the bar where I waited on customers. He seemed very confident, but I didn't think he was cute or anything, on account of him being twenty-seven and a lot too old for me. But he was always very sympathetic about my strict home life. Mostly, though, I remember he wasn't a very good tipper.

Then my section got changed, and wouldn't you know, he moved his seat. I mentioned that to my boss Marcie, like it was kinda strange, since, honestly, it doesn't really matter *so much* who serves your bacon and scramble.

Marcie just shook her head and said: 'Honey, did you ever

think that maybe he keeps coming back here because he *likes* you?'

And I just thought . . . He *likes* me? I felt all fluttery.

'You be careful of him,' Marcie added, pointing her notepad when she thought Blake wasn't looking. 'He lives out in the desert. Cute as a button, but he'll have you livin' barefoot out in the wilds with ten other wives, fixin' his morning grits.'

I was surprised Marcie thought Blake was cute. It kind of upped his stock. I also thought escaping to the wilderness with a bunch of other women didn't sound so bad. Maybe even a little romantic. Didn't turn out that way at all though.

I put my uniform back with the modest clothes. Then I clutch a handful on their hangers and pull. Dresses and shirts slip half free untidily. I push up a batch of hangers so they unhook and clatter noisily to the floor.

There are still a good lot left inside the wardrobe, and I sorta scream at them. Don't ask me why. I couldn't even really tell you what I was saying. Only I enjoyed saying it loud. I'm not one for even raising my voice, as a rule. Girls are seen but not heard, the way I was raised.

One time, when I was a little girl, my momma told me, there was an episode where I was speaking in tongues. It happened right after Papa came back from a work trip. The excitement had gotten to me, Momma said, on account of his having been away so long. Momma and Papa had a whispered argument about it. I'm not too sure of the details. But it was something about my momma making him discipline us kids when he got back from his trips. What I could make out was my momma saying: 'She's a born liar, a born little liar. If you don't do something, she'll end up a whore.'

Don't know why I'm thinking about that now. Anyways, I screamed and screamed into the closet and it sure felt good.

I realized, somewhere along the way, I was still holding the empty cologne bottle, so I threw it into the corner of the bedroom. It smashed into a great pool of glass.

I looked at that for a while. Then went into the kitchen.

Usually we wait for mealtimes. This is a house rule, mostly enforced by Rachel, since she cooks.

But Rachel isn't here.

So I walk right on in, like it's my very own place, and pull open the freezer. Inside, all neatly stacked, are the cartons of ice cream Rachel picked out from the store.

I take out a large carton, and rip off the top. Then I push my fingers right into the vanilla fudge ice cream. It's cold enough to hurt. I eat a big glob, filling my mouth until my head throbs.

There are five grooves cut into the perfect whipped surface now. I look at them for a long time.

That's when I hear a knock on the front door. More like hammering, in actual fact. As though someone has been there a good while and has got themself worked up.

I walk to open the door, still holding the vanilla fudge carton. Two police officers stand on the other side. Two men. I don't recognize them.

I lick ice cream from my fingers.

'Hello?' I say. 'Can I help you?'

One of them looks down at my bare feet. I follow his gaze, and realize I'm bleeding. There's a gash right between two of my toes.

'Is everything OK, Ma'am?' he says. 'Someone called up about a disturbance.'

'Everything is fine,' I say. 'There's no disturbance.'

I look at my foot. A great deal of blood is pooling on the floor now.

'Was someone shouting?' asks the other officer uncertainly.

'Oh, well,' I give them my best smile, 'I trod on some glass. Musta' been that.'

'Real colorful language was reported to us,' says the first officer. He reddens. 'Sacrilegious things. Also, um, noises. Sounds folk usually prefer to keep private, if you catch my meaning.'

I don't, so I just look at him.

'Is anyone else here with you, Ma'am? Your husband?'

'It's only me,' I say. 'My husband is away on a work trip.'

'Would you mind if we confirmed that, Ma'am? We had a very concerned neighbor contact us. They were fairly certain there was some kind of domestic abuse taking place.'

'You're not allowed in without a warrant,' I say, a feeling of elation surging in my chest. 'I don't want you to come in.'

The words come out, just like that.

I can choose now. I am free to choose.

The first officer rubs the back of his neck. He glances at my foot again. A lake of red blood is pooling on the fake-wood vinyl floor.

'I think we'd better give you a ride to hospital,' he says, finally.

That idea makes me feel tight all over.

'Do you know a police lady by the name of Officer Brewer?' I ask the men.

They exchange glances.

'I have some information for her,' I tell them.

'We can certainly help you with that, Ma'am,' says one politely. 'Maybe we can make a call on the way to getting your foot fixed.'

'I need to speak with her personally.'

'I don't think—' says the same policeman.

'It's real important,' I tell him. 'Someone was murdered recently. A man named Blake Nelson.' I look at both of them in turn. 'I know who did it.'

41

Rachel, first wife

Detective Carlson looks less intimidating now he's not wearing all his guns and whatnot. Still got that cocksure air about him though, all bad language and posturing.

'We think we've got a pretty good deal,' Carlson is telling me, rubbing the back of his shaved head. 'It won't be there for very long. Plead guilty to murder and we can take the death penalty right off the table. We can also petition for at least part of your sentence to be in a psychological facility.'

'What about the others?' I ask. 'The other wives?'

'They'll get immunity from prosecution for bigamy, like you wanted.'

The door opens and we all turn. It's the last person I expect to see. Tina is standing in the doorway, Officer Brewer is at her side.

'What do you think this is, a meet 'n' greet?' growls Carlson. 'Get her outta here.'

'I'm afraid I can't do that,' says Brewer, with a faint smile on her face. 'Miss Keidis has asked to represent Mrs Nelson.'

'What the . . .? Is this a joke?' Carlson's eyes narrow. 'Miss Keidis, you got no legal training. Not to mention you're a suspect.'

'So long as Mrs Nelson agrees, she can be represented by a

friend,' says Tina. 'An' I may be a suspect in your mind, but no charges have been made, which makes me a regular citizen, like you.'

'I think you need to brush up on the law,' says Carlson, with a throaty laugh. 'We're not here to play games, Miss Keidis. Mrs Nelson here has her legal counsel. Your services are not required.'

Tina pulls up a chair next to me, close enough I get a waft of the dime-store shampoo she insisted Blake buy for her. I see Carlson's eyes drop automatically to her cleavage, then pull themselves back up again.

'Do you know how many times I been arrested, Detective?' Tina demands.

He doesn't reply.

'Forty-three,' she tells him. 'So I know a thing or two about the law. More than some lawyers even. An' certainly more than your boy here. You think I don't know how you old-style cops work? You see someone new to the system and make God damn sure their representation is Ol' Plea-bargain-Steven over here?' she jerks her thumb in the direction of my mousy lawyer. 'Yeah, I read your file, buddy,' she adds contemptuously. 'Four cases to your name and each last one of 'em you talked into makin' some half-baked deal with the cops. What sort of defence attorney is that? I sure hope Boss Hogg here fronts you more than a beer and pretzel for your trouble.'

To my surprise, Carlson isn't mad or insulted. He's sorta got a half-smile, like *'Ya got me.'*

'I don't drink,' says Steven. 'And I resent the implication—'

'You need to shut your damn mouth,' says Tina. 'The grown-ups are talking.'

She glares at Carlson, whose expression has shifted, as though adjusting to dealing with an equal.

'Watch your language, please,' he says. 'This is a police station, not a bar.'

'Forty-three times,' says Tina, waving fingers, 'so I know there's no law against cuss words in here. I can speak how I like.' She flashes him a grin that shows her dental work at the back.

Tina turns to me.

'Looks like Carlson here was one of the officers who pulled over the Homestead,' she says. 'He's compromised, see? It's on record that he had trauma counseling 'cause of the raid. I got it out of one of the cops out there. Which means we can get your interrogation written off,' she says. 'Not valid.'

There's a look of defeat on Carlson's face, tinged with be-grudging admiration. I feel a slight smile lift the corners of my mouth and push it back down.

'That's not a good idea,' interjects Steven, shooting a fearful look at Carlson. 'You don't want to rile anyone up at this stage and make yourself look bad. They're offering you a good deal.'

Carlson and Tina completely ignore him. Their eyes are locked on one another, like a battle of wills.

'Your client has to agree to be represented by you,' says Carlson. 'Mrs Nelson, you do understand, that if you accept Miss Keidis as your counsel, you won't be able to control what she sees in this room?' He gives me a long look. 'You strike me as a reserved sort of person,' he continues. 'I'm about to present some very sensitive information about your past. You sure you want your sister-wife here to see it?'

I glance at Tina. Swallow. All my prior feelings of triumph melt away. There's no way I can let her see my private things. My therapy notes.

I'm standing by an open grave at night. Holding a shovel. One of the girls from the white bedroom is in the grave. She's touching herself, moaning in pleasure. I toss earth onto her face.

'I'm sorry,' I whisper. 'I can't. I can't.'

Tina kinda shrinks in her chair. The look of disappointment on her face is worse than if she yelled or screamed. But she rallies and starts talking fast.

'Rachel,' she leans in, 'we went out to Waynard's Creek. Lots of people have been looking for maps of the Homestead. Tryin' to buy it. I think there's something goin' on,' she concludes. 'Somethin' bigger than all of us. Somethin' that mighta just got Blake killed.'

For a moment I picture believing her. Imagining that our husband was murdered by some cops-and-robbers-type plot, and not by one of his own wives. But I know that's not the truth. Real life isn't like that. In real life, the worst and most unthinkable things happen to good people.

'Please . . .' I can't call the right words to mind. The ones that make the bad thoughts go away.

'I think we should take a break,' says Tina. 'Let Rachel have a think over.'

Before Carlson can answer, the door opens. We all look up. A policeman I don't recognize is there, frantically waving a plastic bag at Carlson. It's the one with Blake's phone inside. The cell I never knew about. Carlson stands, looking annoyed at the interruption, and walks to the door.

I'm wondering what this could mean. What they've found from the phone. That's when I look across to Tina. Her mouth is wide open in shock. She rises halfway to her feet, as though she wants to run across the room and snatch the phone back. Then sits back down, face stricken.

She's seen the phone before. She knows something about it.

'What is it?' demands Carlson. 'We're in the middle of something.'

'Tech results are back,' says the officer, glancing over to us.

'And?'

The officer leans in close, so I don't hear what he's saying.

Carlson swings around, a triumphant grin on his face.

'Oh Miss Keidis,' he grins, 'you've been holding out on us.' He nods to the phone. 'Guess you recognize that?'

When Tina doesn't answer, Carlson removes the handcuffs at his hip.

'What, no wisecracks? No bad language?'

Tina turns to me. 'I'm sorry,' she says.

'For what?' I demand.

Tina is white as a sheet.

Carlson is heading toward Tina, handcuffs outstretched. It feels like a dream.

'Miss Keidis,' he says, 'I'm arresting you for the murder of Blake Nelson.'

42

Tina, sister-wife

Detective Carlson has made some excuse to duck out of the interview. Which means he and Brewer have some good-cop, bad-cop schtick goin' on. 'Cause here I am with Brewer, and she's not even askin' me anything important.

She's put a pack of cigarettes on the table and told me I'm allowed to smoke if I want. Like I can't see through a smile and twenty Luckies. It's a shame, 'cause I kinda like Detective Carlson. He's sorta cute, in a swaggery cop way. Broad-shouldered and dependable-looking, but not all health and fitness like a lotta the guys in Vegas. You get the impression Detective Carlson works out at the gym and then has a burger and a few beers afterwards. Plus he doesn't judge, like you can tell Brewer does.

'You're wastin' time,' I say, frustrated. 'There's a killer out there and you're lettin' 'em get away.'

I've already used my one phone call. Left a message for Emily, since she's not picking up the phone.

Brewer is shifting papers. I wonder idly if you get glowing skin like hers from good living, or if you're just born with it.

Brewer opens a file, frowning at where some other cop has marked a greasy fingerprint.

Straight away I see my old Nevada headshot. The picture they

took when I was on twenty wraps of meth a day. I wasn't workin'
over casinos anymore. Didn't have the brainpower for it. 'Stead I
was on the streets, hustling guys.

'Mind telling us how you and Mr Nelson met?' asks Brewer.
'You don't seem his regular type.'

I guess she's referring to Rachel and Emily. Fair-haired butter-
wouldn't-melt girls, the pair of them. Godly from the toes up.
Men like Blake might go looking for a little fun with a ten-
dollar Vegas hooker. They don't wind up marrying her.

I narrow my eyes at her.

'We met when I was in rehab, and he saved my soul.'

'How did his other wives feel about that?'

I laugh and it comes out like a snort.

'How d'ya think?'

'Your police record suggests you were something of a career
criminal in the casinos,' observes Brewer.

'I never got caught for that.' I give her my best shit-eatin' smile.

'No,' she closes the file. 'But you did get caught by vice.'

Uh-oh. Here it comes.

I rub at my wrist, where Carlson took the cuffs off. 'Like I say,'
I tell her, not looking up, 'I did my time.'

Brewer's mouth twists. 'Over forty arrests, all in all.'

'Yeah, so? I did my time. I was an addict back then. I'm a
different person now. I been baptized.' I give her a grin wide
enough to reveal my gold tooth at the back.

Brewer doesn't return the smile.

'Miss Keidis, I'm going to show you some pictures.'

She slides some images across the table. At first I think she's
showing me some snuff-movie stills, or somethin'. There's a dead
guy, eyes bulging, a belt wrapped tight around his neck. It takes
me a moment to realize it's a picture of Blake.

'You fucking sick bitch.'

I shove the pictures back at her so fast they scatter onto the floor. And I can't help but see them a second time. My Blake. Red-faced with his tongue lolling, three times the size, from his mouth.

'What the fuck is wrong with you?' I'm kinda hyperventilating.

Guess Brewer was the bad cop after all.

'I dug a little deeper, read some of your old police transcripts,' says Brewer. 'Of those forty-plus arrests, over half involved a particular fetish.'

OK, I'm screwed.

'A few things earned more cash,' I admit. I reach across for the cigarettes and shake one out.

'Strangulation,' says Brewer. 'Erotic-asphyxiation, if we're using the correct medical term. You choked guys with their own belts, right? For money.'

I find myself wishing Detective Carlson was here. I understand cops like him. They play the tough guy but they're alright underneath. Carlson's the kinda man who'd bend the rules to getcha another blanket, or phone call, or whatever.

Brewer slides the phone toward me. The screen is unlocked, a frozen still of a man on a bed in view.

My heart skips. *Blake.*

'Would you mind giving me your account of what is happening in the video?' she asks.

I let out a breath. Light the cigarette. Suck in smoke.

'Blake liked to be dominated,' I say. 'It was . . .' I spread my hands, 'his thing. He liked,' I wipe eyeliner from the corners of my eyes, 'he liked for me to tell him how bad he was. That he was a sinner. That he needed to be punished.'

Brewer watches me steadily.

I inhale deeply, tryin' to savor the blast of smoke. Truth is, it's not as satisfying as I'd hoped, but I pretend to myself it is.

'Um. He got off on havin' a belt around his neck,' I say. 'I'd adjust it so there was some pressure there. Enough to, uh, raise the skin around it, but not to restrict the airflow.'

'Not enough to suffocate him?'

'No. He liked me to do that personally. Whilst he was, um . . . Whilst I was jerkin' him off.'

Brewer's face looks pained.

'So you'd have one hand on his throat. Another . . . on his groin?'

'Um.' I frown, looking down. 'Yeah.' I fiddle with the cigarette.

'And you'd be choking him?'

'Yeah.' I've morphed back into that other Tina. The one I had to become to survive it all. The other Tina sorta sees things happening from a long way off. Detached, removed.

'Until he passed out?'

'No. We had a safe word. But he never needed to use it. I was practiced. Knew the signs.' I shoot her a half-smile. 'You don't build a business from killing your clients, right?'

Brewer lets out a breath. 'You'd be on top of him?'

I nod. 'I'd kinda straddle him.'

'One hand on his throat. Choking him. At what point would you know to stop?'

'I think you know the answer to that, officer.' I draw in smoke furiously. The cigarette is tasting better.

Brewer looks less embarrassed than I might have imagined.

'Right. You'd choke him until he ejaculated?'

'Got it in one.' I wink.

'So, as far as you're concerned, the sex was consensual. In fact, it was requested by Mr Nelson?'

I nod, inhaling more smoke.

'For the tape, please,' says Brewer.

'Yeah.'

'You see, Miss Keidis,' says Brewer, 'we assumed someone hit your husband from behind. Knocked him out, then strangled him. But I checked with forensics, and they can't be specific about the order those things occurred.'

'That so?' The cigarette is down to the butt now. I can feel the heat in my fingers.

'There was never a point,' Brewer is speaking very carefully now, considered, 'never a time in your sexual encounters, when you used undue force? When things went wrong?'

I suck the last from the cigarette, causing the butt to crackle, then pull a fresh one from the pack and light it from the last.

'No,' I say. 'No, officer. There was not.'

But I can see from her face she doesn't believe me.

43

Rachel, first wife

When Brewer comes back into the room, she looks flushed, as though she's just had a difficult conversation. There's a file in her hand. The kind I remember all too well. Lotta those files around when the Homestead was raided. One for each of us kids.

'You arrested Tina,' I say, feeling hot. 'Aren't you going to let me go?'

'You're still a suspect.' Brewer seats herself opposite me, places the folder carefully on the table. 'Hmm,' she says. Her tanned forehead is tight in a frown again. I guess no one taught her the way to avoid wrinkles is to keep sweet thoughts in your head.

'Mrs Nelson,' she sits back slightly, 'I've been on the phone with your therapist.'

I feel myself sitting straighter.

'She's refusing to share all the choice details until we have a warrant. But she was at liberty to offer her own opinions, and a little more insight into these bad dreams of yours.'

Brewer leafs through some handwritten notes, though I get the impression she isn't reading them.

'Madeline Overbacht,' she says, 'seems to think your upbringing at the Homestead might have had an effect on your memory.'

This brings me up with a start.

'She never told me that.'

'Apparently it's common in cults,' says Brewer, glancing down at the pages, 'when members partake in a prolonged meditation, or prayer. It changes the brain.' She taps her head.

I have a memory of us girls on the Homestead, how every hour a bell rang and we would join hands, kneel and pray to the Prophet. Even now when a bell rings, I have to chase away the urge to hold hands with the nearest woman.

'Constant prayer releases chemicals,' continues Brewer. 'It's a reason why victims stay in cults for so long. They become addicted. A little like drug addicts.'

I glare at her, insulted. She's comparing me with Tina.

'Same as drug addicts,' she continues, 'there are side effects. Withdrawal, if you will. When you regularly flush the human brain with unnaturally large quantities of chemicals, it takes time to rebalance. Sometimes the rebalancing is never quite complete. You bend the receptors.' She mimes with her fingers.

'What has this got to do with Blake?'

Brewer raises a hand. 'I'm coming to that, Mrs Nelson. Bear with me.' She gives me a little smile. 'Let me read here, for you.' She frowns at the words again. 'Some former members who have used these prayer techniques for several years report a wide variety of deleterious side effects,' she says, 'including severe headaches, involuntary muscle spasms, poor sleep, and diminution of cognitive faculties, like memory, concentration, and decision-making ability.'

She glances up.

'Sound familiar?'

I don't reply.

'You get bad headaches, right?'

'Migraines. Yes, I do.'

'Any other symptoms?' she suggests.

I shake my head.

'What about poor sleep?'

I feel myself flush.

'Only . . . you told *us* the nightmares were about a clinic. But you told your *therapist* about a *new* recurring dream, 'bout a room with white beds. You've only been having this particular image the past year or so. Ms Overbacht let that detail slip by accident.' Brewer flashes me a smile.

Blake's hand is behind the girl's head as she lies on the bed, sighing in pleasure.

'Does it feel good?' he whispers, moving rhythmically. 'Can you feel the heavenly fire?'

'Yes!' she moans. 'Yes! It feels good!'

Brewer is looking at me. A hard stare.

'So is this graveyard dream a new one, or did you think you shouldn't mention it to your therapist?'

My heart is pounding. 'I don't know. I barely even remember the sessions . . .'

Brewer taps her pen on the table. 'Ms Overbacht was surprised to hear you were still having nightmares. She told me she urged you to seek some extra counseling for that particular aspect of your recovery. Even made the appointment herself. I checked it out. You never showed.'

'I didn't . . . I don't hold with that dream-analysis stuff,' I say. 'There's no reason dreams need to mean anything at all. I wanted to move on.'

Brewer tilts her head.

'And did you, Mrs Nelson? Move on, I mean?'

44

Emily, sister-wife

My foot doesn't hurt much now. The police officers wrapped it up in a bandage and helped me out to the car. They drive me through the streets of Salt Lake City, passing by the strip malls with their boxy parking lots and concrete tower signs. There's a Little Caesar's Pizza, a Taco Bell and a pink-fronted nail salon, alongside a store selling discount ladies' clothing. I bought my wedding dress in a place that looked a lot like that, without Momma even knowing.

I last saw my momma before my wedding. She said a lotta mean things. Like I was dead to her, shouldn't come back. I didn't take her seriously. I thought as soon as she saw the pictures, me in my beautiful dress, she'd come around. Didn't work out that way though.

Momma wasn't at my wedding, of course. Only family there was Blake's mom, and she only showed up to try and stop it happening. She didn't look at me, just grabbed Blake's arm and started talking scripture at him, so fast you could barely understand her.

It was real awkward, standing there whilst your fiancé's mother tries to talk him out of marrying you. I remember looking down at my finger and seeing I'd bitten all the skin around the nail.

I watched as Blake took his mom's hand away, shook his head. Walked away toward the Temple.

I didn't know what to do. I'd never been inside the building before, and I was nervous I had to go in a certain door or something. And Mrs Nelson looked like she might need some help. A ride home maybe. I was thinking how I should go ask Blake what to do, when Mrs Nelson sorta came at me so fast I had this bad urge just to run.

'Your garments will show through that,' she said, pointing at my dress.

I literally had no idea what she'd just said. Only I had the most horrible feeling. My momma had always told me that pervert stuff happens in a Mormon church.

My mouth was dry, but I managed to say: 'What garments?' It all came out wrong. Like a stammer. Just like it used to happen at school when the girls would say mean things to me.

Mrs Nelson blinked, as though I'd said something unfriendly.

'Your garments,' she said patiently, as though I'd only misheard her. 'Your holy garments.'

She looked into my eyes as if hoping to see something there.

'Don't tell me,' she said slowly, 'my son never told you.' She closed her eyes like she was summoning some inner strength, leaned in close and whispered: 'They can rent you something inside to cover up.' Then she stalked away dabbing her eyes. It was only later I realized she'd maybe done a nice thing. Like she'd given her blessing in the only way she knew how. Rachel doesn't agree. Thinks Adelaide was hoping I might back out last minute.

I'd known, of course, that Mormons favor very modest wedding dresses. Blake mentioned I should have my arms and chest covered. I'd thought at the time he was being mean about my clothes, same way as my own momma always is. No matter what

I wear, she always makes me feel like I'm in white after Labor Day.

'You can see your bra strap!' she'd hiss. 'You want people to think you're a whore?'

Anyways, I had gone to the wedding boutique I'd always had my eye on ever since I was a little girl. It's on the corner of Murray Street, and every time I went downtown with my momma, I'd sneak a look through the window, sideways, so she couldn't see. It wasn't the kind of store she'd approve off. The frontage had a big lit-up sign, saying 'Fantasy Bridal', jutting over glass windows filled with frothy dresses. I don't know why but they always reminded me of rows of fluffy ducklings, all lined in a row.

I once asked Momma why it was called Fantasy Bridal, and she got this real mean look on her face, and said: 'Because weddings are a fantasy, before all the hard work begins.'

My momma was married young, and spent pretty much my whole girlhood telling me what a mistake it was. I didn't look openly at Fantasy Bridal after that, but I'd sneak little glances. Don't laugh, OK? But one time, when it snowed, it looked so beautiful, all crisp and clean outside, and I pretended I was an ice princess and the store was my very own wardrobe.

In any case, I went inside before my wedding to Blake. The women were real kind, and I think they could see I was nervous. And, of course, I was all alone. They kept asking about fit, and when was the big day, and would I need a dress a little bigger by that time. So I guess they thought I was what my momma calls a 'shotgun wedding'.

I told 'em, all proud, that I was marryin' my childhood sweetheart, and he'd sent me a rose every day since we were five years old. One of the women wiped a tear away, I remember. Then I explained to them it was important my dress covered my arms and chest, because his family were real conservative people, on account of their religion.

The lady with puffy hair asked, straight out, 'Is it an LDS family, sweetie? Mormon?'

And I said, 'No, Ma'am, they're just real religious folk.'

I wish I hadn't a said that. Only I was nervous, because this wasn't a Mormon part of town, and I didn't want word to get back to my momma that I was shopping for wedding gowns. In any case, the ladies were Catholic ladies, and they were as clueless as me when it came to dressing for Temple.

They brought me all the dresses I could afford for my budget. I'd come with my entire savings – all my Saturday job money saved since I was fifteen, and the diner money and tips after that. So I was eyeing up the big poufy dresses, with big skirts. But the nice lady steered me away from that aisle toward what she called 'pocketbook-friendly dresses'. I so liked the sound of that, I didn't figure right away she meant cheap.

Eventually I saw the one I wanted. It was fitted in folded layers to mid-thigh and then held with a big white flower and spraying out at the feet. It had a halter strap decorated with lots of little white roses and I remember putting my hand out to stroke them.

'Perhaps your in-laws wouldn't mind,' said the store lady kindly, 'if you wore this one. You're such a slip of a thing, you'd look like a little fairy.'

'I'm not sure,' I said, drawing my hand away, remembering the disapproval on Blake's face when I talked of dresses and crowns. 'It's an important ceremony. I want to look right for my husband.'

I felt very grown-up saying that. I remember standing a little taller.

'This one then?' suggested the store lady. I got the feeling she was a little tired of me being in the store at that point and wanted to close up. The dress she held up had see-through lace sleeves and a lace section fitted across the chest. 'It's very classy,' she said, 'modest too.'

'Yes,' I told her. 'That one is perfect.' And I honestly thought it was. Until Blake's mom told me different, on my wedding day.

My face must have looked an absolute picture of misery as I walked into the Temple. I felt like everyone was staring. My wedding dress, with its lacy chest panel, now displayed a solid six inches of faded white nylon, limp from too many washings. It had been loaned from the Temple last minute for eleven dollars and fifty-four cents.

From out of the car window, the discount ladies' clothes store zooms out of view, replaced by a sign for Midtown Plaza, with Dreams Travel Agency, Lotus Massage and the McKabe's Food Market all in the same lot.

There's a crackling sound from the front. The policemen driving us is speaking into his radio. I don't hear the response. We turn a little too fast around a corner.

'Yeah,' he says, hands threading the steering wheel, 'we're bringing her in now.'

45

Tina, sister–wife

I'm sitting, drumming my fingers on the table. Brewer has left the room. Carlson is back. He's brought me a coffee and slides it across the table without a word. I take it gratefully. He raises the pack of cigarettes, waves them.

I shake my head. 'I'm good, thanks.'

He sets them down, stares at the pack.

'I gave up for a while,' he says. 'Hard to make it stick.'

'What happened?'

'Ah, life. Life got in the way.' His eyes lift to mine.

'You can smoke one if you want,' I tell him. 'I won't tell on ya.'

'Not while I'm on duty,' he says. Carlson pushes the cigarettes away, sighs. 'So, you gonna tell me about it?' he asks.

'Tell you about what?' I feel an ache of shame that is unexpected. Like Carlson knows I'm disgusting now. Why should I care?

'Aw c'mon, Miss Keidis. Gimme a break here. Brewer out there,' he jerks a thumb to the door, 'she thinks you did it. Wants to let Mrs Nelson go, get you booked 'n' bailed. But you and I both know you didn't murder your husband, right?'

Unexpectedly, I'm struck by an urge to cry. Takes an effort to drive it back.

'So help me out,' he concludes, hands outstretched, pleading.

I consider him for a minute, tryin' to work out if he's playin' me.

'I don't help cops,' I say finally.

'You gonna go to jail for some honor-amongst-thieves bullshit? 'Cause I'm gonna level with you, Miss Keidis, you seem more intelligent than that.'

Carlson flicks the bottom of the Luckies pack, nudging two cigarettes higher than the rest. He passes one to me, lights it, then touches the flame to his own, pumping in smoke whilst it dangles from his lips.

'Does this mean you're off duty?' I tilt my head, smiling.

'Means I trust you not to tattle.' He smiles back. 'Am I right?' I nod.

'Thought so. I wanna help you, Miss Keidis. I think I might understand your situation a little better than the others.'

'I'm listening.'

'Miss Keidis,' he says, 'a big part of this is all gonna come down to whose idea it was to play bedroom games with strangulation equipment. I'm guessing it was at your husband's request, right? His preference?'

I pick at my nail polish, smoke coiling from the cigarette between my fingers.

'Yeah,' I admit. 'He liked that stuff.'

'This was something you knew before you got married?'

I blow out more smoke, shielding my face. 'It wasn't discussed, but I guess I knew,' I say. 'A few years on the block and you learn to pick out men who want certain things. Certain special services.'

'So how soon, after your wedding, did Blake request your special services?'

'Pretty much straight away.' I feel a little tinge of something bad, remembering that. I'd been so naive, thinking Blake loved me for myself. Of course there was something else I would have to bring to the relationship. Later on, I kinda did it for Emily too. Like I should deliver everything Blake wanted, since I got the impression she wasn't so into it. Rachel, we all knew, was a lights-out-pretend-it's-not-happening arrangement.

'That must be hard for you. 'Specially now he's dead,' says Carlson.

'What are you, Oprah Winfrey now?'

'In my experience, grieving is a complicated thing.' He shrugs. 'You grieve for what was, and you grieve for what wasn't, and also for what might have been.'

'That's real pretty.' Something occurs to me. 'You lose some-one recently?'

'Ah, not so recently. But yes. My wife died, 'bout three years back.'

'I'm sorry.'

'It's OK. I've kinda gotten used to it.' His eyes drift to the window.

We share a companionable silence. I'm glad Brewer isn't here.

'You mind telling me what the appeal was?' he asks after a moment. 'I mean to say, I get the impression you're not as into the religious part as the others.'

'I've been a good Mormon, Detective,' I say, on the defensive. 'I followed the rules. No alcohol, caffeine, nicotine. No blowing guys in alleys for five bucks, the whole deal.'

He smiles at that. 'When I was at high school, I played soccer,' he tells me, drawing on his cigarette. 'Something my old man wanted me to do.' He waves the cigarette like he's dismissing it. 'I followed all the rules too.' He smiles again. 'Never liked the sport though.'

Carlson looks sorta cute when he smiles. Younger.

'I just wondered why that particular line of faith?' he says.

'Yeah, well. Turns out me and God is like every other man in my life. It's complicated.'

He doesn't laugh this time. There's a pause. I wipe at the corners of my eyes.

'You're right, it was hard, that bedroom stuff.' I sniff, after a moment. 'I thought . . .' My voice gives way. 'I thought we'd be like a normal married couple, you know?' I wipe my nose with the back of my hand. 'I mean, normal as you can be in a plural marriage, right?' I swallow, sniff again. 'I knew I'd have to share him. I was prepared for that part at least. Thought I was. But I didn't want to bring any of my past with me. My life had been so *bad*,' I say. 'So messed up, and dirty. I wanted to be pure. A fresh start. I guess I was expectin' too much.'

Carlson doesn't reply to this, but his expression is sympathetic. I wipe tears.

'It didn't even *work*,' I say miserably. ''Cause, I couldn't make him happy. He'd have these kinda black days where he'd just lie on the couch.' I sniff. 'An' he was under so much stress, tryin' to keep the three of us from fighting, 'cause we couldn't get along.'

'You'd come out of rehab. You were vulnerable,' he says. 'It's not your job to make your husband happy. That's his job.'

I sniff again, smile up at him. 'Thanks.'

'You know, something did occur to me. You think it's possible one of the other wives saw the content of Blake's second phone?'

'No.' I sniff. 'I mean, I don't see how. He kept it in a locked box.'

'Phones nowadays tend to automatically sync with cloud servers,' says Carlson. 'Think Blake was tech-savvy enough to turn that function off? I mean to say,' he adds, 'if Rachel or Emily had access to internet, maybe they coulda—'

'I know what you're tryin' to do,' I interrupt, feeling myself growing redder at the thought of those files somewhere in the cloud. 'You're tryin' to put pressure on me. Get me to say that Rachel got mad about those videos and killed Blake.'

I tap the ash. Point the cigarette aggressively.

'Well, I'm tellin' you,' I say, waving the burning tip, 'no one hated Rachel more than me. Maybe she even could kill some-one, I don't know. Buttoned-up gals like that . . . You never can be sure, right? But Rachel is the most devout person you ever did meet. She believes, and I mean *believes*, that she will spend all eternity with Blake. Like *for-ever*. He is the one who pulls her into the afterlife. Him. You really think she would risk her eternal soul, and murder the man she loves, over what? A little jealousy? A disagreement?'

I tap more ash to make my point.

'You're barking up the wrong tree,' I say. 'It wasn't Rachel.'

'Miss Keidis.' Carlson looks at me steadily. 'Can you really be so sure of that?'

I nod my head. 'No way on God's green earth did Rachel Nelson kill her husband.'

46

Rachel, first wife

They've left me sitting alone in the police interview room for what feels like forever.

After the longest time, I pull Brewer's file on the desk toward me, and open the cover.

Right on top is an old picture of Blake. I guess his mother must have dug it out from our college days. Blake's looking young and preppy, his hair true strawberry blond, with his light blue eyes smiling out.

There's an ache in my heart. It must be from around the time of Blake and my initial dates. He had taken me on my first ever visit to an ice-cream parlor – a creamery on the Brigham Young University Campus. Blake was absolutely lit up that I had never been anywhere like it before. He even paid for a five-quart tub so I could try the peanut butter cup. It was one of the jokes at our wedding. His brother said he knew I was The One, since Blake had willingly spent two dollars extra.

I'm caught by a rush of emotion. How my stomach would fizz, every time I saw his number pop up on my phone. Everything was perfect, so long as I kept Rayne Ambrosine buried where she belonged.

A graveyard at night. A shovel.

Blake is gone now, I think, looking at that smiling college boy. *Blake is gone.*

I turn the photo of Blake over, and notice Adelaide has scrawled on the back.

Blake, aged twenty-one, first day at college.

I shake my head. Blake never did graduate. Just didn't have the head for economics. I used to help with his essays, but I couldn't sit exams for him.

The door handle turns and I shut the file quickly and push it back.

It's Detective Carlson. My heartbeat picks up. I don't like him one little bit.

'Officer Brewer and I have been having a disagreement,' he says, sliding out a chair and sitting down, legs splayed.

I don't answer.

'The way I see it is something made you mad that night. You lost your temper. There was a weapon to hand. Our best guess is some kind of hoe or garden implement. Sharp but not knife-sharp. You're a strong woman,' says Carlson. 'All that hauling wood and digging. Maybe your first thought was to make it seem like suicide. Or one of the sex games you knew your husband liked.'

'Excuse me?'

A white-carpeted room, starched linen, crisp sheets. The blond lady lies naked on the bed, with Blake on top of her. She's pretending to enjoy it, but she doesn't. Twisted. That's what people say about her. She's twisted. Jealous of the younger girls.

'Don't play dumb with me, Mrs Nelson. You think anyone would believe you didn't know? You were in the same house, for Chrissakes.'

The blond woman turns her head, looking at me. She whispers in Blake's ear. They're making plans for me. Hatred boils inside of me.

I want to lash out, strike at her with something from her hospital trolley. Make her hurt in her private parts.

The door opens and Brewer enters, looking flushed.

'You didn't come get me,' she says to Carlson, and I can see from her face that she's mad but doesn't want to show it.

'Yeah, I got a few questions for Mrs Nelson, didn't wanna bother you.' Carlson leans back in his chair again and I see Brewer's eyebrows and mouth tighten fractionally, in dislike.

Carlson nods to me. 'Mrs Nelson here is trying to convince me, she didn't know nothing about the video on that phone. I was thinkin' that doesn't sound very likely in a home that's, maybe, sixty feet square. Everyone sleeping up in the hayloft. Bedrooms divided up by a single sheet of plasterboard you could punch a hole through with your finger.'

Brewer looks at me, her amber eyes sympathetic. We share a moment. Like we are both dealing with this jerk.

'Mrs Nelson, are you saying you weren't aware your husband had certain . . . tastes?' she confirms.

I have an awful queasy feeling. The rush of my past life coming back to haunt me. How would I even know what's normal and what isn't?

'I don't know what you mean,' I whisper.

Compartmentalize. To keep you safe.

Brewer looks uneasy. Carlson shoots her a look, like *I told you.*

Brewer blows out air, causing a puff of shiny dark hair to dance momentarily above her tanned forehead.

'You're aware of the damage to your husband's body,' she says. 'Frenzied injuries to the groin.'

Tan-color sand changing to yellow. Boulders the color of cinder toffee, honey-hued with brown edges like they'd been burned in the pan. Men are carrying me. Blood dripping.

A hospital bed, my legs in stirrups. She's doing something to me and it hurts. I'm sweaty, feverish.

'You're not going to try and run away again, are you?' says the blond lady, looking up. 'I can't help you if you do.'

Brewer is still speaking. 'Ring finger and wedding band hacked off,' she says. 'It sure seems to me the kind of wounds a wife might leave. From what I've heard about Mr Nelson, I might even agree that he deserved it.'

I don't answer that. How can I?

'Mrs Nelson, we're going to ask you to watch something from the phone we found,' says Brewer. 'I'm going to warn you, you may find what you see distressing.' She's watching my face keenly. 'Assuming, you've not seen this before.'

'You want me to look at pictures?'

'There's . . . video content,' she says. 'Involving your husband.'

'Blake and I never made home movies,' I say, a little too quickly.

Brewer is turning a laptop screen toward me. Something about the grim look on her face puts the absolute fear of God into me. I don't know what I'm expecting to see. But in actual fact I'm relieved when it's nothing more than a frozen image of Blake, from above. I catch a set of pink fingernails and realize Tina must be holding the phone, filming.

I look closer and trepidation rises again.

Blake is lying on a bed with a look on his face I've never seen before. Expectant, frightened . . . excited. A coiled belt lies on the pillow next to him.

'What is this?' I demand, sickened.

Brewer leans across to press play. 'I think you should just watch.'

47

Tina, sister–wife

Carlson stubs out his cigarette.

'Forget about motive for a moment. Let's just figure between us the facts, 'K? No harm in that, right?'

I nod.

'Forensics can't be too specific about time of death. They place it between late evening and early morning.' He pauses. 'You wives were all too mad with one another to stay in the house in the first part of the evening, right?'

'It's a small place.' I give him a little smile. ''Specially when you're crammed in with three women who hate each other. Um. Lemme see. Emily went for a walk at one point. Rachel went out to do something with the storehouse.'

'So,' says Carlson, 'Emily Martinelli went out on her lonesome, around the time Blake went out fishing?'

'Yeah. Right after Blake drove her back from the hospital. But you seen Emily, right? She's, like, sixty pounds soakin' wet. Not to mention, she's so squeamish she won't even shape hamburger patties. I mean, come on? Emily hack a man's finger off?'

I shake my head at the thought. Emily's face crosses my mind. The expression she had sometimes, when she thought Blake couldn't see her.

'What about Rachel. You're certain she was in the storehouse the whole time?'

'Well, that's what she told us.'

'But you couldn't be sure?'

'Well, Detective, Rachel doesn't *lie*, you see. Part of her religion. So if she said she was goin' out to the storehouse, you can more or less take her word that's where she went.'

'But you couldn't see her? Hear her?'

'Well, you could hear the canning machine a mile off. But the storehouse is a little further out from the house. Once someone is inside, you can't see what they're doin'.'

'How long was she out there for?'

I frown, tryin' to remember.

'We didn't have clocks or phones or stuff like that. It's hard to pinpoint time. All I can say was she came back before it got dark.'

'Was she out there longer than usual, in your opinion? I mean to say, what does Rachel generally do in that storehouse?'

I sigh. 'Detective Carlson, I figured you for smart. So I know you searched that storehouse, and likely found, oh I don't know, maybe a big old canning machine, and a lotta jars of canned produce. Right?'

Carlson ignores my sarcasm. ''Bout enough food for End of Days,' he says, shifting on his chair. 'All neatly stored and labeled. So she'd be out there for what? Hours?'

'There wasn't really a usual amount of time. It depended on the harvest.'

A really uncomfortable feeling prickles at me. Like I've made a betrayal.

'Did you or Emily ever go out to that storehouse?'

'No. That was Rachel's domain.'

'She didn't like anyone else out there?'

'No. I don't happen to have a great interest in picklin' carrots.' I shrug. 'We're all different, I guess. Not to mention Emily and I were both scared of that canner. It was old factory equipment that Blake hillbilly-fixed. Rattled like it was fixing to go into orbit.'

Carlson considers this. 'Did Rachel like to go out to her storehouse at night, Miss Keidis?'

I hesitate.

'Only, we found evidence someone was in there the night Blake died. Your generator meter reported a surge of usage around midnight. From what we could see, the only equipment at the ranch to command that kind of energy was a big old canning machine out in the storehouse. That's maybe a five-minute walk to the river.'

He pauses for this to sink in.

'Little unusual, right?' Carlson adds. 'That someone would go for some late-night canning?' He leans forward. 'Does it sound likely to you that someone might have gone there to wash up? A canning machine is essentially a hot-water bath, right? Could be used to rinse out bloody clothes.'

I picture Rachel's battered Survive Well. The grande 41-liter pressure canner, which looks a little like a bomb-disposal unit – all inch-thick steel and lots of little black gaskets on the top. It runs off the generator, and consumes around a third of our total electricity. I saw it in action one time, shaking all over the floor, with steam hissing angrily about. Like it had all Rachel's grudges and angry feelings locked inside, ready to blow.

Carlson's right though. Squirt of bleach, and I think you could use that canner to wash clothes. Hell, all that pressure might even work better than a washing machine. It ran loud though. I wonder if I could have slept through that. Maybe.

'I'm not a freakin' laundry worker,' I say, suddenly agitated.

'So I wouldn't know, would I? You know what? I'm done talking. This feels like a setup.'

Carlson meets my eye.

'Your call,' he says. 'I'm sure you've realized by now that whosoever murdered Blake would have been covered all over in blood. If that had been me, I might have thought to take off my clothes and wash them.'

We both look up as Brewer enters the room.

A nasty ache is slidin' around my guts. Like there's something real bad about to happen.

'Well, you sure make some interesting points, Miss Keidis,' says Brewer, sliding into her seat.

Shit. She was listening?

'And you have, of course, confirmed,' she continues, 'a few highly relevant things. Firstly, that you yourself are not so convinced as Mrs Nelson that you'll be joining your spiritual husband on the other side of the veil.'

Her amber eyes flash.

'Second, that no one was watching *you* at the time Blake Nelson could have been killed.'

I turn in horror to Carlson.

'You fucking jerk,' I spit at him. 'You set me up?'

He shakes his head. Shoots a dirty look at Brewer. 'You'll be happy to know we're letting you go, Miss Keidis. Though you may be called to give further evidence at trial.'

'What?'

I feel as though the rug has been pulled from under me.

'You found the killer?' I say, not sure how I feel about what this could mean. 'You found Blake's killer?'

Carlson pauses for the longest time, like he's choosing how to answer. Eventually he says, 'Your sister-wife has confessed.'

48

Emily, sister-wife

'So let me get this right.' Brewer's amber eyes are trained on me, like she's trying to catch me out in a lie. 'You followed your husband out to the little stream where he fishes?'

'That's correct.'

I'm pleased with myself. I sound exactly like someone on TV.

'You used a belt to strangle him. Then attacked him with a gardening tool? That right?'

'Yes siree.'

'Right.' She can't quite look at me.

'A little groundbreaking axe,' I explain. 'Sorta curved. For breaking up hard soil.'

'Well that would certainly fit with the wounds on the body. What doesn't fit is where you tell us you disposed of the weapons.'

She looks at me. I wait for her to continue.

'When we looked over the ranch, we found a blood trail – your husband's – leading to an outside storehouse. What can you tell us about that?'

'Um, well, like I told you, I don't remember much.'

'Right. You were in emotional distress,' says Brewer flatly.

'Emotional distress,' I agree. 'I just kinda wandered around, I think. I mean, I couldn't believe it was all happening. I think

I went up to the storehouse and then back down to the river afterwards. Threw everything into the stream.'

'You think?'

'It's all a blur.'

'You realize it's very unlikely that at least one of those items wouldn't have washed up somewhere?'

'God moves in mysterious ways.'

Brewer wears an expression I've seen before. On my teachers at school, when they couldn't explain something they thought was very simple.

'Please don't do this,' she says.

'That's the point,' I tell her. 'I did do it.'

'Emily,' she says gently, 'what can you tell us about the other wives? Were they good to you?'

'Oh, yeah,' I say, nodding. 'They're real good wives. Especially Rachel.' I see my eyes, round and earnest, in that reflective mirror opposite. 'She volunteers and whatnot. Cans all our food. We got enough for End of Days in the storeroom out back.'

'You know they've left you here to take the blame?'

I don't answer that.

'What about you?' asks Brewer. 'Are you a good wife?'

I look down at my fingers. The tiny wedding ring that Blake had to have specially made, on account of the ones in the store not fitting right. He was mad about that, as I recall. Fifty bucks.

'No,' I say. 'I'm not.'

There's a long silence. I don't know if Brewer expects me to say anything. She kinda sighs.

'After you threw the belt and the axe in the river, you went back to the ranch and got into bed?'

'Yes.'

'You didn't, for example, go to the storehouse. 'Cause *someone* went there, that night. We've taken a good look in the place, and can't really ascertain a link to the crime. My thoughts are the killer would have had a lotta blood on their clothes. Maybe used some equipment there to clean themselves up.'

'I don't remember that part so well.'

'What about the missing fingers?'

I have a horrible lurching feeling. A memory, actually. About those fingers. In the car coming back from my wedding, when I looked across at the wheel and noticed for the first time that Blake had red hair on his knuckles. I had been telling him how my momma was saying it wasn't a legal wedding, and polygamy was *illegal* and I was going to jail and then hell. I was even laughing a little. But Blake said: 'A Temple Sealing is a legal marriage in *God's* eyes. I told you, honey, we're outlaws, living God's word.'

I couldn't answer. I mean, I was just straight out shocked. I had thought the outlaw thing was just Blake being colorful. Not to mention, I'd spent the last five hours saying these weird vows, and promising I'd gut myself with a blunt knife if I broke them, and he was now telling me it wasn't even a legal wedding.

I just came right out and asked how the Temple even allowed that, if it was so holy and all? And Blake said the Temple didn't care to check in great detail who had already been sealed to whom.

I had looked back at his hands on the wheel, with that scatter of red hair, and thought it looked just like something I once saw on National Geographic, about some endangered orange monkeys.

'What about the fingers?' I ask Brewer.

'Your husband's ring finger was missing,' says Brewer. 'Hacked away from the hand. We never did find the digit, or his wedding band either.'

'I must have thrown it in the stream,' I tell her. 'With the belt and the axe. Like I say, I wasn't—'

'You weren't thinking straight. You said that already.'

Officer Brewer seemed all small-town cop, but now she's gone into a real interrogation. She fixes me with her funny-color eyes.

'How tall are you, Miss Martinelli?'

'Five two, maybe.'

She nods. 'Forensics estimated the height of your husband's attacker based on the angle of the blow to his head, assuming he was sitting in his fishing chair at the time. They give about ten-to-one odds it was a woman who killed him, but I still think you'd be a little on the small side to pull it off. Your late husband was what? Six feet tall? Physically fit?'

Brewer rubs her tanned forehead.

'You somehow hauled him by the neck to that little juniper tree, and hanged him from it?' She shakes her head. 'I just don't see it.'

'Well, that's how it happened.'

'Miss Martinelli, are you aware that if you confess to this crime you risk the death sentence?'

'It's different in the afterlife,' I tell her. 'No pain, no suffering. Any problems Blake and I had, God would work them out.'

Brewer has this real exhausted look on her face.

'Here's what I'm struggling with, Miss Martinelli. I don't believe a word of your confession. But our officers have been over the ranch.'

She pauses.

'The strangest thing is, your story might be whack, but some pretty key parts more or less fit,' she says. 'So either you really did kill your husband. Or you've a pretty good idea of who did.'

49

Rachel, first wife

I walk out of the police station in a daze.

The two realities are fighting it out in my brain. The things Tina did to my husband. What Emily was capable of. I lived with them both, cooked for them, cared for them.

Turns out I never knew either of them at all.

It feels very much like when the Homestead was raided. Like everything I ever knew, or depended upon, gone, *poof*, in a puff of hot air. As though the ground beneath my feet might drop away at any moment.

Did I not see? Or was I not looking?

Officer Brewer's words float back to me.

It seems your husband picked vulnerable women.

Emily and I had our differences. But after Tina came along I'd honestly thought it got easier. We even had conversations about God and whatnot. Prayed together. All along, she must have had this hatred of Blake brewing.

I guess she musta seen the same thing I saw on Blake's phone. She always was the most terrible snoop. Maybe it made her mad. Everything she'd gone through. Blake acting all cock of the walk, telling us we weren't good enough. When all the while behind closed doors, he was letting Tina beat up on him.

This is what confuses me most. Because surely if Tina used to

. . . what? Choke him half to death? I can't get this clear at all. Why did the police let Tina go? Maybe she batted her lashes at Detective Carlson and he decided she was innocent. Men are like that, outside the Homestead. You can't trust them.

I'm overwhelmed with this. I try to push it away, close the lid. Only now, it's like my boxes are splitting at the sides. Seeing that video of Blake . . . It's done something. Pulled a crank, pushed a lever. Set something tumbling into motion that is firing thoughts I haven't had in a long while.

Pictures roll in from somewhere else.

I see Emily in a blind fury. Something she could hardly control. Like, she's been a good girl for all this time, and something needs to get out. To scream and shout.

A strange dark feeling comes. Like an old knowledge.

I guess Emily must have walked out to where he was fishing. Blake took waders to fish. His regular clothes would have been neatly folded in a pile, back from the stream. The belt would have been coiled on top in a perfect circle.

I can picture him sitting there, very still, his line in the water, his back to the dirt-track approach. In my mind, I see Emily approach, axe in hand.

Then what? They talk? Fight? Blake sends her away, 'cause she's scaring the fish. Turns his back. And just as she's leaving, something furious kicks in. She swings the axe into the base of his skull, and he hits the dirt, bleeding.

A funny feeling is gnawing at me. Like how can I see this all so clearly? Why does it feel like *a memory?*

Ever since Blake died, I feel as though someone is peeling up corners of my mind, like the label on a jar. They're picked at the edges, but now they've got a good hold, and the label is starting to roll back. Sometime real soon, the underside will be exposed.

I climb into the driver's seat of our car. I see Tina emerge from the police station. Then she stops. Detective Carlson is waving her down, he wants to tell her something. I watch them, trying to figure out what they're talking about.

I'm struck by a flat calm. Like the eye of the hurricane. That's when something else occurs to me.

What if Emily is innocent? In which case, in *which* case . . . Nerves bubble up now in all directions. What if she got herself arrested for that exact reason? To put herself where neither Tina or I could get to her?

Now I'm flat out scared.

Because Emily knows. She *knows*. What's more, she won't be able to help herself. Sooner or later, they're going to get it out of her. Emily's gonna tell the police everything.

50

Tina, sister–wife

'Hey! Miss Keidis! Wait up!'

I turn to see Carlson, kinda jogging outta the station. I glance to Rachel, sat waitin' in our beat-up Chevy.

'Can I help you, Detective?' I make it sound real sarcastic.

'I need to talk to you,' he says. 'It'll only take a minute.'

'I don't have a minute.'

Carlson sighs. He looks younger out of the harsh lights of the interview room. Early thirties, maybe. Guess he musta gone bald young.

'Look, I'm not here to fight with ya,' he says. 'You're smart, I get it. You know the law. I don't underestimate you, like some others might.'

This takes me slightly aback.

'But I want to ask you, before you bust out of here, with Rachel Nelson, if you can really be so sure she isn't a killer?'

'If I thought she was, do you really think I'd be gettin' in a car with her?'

He sighs, rubs his shaved head.

'Look. Your girl in there. Emily.' He jerks his thumb back. 'There's a lotta holes in that story. But if she's not interested in pickin' 'em open, there's nothing I can do.'

I glare at him. 'Whaddya want, Detective?'

'When we raided the Sunshine Homestead . . .' He fights for the words. 'It was the worst thing I have ever done,' he concludes, looking me right in the eye. I take this in, 'cause I'm guessing Detective Carlson has seen some bad things. 'Those little girls we rescued, they were terrified of us.' His eyes tighten, remembering. 'They didn't know . . . They didn't realize, it wasn't right for your daddy to marry you off at fourteen. That we were *helping* them. I mean, they were screamin', cryin', tryin' to get away from us.'

There's a haunted look to him.

'We were the monsters, you know? Chasin' around scared little girls. It was so bad, so bad. But we couldn't leave 'em there either. With all the roaches and perverts. An' the mothers like zombies, all dead inside.' He mimes around the eyes. 'It was the closest thing to hell I ever wanna see.'

He looks so sad, I want to put my arms around him.

'We found out later their Prophet told 'em outsiders were devils who'd take their children,' he says. 'And we just went and marched on in and proved him right.' He gives a humorless laugh. 'I sometimes even wonder if that tip-off was from the man himself,' he adds. 'If people are muttering, thinking of leaving. Well, send in a pack of cops to take their kids.'

He heaves up a big sigh.

'I'm sorry,' I say. 'Really. You did your best.'

He collects himself. 'What I'm tryin' to tell you,' he says, 'is there *were* no happy endings. Not months later, not *years* later. There were second-generation kids there. Kids who knew nothing but the inside of that compound. Raised on a one-hundred-percent diet of ignorance and crazy talk. Most a those teenagers could barely write, barely read. Hell, you want my opinion? It'll be a straight millennium, if you're *lucky*, before you assimilate those people and their children into anything approaching the normal world.'

'You sayin' it's too late for Rachel?' My voice is softer now.

'I'm sayin' I never met a single one of 'em who managed to pull their life together. Whether it's drugs, or another cult, or what have you.' He takes a breath. Glances at the car, where Rachel sits staring into space. 'You'll always be an outsider to her,' he says. 'You're not one of 'em. They call us gentiles,' he adds with a smile. 'Sounds kinda nice, until you realize they mean we're all damned, right?'

'Rachel doesn't think that.'

'You don't sound so certain,' observes Carlson, looking at the car. 'From my standpoint, we've got a murder victim, and someone with a motive and means.' He sorta huffs from his nose. 'A person raised with severe emotional dysfunction, who has voluntarily recreated those antisocial conditions in her own family. I know what you likely think of me. I'm another over-worked cop who doesn't care. But I got into this job to see justice done. Miss Keidis, I want to be real frank with you. I'm a police detective. I've seen a lotta bad stuff. Fourteen years has taught me the most obvious answer is usually the right one. It's not like on TV, where you get a twist in the tale.'

He lets out a long sigh.

'I'm tellin' you this because I think you've got more up here than the others.' He taps his head, catches my eye. 'Put it this way, I'm not wasting my breath with Miss Martinelli.' He pauses. 'In my mind, we got our perp. An' she's not sittin' in that police station.' He looks meaningfully toward Rachel. 'Not a hell of a lot I can do about that. I gotta do what I'm told. If it were up to me, however, I think there's a motive worth investigating and a good deal of evidence that hasn't been collected. The state has pulled the plug on this whole inquiry. They got their confession.'

'You sayin' I should look into it?'

'I'm not allowed to say that. But I'm here in whatever capacity I can be, which, you have to appreciate, isn't much.' He gives me an apologetic look. 'I'll listen. If anything . . . occurs to you, be sure to let me know. If you find something we coulda overlooked, then bring it straight to me. I'll take it seriously, you can be sure.' He looks dead at me. 'And, if you insist on continuing to cohabit, Miss Keidis, I'd sleep with a gun under your pillow and one eye open.'

'Thanks for the tip,' I say. 'I think there's more to this.'

He spreads his hand. 'Your call.' He turns to leave.

'Wait,' I say. 'There is one thing.'

'Oh yeah?'

'I got this phone number.' I fish in my purse and pick out the piece of paper Marsha gave me. 'I've rung it at least ten times, but they don't answer. The name is Dakota Jessop. I think she might have met with Blake before he died.'

Carlson examines the picture, staring hard at the face.

'Any idea who she is?' he asks.

'She maybe works for a real estate company,' I tell him.

'Looks like one of the Homestead folk,' he says after a moment. 'That quiffed-up hair and the old-fashioned dress.' He taps the prairie-style cotton collar, meeting with a home-stitched yolk and puffed sleeves. 'Don't recognize the name, but there were two thousand of 'em, and they lied about more or less everything important.'

There's that distant look on his face again, remembering horrors. He takes out his phone, snaps the image and the number.

'I'll take a look into it for you,' he says. 'Can't promise nothing.'

I nod my thanks and start walking back toward the car.

I'm still turning over his words as I slip into the seat next to Rachel.

'What was Detective Carlson talking to you about?' asks Rachel, looking across.

'Nothing.' I look straight ahead. 'We should probably hit the road.'

51

Emily, sister-wife

The door opens and Detective Carlson enters. I like him because when we first met, he brought donuts, and his little belly reminds me of a waterbed, the way it wobbles around over his belt. Like there's solid muscle fighting the chubbiness, and it's an ongoing battle.

Without asking permission, he slides himself into the seat next to Brewer. I see her flash him a look of annoyance.

'I won't be a minute,' he says. 'Only I had somethin' I wanted to run by Miss Martinelli. You were playing detective, is that right? With your sister-wife?' He glances at Brewer. 'According to Miss Keidis, the pair of 'em went out to visit with Rachel's cousin. Got some name and number of a mysterious lady who they think Blake might have been meeting with.'

I shrug, I'm not so interested now I can see he doesn't have any desserts. 'The number didn't work,' I say. 'Just voicemail.'

'Same for me,' says Carlson. 'But I ran it through our system. I don't know who your little claw-haired lady might be. But her telephone number is for a very unscrupulous real estate firm. In Vegas.'

He waits for this to sink in, eyeing me up. I don't say anything, but I feel a surge of excitement. I *knew* there was a story here.

'No convictions yet,' continues Carlson, 'but our cop friends in

Nevada have been tryin' to bust 'em for all kinds of wrongdoing. Las Vegas Real Estate is well known as a mobster firm. We just can't catch 'em.'

A mobster firm. I wonder if Tina knew that, since she works in real estate.

I start turning it over in my head. It doesn't make much sense, I decide. I mean, why would a religious lady join a real estate firm? Especially a bad one, like Detective Carlson is suggesting.

Now I think about it, Blake had some papers he tried to hide from me. Land maps and stuff. In the end, he wound up keeping them at his work in the Temple, since I was such a good snoop.

I consider sharing this with Carlson, then decide against it. I'm tired of everything being about Blake.

Carlson glances at Brewer, who looks less mad at him now.

'You know this could change things for you,' says Carlson. 'If Blake was mixed up in something illegal, I'll bet Rachel would have been mad, right?'

'You're forgetting Tina,' I point out. 'She works in real estate. She's from Vegas. If you ask me, it woulda been her who made the introduction, right?'

I'm thinking how Tina went all quiet about that real estate firm. Like maybe she remembered it.

'Sure,' Carlson seems animated. 'So talk to us. Why would Tina do that?'

I suddenly realize what they're doing.

'You can't trick me,' I say, annoyed. 'I told you, I did it. I killed my husband.' I lean forward with my elbows on the table. 'In any case,' I say, feeling tired, 'I'm done talking. I want to go back to my room.'

'You mean your cell.'

I glance at the clock.

'Yeah. It's nearly lunchtime. The man on the desk told me they'd get more pot roast.'

Brewer lets out a long sigh.

'You're not gonna be staying in the police station for much longer, Emily, you know that, right? That's been explained. Technically, you're on remand now. Unless you post for bail, you'll be put in jail while you await trial.'

'I told you, I don't want bail.'

Brewer's mouth is turned down at the edges, like she's real sad about something.

'Emily,' she says, 'prison isn't a nice place. Why don't you just . . . talk to us for a bit. I know you've got a great imagination. Tell us what you think might have happened to Blake, if you hadn't got to him first.'

'I'm allowed visitors, right?' I say. 'In the prison?'

'Yes. Like I outlined before, there are visiting hours . . .'

'OK. Then I'm done talking.'

'No point in keeping you here if you're not talking to us, Emily. Carlson here thinks you only came in to confess when you thought Rachel might be charged. He puts these things together. Kind of man he is. Thinks you're trying to confuse us. Give us the runaround.'

She pauses, looking at me.

'But here's what I think. I think you're estranged from your mother, whose good opinion matters to you deeply. I believe you're hoping this whole confession business will bring her in.'

I try to look at her steadily, like I'm a detective on a crime drama, but I feel my face twitch.

Officer Brewer leans back and sighs.

'Here's the problem.' Her face softens. 'We tried to get your mother down here. Called her up, explained all that was happening. Got nothing, so I went in person to her cabin in West Valley.'

Brewer is being polite, I notice, saying 'cabin', not 'mobile home'.

Again I feel that face twitch. I raise my hand to my cheek. Maybe I can push it down.

Her amber eyes settle on mine.

'It's not my place to say your mother isn't a nice person,' she says. 'But what I will say is, you play this confession card, to get her to come see you, chances are you'll be playing it right up to when that lethal injection slides into your arm.'

There's a knife twisting up my insides and I hate Brewer for putting it there. What she's saying isn't true, in any case. She doesn't understand.

'Well, I guess that doesn't even matter, 'cause I'd choose a firing squad,' I say, petulantly.

Brewer blinks.

'According to Utah State Law, I'm entitled to ask for one, if convicted of a capital felony,' I continue. 'Because of blood atonement.'

There's a pause as they all stare at me.

'Miss Martinelli, would you mind translating for the non-religious folk in the room?'

'The Book of Mormon,' I tell her, 'says that murder is one of the unpardonable sins. But it can be forgiven if you die by shedding blood on the ground.'

Brewer rests her temples on her fingers.

'You're telling me you're approaching this like a state-sanctioned suicide? But you're particular about your manner of death?'

'Blood atonement is the only way someone like me can get to heaven.'

'You truly believe you'd be forgiven for killing your husband, if you're executed by firing squad?'

'I'd be forgiven for *all* sins,' I say. 'It's not just me that thinks it,' I add defensively, since she is shaking her head like I'm saying something dumb. 'Why do you think we have firing squads in Utah?'

Brewer looks suddenly strained. Exhausted. 'You know, I never thought to ask.'

52

Tina, sister-wife

Rachel drives us out of the cop parking lot without a word. Carlson's warning is piping away at me. Like, *get out of the car!*

I feel like I've worked it partway out. Of *course* Emily has confessed. This is Miss Drama Queen we're talkin' about. She most likely saw all the attention Rachel was gettin' and decided she'd have herself a slice of the pie. What Emily doesn't realize is, if the police take her seriously, there's no money for bail. Not a dime. We were in debt when Blake died. So they'll toss Emily in jail whilst she waits for the court hearing. The idea of that makes me feel cold all over.

I sigh, press the heels of my palms against my eyes. It doesn't bear thinkin' about, what'll happen to weird little Emily in jail. She'll be wishing Blake back.

Rachel still hasn't said anything as she drives us away.

'You OK?' I ask. I'm starting to feel real uneasy now.

She doesn't answer. Instead she spins the wheel and pulls up on a deserted street. I glance at the passenger door.

She sits in the driver's seat, staring straight ahead.

'You lied to me,' she says quietly.

I get this real creepy feeling, like I want to get out.

'What are you talkin' about?' I manage. That's when I remember. I'm fairly sure there's a rifle wedged under the driver's seat.

Blake always kept one in case of carjacking. From how he made it out, that was pretty common for Utah – the gun, not the robbery. Did he keep it loaded? I can't remember.

'You strangled him,' she says. 'You put the belt around his neck. How could you have done that?'

I hesitate. She's not making any moves for the weapon. Her hands are gripping the wheel tight.

'I didn't—' I begin.

'Don't lie to me!' her voice comes up at a volume I've never heard. 'Good people don't lie!'

She's still not making eye contact. Her face looks crazy. My mind starts tracking where that gun might be.

'Rachel, calm down. Let's drive to a diner or somethin'. Talk about this.'

I have this real familiar feeling of threat. Just like when I was in a car with some crackhead John looking to beat up on me. I'm wondering if I could unhook my seatbelt, real quiet, in a way she wouldn't notice. Make a dive for the door. If she's got a gun under her seat, it's likely a bad idea to make myself look guilty.

A public place. Get to a public place. That's what we used to say to one another in Vegas.

She turns to look at me. Her eyes are full of tears.

'Just tell me the truth,' she says. 'Please.'

I weigh up my options.

'My past life,' I swallow. 'Before I was baptized. I . . . I did those things. To men. For money.'

'You killed people?'

'No!' I'm outraged. 'No. How could you think that?'

She makes that strange expression she always does when she's wrong and can't admit it. I carry on talking.

'Cutting off the air, it gives some people a high. They like it,' I say.

'Men *like* that?' Rachel looks as though I just blew her mind. Her face shows raging panic.

'Not all of them. Some. A few. It's, like, a fetish.'

For all her long words, I'm pretty sure Rachel doesn't know what that one means.

'A weird thing some guys like,' I interpret. 'Not commonplace.'

She pauses for long enough for me to know what's coming next.

'Did . . . Did Blake like it?' It comes out as a whisper.

I nod, a lump in my throat. 'Yes,' I say. 'He did.'

Rachel sits heavily on her seat. She's still for a long moment, staring blankly ahead. Then she puts her head in her hands and sobs.

'I always knew I wasn't enough for him,' she says, through her tears. 'I never could have done anything like that. Not even if he'd asked me to.'

I venture nearer in my seat. Put a tentative hand on her back.

'You were enough,' I tell her. 'It's him that was at fault. He wasn't brave enough to be honest with us.' I glance at Rachel, trying to read her expression. 'You know,' I add, 'Blake never told me, before we were married, he liked that stuff.' I touch my neck. 'I never expected it was something I'd ever have to do again.'

Her blue eyes look up at me, kinda soulful, acknowledging, I think, that I was not a little betrayed by it all. Traumatized and let down in my own way.

'He needed us to make him feel complete. But he loved you. He loved all of us.'

She absorbs this, the sobbing subsiding. Rachel wipes away tears. More flow in their place.

'Did you like doing it?' she asks, looking up at me.

'No. Not really,' I admit. 'Not at all, actually.'

She kinda laughs.

'I never liked cooking either,' she says.

We both giggle, in a slightly hysterical way.

'All I wanted was a family,' Rachel says. 'I guess I pushed too hard. God had other plans.'

'You got a family,' I say. 'Up until today we were livin' in the same house, eating meals together, fighting with one another. Sure beats what I had growing up.'

She looks uncertain.

'That's because of you,' I add, looking into her sad blue eyes. 'If it hadn't been for you runnin' the household, I'd be downtown in a gutter, out of my mind on whatever drugs I could score. Emily would be, I dunno, in some institution. You're our glue. OK? Even though Blake is gone.'

'Thank you,' she breathes. Her eyes have lost their desperate look. Then, suddenly, that vulnerable side is vanished and she's cold, orderly Rachel again. 'I just can't understand it,' she says sadly. 'If you didn't . . .' she stops herself.

'If I didn't do it?' I fill in.

She ignores this. 'I thought things had gotten easier for Emily,' says Rachel, shaking her head.

I kinda laugh without meaning to. 'Rachel. Are you serious?'

Her expression doesn't change.

I sigh. 'Rachel, I loved Blake and all. But even you must have seen he was a little crazy at times. I mean, all that stuff about storing a thousand gallons of water. The way he kept enlarging your storehouse so it fitted three years, then six years. Then he was planning space to hold animal feed for animals we didn't even have.'

'You have to be prepared when the end comes. That's our religion. You're new to it.'

'Rachel,' I say patiently. 'I have met Mormons before. Believe

it or not, we have 'em in Vegas. Many Mormons have large pan-
tries – storehouses even. Not so many live out in the desert with
a plan. And remember when Blake got started on the subject
of government and conspiracies and medical records?' I rub my
temples. 'I don't think Emily was finding marriage easy, is all.
Maybe she even felt cheated. Like she'd been promised a normal
life and gotten Blake's version of it instead.'

Rachel shakes her head mournfully and tears spring into her
eyes again.

'Emily should have come talked to me,' she says. 'We're sister-
wives. Sealed together for eternity.'

Luckily, she isn't looking the right way to see the expression
on my face. Rachel is looking forward, shaking her head.

'How could she have done that to us? I don't know if I can
ever forgive her.'

53

Tina, sister-wife

I'm staring at Rachel in disbelief.

'You don't really think that Emily did it?' I ask her, open-mouthed.

'Well,' says Rachel evenly, in this maddeningly practical voice, 'how can you be sure she didn't?' There's just a hint of accusation there, but I let it ride.

'Well, first of all, Emily is about the size and weight of your average June bug,' I tell her. 'Second, we *know* her. Yeah, she's a big old liar. But she wouldn't kill someone. She's not got it in her. Emily just wants a little attention, is all.'

As I'm sayin' it through, it occurs to me that Officer Brewer is no dummy. I don't figure she'd have arrested Emily unless there was something to go on. Gettin' bawled out for wastin' resources isn't her style.

So what if . . . My mind is ticking like a goddamn clock now. What if Emily knows . . . *somethin'*. Like she saw somethin'. Covered it up. Now, that I could believe. Only question is, would she have covered for Rachel? Comes down to who she hated worse, I guess. Her wife or her husband.

Rachel's shaking her head like she's tryin' to dislodge somethin'.

'You act like you're this great judge of people,' she says. 'No one knows anyone else for certain. That's between them and God.'

'You got major trust issues, you know that?'

'Oh really?' she hits back. 'Coming from someone who won't rely on anyone, for anything? Got to do it all by yourself, don't you? Did it ever occur to you to ask me for help managing Blake? Or am I too darn provincial to offer advice on a man I've been married to a little over six years?'

I don't have an answer to that. I'm actually a little shocked.

'Just let's say you're right, and Emily is innocent,' says Rachel, changing the subject. 'Then what exactly do you propose happened out at the ranch?'

There's an uncomfortable pause. For a long moment we just stare at one another. Rachel looks away first.

'We know Blake met with a blond woman, just before he died,' I say. 'That was real out of character for him, right?'

Pain flashes across her features.

'You can't really believe there is some fourth wife out there?' she asks. 'A killer?'

'Love and money, isn't it? The two reasons people kill. Didn't ya ever watch *Law & Order*?'

'That show has a lot of bad language.'

'Sure. OK. Point is, maybe Blake got interested in someone. She was a little crazy, like, I dunno, *Fatal Attraction* or somethin'. It's a movie,' I add.

'That all sounds a little far-fetched to me,' says Rachel sensibly. 'Besides, no one knew about that ranch but us. It's not like Blake coulda gotten someone out there in secret.' She sighs. 'I think you need to deal with your grief. I think you're hoping to distract yourself, with this whole,' she waves her hands, 'cops and robbers. You're hurting. You need to process it.'

This was always the part of Rachel that made me mad as hell.

She's so wantin' to be the good girl, obey the rules. Emily and I always came last to that.

'That's our sister in there,' I tell Rachel. 'Emily doesn't know what she's getting herself into. With no bail, they're gonna lock her up. Sure, she'll have a different-colored jumpsuit and a bigger plate at dinner, on account of not yet being convicted and all. But take it from me, prison is *not* a place where Emily will do well.' I let out a breath. 'She's family. You don't give up on family, right? Even if they're stupid-ass enough to confess to a crime they didn't do?'

Rachel's mouth twists, like she's maybe a little more admiring of me than she was but won't admit it out loud.

'The police won't convict Emily if she's innocent.' Rachel says it like she's tryin' it on for size, the idea of the cops as the good guys, but she's struggling to really make it stick.

I shake my head, frustrated. 'Cops don't solve crimes, Rachel. They close cases, to make their numbers up. Somethin' like this. Somethin' *complicated*. This goes straight in the bottom drawer. Believe me. They got their confession.'

We're both a little quiet for a moment, thinking of Emily.

'All I know is there's something not *right*,' I tell Rachel. 'Blake meeting with mysterious blonds. Tryin' to buy the Homestead property. Your cousin told us that land was in hot demand. Lotta people askin', not just Blake. That's a motive, right?'

'You spoke with *Marsha*?'

'Relax,' I tell her. 'She didn't say nothing bad about you.'

It's a joke, but Rachel does visibly relax.

'Blake knew I didn't like the idea of buying the Homestead,' says Rachel miserably.

By rights, I should be mad. Neither of them told me or Emily *anything* about a land purchase idea. But Rachel looks so hurt, I feel bad for her.

'Blake had an idea in his head that buying the Homestead land could help my nightmares,' says Rachel, and I can tell she's doin' her usual thing, tryin' to explain away our husband's unreasonable behavior. 'Like maybe if I confronted my fears, you know?'

I consider this. 'Sounds like Blake,' I tell her. 'Making something to his own benefit sound like he was being real caring. Not to speak ill of the dead, Rachel, but I think our dearly departed was more interested in payin' off his debts and maybe gettin' in a few more wives than playing psychologist.' I glance at Rachel's face, but it's hard to know what she thinks about that. 'Did Blake ever talk to you about someone named Dakota Jessop?' I ask Rachel. 'A realtor, maybe?'

Rachel shakes her head blankly.

'Blake left her number with your cousin Marsha, who passed it on to me and Emily.' I nod to my purse, currently sat on the floor of the car.

Rachel's face does that thing again. 'Can I see it?' She takes my purse without waiting for an answer and rummages, in exactly the way I might do if I was with a fellow junkie and didn't trust them to give me my fair half. 'This?' she holds up the folded paper and starts to open it.

As the Xeroxed image of Dakota emerges, Rachel's reaction is kinda animal. A jolt of fear. I never seen a human being look so terrified, and I seen a lotta stuff.

'I know that woman,' she whispers. 'I *know* her. She ran the clinic.'

54

Rachel, first wife

Words can't describe my reaction to the picture.

That face. That *face*.

The sensations it invokes are physical. Like an immediate needle pain to the groin. A choking terror. I'm struck by a memory which is visceral.

I'm in a place between waking and dreaming. Men are carrying me over butterscotch earth. The flat amber-yellow rocks clatter beneath their feet. In my semi-conscious state, I have half a mind they're taking me straight to hell. Then I smell the bleach and realize I'm in the clinic. My whole world is pain. Hot awful pain. A familiar coil of fear unravels.

For a moment I consider not opening my eyes. But when I hear her voice, I can't help myself. They pop open all by themselves.

'Sit down,' she's telling someone sternly. 'You want your husband to know you made a show of yourself?'

She's over the other side of the room. I feel my fists bunch.

Please God. Don't let her notice me.

I roll to my side, looking away, my heart beating fast.

That's when I notice there's someone in the bed next to me. A young dark-haired girl. My age, maybe. She's curled in a ball on her side, hands clamped between her legs, like her downstairs hurts.

'Rayne?' Her eyes settle on mine.

I recognize her now. She's a half-sister of mine. Melissa. We used to play together as girls before her family got reassigned to the big house. She has very pretty sea-green eyes that contrast with her almost-black hair.

'Holy heck.' Her eyes boggle. 'You must be in some trouble.'

I don't answer that. Misery ripples through me.

She reaches out a hand and locks her pinkie in mine.

'It's OK,' she tells me. 'Brave like Jesus, right?'

I manage a smile. This was one of the games we played as girls, daring each other to be as brave as the boys.

'Brave like Jesus,' I whisper.

There's a weird sound from the other side of the room.

'Poor girl,' says Melissa, her eyes trained behind me. 'Aunt Meg is always hardest on the pretty ones.'

I don't know where these thoughts are coming from. All I know is I don't want to share them with Tina.

Instead I say, 'I was afraid of her.'

I'm looking at Tina's tanned hands, rather than her face. Her pink polish is chipped at the edges.

'You know her?' Tina sounds excited.

The image is pixelated. Like someone blew it up large from an old photo and Xeroxed it a couple of times for good measure. But you can still see the claw-like hair, plaited around her ears, and the set of the eyes. She has a real peculiar smile on her face, which is also familiar. Like I can see her face smiling down at me, but not in a nice way.

Aunt Meg. Now I remember the name, it seems impossible I ever forgot it.

'She's from the Homestead,' I say. 'Like a nurse or something. I think her name is Meg. Aunt Meg, we knew her as.' It's hard to say it aloud.

'Huh.' Tina frowns at the picture. 'So she changed her name?'

'Most of us did that,' I say, 'when we left.'

'Well, she's got blond hair,' Tina points out. 'Maybe it was her Blake was meeting.'

This idea fills me with the most awful feeling.

'Do you think she and Blake could have been courting?' asks Tina.

A white bed. Naked women, tumbling limbs. Hands are all over Blake's naked back, touching, stroking.

'Does it feel good?' he asks. 'Can you feel the heavenly fire?'

Meg's face, underneath Blake's naked body, her cold eyes fixed on me.

'She's married already,' I tell Tina. 'You can tell by her hair.' I feel reluctant to touch the image. 'See at the top where it's plaited behind the crown? Only married ladies do that.'

Tina lets out a long breath, like she's real relieved. 'So a woman from the Homestead is working in real estate. Selling the place. Sounds corrupt, if you ask me.'

'Everything about the Homestead was corrupt,' I tell her. 'The whole business was like a pyramid scheme. The Prophet ripping off his people. Did you call the number?' I ask.

'Sure I did. Bunch a times. No answer. It's a Las Vegas dial code, though.' She taps the paper thoughtfully.

I screw up my face, trying to think.

'The Prophet went on the run to Vegas,' I say uncertainly. 'They had a lot of safe houses there.'

'Safe houses?'

'Like . . . Secret houses owned by members of the Church. They're all over the country. A network. That's how come he was able to escape arrest for so long.'

We both ponder this. Tina's cell phone beeps. She takes it out, and her face sorta lights in a smile. As if some cute date messaged her back.

'It's from Detective Carlson,' she says.

I roll my eyes.

'He says . . .' She pauses to read. 'He's looked into Dakota's number for me.' Again that smile. 'An' guess what?'

'What?'

'He's got a location for Dakota's firm. An actual office address.' Tina looks at me, real determined. 'I'm goin' to Vegas,' she says. 'Find out what Blake got himself into.'

'Isn't that dangerous?' I ask her.

'I can take care of myself.'

That's when I realize. If Blake was trying to buy the Homestead, there could be pictures, maps. There's no way I can let Tina go look through whatever real estate documents are out there. She's smart enough to put two and two together.

Now something else occurs to me. Like why is *Tina* so bent out of shape on poking around in this stuff? It strikes me as not a little suspicious.

'Hey,' says Tina. 'You hungry? How 'bout we go to that diner Blake said was too expensive? Grab a bite before I hit the road.'

I don't like this idea at all, since there is plenty of canned soup and pasta back at the house, and we've agreed to be careful with what little money we have. But I don't want Tina out on her own, prying into Blake's things.

'OK,' I say slowly. 'Sure.' I put the car into drive, pull out, turning over what to do next. Talk her out of going, I guess. 'We can talk about Vegas over lunch,' I tell her.

'Sure,' replies Tina. She turns her head to look out of the window, a ghost of a smile on her pink-lipsticked mouth.

55

Emily, sister-wife

When I was a little girl, I loved the confessional booth in the Catholic church. Pouring my stories through that little grille, and hearing the priest gasp and tut. Visiting the Bishop in the Mormon church wasn't the same at all. Especially since I always got the strong feeling Bishop Young didn't like me too much.

I feel like that now. He's sitting across the plastic police table from me, scowling from under his big eyebrows. We're in a back room with a smell of grease and a balled-up Crown burger wrapper smeared with fry-sauce in the trash. My chair has a crack right in the middle that pinches my leg if I sit wrong, so I'm leaning on one side, trying to look like I'm listening.

Bishop Young is lecturing me on blood atonement. How it might not work. Least I think that's what he's saying.

'Then why have it as an option?' I point out. 'Why let people request a rifle range?'

'It's not an *option*,' says Bishop Young, sounding cross. 'This isn't a cafeteria where you pick and choose your manner of death. This is serious. You have a duty to defend yourself in court and honor the life God gave you. Suicide is a sin.'

He leans over the table.

'Emily, I think you never really understood the LDS faith. There are two kinds of heaven, not just one. You can't get into celestial heaven through blood atonement.'

I am actually insulted.

'I do too understand,' I say, listing on my fingers. 'Three heavens. There's the telestial heaven for people who are nice enough people, but not godly.' I always pictured this as a homely kind of place with a lot of television sets. 'Terrestrial is for Mormons like you, who go to church but only have one wife. Then there's the best sort, for plural-marrieds who have at least three wives.'

'You haven't understood it at all,' says Bishop Young angrily. 'The Church hasn't held that policy for many years. *Celestial* heaven is for those who have lived a righteous life and accepted the teachings of Jesus Christ.' I'm guessing by his smug expression he considers himself a shoo-in. 'Polygamy doesn't come into it,' he goes on.

I'm getting bored now. That's when Brewer comes into the room holding a pamphlet. I recognize it. The front reads *Christian Domestic Discipline Marriage*. There's a smudgy black-and-white Xerox of two conjoined wedding rings.

Bishop Young looks nervous.

'I thought it might be beneficial to have your bishop present,' says Brewer, sliding into a chair. 'Clear a few things up.' She taps the pamphlet. 'I'll get right down to it. Did your husband believe in physically disciplining his wives, Emily?'

I look across at Bishop Young.

He clears his throat.

'We talked about an understanding between Christians,' he explains to Brewer, 'that the Bible gives a man permission to discipline his wife.'

Brewer looks at me. 'Did Blake hit you?' she asks quietly.

245

'Um. Yes.' I swallow, eyes switching back and forth between the people in the room.

'And where would he hit you?'

'In the bedroom.' My voice is all scratchy, like a whisper. I can see Bishop Young's face growing darker and darker.

Brewer looks very sad.

'I meant, on what part of your body did he hit you,' she says quietly, her mouth turned down at the corners.

'On my butt.' I'm looking down at the table. I kinda wish the ground would open up and swallow me whole.

'With his hand?' confirms Brewer. 'Or something else?'

'His hand.' I nod, still not looking up. 'Sometimes a belt, if I'd been real bad.'

'His own belt?' I guess she's thinking of how he was found.

I nod.

I have this real icky image. Like I would walk around the house afterwards feeling as though everyone must know. As if they could see inside of me. Blake, making a show for Tina, like he always did after.

'Some couples find this dynamic works in their relationship,' interjects Bishop Young. 'Blake and Emily wanted to explore it as an option.'

'Uh-huh.' Brewer arches an eyebrow. 'Like *Fifty Shades of Grey* kinda thing?'

'Christian discipline is *nothing* to do with . . . with . . . *bondage*, or *unnatural sexual acts!*' explodes Bishop Young.

'Right,' says Brewer, raising her voice, 'forgive me, how perverted. It's only about abusing women, right?' She shakes her head in disgust and looks at me. 'To be very clear,' she says, 'it is *against the law* to physically abuse your wife, with your hand or foot, or any other part of you, no matter what the Bible has to say on things.' She turns to Bishop Young, eyes fiery.

'In breaking news, stoning is now outlawed,' she tells him.

'Young lady . . .' says the Bishop, drawing himself up so rigid his chins wobble and addressing officer Brewer.

'You call me young lady again,' says Brewer, 'I'll have you in handcuffs so fast your head will spin. What I'm interested in getting to the bottom of is whether Emily could be charged with culpable homicide, as opposed to murder, which may be possible if we can establish that she was a long-standing victim of physical abuse.'

Bishop Young shakes his head in disgust. 'It is the fashion now, to blame men for situations that women create. I can see how tempting it might be, to play the victim, take no responsibility for your own actions. Marriage is a two-way street, and in successful marriages, wives welcome their husbands with an open heart.'

'Are you seriously suggesting,' says Brewer, 'that—'

I get mad then. It's exactly like it was back at the ranch, with everyone fighting, like I'm not even in the room. I put my fingers in my ears and scream.

56

Tina, sister-wife

A waitress arrives with our food. A Cobb salad for me. A club sandwich for Rachel.

'I just think it's a bad plan,' says Rachel as our server walks away. 'In fact, it's no kind of plan at all. What, you just . . . drive five hours to Las Vegas, and what? Knock on the door of some mobster real estate firm?'

I twirl hair around my finger. To my mind, Rachel is a little too invested in stoppin' me findin' Dakota.

'It's no bad thing to keep busy in times like these,' she tells me. 'Clean the house and whatnot. I get that. But this whole idea seems silly. Not to mention a little dangerous. I mean, isn't Vegas like a trigger for you? You know. For drug use?'

'Are you frightened I might find something out about Blake you don't want to know?' I suggest, because I don't want to admit she's right.

She sorta deflates, knitting her hands around her Mountain Dew.

'Maybe,' she says. Rachel eyes my salad. 'You remember that welcome dinner,' says Rachel. 'Where Blake introduced us?'

I roll my eyes.

'How could I forget? I shoulda known, then.' I spear a forkful of bacon. 'He was such a tightwad. Kirker's Diner for a romantic night out.'

'Cash only,' says Rachel, with a slight smile. 'He liked cash only. Less risk of computers tracking your whereabouts.'

'Oh.' Makes me feel a little funny that she knows that and I don't.

Rachel picks up her sandwich with both hands, but doesn't take a bite.

'I thought you were being all superior that dinner,' she admits, kinda hiding behind her food, 'ordering salad, when we all had, like, cheese steaks and the chicken fry.'

I pause with a fork halfway to my lips.

'You serious?'

'Uh-huh.'

'I always thought you saw me as this lowdown junkie scum, not fit to enter your house,' I reply.

'Maybe I let you think that. Maybe I was a little jealous. Blake was always goin' on about how sophisticated you were.'

I chew my salad, swallow. The crispy bacon has been deep-fried and doused with enough vinegary dressing to make my cheeks sweat.

'He did that, didn't he?' I say. 'Blake never stopped tellin' me what a great mom you'd make. He knew how to hit ya where it hurt, right?'

She nods, and bites into her club sandwich.

'I still don't think a road trip is a good idea,' she says, between chews. 'For one thing, you're not allowed out of the state. That's a condition of our bail.'

'You know the state that doesn't keep close tabs on criminals? That would be Nevada. Vegas is like the crime capital of America.'

'What would you do for money?'

'I got a credit card. I'll use it until it runs out.'

You can tell by Rachel's expression she doesn't like the sound of that at all.

'It wouldn't be safe,' she says. 'Out all alone on the road.'

'I used to drive it all the time. Besides, there's a rifle under the seat, right?'

She does a funny sorta double take. 'Blake kept one,' she says, 'to protect us. It's not loaded though. I made him take the bullets out, after that news story about a gun misfiring and killing the driver.'

She looks at me just a little too long, like *she's* wonderin' if *I've* been wonderin' 'bout that gun.

Rachel regroups first. 'I don't think going to Vegas is a good idea. We should leave it to the police.'

I shake my head at her naivety. 'Yeah right. The cops rang the number and got no reply, same as I did. Maybe they even left a message. An' good luck with that, 'cause last time I checked, mobsters don't return calls. They ain't goin' in person, take my word for it.'

'Why not?'

'The offices are over state lines,' I explain. 'In Vegas. Five hours' drive. An' it's out of their jurisdiction, they gotta liaise with Nevada State, yada yada yada.' I wave my hands. 'Chances are, by the time they get it together to find Dakota, *if* they even decide that's worth doin', she could be long gone.'

I rake a hand through my hair.

'Not to mention it's a mob firm,' I conclude. 'Everyone in Vegas knows 'em. Those realtors are the ones who own casinos. They got more power than the cops, if they wanna cover some-thin' over.'

Rachel is silent for a moment.

'It's all about the Homestead land, isn't it?' she says eventually.

'Maybe. Maybe Blake got mixed up in somethin' dangerous. Whatever's goin' on, this Dakota person likely knows something, right?'

'You sure you don't want to drive to Vegas so you can inject marijuana?'

'*Inject* marijuana? Jeez Louise, Rachel.'

'Are you really so certain Emily didn't murder Blake?' she asks quietly.

I close my eyes. Fatigue is setting in now. The kind of fat exhaustion I used to feel if I left it too long without drugs.

'Would you blame her?' I ask Rachel. 'If she had?'

There's something real funny in Rachel's expression. Like she's looking for something she's lost.

'Come on, Rachel,' I sigh. 'You know what Blake was really like, don't you?'

A feeling of despair settles over me. I need to get up, take action.

I pull out my pocketbook. Throw down bills.

'I'll drop you back at the safe house,' I tell her. 'I won't be gone more than a day.' It unnerves me, how easily I've slid back into my former self. Making promises I know I'll never keep.

'Hey, wait,' Rachel grabs my arm, a desperate look on her face. 'Wouldn't it be best if I went to Vegas?'

'*You* want to go? Alone?'

'Um. Sure.' Rachel's fake-casual tone is terrible.

'You never even made that trip before, Rachel,' I say. 'Even if you left right now, you'd arrive in the early hours of the morning.'

'So would you.'

I shrug. 'I'll catch a few hours' sleep on the roadside. Arrive at dawn. I used to drive Vegas to Utah regular. Did it all the time.'

'Well then, I guess you're tired of it by now.'

Neither of us are gonna come right out and say it. That we

think the other one could have some dark motive for looking through whatever Blake might have gotten involved in without the other one present.

'We'll toss a coin,' says Rachel. This is typical of her. So goddamn righteous she thinks Jesus will turn her quarter the right way up.

'No,' I say. 'There's only one fair way to resolve this.'

'Which is?' her blond eyebrows rise in challenge.

'We both go.'

'OK.' She locks eyes with me.

'On one condition,' I add, playing my advantage. 'Excuse me, miss?' I wave at the waitress. 'Can I get two coffees to go?'

'I don't drink coffee,' says Rachel.

'Rachel,' I say, 'have you ever heard the expression, "what happens in Vegas stays in Vegas"?'

She shakes her head in disbelief. 'Like God doesn't see what's goin' on in Vegas? What are you saying?'

'I'm sayin',' I tell her slowly, 'I'm gettin' you a double espresso. You're gonna drink it. That's the only way I'm goin' to Vegas with you.' I flash her a grin. 'Five hours might be enough to get you talkin'.'

57

Emily, sister–wife

When I'm done screaming, I take my fingers out of my ears and open my eyes. Brewer and Bishop Young are both staring at me. Bishop Young looks a little frightened. Brewer looks like she hasn't made up her mind if I'm crazy or something else.

'Blake wasn't a bad man, like you're making him out to be,' I say, feeling mad. 'He wasn't like that. He was trying his best.'

I eyeball them both. Brewer's mouth twists.

'I mean to say,' I spread my hands, 'Blake didn't always know what to do. It's not like you see how to be a husband to three wives on TV or anything. People don't write books for people like us. We can't live out in the open like regular married people.'

They're both sitting with stunned looks on their faces. Since there's a space to speak, I decide to keep talking.

'Blake tried taking me to the clinic,' I explain. 'He tried praying. Bishop Young told him about the discipline thing. So he tried that too. But he didn't *like* doing it. It made things even more awkward, as a matter of fact. I don't think Blake *wanted* to do it at all. He just, you know, felt he *should.*'

Brewer purses her lips, like she doesn't believe me.

I face her. 'So quit making out like Blake was some monster.'

Brewer has a pleading expression.

253

'Emily,' she says. 'You may not have thought you were in an abusive relationship, but I worked in domestic abuse crime for a long time. If I had a dollar for every beat-up woman who told me her husband wasn't a bad man, I sure as hell wouldn't be drivin' to work in a rusty Ford with wind-up windows.'

'Blake asked me if I consented to be disciplined, and I said "yes".' I fold my arms in front of me.

'Did he always ask your permission? Every time?' Brewer says it like she knows the answer.

'That isn't the principle of Christian discipline,' interrupts Bishop Young. 'It is the responsibility of the man to decide when punishment is appropriate.'

'In other words, he took you off for a spanking when he thought you were out of line?' asks Brewer, not bothering to look at Bishop Young.

I chew my finger.

'Were there times when you asked him not to hit you, and he did anyway?'

'Yes,' I say, eyes glued to the desk. I've got a bit of skin in my teeth now and I work at it. 'Mostly 'cause I was talking too much. Blake was under a lot of stress. Money troubles. And,' I glare at Bishop Young, '*he* was threatening to excommunicate our husband,' I explain.

Brewer looks back and forth between me and Bishop Young.

'That true?' asks Brewer. 'You were going to kick Mr Nelson out of the Church?'

'The Nelson family have been part of the Tucknott Church a long time,' replies Bishop Young. 'Whilst Blake kept his plural marriage discreet, I was willing to turn a blind eye. But buying up a big plot for the purpose of taking more wives was a step too far.'

'So, to clarify,' says Brewer slowly, 'you were planning to

excommunicate Blake Nelson *if* he bought that land.' She leans her chin on her fist, like she's real interested.

'I hoped it would never come to it. But yes. Adultery is a sin. I have a congregation to protect.'

'Emily,' says Brewer. 'How about you just . . . talk to us about what you went through? There's a growing precedent for domestic violence to be taken into consideration in murder cases. Not in Utah just yet, but it's worth a shot, right?'

'Blake Nelson was a good man,' interrupts Bishop Young. 'Would you really want to put his family through all that, Emily? Sully his memory?'

I look into Bishop Young's fat face, thinking how he only ever got me into a whole heap of trouble. Since the first evening I met him, as a matter of fact, right before I married Blake, when Bishop Young gave me my official recommend card. He explained it was like a security pass into the big white Temple church that lasted for life. Bishop Young took so long explaining what an honor it was, I got home late and Momma went crazy. She hadn't seen the dress mashed in my closet, so she got it all wrong. Started screaming that no man would marry me if I wasn't a virgin, and she always knew I'd give in and whore myself before even going on one real date.

I got real mad then and told her that the boy from the drug-store *was* a real date, and he'd bought me a snow cone and a full-size Coke, and she just said, 'What kind of date is it where a boy makes you walk four blocks to his house?'

I *had* been planning to surprise Momma in the morning, dressed in my wedding gown. Telling her my husband-to-be had an honest-to-God *revelation* about me. Instead I went to my room and balled up the dress right in its plastic wrapper and ran out of the house with it under my arm. I think Momma saw it, but maybe she wasn't sure what it was, because she didn't try and stop me leaving. I spent the night in the Our Lady of Lourdes Church five blocks west of Sugar House, hunched in a corner with my dress for a pillow, with all the hobos snoring on the floor around.

I sigh. I like Brewer, I do. I wish I could help her.

'I'm sorry,' I tell her. 'I just . . . I want to atone for my sins.'

58

Rachel, first wife

It didn't take Tina too long to convince me to go to Vegas. Because the truth is, when I considered the alternative – going back to the ranch – I felt the walls of my world were falling away. So we got more or less straight on the road, in Blake's old Chevy. Didn't even stop for clothes. Kind of reminded me of when I ran away from the Homestead, that second time. The time I actually made it.

Our car holds the acrid scent of nail polish, and I glance across to see Tina's fingertips on the steering wheel are fresh-painted. She must have reapplied whilst I was in the bathroom in the diner.

Tina drives us west, past the mighty crater of Bingham Copper Mine. I lean out the window to look. From what I've heard, a lot of boys from the Homestead wound up working here. Even from this distance, the thing is jaw-dropping. It's got to be at least two miles across, with concentric circles going deeper and deeper into the earth, like an amphitheater for giants. I always pictured the mine as orange, but it's beige, with a white crust, like salt.

'Incredible, isn't it?' Tina looks across, catching the direction of my gaze. 'Guess all those mountains hold a lotta copper. From what I've heard, you can see it from outer space.' She blows hair from her face. 'Is it any wonder men start thinkin' they're gods,' she adds, more to herself than me, 'when they got tools to dig out the side of the world.'

I can tell she's thinking of Blake.

We rumble along the interstate, and I think how beautiful it all is out here, and how I never really got to see it. I was so concerned with making the perfect home. The amber and yellow sand stretches out for miles, dotted with balls of green grass. Mountains of layered red and pink rock fork up in different shapes, jagged peaks and flat summits. It's such a long drive, it gives me time to think.

Images are drifting in and out of my brain.

Blake is on the white bed. The women are arranged at the foot, wearing loose white robes.

'You have to be comfortable being undressed,' he tells them. 'Your nakedness is no sin in this room.'

The women pull off their robes. Only now I can see at least half of them aren't really women. Two are barely of age, high-breasted with sparse tufts of pubic hair. Blake lounges, watching, a hand on his crotch.

'God wants you to be sexually excited,' he tells the girls. 'Help each other. Go on.' He nods.

The girls start touching one another, stroking, fondling. A few look resigned. Others confused.

'I'll tell you,' says Blake, 'you ladies are lucky you don't know what faithless men are like.'

'We're grateful we don't,' murmurs a brunette girl, obediently, glancing at the others.

Blake beckons the dark-haired girl. Now I can see her face, the sea-green eyes. It's Melissa.

'Come over here,' he says. 'You can show the others how to give me comfort.'

'Incredible, isn't it?' Tina glances across, interrupting my thoughts. 'I used to make this drive in the early days of courtin' Blake. Nothing but me, a flat ribbon of road, and rolling pink-red desert. I'd feel this *joy*, you know? I remember thinking this landscape couldn't be an accident. Something this beautiful couldn't just be some random event. Maybe that was even what convinced me to convert to the faith, in the end,' she considers.

I smile at her. I've never seen this side to Tina before. Breeze flapping her dark hair as the road zooms under us, she looks as though she's flying.

We're about halfway to Vegas, when Tina makes a sudden dramatic stop.

'Just thought a somethin',' she says. 'Wait here.'

I sit in the car watching her go. Then I lean across and check Blake's gun is still where he left it, under the driver's seat. Glancing to make sure Tina's out of sight, I scoop it out and toss it under the seat in the back. Then I remember, Blake has a hunting rifle someplace in the trunk too.

I'm turning around to look for it, when the door pops open.

Tina swings into the car and drops something into my lap. It's a phone.

'Hey,' she said. 'What were you doing?'

'Nothing. I thought you said we couldn't use phones,' I say, changing the subject. 'The police will track us.'

'It's a burner phone,' says Tina. 'A phone that can't be traced,' she explains, seeing my blank expression. 'We can use them to talk to each other. Little somethin' I learned in my hustlin' days,' she adds, flipping a strand of black hair off her face. 'Not as dumb as I look, huh?'

'I never thought you were dumb.'

She tosses me a look. 'Yeah right. Look,' she glances across at me from the passenger seat, 'I'm gonna be straight with you. I used to be a real bad person. Full on mean. I kinda had to learn it, to get by, you know? Sorta blank out my emotions. I learned not to care. Not about myself, but about anyone. I'd lie, I'd steal, just for my next fix. I even . . . I even rolled over some of my friends.'

'No one's perfect,' I tell her. 'Jesus will forgive you, but first, you've got to just forgive yourself.'

Tina glances at me, then looks back to the road. 'You know that is the Mormoniest thing you have ever said to me?' She takes a hand off the wheel and scratches the side of her nose with a pink fingernail. 'I'm just sayin' we're headin' back to where I grew up, and you might see an ugly side to me. You wouldn't have liked me back when I worked the strip.'

'I don't like you now.'

To my surprise, Tina throws her head back and laughs, revealing a little clutch of cheap metal dental fillings.

'I been waitin' over a year to hear you own up to that,' she says. 'Least you're being honest, *finally*.'

She taps her bright fingernails on the wheel, puts her foot on the gas.

'OK, let's go over the plan,' she decides as we speed away.

'*You* have a plan? What is it? We drive on over there and knock on the door?'

'Don't be such a wise-ass. Look, if we're gonna get along, you need to cut that shit out, right? I mean it. Quit with the snarky comments.'

'Well then, you need to stop being so . . . so *blunt* about everything.'

I'm not sure where this frankness has come from. I guess it has something to do with the coffee.

'Alright,' she says. 'Truce. We'll pretend we like each other.

And, as it happens, you're right about the plan. We go knock on the door. More or less.'

A prickling feeling lifts the hairs on the back of my neck. I'm wondering just how deep Blake got into Homestead affairs, and how the heck I'm going to hide it from Tina.

59

Tina, sister–wife

Last night, I kinda regretted giving Rachel the coffee. On the road, she had gotten this glittery-eyed look which was a little scary. Plus, when we pulled over around midnight to get some sleep, she talked non-stop about our relationship for a full hour, and took no hints I was trying to get some rest.

It's early morning now, still dark, and she's passed out in the passenger seat, doing this heavy-breathing thing, like her body wants to snore but her mind won't let it.

I figure we're maybe an hour from Vegas. The landscape changed a while back. The pretty rainbow of Utah's mauve-striped mountains and honey-color sand hardened up, getting redder. Meaner. The parched grass got more attitude, stickin' up all punky in little pale tufts.

I'm pretty sure even the air is different. Utah is placid, like it's chewin' the cud. Nevada air has a little zip to it.

I glance at Rachel. Maybe the land makes the people, and not the other way around.

I turn on the engine and pull out, trying not to wake her, but she comes to, blinking her eyes groggily.

'We'll be in Vegas by sunup,' I tell her, watching the road fly past as we pick up speed.

'H'OK,' she says, rubbing her eyes. 'Great.'

For a long time, we drive in silence. It's nice. Like we're actual buddies. Feels strange to be making this journey again with Rachel. Like my life in reverse.

In the distance, the sun is peaking above the horizon.

It's getting light when Rachel speaks.

'If this Dakota person is in real estate, then wouldn't you know her?' she asks, in this real unconvincingly casual voice.

'No,' I snap. 'I mean, why would I?' I look across, tryin' to figure why this is the first thing she's said.

'Just a thought.' She's backtracking. 'It's a small world right, real estate?'

'No,' I tell her. 'Real estate is a very big world. Lotta people buy property. Even our husband.' I smile at my own joke. 'Look, this isn't gonna work if you don't trust me.'

'I'm sorry,' she says. 'It isn't personal. I know it's a . . . problem. My upbringing, I guess. It was drilled into us. Only blood family counts. Blake didn't like it either. I'm nervous, is all. I've never been to Vegas before.'

I'm shocked into silence. Rachel has just voluntarily owned up to a vulnerability.

'It's OK,' I say. 'I'll take good care of you. This doesn't mean we're friends though.'

'OK. There is one last thing,' says Rachel, as Vegas glitters on the half-light horizon.

'Right!' I smack my forehead. 'We need to get you some new clothes. You can't walk around Vegas like you wandered in from Hicksville. Don't worry, there's a mall on the outside of town. We can make a stop.'

'I wasn't referring to that,' she says, frowning. 'I meant, what if you're wrong? What if Dakota is a regular realtor?'

'With a prairie dress and claw-hair? Are you kiddin' me?' I

look over at Rachel. 'You gotta do something with your hair too. So it doesn't look so Mormony.'

'It doesn't look *Mormony*,' she sounds like she's insulted without knowing why.

I shake my head. 'Jeez Louise, Rachel. You never noticed that women in Utah have a particular look? We're incognito, remember? Absolutely no one in Vegas has long mousy hair with home-done highlights plaited down their back. Nothing says Utah out-of-towner more than that getup. Trust me.'

'I have my hair up for the road,' she says, touching it lightly with her palms. 'I'll shake it out in a more regular style.'

'Rachel, I hate to tell you this, but your hairstyle is regular for an eight-year-old girl. No offense,' I add.

'It's OK.'

We're hitting the first few blocks of Vegas now and I figure Rachel must realize my point. Since this is party town, there is a mess of dressed-up people eating breakfast burritos and downing Bloody Marys in roadside places. Every girl has bleached or dyed hair, blow-dried straight, or framing the face with curls.

'I'll do your makeup too, if you like. And we'll get you somethin' nice to wear,' I tell Rachel. 'A big butt doesn't have to write you outta good clothes. Look at Beyoncé.'

'You know, this is what I mean about blunt.'

'This is good. We're communicating.'

On the road ahead, I see the downtown gas station I remember from my Vegas days.

'Give me a minute,' I say, swinging the car into the lot and turning off the engine. 'I'm gonna fill up.'

'Didn't we do that already?'

'Better to be prepared. And I'm maybe a little nostalgic,' I confess.

Rachel just nods. It's good she has so much on her mind too. Because she barely even looks up as I go into the gas station. So she doesn't see me buy a box of bullets for the gun in our car and slide them into my purse.

60

Emily, sister–wife

When I was at high school, there was a boy I liked called Peter Brown. He sat near me in class, and did all these doodles of old-style cartoons on his notebook. I used to pray every night that he would notice me, but he never did.

And you know what? Right after I got engaged to Blake, I ran into Peter downtown and he asked me out on a date. Said something about how different I looked.

I have the same kind of feeling now. Mr and Mrs Nelson, after all those years of pretending I didn't exist, have come to visit. Detective Carlson says they want to pay my bail, but only under certain conditions.

'My momma's gonna come down and post bail,' I told Carlson. 'She'll be here real soon, you'll see.'

I could tell he felt a little sorry for me then.

The Nelsons are waiting, looking real uncomfortable.

Mr Nelson wears a suit, which strikes me as a strange choice, given the occasion. But I guess he doesn't have a lot of clothes, besides the overalls and cotton shirts he wears to the store. Mrs Nelson is in a perfectly ironed check dress and matching shoes, with her hair sprayed up in its usual poufy style. I never could get my hair that high, on account of it being natural blond and very limp. I used to pray for mousy hair which could be bleached and teased up.

But Mrs Nelson's hair doesn't look so perfect today. There are tufts where the hair is breaking away in clumps. Like she's stopped being so careful with how she applies the bleach. She's not wearing her usual perfume either.

They are both very serious, and I feel sorry for them then. Mrs Nelson looks broken with sadness. She won't look in my direction at all, like she's frightened if she does she'll lash out or something, start screaming at me. Her eyes are fixed hard on the table. Mr Nelson clears his throat.

'We've come to talk to you,' he begins. 'We want to post your bail. It's a large amount of money. A very large amount of money. I can get it, but it won't be easy.'

'You want to pay me off, so I don't say bad things about Blake in court?'

Mrs Nelson jerks in her chair. *Ha.* Guess they don't think I'm too smart. Mr Nelson sucks his cheeks, making a saggy spot where he's missing teeth on one side. According to Blake, Mr Nelson lived with tooth pain for two years straight, despite having dental insurance, because it cost thirty dollars in gas to make a round trip to the nearest clinic.

Mr Nelson toys with the cuff of his shirt.

'We know you and Blake were having problems of a . . . sexual kind,' he says, looking directly at me. 'And that Bishop Young gave you some . . . advice. Lawyers twist things like that. Make things sound perverted.'

I have an image of them both in court, straight-backed, whilst their family reputation is dragged through the dirt. For some reason it brings a little smile to my face.

'The truth is,' says Mr Nelson, 'Blake never did care to listen to our opinions.' His face sorta twitches. 'Married Rachel without even consulting with us.'

My eyes open wide. I didn't know that.

'Then went headlong into this . . . this *adultery* justified by scripture.' Mr Nelson has this strange way of not quite looking at you when he talks. 'Brought shame on the family who raised him. Never worked a hard day in his life.' He shakes his head. 'After everything his mother did for him, and it was never enough.'

Mrs Nelson puts a hand on her husband's arm. He looks at it, as though he's puzzled. She drags her eyes to mine, but it looks like it takes some effort.

'Bishop Young told us,' she says, her features twisted in hurt. 'He said you might see yourself as . . . as kind of a victim.'

I don't know how to answer that, so I just stare at her. She looks away again then, as though she might lose control.

'We tried to explain to our son, that polygamy is wrong,' says Mrs Nelson, looking back at the table. She wipes away tears, but real careful with the bottom of her finger, so as not to smudge her makeup. 'He wouldn't listen. It felt like . . . we'd lost him. Now we're losing him all over again.'

She breaks down into this weird singsong sobbing, and gives up on the makeup dabbing. It's kinda shocking to see her this way, since Mrs Nelson is always so in control of herself and well turned out. It's like seeing Spiderman with a beer in his hand, or something. I expect Mr Nelson to put his arm around her, or comfort her, or try to make her feel better. But he pats her on the shoulder in this real awkward way, like she's a dog. Mrs Nelson sorta flinches away.

I look at them both, trying to imagine how they ever had five children together.

'You're not gonna drag his name through the dirt, are you?' whispers Mrs Nelson, managing to raise her eyes to my face. 'We've worked so hard . . . For his brothers and sisters.' Her face is white. 'I raised them all to respect God and family.'

'The devil,' says Mr Nelson, suddenly. 'The devil tempted him away. That Rachel, or Rayne, or whatever the heck she calls herself.'

His lips press completely flat.

'She convinced him to buy the old Homestead plot on the state limits. Ten thousand acres! Who in the name of Sam Hill needs that amount of land? Blake wanted *me* to loan him the down payment too. As if it wasn't enough I acted as guarantor for that ranch of yours.'

Mr Nelson catches my expression.

'Oh, he didn't mention that? No, I don't expect he would. Blake always liked to play the big man, taking care of business, but the truth was, none of the banks would give him credit. Last I heard, Blake was cooking up some kind of half-baked deal to buy that land with an out-of-town firm. I-talians. Mobsters.'

He's forgotten I'm Italian heritage. Mrs Nelson glares at him, and he stops talking.

'We want you to know, we are trying to forgive you.' Her voice gets all throaty. 'We want to believe you're trying to do right. After . . . After everything.'

I look back and forth between them, not sure what the heck they're getting at.

'We know Rachel drove you to it,' continues Mrs Nelson. 'She has some *hold* over you. She wants you to say terrible things about my boy.'

I get mad. 'Rachel can be real mean,' I say, 'but she takes care of us. Never saw you do that, Mrs Nelson. You're always doing people down. Blake always felt he was never good enough for you.'

She stiffens in her chair. Two pink spots appear in the middle of her cheeks.

'That isn't true,' she says, holding my gaze determinedly now.

'I was very proud of Blake. I never told him enough. I wish I'd had the chance to tell him . . .' Her voice breaks and she starts shaking her head raggedly, side to side. Her big hair doesn't move an inch. She swallows. 'We can help with a lawyer, if that's what you want. Get you the best outcome.'

'I only want one outcome, Mrs Nelson,' I say. 'I want to atone for my sins.'

Mrs Nelson looks at Mr Nelson, with this agonized expression.

'I would have thought you'd have more dignity. It's bad enough . . .' her voice chokes up. 'It's bad enough he's gone.'

I'd been feeling sorry for Mrs Nelson until now, but that feeling vanishes away.

'Your son broke my heart,' I say, in a formal kind of voice. 'He never told me the truth, about the life I would have. I spent the last four years bathing with a cup and a faucet. And you know what else, Mrs Nelson? I think you were downright cruel to him when he was growing up.'

I have an image of my momma, locking me in my bedroom until my father came home. All those stories she told me about princesses.

'I think you should have let him be who he wanted,' I tell her. "Stead of forcing him to be something you wanted. He would have been a lot happier, and you would have saved us all this big mess.'

Mr Nelson stands. His hands are shaking.

'Make your choice,' he says. 'We won't be extending this offer a second time.'

I look back and forth between them. Mrs Nelson has a hopeful look on her face, but Mr Nelson looks plain mad.

'No thank you,' I say. 'I don't need your help.'

61

Tina, sister-wife

Vegas early morning is a funny kind of place. Like a zombie town. Plenty of people walkin' about, but not altogether there, if you catch my drift. The bright lights are still on, but they got a bargain-basement look to 'em, like they're not quite the real deal.

Rachel has got this dazed expression, seein' Vegas for the first time. I think she couldn't quite get it in her head that women could dress that way and go outside. I got a little concerned she might bail on the whole idea of finding Dakota. Particularly since even at 7 a.m. she looked so out of place in her plain old jeans and shirt. It was one of the reasons I sent her off alone with the credit card to get some regular clothes, since the stores here don't sleep, but the real estate business does. I also had an ulterior motive.

I wanted to load the rifle under the driver's seat with the bullets from my purse.

Now Rachel's been gone a lot longer than I expected, and here I am in Vegas with the old temptations on all sides.

Be honest, a snarky voice says. *That's why you wanted to come here so bad in the first place.*

It's hot for the morning too. Especially for fall. I'd forgotten that about Vegas. In these parts, the weather kinda lazes around, doin' its own thing. Little hotter, little cooler, changin' its mind once in a while, no big deal.

In Utah, the seasons arrive right on the clock. Blazing sun, pouring rain, freezing snow. On time, as ordered.

I notice an unfamiliar blond lady, on the edge of the parking lot. She's acting a little suspicious, like she's worried she's being followed. I watch her snake around the cars.

Last time I was here was with Blake, right before we were married, I convinced him we should have a bachelor party, the two of us. For all he seemed real serious with his other wives, Blake was more fun than he let on. So for one night only, he let me tour him round Sin City, shootin' tequila and seein' shows with more on display than feathers, if you know what I mean.

'Course Blake didn't get *drunk* or anything like that. But he did choke down a single tequila. I remember staring into his eyes, sayin' I was waitin' for him to take off like a rocket. He only laughed and said that was how he felt all the time when he was with me.

He told me some other stuff too. About his mission in Mexico. I remember feeling so bad for him. I've been incarcerated waiting for sentencing and, honestly, what he went through sounded worse. Dawn to dusk thinkin' only of God. Least in jail you're allowed freedom in your own mind. You're not set on this impossible task and told you're not godly if it doesn't get done. That was what broke him, Blake said. He'd started getting stomach ulcers and skin rashes but soldiered on, desperate to get at least one conversion to the faith. Then his group got told of a boy in Washington who'd gotten four baptisms in a week. Blake fell apart.

I remember telling him he was a good man. God hadn't forsaken him.

All that feels like it happened to somebody else now. Like

I can't even get myself to feel how I felt. But you know what I can remember? The drugs. That mad desperate life where nothing mattered. You may think this is crazy. But I just can't do normal. It freaks me out worse than anything. The thing with growing up with half an eye on danger the whole time is when the danger goes away, you're kinda left with nothing. It makes you twitchy.

That's why the drugs and the hustles, I guess. Just got so sick of thinkin' all the time. About what to look out for, who was gonna come through the freakin' door. I thought I was so smart, pulling these three-dime scams and hustlin' out-a-towners for lines of coke, and then, before I knew it, I was sucked in. Turns out there are other ways to lose at casinos than gambling.

The blond lady seems to be walking my way. I'm not really paying attention. Another memory has come back from the early days. Our wedding night. Blake had wanted me to do him a striptease in some cheap bra set he'd bought. I'd tried not to mind he was treating me like a whore.

I flip the car key in my hand, check the time on the big clock above the mall.

Rachel has been gone over two and a half hours now. How long does it take to buy clothes? I flip possibilities in my head.

Fuck it. I'm goin' downtown.

Then I realize the blond lady on the other side of the parking lot is Rachel.

Wow. I can't believe it. Rachel has cut her hair. It's shoulder-length, sparkling with professional highlights, with a cute wave.

'Sorry I was so long,' she says. 'I had a moment of madness. Saw a hair salon in one of the casinos, and I just thought why not?'

'Hey. You look great.' I close in. 'Lemme see. Uh-huh, you let them redo your highlights?'

'I more or less let them do what they wanted,' she admits. 'I put it on the credit card, like you said. Something about this town,' she says. 'I feel kinda reckless.'

'OK, well congratulations. You look normal. Let's go.'

'We have an appointment?'

'I got a plan.'

62

Tina, sister-wife

Both of us are nervous as we approach the skyscraper building where Las Vegas Real Estate keep their offices. A shiny silver list fixed to the exterior places them on the third floor, below and above a whole bunch of other official-sounding firms with very nondescript names.

We pass through big doors into a slick lobby full of modern art. A big glass wall looks out onto the palm-lined sidewalk and a giant billboard advertising a local injury lawyer.

A model-gorgeous receptionist sits behind a slab of polished concrete acting as a desk.

'Excuse me,' I say as we walk in, 'Ma'am?'

She looks up, her blond chignon not moving a millimetre.

'We're here to see someone at Busby Allsop,' I explain, calling to mind one of the firms on the list outside.

Rachel's eyes widen. Probably I shoulda explained my plan to her. I guess she's wonderin' why the hell I'm askin' for a different firm to Dakota's.

'OK.' She lifts the phone. 'You have an appointment?'

'No, but we're looking for representation for a legal case. Perhaps you might pass on that message?'

She nods, presses a button, and speaks into the receiver.

'Uh-huh, yes.' She looks up at us. 'Go right up. Floor four.'

She buzzes us through.

'Thank you kindly, Ma'am,' says Rachel. 'Heaven bless ya.'

'You can't keep blessing people,' I hiss. 'In Nevada, they'll think you're a crazy.'

'Why did you get us in to some law firm?' whispers Rachel. 'How is that gonna help us?'

'Relax, I used to do this all the time. We're through security, right? We get out on floor four, and take the stairs to level three where Dakota works. No appointment necessary.'

Rachel says nothing as we get into the polished elevator, but sorta jumps every time the carriage stops.

Everything goes smoothly and we make our way to Las Vegas Real Estate.

Rachel whistles. 'Sure is a lot of money round here,' she says, taking in the slick photography of huge buildings and mansions. She nudges me. 'Look.' Rachel points. There's a half-open door with a bronze plaque. It reads:

Dakota Jessop.

I take her hand and pull her through.

Inside is the office of a man who sells smart condos, but not penthouses. A wide mahogany desk and big leather chair, both three shades too bright to be real. There's the kind of computer you can tell is slow just by looking at it, and a keyboard where the return symbol is worn away to a shiny grease-edged thumb-print. A tube of Screenies sits ready for action, with a fresh wipe sticking up for duty.

A man stands at a bookshelf on the far side. He turns as we enter.

He gives no indication he finds our sudden entry anything less than delightful.

'Can I help you ladies?' He smiles, politely taking in both our faces.

'Yep,' I say, 'we're looking for Dakota Jessop.'

His pleasant expression deepens fractionally.

'Well you found him,' he says, straightening his suit jacket. 'I'm Dakota Jessop.' He looks us up and down. 'How can I be of service?'

63

Rachel, first wife

Dakota's office couldn't be more family man if he tried.

There's a picture of three smartly attired children on his desk, and a blond smiling wife. The boys wear suit jackets and their hair is neatly center-parted with gel. The little girl is dressed like she's going to church or a wedding.

His certificates of real estate qualifications fill the wall. There's a photograph of him too, I guess on his mission. He stands smiling with two other boys, arms on one another's shoulders, in the regulation smart black suits and white shirts. They look so young to be dressed as men, my heart suddenly aches for Blake.

'You sure you're in the right place?' says Dakota, frowning in concern. Tina's face is creased in perplexity.

'I'm sorry,' says Tina, 'I just . . . I was expecting a girl, is all.'

Dakota's warm smile doesn't falter for a moment.

'You'll have to take that up with my mom,' he says. 'I guess she never counted on Dakota Fanning getting so famous.'

'We'd like to know,' says Tina, 'what business you had with our husband.'

She seems caught halfway between accusing and backtracking.

'Well, Ma'am,' says Dakota, with a polite smile. 'You'll have to tell me who your husband is.'

'Blake,' she says. 'Blake Nelson.'

Dakota frowns in recognition. I'm suddenly panic-stricken he knows about Blake's murder. It was all over the local news. Could it have traveled as far as Vegas?

'Red hair,' I supply. 'Kind of cute-looking. He would have been here the week after Labor Day.'

'Oh yes. Well, I couldn't say if he was cute, of course. He was here about the land purchase, wasn't he? Would that be right? I did wonder . . .' His eyes rove back and forth between the two of us. 'Now I understand, I think.' He scratches his head, still looking back and forth, then seems to come to a decision. 'Do you ladies have any ID?' he asks. 'Anything to prove you are who you say you are.'

Relief rushes through me. I scrabble in my purse, produce my driver's license. Tina does the same, but I get the sense she's more guarded about the idea, and she snatches her ID back the moment Dakota has scanned it.

'Well, I'll help you best I can,' says Dakota, having assured himself of our identities. 'You ladies are in a plural marriage, is that right?'

The old fear seizes me. Tina nods.

Dakota glances at the picture on his desk. 'Blake Nelson said he wanted somewhere his family could feel safe,' he explains. 'Not to have to live in hiding.'

I'm looking at Tina, confused.

'The laws in Vegas are different to Utah,' says Dakota. 'Polygamy isn't illegal here. Your husband was hoping to find you a premises where your family wouldn't be outside of the law.'

He ducks behind his desk and gestures at two guest chairs. 'Please have a seat.'

I sit heavily. The thought of Blake looking for somewhere for us to live happily together has hit me hard. I wipe away a few tears.

'Excuse me,' I say. 'It's just . . . Blake died. Very suddenly. We're here to manage whatever he left behind.'

Dakota's smile drops away.

'I'm so very, very, sorry to hear that.' He opens a drawer and removes a box of Kleenex. 'Here.'

'Thanks.'

'Well, you know, he loved all three of you,' says Dakota. 'This whole business was for you. To keep you safe and happy.'

'Thing is,' says Tina, 'we don't know what business that was. We were kinda hoping you could tell us.'

'Well,' says Dakota, 'there was talk of a mutually beneficial arrangement between ourselves and your husband.'

'In English.'

'A deal,' says Dakota. 'For the Homestead land. Our organization is . . . extremely keen to purchase it. We're not the only ones of course.'

'I don't get it. Who would want a scrub patch of land, in the middle of nowhere?'

'Well,' Dakota straightens his glasses. 'For a start, it isn't a bare patch of desert land. That plot has hundreds of thousands of dollars of amenities. Roads, gas pipes, supplies of that nature.'

Tina is looking at the real estate photographs. 'You build casinos, right?'

'That constitutes a large part of our portfolio.' Dakota adjusts his glasses.

'But gambling is illegal in Utah,' I say.

'That's correct,' says Dakota. 'But not in Nevada.'

To make his point, he stands and moves to a map on the wall. 'The Homestead land is right about here.' He lets his finger trail the great long section of Utah that borders the Nevada state.

I stare at the map. I never knew the Homestead bordered Nevada.

'Border-town casinos make a lotta money,' Tina tells me. 'I mean, it's small fry to Vegas. But gaming and slots always make good money. You get a lotta Mormons come to gamble, right,' she shoots Dakota a glance to confirm. He nods. It strikes me Tina is very well informed on the subject.

'Wendover is the nearest legal casino to Salt Lake City,' says Dakota. 'It makes $63 million per annum. Ninety percent of visitors make the hour-and-a-half drive from Salt Lake City, and most of those are Mormon.'

I clear my throat. 'Your company wants to buy this land? Put a casino there?'

'I'm not at liberty to share that with you, I'm afraid.' He looks genuinely distressed.

'So you're sayin' this plot is worth money?' Tina confirms. 'Like what? Thousands? Millions?'

'That would all depend on what someone was prepared to pay,' he says.

Tina fixes him with a look. Dakota unfolds his hands.

'The property is a thorn in the state government's side. They employ a sheriff to guard it, the local town is taxed on it. We would expect to broker a good price. But it's all theoretical. We can't buy it.'

He adjusts his glasses.

'Why not?' I ask.

'Well, because of the secret cemetery,' says Dakota.

64

Tina, sister-wife

'The Homestead land can't be bought,' explains Dakota. 'You can't sell a plot with dead bodies on it, see? Not without gettin' 'em exhumed. Law won't allow it. And no one could find that cemetery.'

'Why not?' I glance at Rachel, but she isn't looking at me.

Dakota clears his throat. 'Only the Prophet and his closest followers knew about it.' He's looking at Rachel now. 'Those people are either dead or vanished, or in the Prophet's case, they're not talking.' Dakota's eyes switch back to me. 'Best guess is some sort of cover-up.'

'But they already got busted, right?'

'Right,' says Dakota. 'Multiple counts of child rape, kidnap, extortion of money from members, aggravated sexual assault. With a rap sheet like that, you kinda have to wonder what's left to hide.'

We're all quiet.

'If they can't find it,' I say, eventually, 'how can they be so sure it's even there?'

'There are records,' says Dakota, 'death records. Well kept, by all accounts. Police went through them with a fine-tooth comb and matched most of the deceased to a large cemetery plot toward the front of the compound. However,' he takes a breath, lets it out. 'Some of the deceased were listed as being buried in a secondary cemetery on the compound. A place kept secret, even to the record-keepers.' He shrugs. 'Problem is, the Homestead is a big parcel of land. Three thousand acres, and a good part of that just wilderness. Take you months, maybe years, to dig through all that plot.'

Just as we're reeling from what Dakota is tellin' us, a phone in the outer office starts ringing.

Shit. Maybe the downstairs receptionist has worked out we never showed at the legal offices.

I put the thought to one side. Return my attention to Dakota.

'So you're tellin' us, Blake was interested in buyin' this land?'

'Well, he mighta had special circumstances,' explains Dakota. 'Former residents are entitled to purchase it, without exhuming the remains. And Blake believed he had access to that category by marriage.'

Rachel's face does something funny.

'On account of the laws about Indian graveyards, right?' I say. 'I work in real estate,' I add, seeing Dakota's expression. 'OK,' I close my eyes. 'So lemme see. Blake is married to Rachel. He still has to involve her though, right?'

'Well,' Dakota adjusts his glasses. 'He would need his wife's birth certificate. Probably a signature too. These things can be somewhat of a gray area.'

We both consider this. I remember somethin'.

'Do you know who this lady is?' I take out the folded grainy picture. 'This paper had your name and number on the back,' I explain. 'In actual fact, we assumed she was you.'

Beside me, I feel Rachel stiffen. Dakota looks at it.

'Yes, this is the person we were all trying to find,' he says. 'All the former Homestead folk swore, right hand to God, they knew nothing about a cemetery. But someone told us this lady might know about some graves. Problem was, no one knew her real name.' He frowns. 'They only knew her as Aunt Meg. She was something to do with healthcare.'

'The nurse,' says Rachel in a weird flat voice. 'Aunt Meg was the nurse.'

'That was it.' Dakota clicks his fingers. 'Well, clinician, they told us, but I guess it was the same thing out there. Self-appointed, we assume, likely zero qualifications. Make of that what you will.' He glances at Rachel, realizing he's talking to a former member, and puts a strong focus on rooting in his desk. 'A colleague did compile a file on that and I think I have the original picture of her someplace here . . . Ah!'

He lifts free a glossy photograph – almost like a high-school picture. Only the students are all young women, in pastel-colored prairie dresses buttoned high to the neck and falling to the ankle. Each last one has swooped-up crown hair, with variations on plaits at the back. Many wear pastel-pink lipstick that looks too old for them, and they're all beaming smiles as though their lives depended on it.

At their center is a radiantly smiling guy with brown hair, in a sharp suit.

'The Prophet and his wives,' says Dakota, looking at the image. 'There are pictures like this pasted all over the compound. Guess the idea was his followers couldn't hardly move without his eyes on them.' He shakes his head sadly, then glances up at Rachel. 'Are you alright, Ma'am? Would you like a glass of water?'

Rachel looks like she's been hit by a truck.

'That's him,' she says. 'That's my father.'

She reaches out a finger and taps a face to the right of him.

'And that's her. Aunt Meg. She was his wife.'

65

Emily, sister–wife

They take me to a special room for my psychiatric evaluation, all soft couches and tables made of wood instead of Formica. Plugged into a low-down socket is this ancient air-freshener thing, all brittle yellow, that makes the room smell like burning flowers.

The psychological lady is very nicely dressed, with gold-and-black-rimmed glasses, and a neat mouth of lipstick. She introduces herself as Miss Truman.

'Hi.' I shoot out a hand, smiling.

'You seem pleased to be here, Miss Martinelli,' she says.

'They put candy in the room,' I explain, nodding to a dish of M&Ms, 'see?' I reach out and take a scoop, pushing them into my mouth fast in case she complains.

Instead she says: 'Help yourself.'

My smile widens.

'So, Miss Martinelli,' she says, 'can I call you Emily?'

'Sure.' I crunch the candy, settling back onto the couch. In the holding cell, there's like this hard bed thing. It gets so boring I want to scream.

She asks me a few questions, about life on the ranch and my reasons for killing my husband. Wants to know about the dis-cipline side of things. How often, how hard. Questions I don't really care to answer. I figure she's getting bored with one-word answers, 'cause she switches topic to the sexual dynamic, as she calls it.

'So you'd all line up, waiting to be picked?' I can tell she's trying to sound neutral and struggling with it.

'Yeah.' I eat more M&Ms. 'Mostly he chose Tina, though.'

'Did that bother you?'

'*No.*' I roll my eyes, crunch more candy. 'I think it bothered Rachel a lot.'

She nods in an understanding way.

'Was there jealousy between you women? Over Blake?'

'Well, we fought a lot,' I say. 'But no one was ever gonna win against Rachel.'

This seems to surprise her. 'Can you tell me what you mean by that?'

I crinkle my nose. 'I just mean . . . Blake and Rachel. That's who the whole marriage was about. Us other wives were just a little color for them.' She doesn't say anything, so I explain some more. 'Blake liked to prod at Rachel, and she did the same to him. They kinda brought out the worst in each other. Love does that sometimes, I guess.'

'What things did Blake like to prod at?'

I shrug. 'I don't know. He wanted Rachel's approval. But then it was like he couldn't forgive her for something either. Like those two things were fighting it out.'

The therapist lady sits back, taps her mouth with her pen.

'That's very insightful,' she says. 'Can I ask how did Blake feel about children? Having them, I mean to say.'

'Well, we all wanted children . . . so . . .'

'About that,' the therapist sits a little forward. 'Did it ever strike you as strange, that none of you wives conceived. Got pregnant, I mean?'

'Well, it doesn't always happen right away,' I tell her. 'You gotta be pure of heart before God blesses you with a baby.'

'That's what your husband told you?'

'Yes.' I feel a little uncomfortable now. Like when I wasn't following the teacher in class.

'Do you understand how babies are made?' she asks. 'About sexual intercourse?'

I feel my cheeks get hot.

'That's not something that's nice to talk about.' I'm kinda writhing in my seat.

'You know for pregnancy to take place, a man has to ejaculate inside a woman?'

'Yes.' I'm looking up at the ceiling. 'I knew that.'

When I look down, she's writing. I'm pretty relieved she's not talking about dirty stuff anymore. That's when my brain kinda hops across to what we were talking about earlier. The bedroom lineup.

If Rachel didn't get picked to sleep in the master bedroom, she used to have bad dreams, sleepwalk even. One time at night, when Tina and Blake were making all these loud noises, I went outside for some air.

I found Rachel digging a hole by her storehouse, moonlight glinting off her shovel.

I think I asked her what she was doing. Got the shock of my life when she turned to look at me. Something was really wrong with her eyes – all flat, like a dead person.

'I need to dig,' Rachel told me. 'Before he sees.'

'What do you need to dig?' I whispered it. Like we were on the same side. I figured she was hiding something from Blake.

Rachel wiped her brow.

'I need to bury her in the red graveyard,' she whispered back. 'Or they'll find out what I've done.'

'Did Rachel talk to you about it?' the therapist lady is asking. I stare at her in shock.

'The bedroom problems,' she clarifies. 'With Blake.'

'Um. Well. It's not like she really knew what to say. But I could tell she was trying. And she felt real sorry for me too.' I'm fiddling with the bottom of my shirt. 'She just said, uh . . . Rachel said it seemed real scary to her too, in the beginning. But you get used to it and then it gets nicer.'

The therapist lady looks real thoughtful.

'Rachel used the word scary?'

I nod. She taps her pen again.

'Did Rachel know that Blake had taken to punishing you, physically?'

A strange ball swells in my chest. Like feelings about Rachel and waiting for my father to come home have got all knotted together.

'I think . . .' I consider my answer for a second. 'I think Rachel is real good at not seeing things she isn't supposed to see.'

66

Rachel, first wife

It's the strangest feeling, seeing that picture.

'It's a photograph of the Prophet and his wives,' I explain to Tina.

'What. *All* of 'em?' Tina is staring. 'That is so gross. They look adolescent.'

'Youngest was fourteen, I think.'

I peer closer. It's a glossy color image of the Prophet, with his sixty wives arranged around him. My father. His hair is swept across his forehead and he wears square outdated spectacles. Seeing his smiling face makes me want to tear up the picture. Hurt him so bad he can never smile again.

'That's my mother,' I say quietly, pressing my finger on a woman right at the back. 'She was second-tier. The Prophet married wives of men he excommunicated, she was one of those women.'

'I don't get it.' Tina frowns at me. 'So Aunt Meg was like . . . your stepmom?'

I can see what she's thinking. *How is it you didn't know who she was?*

'It wasn't like that,' I explain. 'The Prophet had over sixty wives. Only ten or so lived in the big house with him. They were the favorites. Lived in luxury. All the latest mod cons. Us regular people had a much harder life, so we didn't associate with them much. Only saw them at prayers in the Homestead Temple. From my understanding, the Prophet wanted to avoid jealousy.'

Dakota takes a step back from us, like he's trying to be polite and not listen in. But, of course, in this small office that's impossible.

My eyes move down to the Prophet. Aunt Meg is maybe late twenties in this picture. A good few decades younger than my father. Her hair is coiffed in the regulation claw shape, curled high above her forehead, plaited extensively around the ears. I try to imagine what she might look like with regular hair and clothes. I left the Homestead ten years ago. Aunt Meg would be around forty now, I calculate.

'So . . . Aunt Meg was one of his wives?' asks Tina.

'The first,' I say. 'She must have been the first. The first wife sits on the Prophet's right-hand side. I kind of remember the first wife did things for the Prophet,' I say. 'Lied for him. She used to say she'd seen him levitating whilst he slept, junk like that. Things to make her the favorite. I guess she had a hard job competing with all those young girls. When it all went to court,' I add, 'I think the first wife was accused of holding some of the girls down, during the marriage ceremonies.'

'Are you sure you're OK?' asks Tina.

'I'm fine.' I shake my head. 'It's just . . . The Prophet's wives tended to go one of two ways.' I glance up at Tina. 'They either left the Homestead, maybe even testified in court, if they were brave, and tried to lead regular lives.' *Like me*, I think, wondering how I wound up so far from this intention. 'Or,' I continue, 'they got kind of radicalized. Like they interpreted the Prophet's imprisonment as the persecution of their living saint.'

Thoughts are wheeling through my mind.

Out loud I say: 'Why would Blake have her picture?' I look at Dakota.

'I'm afraid I have no idea,' he says with a shrug.

'I guess Blake was looking for her at Waynard's Creek,' suggests Tina. 'Hoped he could ask her the location of the secret graveyard. Then used the paper to scribble the real-estate-firm number on the back.'

Relief floods through me. Of course, that makes sense. They never met. Please God let that be true.

The image of Aunt Meg, naked beneath my panting husband, flashes up.

You're not real, I tell it savagely. *Get back in your box.*

Something else strikes me, at the same point Tina says it out loud.

'Why would Blake be looking for the secret graveyard?' she asks. 'If he wanted to buy the land, he has a legal entitlement because of his marriage to a former resident. Why go hunting for dirty secrets?'

'Blake was very devout,' I say. 'Perhaps he wanted to make sure there was nothing on that land that could endanger our souls.'

Or perhaps he wanted to have a hold over you. Something to make you a supplicant for the rest of your life.

Tina is looking at me, like something doesn't add up. I move my eyes back to the picture. Dakota shuffles his feet, like he wishes he were somewhere else.

'Where is the Prophet now?' asks Tina. I get the sense she doesn't want to use the word 'father'. I think Tina probably hasn't really absorbed how twisted my childhood was until this moment.

'In prison,' I say. 'He's in prison now. Fifteen counts of

underage rape. He's there until he dies.' I turn to Dakota. 'Your colleagues ever find this Aunt Meg person?'

'Nope.' He shakes his head. 'Not to my knowledge.'

Just like that, the old fear comes flooding back in.

If Aunt Meg is still out there. If she got in contact with Blake . . .

I close my eyes, but it's no good. There are no more boxes left.

67

Tina, sister–wife

Rachel is steadying herself on a desk. She looks like she might puke.

'Sir,' I put on my best voice. 'Did Blake agree a deal with you to buy that land?'

'I'm not allowed to tell you that,' says Dakota. 'Our records are confidential.'

'We have his certificate of death,' I say. 'The law of Nevada states that you have to release any documents relating to a deceased individual on presentation of a death certificate, either to a legal relative making the request, or a police officer.'

Rachel manages to cast me a little look of admiration. She's rallying.

'We've come all the way from Salt Lake City,' says Rachel. 'That's a long drive.'

Dakota hesitates. His gaze falls to the picture on his desk.

'I can't help you,' he says, casting a glance toward the door. 'But it so happens I'm gonna step out to get myself a sandwich. I'll be gone for twenty minutes or so. You can make your own way out, and please don't look in that big green cabinet over there, 'K?'

Rachel and I nod silently, hardly able to believe our luck.

'Heaven bless you,' whispers Rachel as he leaves, and this time, I don't correct her.

As the door clicks gently shut, we race to the filing cabinet.

'Why do you think he's helping us?' asks Rachel, as we locate the drawer labeled 'M–N'.

'He's plural married,' I say. 'Did you notice how he's got a picture on his desk only he can see? I got a glimpse of it when we came in. The women are arranged so they could be aunts, or what have you. But I'll bet those ladies are his wives. He has four.'

'But it's not illegal in Nevada, to have more than one wife,' says Rachel.

'Just 'cause it's not illegal doesn't mean people don't judge,' I say.

I roll out the drawer. Rachel and I exchange glances. I don't know what I'm hoping to find, but I'm suddenly determined to leave with something.

'Here,' I say, feeling cold. 'Blake Nelson.'

It's a plain manila file. Rachel flips it open and lifts free a little clutch of papers. Realtor-type things.

Relief registers on her face.

'Not what you were expecting to see?' I'm eyeballing her.

'Oh, I just . . . Didn't want any more bad memories,' she says. 'I'm relieved it's just realtor things. No more family portraits.' She manages a dry laugh. 'Here,' Rachel says, pushing me the notes. 'You can take a look. You're better with these documents than I am.'

'Is that supposed to be a compliment?'

'Sure.'

'OK.' I leaf through. 'Well . . . It looks as though Las Vegas Real Estate were offering Blake a deal. They'd front the money to buy the Homestead, and Blake would purchase it using his, uh, connections.' I snatch a look at Rachel. Her face is expression-less. 'On completion of purchase, Las Vegas Real Estate would pay Blake a fee for his involvement . . . Ten thousand bucks.'

'But he wouldn't have gotten any part of the land?'

'No.'

We're both quiet.

'Doesn't sound like Blake, does it?' says Rachel eventually. 'Casinos, mob firms making him payouts. For all his faults, Blake had conviction.'

It's the first time I've heard her admit Blake wasn't perfect.

'More to the point, he would have wanted the land,' I say, turning the papers. 'No evidence to suggest he took the deal,' I add. 'Maybe he turned 'em down.'

I look at Rachel to see if she's as mad as I am. We were all living on tinned meat for dinner, and Blake had been offered this big stash of cash he never told us about.

'He never told you about any of this?' asks Rachel. 'You're in real estate.'

'No.' I'm smarting about that, but I kinda don't want Rachel to see. I can't quite tell if she's sympathetic or smug.

'If Blake was entitled to buy the land through marriage,' Rachel continues pointedly, 'wouldn't that mean you could too? If Vegas allows plural marriages, you have the same entitlement to buy that land, right? Through marriage.'

I shoot her a withering look. I don't like what she's implying at all.

'Blake and I had a spiritual wedding,' I say. 'Not legally bind-ing anywhere. So you can quit thinking I had some black-widow plot to get a hold of the money our husband *didn't* have. In case you'd forgotten, the person who paid most of our bills was me. You're welcome, by the way.'

Rachel looks away, starts leafing through more papers.

'ID,' says Rachel. 'Proof of address.'

The first is a copy of Blake's driving license. I catch my breath to see the familiar features. He was younger then, his copper hair a lighter shade, less freckles.

He's got that look on his face, like he's embarrassed to be posing but knows he should be smiling too. For a moment I smile back at him.

'I went with him to get that picture taken,' says Rachel, in a soft voice. 'It feels like a lifetime ago.'

We're both silent.

'He wasn't perfect,' I say eventually. 'But he was ours, wasn't he?'

Rachel nods, wiping away tears. She peels away some other papers.

A batch of photographs. Realtor shots, and documents.

'This isn't complete,' I say. 'The map is missing. You always get a map and land boundary upfront. It's gone.'

I turn over what that this might mean. A secret cemetery. A missing map. And something that got a man killed.

'Is this the Homestead?' I shuffle photographs.

Rachel takes a quick breath. She nods, her eyes glued to the images.

The first thing that strikes me about the Homestead is it's reminiscent of a downmarket winter resort. All the log cabins and roads have the exact same layout and building materials. Like a low-rent 1950s Disneyworld that's been left to rot. There's no individuality to anything, not so much as a front door or a mailbox is out of the common style. The same is true of the interiors. Corridors lined in the same cheap green carpet. Round brass door handles on every plain rectangular door.

'Kinda creepy,' I breathe, turning pictures over. 'Like a ghost town.'

There are vast expanses of empty corridors, littered with over-turned chairs and scattered documents. Like everyone left in a hurry. Interior room shots are depressing, dark with mildew climbing the wall, and the barest furnishing.

There's something almost high-school-like about it. Room after room, with hardly any difference. Then the images take on a different feel. There's a vast three-storied log cabin, reminding me a little of the advertisements you see for ski lodges in Whistler.

'That's the Prophet's house,' says Rachel. 'We weren't allowed inside.'

More pictures show a spacious kitchen, like something between a catering facility and a Shaker-style domestic place. White carpets and broad stairways.

I glance at her. She looks to be in a kinda trance as I turn over another picture.

A large bed with a headboard with 'Keep Sweet' carved onto it. More bedrooms, basic, but far nicer than the previous accommodations.

Then several images of a white room. I look at them for a long time. Everything in the room is snowy white, from the high curved ceiling to the carpet. Wood paneling lines the interior from waist height and the same decorative effect is seen on the arched door. It kinda reminds me of the sort of nursery a mobster's wife might have, all pure, soft and spotless.

In the center is a white bed. All high up and weird-looking. It's high off the ground with a kind of padded footstool, long and poufy.

There's a sacrificial feel to the bed, which gives me a nasty feeling. It's a single, with white wood sides hanging down, which can be raised to form barriers.

'Oh my heck,' Rachel whispers. 'That's it. That's the bed in my dream.'

From the window behind us comes a flash of light. Blue. Pulsing.

Shit.

I move to look out, but I already know. Three cop cars have pulled up.

68

Rachel, first wife

Tina is a total professional at evading the police. I can't help but get swept up in it all, as we're racing down the back stairs. I should be frightened, but I feel a little giddy.

'This way.' Tina leads us all the way down to a basement parking lot. 'Cops'll be watchin' the exits,' she explains. 'They know we came in on foot. So best way out is by car.'

'Wait. You're not gonna . . .'

Tina's gaze fixes on a little Ford. She fishes in her bag and pulls out a compact hairbrush. Then she unfolds it, places the rubber section over the lock and slams a fist into it.

'These old central locks can be busted with a half tennis ball,' she explains. 'Purse-size hairbrush does the same thing, with the advantage it looks innocent if anyone searches your bag.'

She opens the door.

'Get in.'

'I can't . . .'

'Then don't,' she says. 'Turn yourself in. I don't mind.'

Her eyes are flicking around wildly, and I have a feeling it's not a good idea to leave her alone with a car in Vegas, on account of her former drug problem.

I slide in the seat beside her.

'What if the police catch us?' I pull my belt on. The old terror is coursing through me, like it never went away.

Don't let the police get you. They'll take you away.

Tina laughs. 'You're scared of cops? You're lucky. Where I'm from, we're scared of the pimps.' She pulls the car into drive.

I'm actually a little disappointed when Tina cruises slowly out of the parking lot. I'd been hoping to speed out in a blaze of glory. But I guess she knows what she's doing. I'm thinking that right up until she stops outside this seedy-looking bar in a part of town that is definitely not a tourist area.

She pauses to take a picture of the car number plate on her phone.

'I'll send the plates to the cops when we get on the highway,' she says. 'Let the owner know where they can come pick it up. No harm done, right?'

'The courteous thief,' I mutter.

'Yeah well.' Tina pushes hair from her eyes. 'I believe in karma, nowadays.' She regards the bar in front of us. 'Cops'll never look for us here,' she says, dragging me toward the entrance.

'Tina, this place is *actually called* Dive Bar,' I hiss, as she pulls me under the neon lighting.

'It's stylistic.'

'Then why is the floor sticky?' I duck under a sign bragging: 'We Never Close!'

Inside, it's dark, low-ceilinged, with beer mats glued all over the walls, and a lot of jagged spray-painted writing. It's hard to read, but one says 'Drink On Your Sins!'

'Tina,' I whisper, 'that's sacrilegious. This is a sacrilegious place.'

'Quit whispering, you'll make us look suspicious.'

Tina pulls me to the bar, which is empty, aside from a female bartender with a pierced lip.

'Hey,' says Tina. 'Um. We're both Mormon.'

The bartender looks bored. 'Show me the garment lines.'

Tina presses her dress to show the lines of her garments. 'See? Her too.' She makes the same manipulation to my clothing.

'OK,' the bartender spins on her heel. 'First drink is on the house.'

She pours us two tequilas. Tina pushes a bill into the tip jar.

'Did she give us free alcohol?' I whisper in Tina's ear.

'It's a Vegas thing,' Tina grins, picking up the two shots expertly with one hand and guiding us to a greasy-looking low table. 'Mormon Tuesdays. Anyone with garment lines gets a free drink. Vegas, right? Sin City.'

I'm processing all this as Tina sits us both down and produces the documents we took from Dakota's office.

'Plus I figured you could use one,' she says. 'Whilst you tell me about this white bed thing.'

Tina lays the photographs out. The shock is gone now, replaced by something else. Relief. There were no pictures of the clinic. Nothing that could lead to the graveyard. Only that awful white bed, with all its connotations.

I pull the pictures toward me. 'I remember things,' I say. 'In pieces. But more things . . . More things seem to be coming back, now Blake is gone.'

I leaf through the images. My eyes glide over the shots of room interiors. Corridors. With all the families gone, they look less familiar than I might have thought. Like a sketch of a memory, rather than the thing itself.

But the room with the bed is exactly as I remember it. Nothing has been disturbed. Just for a moment, I allow myself back there.

Aunt Meg. Aunt Meg's face.

I can't do it. I lift the tequila and gulp it back. It burns. I choke and cough. Tina slaps my back.

'Remind me never to do that again,' I gasp.

'Not a problem,' says Tina. 'You only get one free. I ain't buyin' ya another. Might get you some hot wings, though, you play your cards right.' She winks.

My eyes drop back to the picture. The tequila feels like it's burning a hole in my stomach, loosening things up.

I'm in the corner of the white bedroom. I shouldn't be here. I was trying to get out when they all came in. I hid . . . I hid behind a curtain. That was when I heard him, telling them to line up, explaining they would feel the spirit. She was there too. Aunt Meg. Orchestrating. Positioning girls. Then standing a little apart from it all, hovering like she was trying to join in.

Her hand strokes Blake's back awkwardly, but he's not looking at her.

A girl is lying under him. She can't be older than fourteen. He's breathing heavily, moving on top of her. She's gasping, tears in her eyes. Aunt Meg holds her shoulders. A terrible sick feeling overwhelms me.

'So tell me,' says Tina quietly. 'You can trust me. What do you remember about that white bedroom?'

'Try to help her, Meg,' gasps Blake, moving faster. 'Don't think about where it hurts,' he tells the girl. 'Think about Heaven.'

But the voice. The man's voice is wrong. That's when it hits me. The bed, the girls.

The man in that white bedroom. It wasn't Blake.

69

Emily, sister-wife

Officer Brewer takes me back to the interview room and talks me all through what I can expect to happen. How I'll be transferred to prison later on today or maybe tomorrow morning. She keeps asking me if I've got anything else to tell her. That's when Detective Carlson comes in. There's a little friction between them still, only now they seem to be on the same team.

'I gotta tell you, this is a first for me,' says Carlson, running a hand over his shaved head. 'I'm usually in the business of proving suspects guilty.' He shakes his head. 'Now Brewer there, she thinks you did it but it wasn't your fault. On account of some domestic abuses and so forth. Me, I think you're covering for someone.'

I don't reply, but Carlson doesn't seem to mind.

'Got something I'd like you to take a look at,' he says, sitting himself down. He takes a laptop from under his arm and opens it. 'I think you should know everything about the person you're covering for.'

He tilts the laptop my way.

'Did Rachel Nelson ever share with you that she visited the state penitentiary earlier this year?'

I am so shocked I don't even answer.

Detective Carlson just nods.

'Went to visit her daddy. That's good old Prophet Ambrosine to you and me. You most likely saw him on the news? Fifteen counts of rape of minors? Life imprisonment.'

I nod slowly. It was a big story back when I was a little girl. Prophet Ambrosine was this handsome guy, very nicely spoken. He had what my momma called a buttered-corn accent. Like when he testified in court, it sounded real gentle and convincing, with a lot of scripture quoted straight from the Bible too, learned by heart. His eyes were very dark brown, almost black. They gave him a doe-like appearance, like he wouldn't harm a fly. My momma said she thought he would have got away with it, if it hadn't been for the sex tapes.

I still can't really wrap my head around that. Like our Rachel grew up there. When we talked about it, after the birth certificate incident, Rachel told me it wasn't so bad as people make out on the TV. Like they lived real poor, but for the most part the children played outdoors and rode horses and such. She made it sound nice.

'Well, Rachel went over to the prison,' says Detective Carlson, 'right around the time your husband was seen having lunch with a mysterious blond lady.'

He pauses for effect.

'Officer Brewer here had a hunch,' he adds, jerking a thumb. 'So we checked it out. Wasn't apparent right away it was Rachel Nelson, on account of Prophet Ambrosine still having so many wives visit.'

He nods at my expression.

'Yup,' he says grimly. 'Lotta ladies still believe themselves his heavenly wives. Visit him in prison and try and smuggle out his word to the little clutch of whackos out by Waynard's Creek. Pretty messed up, right?'

I just nod.

'What we have here is footage of Rachel's visit,' he presses play. 'Not good quality but enough for you to get a picture.'

I lean forward, fascinated, despite myself. It's a visiting room with a number of tables. A tall man in an orange jumpsuit is sitting at one, his hands cuffed in front.

'You can see that burn mark on his neck?' Carlson points, a little like a zookeeper showing the animals. 'The so-called Prophet tried to hang himself a few days after incarceration.'

'He doesn't look how he looked on TV,' I say. The change is scary. He looks like a crazy old man, with a shaved head and sores on his face, the dark eyes look insane.

Even in the jerky footage, I can tell Rachel is real nervous. But as she approaches the table where the Prophet sits, the nerves seem to melt away. Like she's just thinking the same as me.

He's nothing but a crazy old man.

As Rachel sits though, it's like a little of the Prophet's old charisma returns. He sits straight, and there's this charming smile on his face. Rachel seems a little wrong-footed by it. Like maybe she came with a plan and the force of his personality has taken her unawares.

'What are they saying?' I ask.

'There's no sound,' admits Carlson. 'The prison guards didn't pay too close attention. One of 'em thought it was a little different to his usual meetings. Recalls Rachel trying to convince the Prophet to let his followers accept charity, on account women and children were starving. Prophet Ambrosine just gabbed on about being God's messenger on earth and Jesus providing for the worthy.'

I sag a little.

'They talk for, maybe, five minutes. Then watch this part.'

Carlson fast-forwards. The Prophet barely moves, but Rachel's body language changes completely. She's upright, gripping the table, like she's been given some real scary news.

'What do you think happened there?' asks Carlson, watching me closely.

I shake my head slowly. 'I don't know.'

Carlson closes the laptop, looks me straight in the eye.

'You sister-wife let you know she made that trip?'

I shake my head slowly.

'Quite a big deal not to tell you, right? Rachel goes visiting criminal rapists and doesn't even give it a passing mention. I mean to say, aren't you wives supposed to love one another?'

I feel my face twitch.

'Did you know your sister-wives are out in Vegas?' tries Carlson. 'The number plate from your family Chevy came up on a state-line police camera. Cops will pick them up any minute now. You can't protect them any longer.'

I look back at him, trying to work out if he's bluffing. It's impossible to tell.

'Well, I fixed you up one last appointment with the psychologist,' says Brewer. 'She's going to assess if you're in a fit state to stand trial.' She looks at Carlson again. 'I just hope for your sake she doesn't.'

70

Tina, sister-wife

Funny thing about being back in a sleazy Vegas bar - nothing's changed, except everything. There are the same sickly green lamps over the pool tables. A couple of scuffed-up balls left on the balding baize. That familiar smell you get when the doors first open – a thick boozy undertone, with a top note of cleaning-fluid spritz.

Difference is, I don't like it anymore. Thank the Lord for tequila though, because whatever Rachel has been keeping in is now spilling out.

'I have a memory of being in that room,' she says. 'Everything is white. There is this . . . bed, laid out, right in the middle. White . . .' She stops, takes a breath. 'I shouldn't be seeing it, and I'm really, really scared. It's His celestial bed.'

'Hey,' I tell her. 'It's OK.'

'I've been having these awful thoughts about that room,' Rachel is saying, holding her forehead. 'Like *dirty* thoughts, about Blake. He was in a bed, with all these *young girls*. Just, you know, having a time of it.'

Rachel's neck flushes red.

'Like a three-way?' I ask.

'A what?'

'Two girls one guy.'

'Um, I guess so,' says Rachel. She sighs out, kinda blows her cheeks. 'Only with about seven women. Girls, in actual fact. Some of them were likely underage. I thought I was losing my mind,' she says quietly. 'Truly. I just had these *pictures*.' She blinks, like she's trying to send 'em away. 'Like a porno film I couldn't shut off.'

I very much doubt Rachel has ever seen a porno, but I'm not about to interrupt.

'One of the girls in the bed was my half-sister,' she says. 'And Aunt Meg – I saw her there too.' This part seems to gross her out especially. 'All, you know. *Doing* it. With Blake.' She rolls the tequila glass around in her hand. 'Only it wasn't Blake. I had it wrong.'

She sorta shakes her head, like she's still not real clear on things.

I frown. 'What do you mean? You had it wrong?'

'I just . . . I don't know. Like I dreamed it or remembered it differently. I saw Blake in that bedroom, when it wasn't him.'

'Who was it?'

'The Prophet.' She pauses. 'I remember it now.' She shakes her head. 'I don't know how it happened, but I ended up in that white bedroom watching one of his Heavenly comfort sessions.'

'Heavenly *comfort*? Is that what he called it?'

She nods slowly. 'It's . . . disgusting. The Prophet would get a clutch of his wives in the white bedroom, and they'd all get naked and . . . get down to it. He'd tell them all it was God's will.'

'You saw this? Wait . . . wasn't this man, like, your father?'

'Yes, but like I said, he wasn't a dad like regular people have.'

'You're speaking to the wrong person.'

'I just mean I likely met him maybe three times my whole life.'

She looks thoughtful. Like she's remembered something even the tequila can't get her to admit to.

'Rachel.' I put my hand on her arm. 'He didn't do anything with you, did he? You can tell me.'

Rachel shakes her head real quick.

'No, that was about the only thing he wasn't guilty of. Relations with his daughters. He had his pick of young girls, so I guess he figured it wasn't necessary.'

There's a pause.

'So what . . .' I ask her. 'You just, *walked in on them*, all at it?'

She scrunches her face like she's tryin' to dredge a memory.

'Kind of. I think I wanted to get somewhere else. I don't remember that part so well. But Aunt Meg was there and she saw me and told the Prophet I had to leave.'

She breathes out.

'It's such a relief, to know it wasn't Blake with those girls. You can't imagine how it's been eating me up. Like I couldn't trust my own mind.'

She frowns down at the table and it hits me just how little Rachel shares with anyone.

'Aunt Meg stayed loyal to the Prophet,' she says. 'She was one of the wives who radicalized others. Those people are still out there,' she adds. 'In Waynard's Creek, in safe houses . . .'

Rachel lifts her eyes to mine, the image of a fanatical wife blazing through both our minds. I switch my thoughts back to Blake, what he might have done. What if he tracked down Aunt Meg? Maybe said the wrong thing and got her worked up.

'So, this Aunt Meg,' I say, thinking aloud. 'If she's the

Prophet's first wife, really believes her husband is some kind of Jesus on earth . . . would she kill for him, do you think?'

'That all depends,' says Rachel.

'On what?'

'On whether or not he asked her to.'

71

Rachel, first wife

The tequila is dredging things up so fast I can't keep pace. Parts are fitting together. The white bedroom. The clinic. But in the middle of it all is . . . *a box*. Like a great void where the memory should be. Only this box, *this box*, is different. It's got a color. Form.

It's a blue shoebox, the kind the Homestead got bulk orders of cheap school pumps delivered in. And it's standing right in the middle of what I need to remember.

'I'm so confused by everything,' I tell Tina. 'It's like I can't tell what's a memory and what's a dream.' I rub my face. 'I think I was in a clinic,' I tell her. 'On the Homestead. I've kind of blanked it out. I don't know. A sort of home-built medical facility. It had a hospital feel, but things hadn't been done properly. I just . . . I remember being in this bed, just feeling *trapped*. Like I would never get out.'

I look up at Tina. I guess that memory of fear must show in my eyes, 'cause she reaches out and takes my hand.

'It's OK,' she says, mouth grim. 'You're safe.' She swallows. 'They kept you in a hospital?'

'Aunt Meg was there,' I whisper. 'I think she did things . . . I don't remember it.' I squeeze my eyes shut, trying to force something concrete. 'I was hot,' I say, eyes still closed. 'Like, so hot

I thought I was in hell. I remember, she told me . . . Aunt Meg said I had an infection.'

I can't tell Tina the next part.

'You've got an infection,' Aunt Meg told me. She held some sharp-looking tongs in her green latex gloves. 'That's why you smell so nasty down there.' She moved to the base of the bed and there was an excruciating pain, like a needle in my groin.

'Was it only you in the hospital?' asks Tina.

I shake my head. 'There was a girl next to me. Melissa. I knew her a little. We used to play together as kids. I think some other girls too, but I didn't see them up close.' I stop talking.

The clinic had a basement. Girls went down into the basement. They never came back.

The image comes to me just like that. *The staircase. Steep and clinical. A smell of bleach and something worse underneath it. That's where she makes them disappear. They go to her basement and don't return.*

'You OK?' Tina puts a hand on my shoulder.

I take a breath. 'I just don't know if I'm remembering something real or a dream.'

'You think you could have dreamt this?'

'That's what my therapist thought. I mean, it sounds pretty unreal, right?'

'I don't know,' says Tina. She lifts her eyes to mine. 'Your whole childhood sounds kinda unreal to me.'

Memories are lifting up, threatening to overwhelm me. My therapist's voice.

What was in that basement, Rayne? Why were you so frightened?

Reflexively, I flip more pictures. There's the familiar panic again. Almost like I can't catch my breath.

'Hey!' shouts the bartender. 'If she's gonna puke, take her out!'

'Check your tip jar, lady!' yells Tina, cupping her hands around her mouth. 'Twenty bucks is code for leave us the hell alone!'

The bartender goes back to polishing glasses, muttering.

'Thanks,' I say. Something about Tina's rudeness is oddly re-assuring. Like she doesn't care about anything, and it rubs off.

I take a breath.

'It's all jumbled up in my mind,' I say. 'Because *before* all that. *Before* the celestial bed. There's this . . . *basement*. With some-thing really, really bad inside.'

I close my eyes because I don't want it to be real.

The box is there again with its lid clamped tightly shut. Blue cardboard, rectangular-sided, planted right in the space between the clinic and the celestial bedchamber.

'I think Aunt Meg took girls down there,' I say. 'I think maybe *I* went down there. Only I don't remember.' I shake my head. 'It's like there's a big piece missing. And if I remember, I'm scared I'll fall apart or go crazy or something.'

Or go to prison, or get killed.

I'm remembering what the Prophet said to me, when I visited him in prison.

'If anyone finds out, they'll toss you in jail just like they did to me.'

Leave it alone, Rayne, says a voice in my head. *You don't want anyone to know what you've done.*

313

72

Emily, sister-wife

They've got me back with the therapist lady again. Refilled the bowl of candy. I more or less make straight for it.

'Would you be able to tell me a little bit about your living arrangements,' she says, 'prior to your husband's death?'

'OK.' I'm slightly disappointed she's not asking about me, but I give her a rundown.

'What the courts are interested in,' she explains, making notes, 'is your state of mind. Whether you were coerced into those arrangements. Whether anyone in that household was domineering, or controlling.'

'Well, *yeah*,' I breathe. 'Rachel.'

'Rachel Nelson?'

'Uh-*huh*.' I roll my eyes to emphasize. 'She says, like, what color the sheets are, how you fold your clothes, what you eat for dinner, everything.'

She makes more notes. I carry on talking, all the mean things Rachel did.

'It's very interesting to hear you talk about Rachel,' says Miss Truman. 'Have you ever heard of institutionalized sociopathy?'

'Is it maybe a medical thing?' I suggest.

She smiles. 'In a way. It happens in young or second-generation cult members. People who are still laying down formative emotions. The human mind will adapt to most any situation. If it has to, it will learn not to register so much empathy. We see that in young men raised in bad neighborhoods, where gangs or the mob are prevalent. It's survival. You simply have to shut some things down.'

I nod, but if I'm honest, I don't really understand what she's talking about.

'In cults, like the one Rachel was in, we see mothers shutting down their natural instincts to protect their young. Instead, they see them as an extension of themselves. They lose their boundaries and can't distinguish.'

I scrunch up my face, trying to understand. For some reason my momma's face pops into my mind.

Do you want people to think you're a whore?

'It becomes normal then, to force children to obey their will,' continues Miss Truman. 'In their heads, they're only exercising personal willpower. Same as a long-distance runner telling the burning lungs and aching legs to quieten off for the final sprint.'

'You're saying this happened to Rachel?'

'Well now, you'd be in a better place to answer that. Did you get the sense, living in a household with her, that she didn't view you as a distinct person with your own needs?'

'Oh absolutely. Sure.'

'How about your mother? Was she like that too?'

She says it a little too quickly for my liking.

'I had the best mother there was,' I tell her. 'She gave up everything to raise me.'

She smiles.

'What's funny?' I demand.

'Nothing. Nothing at all. Would you like some more candy?'

I take some, pacified, noticing how it leaves bright red and blue food dye on my hands. Guess my palms must be sweaty.

'You mentioned to the police that Rachel told you about some bad dreams she had?' tries Miss Truman.

'Not *told me* exactly. She used to walk around the house at night sometimes. It was pretty creepy. She'd come out with all kinds of stuff, about boxes. Um,' I look up to the ceiling, 'a white bed, she talked about.'

Miss Truman leans back, as if considering whether to tell me something. She taps her pen against her red lips.

'I followed the trial of the Homestead's so-called Prophet,' she says. 'It was in the newspapers. They ran pictures of a white bed used as evidence. Documents were found showing the Prophet ordered this bed to be constructed for his marriage ceremonies. He asked for raised sides and plastic sheets. To clean up what he did to those poor girls.'

I glare at her. The most horrible feeling is swirling around my insides.

'I think I'd like to go back to my room now.'

'Emily,' says the therapist. 'If you're not telling the truth, if you didn't kill Blake, that means one of your sister-wives did. That's important. We could help her. Rachel.'

'Help her how?'

She's about to answer, when the door opens. Brewer stands there, looking a little out of breath, like she's run here.

'Can I help you?' Miss Truman says it all sugary, but you can see she's annoyed.

Brewer walks into the room, holding a printed list.

'Miss Martinelli, could I trouble you for a detail?'

I don't know how to answer that.

'You're a good detective, right?' says Brewer. 'Top of your head, might there be a place where your husband kept private documents, away from your property?'

I guess that means they searched and found nothing.

'Blake had a second job,' I tell Brewer, feeling a little pleased that she wants me to help with her inquiries. 'He took work as a janitor at the Temple, on account of money being tight.'

What I don't tell her is how Blake kept documents there. Real estate things. Rachel's birth certificate was mixed in, but I didn't get a good look at them all. They would be in his locker in Temple.

Instead I say: 'The police can't look in Temple, can they? You're only allowed in with a handwritten recommend from the Bishop.'

'We could obtain a warrant with reasonable cause.'

'Do you have reasonable cause?'

'I thought you could help me with that too.' She waves the papers in her hand.

I'm getting a little suspicious now, wondering if this is all a trick.

'When we searched the ranch,' she says, 'everything was catalogued. Nothing incriminating was found. But your husband had a lot of . . . equipment in his barn.'

I get the impression she just stopped herself saying 'junk'.

'Took a long time to get that all logged,' she says. 'Now the report is in,' she waves the paper. 'Something caught my eye. Your husband looks to have gotten hold of a set of some pretty fancy electronically operated padlocks.'

I remember Blake bringing those locks back from an office that had gone bankrupt. He told us all how technology was the start of the apocalypse. When the end came, Blake said, those men would be trying to sell us their godforsaken technology as scrap metal, and it wouldn't even be worth one sack of our dried peas.

Brewer is still talking. 'We found three of 'em in a box that once held four. Any idea where that other padlock could be?'

Things are coming together in my head. This must be how Cagney feels when she realizes how the criminal did it.

Fingerprint access.

Blake talked about that when he brought the locks home. How the government had a plan to control all the doors and only let in people who agreed with what they thought. Which was some religion where you believed in aliens. So Blake was going to keep us safe by figuring out how they worked. Then we could override them.

Those electric locks were fingerprint access.

It hits me like a freight train, how it all connects.

Blake's fingers. Blake's fingers were missing.

73

Tina, sister-wife

I'm tossing up the idea of lining up a second shot of tequila. Rachel is comin' out with all this *crazy* stuff. And the Homestead is so damn freaky, I can hardly wrap my head around it. The idea of all those children crammed into those dirty rooms. Secret beds for teenaged brides. It makes my skin crawl. I mean, I thought *I* had it bad, in my mom's junkie apartment.

All this time, I've been mad with Rachel for not being open. Now I kinda wish she'd close back up.

It sorta hits me then. She's been protecting us from it. Like a mom would do. Well, not like *my* mom, but you know what I mean.

So Rachel is talkin' 'bout this clinic, and she thinks maybe she was kept there. This freaky nurse-lady did stuff to girls there. Like took 'em down to a basement and maybe vanished 'em or something. I can't take it all in.

Rachel looks up at me. 'And it's like someone has taught me not to think of it. Like this same phrase pops up. By the power of Jesus Christ,' she adds, more to herself than me, 'I command you to leave me alone.'

I get the impression somethin' profound has occurred to her, but she doesn't share it.

'You been carryin' all this stuff around on your own?' I say.

'I'm sorry. For real. I been a shitty wife. Guess I was so buried in my own things, and you seemed so in control . . .'

She doesn't answer, rolling the tequila glass between her small hands with a far-off look.

'OK, so a clinic,' I say. 'And this lady with the claw-hair. The one they think has information about the cemetery. She's a nurse. Something there all fits together, right?'

Rachel doesn't reply. I figure maybe the alcohol is botherin' her insides.

I lift my shot of tequila and down it.

'Is that why you were so freaked, when the cops wanted to show me your therapy notes?' I ask. 'You thought I'd think you were a nut?'

She waits so long to answer, I figure the tequila might be fuzzing up her brain. Finally she speaks.

'I told the therapist . . .' she takes a breath, like she's fighting an overwhelming sense of betrayal. 'I told her I was . . . assaulted,' she says. 'When I was fifteen.'

Right away, I know when Rachel says 'assaulted', she's talkin' a whole lot more than wanderin' hands. Her eyes meet mine, hesitant, like she thinks I won't believe her.

'Hey, me too,' I say, sympathetically. 'Sucks, huh? My dear old mom used to have all kinds of trash in the house. Dealers, pimps. They'd all get high together and she'd pass out. Only a matter of time before somethin' happened. I was lucky, it only happened once,' I add. 'I went to the cops, and they didn't believe me.' I blow hair from my face. 'They thought I was trying to trick them into giving me free state accommodation.'

'Mine was my cousin,' she says. 'His mom said it was my fault, and slapped me until my nose bled. Said if I told anyone, she'd kill my sisters.'

I whistle. *Poor Rachel.*

'Makes you feel dirty, don't it,' I say with feeling, looking at Rachel. 'Makes you feel dirty that it happened to you, and stupid for not being believed.'

She nods, her expression lighter. I reach across, take her hands and hold them. We're silent for a moment.

'The weird thing is, it wasn't all bad at the Homestead,' says Rachel. 'We were family, working together for the same thing. A lot of the time, I remember being surrounded by *love*. The hardships brought us closer in prayer. It was uplifting. I miss it.'

I squeeze Rachel's fingers tight.

'I know how you feel,' I tell her. 'You get that same thing when you get high with the same crew. When you're all on the skids together. Just you and your buddies against the world, right?'

Rachel smiles. I had kinda been expecting her to get offended. The old Blake-Rachel would have.

'It wasn't your fault, you know,' she says. 'When Blake went into his black moods. It wasn't you. It was just . . . a part of who he was.'

We're both silent for a while, lost in our memories of Blake.

'So what do we do now?' asks Rachel. 'I mean, aren't we fugitives, or something?'

'Nah.' I'm playin' this down, because if those three cop cars were for us, someone thinks we're kind of a big deal. 'We'll avoid the interstate, just in case,' I add.

Rachel gives me this real warm smile.

'I'm glad I came with you,' she says. 'I'm glad I . . . saw all this.'

'That's the tequila talkin'. You'll be tryin' to make out with me next.'

She grins. 'You should be so lucky.'

'So what about this lady. Aunt Meg, I mean. She could be

part of this, right? Something . . . sinister. Should we try and find her?'

Rachel's smile vanishes. I get the sense she's choosin' her words real carefully.

'Anyone from the Homestead is a ghost, so far as regular society is concerned,' she says. 'Especially the women. No job, no social security number, no nothing.'

'Well then, what about we pay a visit to the Homestead? Maybe it would jog your memory. It's the big abandoned place off the main highway, right? You might even be able to find this cemetery everyone's looking for.'

Something happens to Rachel's features. Like a microexpression. Just for a moment, I feel like there's this . . . *rage*. Then it's gone so fast, I wonder if I saw it at all.

I'm struck by this thought that Rachel knows something she's not sayin'. It's real intuitive, like in my gut.

She doesn't want anyone to find that graveyard.

'I've got bad memories of that place,' she says coldly. 'I'm not going back.' Her tone tells me to drop it.

I feel abandoned. Like I've found her and she's left me. The bar feels cold and deserted. Just me all alone here.

'You OK?' I say, trying to pull her back. 'You look pale.'

'I think the coffee wasn't a good idea.' She puts a hand to her forehead. 'I've got a real bad headache.'

An' then she isn't there at all. Rachel has slipped into that strange void she goes into sometimes. Demons in the closet, Blake used to say. Rachel has a lotta demons in the closet.

'Come on,' I say, knowing it's best to let her be when she's in this kind of mood. 'Let's get back to the car.'

I'm getting to my feet when I realize something.

'Hey,' I say, 'pass me back that file, wouldya?'

Rachel slides it over.

I leaf through. 'So we know parts are missing,' I tell her. 'Maps and things. Stuff you'd expect to find in a complete file.' I tap a stack of photographs on my mouth, something pretty huge dawnin' on me. 'Do you remember,' I ask Rachel, 'that lately Blake had taken to keeping paperwork in his locker in Temple?'

74

Rachel, first wife

I *do* remember Blake getting real antsy with Emily poking around in his things, right before he started taking papers into work with him. Then he got all animated about the government, and federal men infiltrating the Church, which meant we were due one of Blake's catatonic couch episodes shortly after.

But Tina is just saying crazy things. Trying to persuade me to burglarize the most holy building on the planet.

'Tina, it's the *Temple*,' I tell her, exasperated. 'Holiest place on earth. Shoot, we can't go in and start poking around. I can't get it right in my mind you would even suggest it.' I'm furious with her. Not to mention exhausted. I just want to go home and lick my wounds. I feel as though I can't walk another step. 'Those papers in Blake's locker are most likely regular household stuff.'

'Then why not keep 'em in the regular household? Why put them somewhere you need a recommend to get in?'

'Because he didn't want us getting in a hot panic about the debt we were in,' I suggest.

'So you think it's just a coincidence,' presses Tina. 'Our husband took some papers to his workplace in Temple. Then shows up dead.'

'We're already in enough trouble. The police know we've skipped bail,' I point out.

'We haven't *skipped bail*,' scoffs Tina, rolling her eyes at my idiocy. 'That's when you don't show up in court, dummy. We just,' she waves pink fingernails, 'misunderstood the boundaries.'

'We need to leave these things to the police,' I say stubbornly.

'The cops can't get inside Temple without a *lotta* red tape,' Tina presses. 'You need to be a member of the Church, with a recommend. No cop is gonna take time from his donut break to get that done when he's got a passable confession sittin' in his cells. Not to mention,' she scoops a fistful of black hair behind her ear, 'if this is some kind of, like, *cover-up*, then someone could get to Blake's locker before the cops. To get in Temple without a recommend, the cops would need an official warrant. But *we don't.*'

I think of my Temple recommend – a handwritten docket with a pleasing likeness to an old-fashioned library ticket. The kind you got slipped into the front of college books. A Latter-day Saint recommend is like a badge of purity, letting you go into Temple, where regular folk aren't allowed. It lasts a lifetime, except in exceptional circumstances too awful to even contemplate.

I'd been so proud the day I got my recommend. It had been after my formal baptism. I had truly felt washed clean. Like God was giving me a fresh start.

Tina doesn't understand. I can't risk losing my recommend.

'It's the *Temple*,' I say. 'You have no notion at all—'

'Yeah? An' you always pull this shit. Like obey the man instead of defending your sisters. You're really gonna let Emily go to prison, without even raising your voice. Pretty little liars don't do so good in state prisons, Rachel, believe me. An' as soon as she's processed, there's no way out. You get that, right?'

Emily found me sleepwalking. Heard me talking in my dreams.

Tina glares at me. I glare back, fists balled, seething. I want to slap her face, pull her hair.

'So what now?' she says. 'You gonna push me down some stairs?'

The bartender is staring at us.

'Nothing to see here,' Tina tells her. 'Just a little *Mormon* stuff we're workin' through.'

The bartender shrugs and begins arranging bottles.

I sag. 'I can't do any more of this, Tina. We just need to grieve, OK? Like properly go through the process. I need to go home. Be alone with my thoughts. Pray.'

'Please,' Tina's eyes are large. 'Please, Rachel. I'll just . . . I'd go crazy not knowing, OK? What if we don't go look, and then whatever those documents were vanish someplace?'

'Just to be clear,' I say. 'You think Blake got caught up in something over that land. Something he was killed for. And there's evidence in his locker at work?'

I'm hoping she'll be struck by how silly this sounds, but it doesn't work that way.

'If the mob are involved in building a casino,' Tina says, 'offing some guy who's problematizing their plans is nothing to them. It's, like, something they do before their cornflakes. What if Blake agreed to take their money, and then refused to have a casino there?'

I'm silent, because it sounds plausible.

'Then there's this Aunt Meg person,' continues Tina. 'We know Blake was looking for her. Maybe he found her. Got her all freaked out that he was goin' to uncover some freaky dark secret at the Homestead. Something about the secret cemetery. She talks to the Prophet and he tells her to take Blake out. We know she'll do whatever it takes to help the Prophet, right? You said yourself this Aunt Meg person vanished away girls in her basement.'

I close my eyes and instantly regret it. The blue shoebox is still there. Only now, inside the cardboard walls is the yellow sand graveyard.

Burial mounds, lots of them.

I scrunch my eyelids tight, pushing it away.

'If we don't look, we'll never *know*,' presses Tina. 'It will haunt me. And if Emily is convicted, she could get the death penalty.'

The horror of this image sits cold on my heart.

'If there was even a chance she didn't do it . . . Please. I'm beggin' you. I got so much bad shit in here.' Tina taps her head. 'Things I did. There's no room for any more frickin' *guilt*.'

I cradle my temples, trying to think straight.

'If I help you,' I say, 'will you leave all this alone? Will you accept that Emily has confessed, there's no . . . crazy conspiracy here?'

Tina nods firmly. 'Shake on it.' She spits on her hand, holds it out. 'I didn't really spit,' she adds, seeing my expression.

I shake her hand.

'Swear,' I say, looking her in the eye. 'Right hand to God?'

'Right hand to God,' says Tina solemnly, raising her hand. 'If you help me bust into Blake's locker, and we don't find nothing, I will leave all this shit alone. OK?'

I breathe out.

'OK.'

'You really think there's something in Temple that could lead the police to Blake's killer?' I say.

'Well, we'll never know unless we look. There's no need even to lie to anyone,' adds Tina with a wink. 'We'll do your thing, you know. We won't tell them the truth.'

I put my hand on my forehead. I can still feel the headache.

327

'If we're gonna do this,' I decide, 'we have to do it properly.'

Tina's face lights up. 'Damn . . . Dang straight!'

'We need you in some different clothes.'

'What?'

'Well, we're planning on getting inside without anyone notic-ing us, right?' I explain. 'Well, you're . . . somewhat noticeable.'

'What?'

It hits me that Tina regards herself as dressing incognito. I guess, compared to the six-inch heels and shorts skirts of Vegas, maybe she is.

'What's wrong with this?' she demands, tugging at a low-cut pink sweater, that draws full attention to her C-cup chest. 'You can't see garments, right? Isn't that what the modesty is for? If some guy checks out my hooties, that's on him.'

'That's true,' I say patiently. 'But a lotta folk are more old-fashioned. How 'bout we get you something a little more muted. Higher cut here,' I gesture. 'Plait your hair for Temple like the others do.'

'You're freakin' kidding me. You expect me to dress like you?'

'If you don't wanna stand out, sure. It's a classic look. Cap-sleeve tee, with spaghetti-string tank vest on the top. All the girls wear it.'

'Yeah, I never got that.'

'It's modest, for one thing. But, you know, a little sexy too.' I give a little shimmy of my shoulders.

'*What?*'

'I'm risking my immortal soul,' I tell her. 'You're wearing the cap-sleeve tee. It's non-negotiable.'

75

Tina, sister-wife

Carlson picks up right away.

'Shit, Tina. Don't you know there are cops out looking for you? You went out of state for Chrissakes! They're gonna lock you up when they get hold of you. Both of you.'

'Come on, Carlson. You think there's something in it,' I say, 'dontcha? Like there might be something more to this?'

There's a pause.

'You got the information I sent, right?'

'A midwife named Aunt Meg?' he says. 'I'm looking into it, but you've not given me a whole lot to go on. You got a full name?'

'Not yet.'

He sighs. 'Tina, I'm gonna take a wild guess, you've not found any fourth wife out there.'

'Not exactly. But we know Blake met with someone right before he died, right, a woman? Well, turns out this Homestead place has a lotta skeletons in the closet. I mean literally. There's some secret cemetery down there that all the real estate people are tryin' to find so they can buy the land. And Rachel is re-memberin' stuff. Like there was a clinic where they did things to women.'

'Rachel told you that?'

His flat tone makes me feel helpless.

'Yeah, but listen. Doesn't this sound like something someone might wanna cover up? Like kill for?'

'You think someone out there with a secret to hide doesn't want it bought? Killed Blake, so no one would go snooping around?'

'Makes sense, doesn't it?'

'It makes about as much sense as Brewer's fingerprint padlock theory,' says Carlson.

'What?'

I hear Carlson make a muffled curse. 'Forget I said that.'

But I'm already two steps ahead.

The set of fingerprint locks Blake brought home, hoping to crack the biometrics.

I'd forgotten all about them. Assumed Blake had too. But his fingers were missing, weren't they? What if he took one of those locks into his workplace in Temple? Fixed it to his locker . . .?

'You still there?' asks Carlson.

'Uh-huh.'

'Don't go running away with anything,' repeats Carlson. 'Lotta wild geese. Like I told Brewer, you can't use dead fingers to open locks.' I can almost hear Carlson shaking his head. 'Not outside the movies. It all sounds like a good story,' continues Carlson. 'When I hear a good story, I ask myself who's got a reason to be tellin' it. 'Specially when I'm not hearing any actual evidence this happened.'

'Blake was meetin' with a realtor who knew about a secret cemetery,' I say. 'That's proof. You can ask 'em.'

There's a long pause. I grab a hold of it.

'You raided the Homestead, right?' I press. 'There were unexplained death certificates, weren't there?' I'm remembering what Dakota said about records.

I can almost hear him cycling through what he's allowed to tell me. What he probably shouldn't.

'Well, we found a good deal of paperwork,' he says. 'Mainly because the menfolk were stupid enough to run straight to it and try and destroy the records. As you might imagine, we found proof of underage marriage. A lot of it. And a whole bunch of other things. Births and deaths.'

'Deaths that didn't match up?' I'm gripping the receiver tight.

'My buddy found a list of names. Around about fifty people were given a special baptism. Recorded as buried in a different graveyard to the rest. He was pretty damn sure these were folk who tried to leave and were caught. Executed maybe.'

'That's a reason to cover up the cemetery, right?' I say, all excited now. 'Someone could be jailed for murder. Maybe Blake got killed for what he knew.'

Carlson sighs. 'Tina, I appreciate a hidden cemetery sounds freaky. But it's actually not uncommon in self-contained communities. They start thinkin' they're all above society, they don't need what we got. Then a few people die of natural causes, and it takes 'em a year or two to figure out they're gonna need a proper burial ground. That's when they realize you need all kind of permissions and so forth to make a graveyard and they've been breakin' the law. So the first plot gets covered up, 'cause they don't want to get busted. They form another one, this time with state permission. The result is a secret graveyard, but the reality is there's nothing more sinister than people's idiocy.'

I'm silent, thinking this through. Much as I hate to admit, it sounds more likely than a murderous conspiracy.

'Tina, if you disregard everything that Rachel says, I think you'll find a pretty boring story. Wife gets jealous, kills husband. I see it all the time. But my main concern now is you're runnin' around with a psycho. A psycho who might be planning to murder you and skip state. Am I to understand that Rachel Nelson has changed her appearance?'

'That was my idea,' I say.

'You sure about that? Or did she let you think it was?'

There's a pause as I remember it kinda *was* Rachel who went all out, changing her hair an' all. I was just planning on buying her some clothes that weren't from a 90s bargain rack.

'I think somethin' could have happened that caused someone to kill Blake,' I say stubbornly. 'We were the only ones out in the desert. But if someone really cared enough, they coulda, I dunno, followed Blake home, or somethin'.'

'No they couldn't.' Again, it's like I can almost hear Carlson shaking his head. 'That's impossible. It's a stretch of empty desert road running for at least forty miles. You think he wouldn't notice a car behind him?'

'His GPS then,' I say. 'He's got a mapping system for work. Tracks his movements. What if someone read his output? Followed the trail?'

Carlson pauses. 'GPS systems don't share journeys with a central system. Let's just say your husband had some super version fitted, by some crazy control-freak boss. Well then, that would point the finger toward someone at his workplace, I guess. Would a canning machine salesman make life-or-death enemies?'

'Could be someone powerful enough to get access to the system from outside,' I counter. 'Someone high up in the mafia, or even the Church. If there's something on this land that's a big deal, that's possible.'

'All of this sounds pretty unlikely. Why would they have strangled him with a belt? Isn't that kind of coincidental?'

'Maybe they had access to his phone.' My arguments are

sounding weaker and weaker. 'Wanted to make it look like one of us did it.'

Carlson sighs.

'I want to help you. I do. But the best thing you can do for yourself is come in. Let us protect you. Rachel too.'

I imagine the police station. The bland halfway house we've been living in. My husband's coffin. There's no way on earth I'm coming in.

I make a last-ditch attempt.

'Look, we *knew* Blake. We know he wouldn't just meet up with some woman. He wasn't *like* that. He didn't have casual female friends who he'd grab a bite with. Kirker's Diner was his special date restaurant.'

There's a long pause. For a moment I think Carlson has hung up.

'I'll talk to Kirker's Diner,' he says. 'OK? If they have security footage, I'll pull it. Take a look.'

'Thanks.' I swallow, deciding to push my luck. 'What about the list of names your buddy found at the Homestead?'

'I didn't file that paperwork.'

'You couldn't take a look?'

Carlson sighs. 'I can't . . .'

'Pretty please.'

There's another pause. 'Alright. *Alright.* I can't go digging out a million files, but I'll give my buddy a call, 'K? See if he remembers anything else. Only because it's you askin'.'

I smile at that. 'You're one of the good ones,' I tell him, 'you know that?'

'I know it. Just don't tell the others.'

'Cross my heart.' I hesitate. 'What happens next. To Emily?'

'I'm afraid to say she's been talkin' about requesting a fast trial. I don't hold up much hope for the verdict.'

'But . . . I mean, she's crazy, right? Anyone can see that.'

'This isn't Nevada, Miss Keidis.' He's reverting to official cop now, calling me by my surname. I'm surprised at how it feels like a loss. 'People don't really believe in crazy. An' they don't take too kindly to husband killers around here.'

76

Emily, sister–wife

I really like Google. The one good thing my therapist lady did was allow me some time on the internet right before I get driven to actual prison. Since I'm not convicted, I have more rights, apparently, and one whole hour on social media is one of them.

Of course, I don't *have* any social media pages, or things like that. All that stuff actually gives me a lot of bad memories, mostly about high school. Before I grew into my looks, some of the mean girls said things, like stick insect and bug-eye.

I had an idea in my head I might start a blog about being in prison, or something. When I started looking at how to do that, though, it made my head hurt. So I mostly look up cake recipes. There's one called a piñata cake, with a candy center and rainbow layers, which is just *for cute*. I really want to make that one someday. I just need to get faster at reading recipes.

I'm so caught up in making the letters join up, I don't notice Detective Carlson slide in next to me.

'Hey,' he says. 'You wanna take a walk? Not much time for that in prison.' I'm about to say no, when he reaches in his pocket. 'Gotcha some candy,' he adds, waving two chocolate bars.

I get to my feet.

'Hey!' a lady police officer is frowning at us. 'She's not allowed out. You know that. I'm due to drive her over to the state penitentiary at five.'

Carlson glances at the clock.

'Ten minutes and I'll have her back,' he promises. 'I'll cuff her if you like.'

The police lady just shakes her head and nods he can take me out. As soon as we're in the corridor, he hands me the candy bar.

'I was working on a theory you were covering for Rachel,' he tells me as our feet make clicking sounds on the rubber floor. 'At a stretch, Tina.' He tosses me a grin. 'You got what we call mommy issues, right? And since Rachel is like a mother figure . . . well, you get my thinking.'

His hand dances to his pocket, like he's thinking of pulling out a cigarette, then away again.

'But then I got Tina on the phone,' he continues, frowning. 'And I dunno. I just can't shake the idea maybe there *is* something in this Aunt Meg business after all. Like maybe she was supplying your husband with a wife, or blackmailing him for something Rachel did.' He stares hard at me for this last part. 'Anyways,' he concludes, 'I promised Tina I'd look into it a little.'

I keep my breathing very steady. We've reached the end of a corridor now. Carlson stops at a reinforced glass window with a view of crimson mountains and cobalt-blue sky.

Between miles of desert and the flat vertical stop of the rock face in the distance, there's a little clutch of rock spires, all jagged and burnt orange. Blake used to say they were nature's cathedral, but I always thought they looked plain mean. Dangerous. All sticking up and pointy, like *don't touch us*. Even the lowdown misshapen ones are squat and glowery like trolls.

I decide I like them better now. They can't help how they were made.

'Sure is a pretty view,' says Carlson.

We stand there for a minute.

'Problem was, "Aunt Meg" is no name to go on, less you wanna find a bunch of cupcake companies,' says Carlson, looking out. 'Brewer and I couldn't find any criminal proceedings, and wound up finding a heap of things relating to the Prophet's trial. I won't go into detail, but suffice to say, there were wedding-night tape recordings that made grown jurors cry.' He taps his head. 'Then Brewer had a clever idea. What if Aunt Meg had Rachel's surname? Like they were relations. So we look for Meg Ambrosine. And whaddya know?'

'What?' I'm intrigued.

'Nothing on our system, but when I put the name into Google, we find a hit on an acknowledgments page of a book. Written around the time the Prophet was convicted. The book is by Moroni Brown and is entitled: *The Truth: A Father's Honest Account*. In his acknowledgments, he thanks Margaret "Aunt Meg" Ambrosine for her truth.'

'What was the book about?' I'm real curious now.

'Ah, basically saying that all the women who testified against the Prophet are liars. Author condemns his own daughter as a fantasist. It wasn't well received,' he adds with a little smile. 'Bunch of one-star reviews and nothing more to go on. However,' he clears his throat. 'Now we had a *full* name. And when we put that into the system, *Margaret* Ambrosine has a record.'

He pauses for effect.

'Margaret Ambrosine was arrested for witness intimidation when the Prophet stood trial. Nothing was brought to charge, but wives cooperating with police found dead crows hung outside their homes. One even had their windows shot out.' He puts his hands in his pockets. 'Margaret "Aunt Meg" Ambrosine also testified against a lot of the wives who gave testimony at the

Prophet's trial. Said they were born liars. I know, right?'

Carlson looks at me again.

'So I talk to my buddy, who filed all the Homestead death certificates and what have you. Back at the time, he found a list of names that he never did get to match, but we dismissed it with all the other weirdness.'

He waits for this to sink in.

'I asked him where this list was found. He can't remember much, but he thinks it was in some kind of medical facility. Like a clinic. And it was in paperwork belonging to a woman, which was very unusual. He didn't remember much else, but when I sent him the photograph of Aunt Meg your sister-wives are running around with, he was fairly certain the documents had been in her possession.'

I wait for him to say more. I can feel my heart beating.

'Problem is, Aunt Meg vanished.' He clicks his fingers. 'Poof. Disappeared.'

My mouth feels dry.

'Do you have anything you want to tell me?' asks Carlson. ''Cause if you do, now's the time. Could be the person you think you're protecting didn't do it after all.'

'Miss Martinelli?' the police lady from the computer room has come out. 'Time's up.'

My mind is racing as Carlson walks me back to the room, like I can't catch a thought. I can't be sure if he's trying to trick me. He gives me one last sorry look before handing me over to the lady police officer, who looks up from texting on her phone, and motions me to wait in a bored way. It's only when Carlson is out of sight, the police lady clicks her cell off.

Her screensaver is a shot of her with her arm around two girls, who are maybe eleven and fifteen. Daughters, I guess. They are all beaming, huddled in close. The police lady sees me looking and pockets the phone with a weird expression.

I make a decision. I need to tell Carlson the truth. Rachel and Tina could be in danger.

'Wait!' I turn to the police lady, catch myself. Arrange my features in a smile. 'I mean, may I please speak with Detective Carlson for just a few more minutes? It's important.'

'I think you've already had enough rules bent for you,' she replies. 'Those pretty eyes don't work on me, sugar pie. You're allowed your last twenty minutes of internet time if you want it. Take it, don't take it, all the same to me. Not a minute over. Then you go to the big-girl prison.'

77
Tina, sister-wife

Salt Lake City is kinda surreal on the best of days. You know those models architects make for new building projects? All straight and boxy, fresh cut out of white foam board, with perfectly circular green trees and wide roads holding a tiny scatter of cars. It looks like that.

So it feels even stranger to be here, dressed as a resident.

'I think you look lovely,' says Rachel. 'You know, they always say, dress modest and people will take more notice of your figure than if you're putting it all out there. I never found that to be true,' she adds, 'but for someone who looks like you, it works. You were hiding that little waist with all the chest going on.' She nods approvingly. 'And your eyes look real pretty.'

I've caught a glance at myself in the mirror. I feel washed out, pale. Like a layer of me has been stripped back.

'I look like I'm sick.'

'No you don't.'

'I'm dressed like a fifth-grader.'

'Well then, so am I. But people aren't looking at us, right?'

Rachel has stipulated the obligatory Utah uniform of spaghetti-strap tank worn on top of a cap-sleeve T-shirt. She brushed all my hair up into a loose bun, and held it back with a skinny black headband. I don't look like myself at all. But I take Rachel's point – no one is looking my way. Not one. It makes me feel a special sorta worthless.

'You changing your mind?' asks Rachel. She kinda pulls at her shirt as she says it. Rachel's real nervous, I realize. I'm not sure she quite bought the theory that Blake might have added a fingerprint lock to his locker at work. 'That wouldn't be allowed,' she pointed out, not really accounting for Blake, who did a lot of things he wasn't allowed to do.

'I'm not changing my mind,' I say. But it isn't true.

'Do you even know why you're doing this?' she asks softly.

Because I don't want to believe you killed him, Rachel. Because the only thing to keep me from going insane is to keep moving.

To Rachel, I say: 'I just have to *know*, OK?' I lift my eyes to the great spire. Ahead of me are the large gold doors of the entrance. Either side are set stained-glass windows. The modern kind. In front are square pillars, rectangular brick. Above is written in sharp metal letters: Holiness to the Lord. House of God.

A whole bunch of people are milling around the entrance, walking through, waiting for family outside, taking pictures.

We walk forward.

'I can't do it,' says Rachel. 'I can't go into Temple and . . . creep about where I'm not allowed. If anyone finds out, I'll be excommunicated. I could lose everything.'

'You promised,' I remind her.

Rachel nods, swallows.

'OK,' she says.

We step through the glass doors, and right away the cool air hits us. Streams of people are pouring past, their Temple recommends at the ready. A security guard stands by the entrance trying to look holy, with a red tabard over his beefy shoulders. He steps forward as we enter, checking we're not tourists confused over where we're allowed to go.

Rachel and I flash our Temple recommends and he nods us inside.

The lobby is bigger than a cathedral, white, serene, with a lotta gold bling inching the whole thing toward gaudy. There are marble floors, a matching marble desk, and a long mural of Jesus meeting prophets on the mount, in muted colors. It reminds me of some of the themed casino interiors in Vegas made of stucco and paint. This would be Heaven Casino. No high rollers and the buffet is one day old.

I glance about. Pockets of people are preparing themselves. There are brides and their families waiting for the Sealing ceremony on one side of the broad lobby. Excited-looking grooms on the other. Young men and women are awaiting baptisms and endowments.

Now that I'm here in my own right, without a ceremony to trouble my nerves, I think it's so beautiful. All these faithful people, coming together 'cause they believe in somethin' bigger than themselves.

I hold out my Temple recommend, and motion for Rachel to do the same. Since she seems to be struggling to walk, I grab it from her unresisting hand, and half drag her to the desk.

I wave our pieces of paper – Holy documents penned by Bishop Young, entitling us to lifelong Temple access. Women get them on their wedding day. Men get them when they complete their mission. Guess that says a lot.

A familiar thrill is rushing through me. I feel the way I used to as a younger woman, pullin' hustles in Vegas. There's somethin' else too. The distraction. I'm not thinking of Blake. The big sad pull way back behind my eyes is covered over.

'We're here for the Smith wedding,' I say.

The orderly barely looks up, just waves us through.

'You lied to an orderly,' whispers Rachel.

'It's a white lie,' I say. 'Else they might be looking to check we go into the personal reflection rooms. This way there'll be less heat. Nothing in the Bible that says you can't lie,' I add. 'Only bear false testimony, right?'

'Bear false testimony *is* lying,' hisses Rachel, as I sweep her past several serious-looking men in suits. 'That's what it *means*.'

'Oh, well, you say potato, I say po-*tah*-to,' I say, emphasizing the Utah burr. 'We all read scripture different.' I grip her arm. 'Bible also says God helps those who helps themselves,' I say. 'Come on.'

We're halfway along the corridor when Rachel stops as we pass a point labeled 'Staff only'.

'Tina, have you noticed?' she says, pointing to the ceiling. 'No cameras. Not anywhere. Remember Blake talking on and on about cameras?'

I pause, because I do remember that. Blake came home almost hoppin' on the spot, talkin' about how the government had in-filtrated Temple, and there were cameras in all the staff areas, filming their every movement. He'd told us it wouldn't be long until they'd figured a way to get inside our minds.

I turn this through, wondering how much of Blake's way of looking at the world has rubbed off on me.

I look across at Rachel. It's impossible to know what she's thinking.

Which kinda brings me back around to what Carlson's been telling me all along. That this is all a wild goose chase. What if Blake's death just comes down to an angry wife mad enough to kill her husband?

78

Rachel, first wife

No cameras. Blake *lied* to us. I am just plain stunned by it. All this time. I'd relied on him to tell me the truth about the outside world. He was supposed to keep us safe. Instead he'd come back with these wild stories about cameras and government conspiracies. I just can't get it right in my mind.

'Come on,' says Tina. 'Let's see what's inside Blake's locker.'

I let her lead me, still burning with my husband's mistruth. Maybe he made a mistake. The cameras were scheduled but not yet in place. But that isn't what he told us.

My knees sorta buckle beneath me. I'm glad to have Tina here. She frog-marches me along. She seems lit up by the whole thing, like there's a wild energy about her.

I'm seized with apprehension as we enter the inner sanctum. When I was a little girl, my mother showed me pictures of the Temple in Salt Lake City. For a long time I was convinced it *was* heaven. The great grand white spires looked exactly as I pictured the Celestial Kingdom. I was a little unclear on where this left the other, lesser heavens. The ones for Mormons who don't practice polygamy. Nice places for sure – I always imagined them as homely, with a lot of comfortable rugs and couches – but without the white and gold opulence of the holiest of holies.

The first time I actually went inside was to be sealed for my wedding. It was a scary and wonderful day.

It feels like everywhere I look I'm reminded of Blake. Like I'm being tortured with memories of him. Because we were happy, back then. Realizing it makes me see how unhappy we were by the end. Or how unhappy he was, I guess. He'd lost a lot of his lightness, in the grip of his need to keep us all safe.

Inside, Temple is the most beautiful place you can imagine. It's all pristine white marble. Mahogany wood banisters leading these incredible stairwells up and all around. Great sweeping chandeliers. It never fails to take my breath away.

'Hey! Excuse me!'

Oh no.

'Excuse me, Ma'am?'

I swallow and turn, to see a young orderly walking toward us.

I see Tina's expression. I assume she'll be mentally cursing, but she is taking this in her stride. Wide smile on her face.

'If you're here for the wedding party, you're headed the wrong way,' he explains.

'Thanks,' says Tina, 'but, as a matter of fact, my husband works here as a custodian. He forgot his sandwiches this mornin' and since I was heading on into town with my sister here, I thought I'd come by and put them in his locker.'

She holds up her purse as evidence.

'Ah, OK,' he smiles. 'That way, down the hall, ladies. There are some big doors at the end, you can't miss 'em. Heaven bless ya,' he adds.

Tina beams her thanks.

'Candy from a baby,' she mutters as we walk away. 'If Mormons ran things in Vegas, I'd be a billionaire by now.'

We arrive at two discreet white doors, labeled 'Staff only.'

345

Tina pushes them open without hesitation. I'm half in awe of her bravery, half terrified by it.

Once inside, we're faced with a row of battered lockers. None of them have the missing lock that Carlson was asking about.

'No fingerprint lock,' says Tina quietly. 'Maybe Carlson was right. Wild goose chase.'

My eyes glide across the names and settle on a nameplate. Blake Nelson.

Even this small evidence of Blake's world fills me up with grief. It's the first time I've realized the box in my mind with his death inside won't hold forever. Now I'm here, I can't trap it shut. My eyes fill with tears.

Tina follows the alphabet to where my eyes are already resting. 'Blake Nelson.'

The rush goes out of her then. Like a balloon sagging.

'Here he is,' she says again, in a quiet voice, her fingertips resting on the metal.

We're silent for a second, both in our own thoughts.

'Do you really think we're gonna find anything?' I say.

Tina thinks about this.

'Maybe,' she admits. 'But we all know Blake took things he didn't want us to see into Temple with him, right?'

'That was just . . . accounting things.'

Tina just arches an eyebrow and shakes her head. 'Well if you say so. We still don't know who he had that date-lunch with though, do we? The blond lady that got all those tongues wagging. Maybe the answer is in here.' She taps the locker.

I don't answer outright. Instead I say: 'In any case, how are we gonna open it?' Ridiculously, this never occurred to me.

The question snaps Tina out of her temporary funk.

'A *locker*,' she smiles. 'Rachel, we just hustled the holiest building in Salt Lake City. A locker ain't gonna give us no problems.'

79

Emily, sister–wife

The police station clock seems to have a deliberately loud tick. Like it's counting down my minutes left in custody and making it hard to concentrate. I'm sitting in front of the piñata-cake picture, waiting for my internet time to be up.

I've had a little time to process things now. Maybe Carlson was trying to trick me after all, putting me under pressure to answer real quick. I try to keep calm. Think what Cagney would do.

Since I'm in front of a computer, I decide I should find out more about Aunt Meg.

I start pushing the keys, typing Margaret Ambrosine, Homestead. Just like Carlson said, the book comes up with her name in the acknowledgments.

Story checks out.

I blow a little hair out of my face, deciding what this means. I start clicking through pages. Nothing, nothing, nothing.

Then a result flashes up.

Whoa! Go Cagney!

Aunt Meg's name appears on some comments site. Someone has posted about a rumor of a sadistic midwife on the Homestead, who made women in labor sit with their legs crossed and let babies die. But not a soul has replied to the thread and it was

347

written way back, by someone with a weird anonymous cyber name.

There's a lot of writing and it's hurting my eyes, so I click back, and sorta scroll down and down. I figure the police must have read this too and ruled it out. No leads.

I look up at the clock and realize I've only got ten minutes left. Must have spent longer than I thought on the typing. I don't want to give up just yet.

Slowly I type in 'Aunt Margaret Ambrosine'.

A few results come up, with the same information I know already. I pout a little, trying a few more variations.

Aunt Meg. Aunt Ambrosine. Meg Ambrosine.

Nothing.

I let my finger sit on the cursor, watching the pages fly by, until they get into nonsense.

Five minutes on the clock. Guess that's that then. Least I tried.

I'm about to go back to cake pictures when I remember Rachel's nightmares. How she'd talk about graves and digging. Keeping it all secret. Then what I remember Rachel saying when she spoke to me in her sleep. What were her exact words?

I need to bury her in the red graveyard. Or they'll find out what I've done.

Carefully, I type 'red graveyard', and 'homestead', then press enter.

There it is. Right at the top. A quote, picked out in the header.

'No such place as the red graveyard. The REAL truth behind lies I was involved in the disappearance of Homestead sinners. By First Wife Ambrosine.'

There's a picture too. My finger freezes over the mouse.

Holy moly.

Looks like Aunt Meg has a blog. I click frantically, but I'm so panicky, it's hard to read things right.

From what I can make of the blog, it's pages and pages of her refuting a lotta accusations, in misspelt English even worse than mine. Aunt Meg denies she was ordered to do away with folk who wanted to leave the Homestead. She also says she never tried to intimidate ex-members who wanted to spill secrets and testify against the Prophet.

I glance up at the clock and my heart sinks. The police lady is already headed toward me, dangling a pair of handcuffs. I'm out of time.

80

Tina, sister-wife

'I thought you said a locker wouldn't give you any problems?' Rachel hisses.

'Well, these Mormon lockers are more secure than you might imagine. 'Specially for a place where no one steals.' I push back a strand of hair that's escaped my headband, and jimmy the unfolded paper clip I keep in my change purse for picking locks.

I glare at the little keyhole, twisting at it.

'These cheap locks usually pop real easy,' I say, frustrated, tugging at the door. 'I never had this much trouble before.'

The locker makes a loud rattling. Rachel glances around, terrified.

'*Tina*,' she's almost sobbing. 'They're going to *find us*.'

'So?' I give the metal another jerk. 'What's the worst they can do? Have us arrested?'

'They can have us *excommunicated*.'

Rachel is a shade of green.

'So go watch the hall. Tell me if anyone's comin'.'

Rachel looks as though she's going to disagree, then silently pads to the door.

'All clear,' she says, sounding calmer.

In desperation, I give the locker one last loud wrench. The

catch bends, and all of a sudden the paper clip sinks deeper, clicking the tumblers open.

'Here we go,' I say. A rush of emotion hits me. Like I've been masking all this stuff. Do I really want to see what's inside?

To my great relief, there's nothing of Blake's. No clothes, or familiar things. It doesn't even smell like him. I think for a moment I've got the wrong locker. There are some papers crammed at the back. I pull them out.

Xerox maps. Land boundaries. Legal papers.

My hand shakes a little. 'Holy smokes,' I say, shaking my head. 'Looks like he did it. Blake actually went ahead and bought that Homestead land.' I look up at Rachel. 'A big down payment had gone through.'

'What *down payment*?' demands Rachel. 'We didn't have any money.'

'Looks like he brokered a different arrangement with Las Vegas Real Estate. A fifty-fifty land split. In return, they *loaned* him the deposit. That's a bad deal,' I add. 'I'll bet those realtors would have fronted the money.'

'That sounds a lot like Blake,' says Rachel quietly. 'Too proud to take a payout from anyone outside the Church. How do you think he planned on paying back the loan?'

'Knowing our Blakey, I'm guessing he thought God would provide.'

I flip papers. A bunch of low-quality pamphlets fall free. Advertisements for backyard mining equipment. The kind hillbillies buy on credit in the hope of striking gold or oil.

'Oh wait, here ya go. I think we have our answer.' I shake my head. 'Blakey, Blakey, Blakey.'

Rachel lifts a few brochures for cheap mining equipment, mini-diggers and mechanical sorters. The text advertises fifty percent discounts and offers for unsecured credit in loud yellow type. At the back are case studies of ordinary men who have struck it rich using the homespun power tools.

'Copper,' says Rachel flatly, waving a stapled set of Xerox pages entitled 'Backyard copper mining'. 'He wanted to get copper out of the ground.'

'Lotta that in Utah,' I say. 'Half the state must have a little in their backyard. But it's no get-rich-quick plan. He woulda had us all pickin' rocks in the blazing sun, right? Whilst he drove some big digger around.'

'Right,' says Rachel bitterly. 'Knowing Blake, it was more a plan to buy a yard full of dangerous machinery he could barely operate, without thinking it through. Leave me to work out whatever subsistence could be dragged out of a backyard copper mine.'

Rachel has it exactly right, and to be honest this is a lot like how the whole marriage operated. Rachel quietly making things work, whilst Blake moved from one crazy scheme to the next, in between bouts of black paralysis.

'Rules out one motive though, huh?' I point out. 'Blake wasn't blocking any casino plans. Las Vegas Real Estate would have gotten the Nevada half.'

'Mining copper would mean digging into the land,' Rachel points out. 'If there were a cemetery near the deposits, it would likely be unearthed in the process. If so, wouldn't someone want to cover it up? I mean, that's a motive, right? Ensuring a crime stays hidden.'

'I guess so.' I read some more. 'The sale agreed was for a little over one hundred thousand dollars. That's a good price for so much land.' I hold up the letter you get right before you exchange. 'He woulda been days away from getting the deeds to his half.'

I'm good at actin' casual, but truth is this really burns that I had no idea. Guess I didn't know my husband well at all.

Besides the exchange papers, there's a thick file of other documents. There are some more pictures of the Homestead, which strike me as a little off. A clutch of pictures of an abandoned hospital. It looks creepy. A pair of bloodstained green gloves have been snapped separate to the rest. I'm just puttin' two and two together – the clinic Rachel talked about – when I feel the picture wrenched from my hand.

'What are you doing with that?' demands Rachel.

'Hey, take it easy,' I say. 'Jesus, are you OK?'

She looks like she's having a heart attack.

'That's it,' she whispers. Her finger touches the image very slowly. 'That's where I was. In that clinic.'

She starts to cry.

'It was real,' she says. 'It really happened.'

81

Rachel, first wife

All I can see is those bloodied green gloves. They fill me with a terror that is hardly real. Like I'm back there and I can never get out.

Yellow sand underfoot. Men carrying me. Blood dripping from between my legs.

We came to a part of the Homestead I'd never been to before. A building. Unlike the other wooden dwellings, this was cinder block, clad in corrugated steel. Automatically I felt a pulse of fear. I knew this was bad.

I'd heard about hospitals on the outside. It was generally frowned upon to visit one unless you were about to die.

The doors opened and there she was. Aunt Meg.

'Bring her in,' she told them, shaking her head.

Inside was like nothing I'd ever seen. All smooth vinyl floors and rows of metal-legged beds. Everything looked very clean and crisp. Almost the exact opposite of the ramshackle log buildings we lived in.

I silently counted ten beds. Beds always gave me a funny feeling. All us girls had been raised with mixed ideas of what happened in them.

The men dropped me to my feet and half dragged me to a bed, blood drawing a slippery skid under my feet.

That's when I saw the plastic garbage can. The lid was half off and it smelt something awful. Inside was filled with blood-soaked paper towels.

I was so afraid. I wanted to go to the bathroom, but I knew I couldn't ask. Aunt Meg drew up alongside me, the blood spot on her dress inches from my eyes. She snapped on a pair of green gloves.

Aunt Meg looked at me. 'You've been a bad girl,' she said.

The familiarity of this picture is jogging things free. The clinic basement. A place I shouldn't have been.

Tina puts her hand on my arm.

'She did bad things,' I whisper. 'Aunt Meg.'

Aunt Meg, walking away toward the basement. She's carrying a blue shoebox.

'It's OK,' Tina says. 'She can't hurt you now. Fucking psycho,' she adds venomously, prodding the image.

Tina's anger makes me feel better. Safer. All us girls were so afraid of Aunt Meg.

Tina flips the photo over. A little square of paper is glued to the back. Written on it in jerky typewriter letters is 'The medical facility.'

Just the sight of it brings a wave of strange memories. The women on the old typewriters at the Homestead, who handled the labeling and filing. I can almost see a stern claw-haired lady, gumming this paper to the photo.

I'm outside, yellow earth under my bare feet. I'm holding the box and I'm scared. The Prophet is hunting me. I stole something very valuable. He wants the shoebox.

Aunt Meg is . . . helping me. She's helping me hide it. She hands me a shovel, raises her finger to her lips.

'I won't tell him. It'll be our secret,' she whispers.

I start to dig.

That's when the door of the janitor's office flies open.

'There you are.' The orderly from reception points to us. 'The hall man tells me you were trying to find the janitor's office, when you told *me* you were going to a wedding.'

He glares at us, accusingly.

'So which is it?'

I turn to Tina, desperate for her to get us out of this.

Tina can save us. I know she can. She has to.

The implications if she doesn't are unthinkable.

'We're widows,' says Tina, her voice getting choked up. 'Plural married. We know the Church doesn't approve, but we just wanted our dead husband's things. Is there anything so wrong with that?'

There are tears in her eyes, and she is trembling. It's such a convincing performance, it occurs to me, uneasily, she could make a person believe anything.

The orderly's lips tighten. 'Your recommending Bishop is on the premises today. Let's see what he has to say.'

The connotations of that are so unthinkable I find myself balling my hands in prayer.

Please no, please no. Don't let Bishop Young find out.

The orderly leans out into the hallway and shouts to an unseen person.

'They're in here!' he calls. 'I'd be obliged if you can straighten this out, sir.'

No, no, no.

But it's too late for prayer. Bishop Young appears in the doorway. The disappointment on his face just plain floors me. I want to curl up in a ball and die.

'We were getting Blake's things,' I whisper. 'I'm sorry.'

'Fortunately I was in my office,' he says. 'So I was able to come in person. Because, naturally, I knew they were mistaken. Rachel Nelson would never, *never*, break the sacred covenants of the Holy Temple.'

He throws a little look in Tina's direction.

'Thanks for your faith in me,' she says, cheerily.

It's not funny anymore. I feel sick now. Like the party's over. I've let Tina lead me all over, stirring up old hurtful memories. And all that's come of it is I've shamed myself.

Bishop Young is shaking his head.

'It's too late for apologies,' he says. 'You have shown utter contempt for our House of God. You have *lied*. Damaged property of the Church. *Burgled*. Needless to say, I will be informing the police. I understand you are both on some kind of bail, so I don't know how that will sit with their arrangements.'

'Don't do that,' says Tina. 'We didn't do nothing. This is our stuff. Technically. We're clearin' out Blake's locker. Right, Rachel?'

I can't bring myself to look at her.

'I'm going to ask you both to leave,' says Bishop Young. 'That I should live to see a Latter-day Saint disrespect their *own Temple* in such a fashion,' he says as a parting shot. 'Least of all you, Rachel. You've let yourself be corrupted.' He glares at Tina.

'I'm here all eternity,' she says, waving. 'Tip your waitress.'

His expression switches to confusion.

'It's an old Vegas joke,' says Tina, helpfully. 'From the old comedians who worked the circuit – "I'm here all week, tip your waitress." No? Guess not everyone gets that one.'

Bishop Young's eyebrows draw together in sour rage. He holds out a chubby hand.

'Kindly hand over your Temple recommends. Your privileges of entering this Temple are revoked. You'll both leave the premises immediately.'

'No!' I feel as though my world is falling in. 'Please, Bishop Young!'

'It wasn't her.' Tina is talking quickly. 'It was all my idea.'

357

Bishop Young doesn't retract his hand.

'Please,' says Tina. 'I'll leave the faith. Anything you want. Just don't hurt Rachel. It means a lot to her.'

Bishop Young shakes his head.

'She has a responsibility to resist temptation,' he says. 'She chose to ignore it. Rachel, I'll be needing your recommend now.'

82

Emily, sister–wife

The police lady I don't like is driving me to the big prison building now. We roll through gate after gate. This must be about the only place in Utah where you can't see red mountains. The blue-blue sky looks a little lost without them. It's got nothing but cream-colored concrete to fix on.

I have a million questions, and no one to ask them to. The idea that keeps bubbling up is this Aunt Meg person is likely a killer. She was involved in making people disappear, and maybe some secret graveyard, and Rachel knows something about it too.

What if . . . Blake found evidence of what Aunt Meg had done, whilst he was trying to purchase the Homestead? Maybe Rachel even told him. What if Aunt Meg met with Blake in Kirker's Diner, asked him to forget all about it for Rachel's sake and he refused? That is absolutely the kind of thing Blake would do.

I need to contact Tina and Rachel. If Aunt Meg is out there, she could come for them next.

The lady officer snatches a look at me, and I must look a little unwell 'cause she sort of smirks and says: 'Real-life prison is not like on TV, is it?'

'I need to speak with Detective Carlson,' I tell her.

She turns back to the wheel. 'You said that already.'

Inside, they bring me behind a reception area, and make me take my clothes off. The guard gets mad when I'm not helpful, and it takes three of them in the end, to stop me kicking. One of them even puts on a hospital glove and pokes a finger right inside my butt, which I'm sure is not allowed. When I tell her that, she scowls and tells me I'm not making any friends.

They give me the smallest boiler suit they have, which is still too big, and cotton slippers that are hard to walk in. They open the door to a long corridor that smells of bleach and bad soup.

'Lucky you,' says the guard. She has a face a little like a frog. 'You made it in time for lunch.'

At the far end, I can make out some big glass panels, with a big cafeteria hall, which reminds me a lot of high school. All these people turn to look at me, and I just have the worst feeling.

All I can think is that I want Rachel. Rachel and Tina.

Rachel might have been snippy with me, and bossy, but she was never actually mean like the girls at school. She never spit in my hair, or stuck half sandwiches to my back.

'I need to speak to Detective Carlson,' I say.

'Listen, princess,' says the guard nastily. 'We know all about you. You've had your fun, dicking us around, getting psychologists and police to spend their precious time tryin' to get you to tell the truth. Right now it's time to meet with the consequences of your actions. You're not special. You're not important. Once we get past this door, you're like everybody else in this prison. Sooner you work that out, the better you'll get along. By my understanding, you're not coming out. You wanna get a message to your detective, have your lawyer call him tomorrow.'

'That could be too late.' I'm almost crying with frustration. 'Please. Rachel could be in *danger*. This person, this Aunt Meg, is out there. She's a killer. She maybe even killed my husband.'

'Oh wait. You're saying now you didn't do it? Right around

the time you got a look inside state prison?' She shakes her head. 'Sorry, it doesn't work that way. You confessed to a crime.'

'What about my phone call?'

'You've had your phone call.'

'Please,' I say. 'I was lying before. I'm telling the truth now.'

'Well now, that's the problem with telling lies, isn't it?' she says. 'No one believes you when you tell the truth.' She takes my arm. 'Come with me.'

'Hold up!' A voice comes from behind us. I turn back to the reception desk.

I have never been more relieved to see a person in my whole life.

Officer Brewer. Officer Brewer is here.

'Turns out we're not quite done with Miss Martinelli,' says Brewer.

The frog-faced guard's face knits all together, eyeing Brewer.

'She's Carlson's arrest,' she says finally. 'I can't hand her to you.'

'Carlson's on his way,' says Brewer. 'Talk to him, if you like.' She takes out her phone, but the lady doesn't take it.

'We processed her,' she says. 'You're too late.'

'She's on remand,' says Brewer. 'Unprocess her.'

'Can't do that.'

'Then let me in to speak with her,' says Brewer quickly.

There's a tense pause whilst the guard decides exactly how difficult she'll get away with being. I regret kicking her in the shins now.

'Twenty minutes,' says the guard eventually. 'That's all. Then I gotta assign her a cell.'

Brewer nods. Takes my arm.

'Carlson pulled the tape,' she says, as she leads me away, 'from Kirker's Diner. We know who Blake was meeting with.'

83

Tina, sister–wife

Rachel loses all her fight the moment Bishop Young's fat fingers close on her Temple recommend. It's plain *weird*. Like she's become a different person. I swear, I could see her facial features change almost. It's as if she's vanished. She's a little girl suddenly, begging for Daddy's approval.

An' you know what. She used to do this *all the time*. With Blake. Like even when he was being a real jerk, acting like the man of the house who knew everything, she'd kinda bail. It makes me mad, thinking about that, in actual fact.

The orderly snatches up the papers we took from Blake's locker. Then they try to shuffle us discreetly out of Temple, but everyone is staring. Bothers me more than I thought it might, actually, since I been hustled out of a lot of places. Probably it's because Rachel is, like, *dyin'* beside me, beet-red, and can hardly raise her eyes to see where she's goin'.

As soon as we're outside, almost before we make it off the steps, Rachel falls apart. Collapses to the lowest white stone step and sobs her heart out. I move to put my arm around her, but then she turns on me, eyes all bloodshot and angry.

'How could you?' she accuses. 'I *told* you we couldn't break in. It's a holy place! You and Emily got some wild ideas in your head, about fingerprints, and some . . . *conspiracy*.'

'I'm sorry,' I say, though I'm only half sorry. She's being kinda selfish, what with Emily in prison. I mean, God knows our good intentions, right?

'I think we should put all of this behind us,' she says, all prim. 'We have to accept that Emily has confessed. She committed the crime. We haven't done anything but get ourselves into trouble.'

'You're *kiddin'* me, right? Emily is innocent. You *know* her.'

'I thought I knew Blake. Turns out I didn't know him very well at all.'

'That's bullshit and you know it. You chose not to see the parts you didn't want to. You knew they were there. Look. Whatever the cops say. However we all may or may not have got along, if they ever get me in court, I'll put my hand on a Bible and say Rachel Nelson did not kill her husband, right?'

'I would never ask you to do that.' She says it in this weird voice. Like she doesn't want to owe me anything. That's when it really sinks in. She doesn't fuckin' trust me either.

'Wait. Wait a *minute*. Are you saying you think *I* might have killed Blake?'

'I'm just . . . processing things. This is all very new to me. The thought that Blake liked . . . certain things.'

'Oh, you think he didn't like those things? Like it was my idea? What, like I coerced him into being strangled?'

'I think you should keep calm.' She casts a glance over her shoulder. 'Let's move away from the Temple. Maybe there's a chance Bishop Young will change his mind . . .'

'Is that all you fucking care about? Your fucking *Temple recommend*?'

'You don't have to—'

'*Fuck off.* I'll swear if I like. It's about expressin' yourself, and . . . and communicatin' emotions, which is something you know *nothing* about.'

'You know, this is why Blake never respected you,' she spits. 'You have to do it all by yourself, don't you? You couldn't have asked the police for help?'

'Why Blake never *respected* me?' The worst part is, she's right. 'Yeah? Well, this is why he never took you to bed, Rachel, because of the goddamn stick up your ass.'

'And it was your *perverted* goings-on that got him killed!'

'Ex-*cuse* me?' I'm mad enough to kill her.

'Just drop it,' she hisses, getting to her feet.

'No, no I won't drop it.' I grab her arm. 'Let's get this all out in the fuckin' *open*. Or is that not how good Mormons do things? You think I went out there, and what? Tempted him into some kinky dangerous shit. It all went wrong, and . . . Well then what? You tell me!'

'I guess you coulda thrown the murder weapon in the river. Like the police said.'

'What about my clothes? Assuming I'm covered in blood?'

'My canning machine in the storehouse. Someone had used it that night. Someone who wasn't me.' Her eyes flick up at me, challenging.

'I cannot fucking *believe* you,' I hiss. 'You just got no goddamn loyalty to anyone, do you?'

'How can I trust you?' she says. 'You lie all the time. For all I know, you and Blake were in that land purchase together.'

'Sure,' I say sarcastically. 'And then I killed him, because that makes so much sense.'

'I don't know how property law works,' says Rachel. 'Maybe there was a lot of money in that casino or something. Maybe . . . Maybe Blake didn't want to build a casino and you did.'

'You've honestly thought about why I mighta killed Blake?' I'm just about done with her now.

'You haven't done the same about me?' Rachel retorts. 'You think I'm dumb enough to believe that?'

'I . . . This is unbelievable. You know what. You're on your own. You always fucking were. Fuck yourself, Rachel Rayne Nelson. And your secrets, and your bullshit. You know somethin'? You think you're so high and mighty, I'm such lowdown trash? You think you were such a *perfect* wife? Marriage is about trust, you sonofabitch. Which means you were the worst wife *ever.*'

I turn around, storm off.

'Where are you going?'

'Eat me.'

'Tina. Wait.' She looks pained. Guilt, I guess. 'You don't even have a car. At least let me drive you.'

'You think I'd get in a car with you? I know how to look after myself. I been doin' it all the while your slimy Prophet was marrying little girls.'

She flinches as though I've physically hit her. I regret saying it. But it's too late now. I'm in full mean-Tina mode. No one gets out unhurt. Just keep outta my goddamn way.

So what am I gonna do now? I'm gonna steal a car, that's what. I'm gonna steal a car and I'm gonna ride straight downtown and I'm gonna pick up where I left off buyin' meth.

And no one, absolutely no one, is gonna stop me.

84

Rachel, first wife

All I can think is I want to go home. The home Blake and I built together, out in the desert. I decide to drive to the ranch, to try and find some peace. I'll fast, I'll pray. Do my best to come to terms with it all.

Truth is, I'm ashamed of myself. For how I never stood up for Tina, even though she stood up for me. Feelings of self-loathing and pain are taking hold of me like icy fingers now. Like all the grief I've been pushing aside coming out at once.

It took my mind off things, racing around, trying to find clues and uncover things about Blake. Cutting my hair, acting like it was all happening to someone else. It was a distraction. Now the rolling loss is hitting me from all directions. The things I have to accept.

We were the only ones out on that ranch.

And I don't quite know what to do with that. Because it must mean I'm guilty of so much. So much pain I could have prevented, if I had only opened my eyes.

Tina's words are haunting me.

Come on, Rachel. You know what Blake was really like, right?

It comes to me, how badly I had treated Emily. She had always been more like a house guest than a wife. And, if I'm being very honest, a house guest who'd outstayed her welcome fairly fast.

If she ventured an opinion on one of Blake's reckless ways to improve the ranch, I always sided with my husband, let him spend the family money on his latest End of Days plan. I recall how Blake and I never took any trouble to hide our affection for one another. That must have been real hard for Emily, especially when she was having problems of a private kind.

When Tina came, it forced me to realize how bad that is to watch. How bad it feels to have someone side with your husband against you. But I never apologized to Emily. Maybe now it's too late.

I turn it over and over in my head, trying to figure how she felt. What drove her to it.

Because I'm certain now, Emily must have done it.

I force myself to picture it. I see Emily pulling the belt tight, feeling Blake's strength fade. She doesn't want to let go. If she does, she'll have to deal with what she's done.

When she finally does, the air has turned cold. The sun is setting. What was once her husband is nothing but a lump of meat.

Curious now, she steps to the front of him, her lips parted. The belt he once used on her is slack around his neck. His arms are limp, powerless.

Emily is gripped by a sudden black rage.

She grabs the gardening axe and . . . she doesn't remember the rest. Only sweat and blood.

I realize with a jolt of shock, the deep anger is mine. The desire to swing a weapon and cause pain. I can *feel* it.

Forgiveness. Forgiveness through understanding.

The images keep coming.

I see Emily's terrified face. The gory axe.

Somehow, she finds the strength to drag him by the belt, winch him to the tree. The juniper is strong yet yielding, as though complicit.

She would go to the storehouse now, I think, to wash the bloodstained clothes. Or was that me, turning the screws on the Survive Well lid, setting it to boil?

I pull the car to a stop. That's when I see, I haven't driven to the ranch.

Ahead of me in the desert scrub are two huge gates, and a wire fence stretching on and out as far as the eye can see. It's a big property.

A notice is pasted to the ironwork.

NO TRESPASSERS
Keep Out. Dangerous Infrastructure.
Utah Department of Public Health.

I've never seen this sign before. I've never seen the main gates from this angle before. But even so, this place is as familiar as breathing.

I've driven right to the old Homestead.

85

Rayne Ambrosine, aged fifteen

I'm in so much pain, I'm sick with it. I vomit into a metal bowl by my bed.

Aunt Meg puts cold cloths on my forehead, but I'm burning up so bad she has to switch them almost as soon as she's smoothed them out.

Her demeanor has changed somewhat. She is concerned. I hazily think this means I am dying. I hear voices. A man's voice, but can't make out the words.

'She needs a blood transfusion,' Aunt Meg is saying.

More muttering.

'I've given her antibiotics. Strongest we have.' There's a little steel in Aunt Meg's voice now. 'She needs proper treatment,' she says. 'More than I can give her here.'

'Take a mind of your tone.' The man's voice is louder now. 'And remember who you are speaking to. Go pray for humility, please, Meg.'

Through the pain, my eyes land on Aunt Meg's face. She walks away grim-faced.

I feel warm hands touch my burning chest and try to flinch back.

'I am laying on hands,' says a man's monotone voice. 'I humbly beseech you, Lord Jesus Christ. Heal this woman if you think her worthy. Bring her back to our fold.'

I recognize the voice now. It's the Prophet. If he's taken time to try and heal me, I know I should be grateful. But all I can think is I need the hands to stop. They're burning me. I try and tune out the heat.

Somewhere between the unbearable warmth and the monotone blessing, the Prophet vanishes away.

Through my slitted eyes, I see a woman arriving at the clinic door. One of the older ones, sagging under the stress of all the babies they'd produced. Hard-faced with a ground-in tiredness; dark circles etched on dark circles. Her dress is frayed at the ankle-length hem, and her lace-up boots are held together with duct tape.

There is a baby in her arms, wrapped in a dirty-looking blanket, but it isn't moving right, and making deep wheezing noises. Like it's struggling for air. A blueish-colored leg dangles free.

'It's like the other one,' she is telling Aunt Meg. 'You helped me before.' She wipes her nose with the back of her hand, and suddenly her face turns very red. 'Because I *can't*,' she says. 'I just *can't*. We got a new wife last week, and there are twenty children in that room, Meg. Half of those are in diapers. The storehouse is empty most days, and I'm just feedin' 'em nothing but rice when I can. The small ones are too hungry to sleep, with this one I'm awake all night anyhow . . .' She glances to the unmoving child in her arms.

'This child is a blessing,' says Aunt Meg. 'You know that. A test of your fortitude.' Her eye twitches in the corner.

The baby starts choking.

'Shh, shh,' says the woman. She tilts the bundle and issues a volley of sharp pats to the baby's back. The choking stops, replaced by a weedy wailing.

Aunt Meg's expression is stony, a faraway look in her eyes.

She nods, 'Give her to me,' and moves to take the baby.

'She needs specialist equipment,' the woman begins babbling as the baby is lifted from her. 'Something to keep her lungs clear. A machine, or something. You have that here?'

'She'll be taken care of,' says Aunt Meg.

'And she doesn't like cornmeal grits,' the woman wipes her eyes. 'Spits 'em straight up. Only takes the oat kind.' She kisses the baby's face as Aunt Meg adjusts her stance to bear the weight.

They look at each other then, and they are both so sad it is unbearable. The mother looks away first.

'Wait there,' Aunt Meg tells her.

She walks across to the door that led to the basement and disappears through it. When she comes back, she isn't holding the baby. Instead she clutches a package of cookies.

'Here,' she lowers her voice. 'These are from the Prophet's groceries. Don't tell anyone I gave them to you.'

The woman nods, wiping tears. She looks rapturously at the cookies, tucks them inside her dress.

'Thank you,' she says, her voice light with relief. 'I can't tell you, Meg . . .' she touches the contraband cookies. A bell sounds.

'You'd better go,' says Aunt Meg, her voice hard. 'Don't want to miss the mid-morning prayer.'

She turns to the wider room, claps her hands.

'Get up, girls,' she says shrilly. 'You of all people need to ask God's forgiveness.'

86

Tina, sister-wife

I've left Temple Square with its wide green spaces long behind me now. Tell the truth, I'm lost, though I can see how Salt Lake City is like a square box crossed over with straight lines for roads. I'm tryin' to stay angry at Rachel, but it's slippin' away from me, and now the other stuff is crashing in.

Idiot, Tina. You fucking idiot.

The rehab lady always told us, first rule of rehab, don't fall in love. When you finish the program, you're *suggestable*, see. Susceptible, to the first smooth-talkin' son-of-a-gun who comes along. You've turned your whole life around and it's tempting to keep going. And silly ol' me, I fell head over heels before I even *left* rehab. As my dear old mom woulda said, that is just classic Tina. Someone tells you 'no' and you've done it before they even finish talkin'.

I recognize a storefront, and I'm fairly certain now I can only be a block or so from Rio Grande. I stick my hand in my purse, like I always used to back in Vegas, turning the dollar bills, re-assuring myself. I've got maybe thirty bucks in bills. Enough.

I've reached Rio Grande now, and right away my eyes light on a little huddle of people who I just know will help me out. I start turning the bills again, not long now.

All of a sudden, a young man in a dark suit steps right out in front of me. Before I can yell or react, he beams this wide smile.

''Scuse me, Ma'am, may I have a minute of your time to talk about the word of Jesus?'

I want to laugh. If it isn't a goddamn missionary, all neat in his black jacket and tie.

'Um, are you OK, Ma'am?' He's staring at me, real concerned, like he genuinely gives a shit.

'Yeah.' I fight back the tears which rush up. 'Um, I'm already a member of the Church,' I add, trying for a smile. 'You're too late.'

He nods in a serious way. 'Do you need a ride?' he asks. 'I don't know if you're aware, but this is a dangerous part of town to be walking alone in, for a lady.'

My eyes glide over to the little pack of dealers, hunched on the curb fifty feet away. Blake was always telling me about revelations. Signs from God. That was how he won me over. He was so goddamn sure we were meant to be together. God had told him. I shake my head a little, smiling.

'Sure,' I say. 'A ride would be good. Could you take me someplace where I could rent a car?'

I'm not actually sure how I might go about that, since I've got a burned-out credit card and zero ID, but if God is really giving me a message, I figure it's time to try him out.

If you're really tryin' to save me from myself, then get me a car, and I'll drive on home and apologize to Rachel.

The missionary shakes his head slowly.

Ha! Guess meth beats miracles.

'You won't get a good rate if you rent on the day,' he says, shaking his head again. 'Tell you what,' he adds, the smile coming back. 'Why don't you borrow my car?'

'Um. What?' I look at him, like *are you shitting me?*

He puts a hand on my shoulder, and somehow I don't mind.

'You're a member of the Church,' he says, 'and you look real upset, if you don't mind my saying, and you need a car. God moves in mysterious ways. Maybe he put me here to help you. In any case, Ma'am, so long as you don't mind driving a beat-up ride, you can borrow my car. I'm staying at a mission house nearby, I don't need it right now.'

'Thanks,' I tell him. 'But I can't borrow your car.'

'Why don't you see it like you're doing me a favor?' he insists, all warm smiles. 'I've not got any conversions yet. Not in four months. At least let me do a good deed for the day. We're all family in the Church of Latter-day Saints. Just bring it back in one piece on Monday.'

I swallow hard, because not even I can stoop to doin' drugs in this nice young man's car. If I accept his offer, I stay clean.

I give him a long look. 'Do you believe that God sends angels to intervene, just when a person is at their lowest?' I glance longingly at the dealers.

'Yes, Ma'am, I do. That's why I work this district.' He holds out his keys. 'My car is over there.'

I roll my eyes up to the heavens and shake my head. *You motherfucker.*

87

Emily, sister-wife

'I appreciate you're of a mind to go before a firing squad,' says Detective Carlson as we sit at a plastic table in the visitor's room. 'But I've got some bad news on that score. Or maybe some good news, depending on how you see it.'

He nods to Brewer, who opens a laptop, turning it so I can see. 'Turns out Kirker's Diner *does* have security cameras,' she says, 'and pretty good coverage at that. Took us a while, but we found your husband there with his mysterious lady friend.'

'Who was it?' I'm leaning forward in anticipation.

Brewer checks the screen, frowns, then fast-forwards. Two people walk really fast to a table and sit. Brewer hits the play button.

'Did Blake make a habit of meeting his mom for lunch?' asks Brewer.

'Uh-huh,' I nod. 'Every second Tuesday. They met at the pancake house on the road into Tucknott. Mrs Nelson liked the fresh fruit stack.'

'Looks like this Tuesday, they made an exception,' she says.

It's only then I make out the people on the laptop. One of them is obviously Blake. Even in the black and white, you can tell he has red hair. The other has very poufy blond hair, styled high.

It's Adelaide Nelson. My heart sinks.

'Guess he took her to Kirker's,' I say dejectedly. 'One of the busybodies from the ward must have seen them from a distance. Blake and a blond lady. Took two and two and made five.'

If it wasn't all so serious, I'd laugh. The Mormon community is so gossipy and bored, this dumb rumor ran halfway around town, that Blake was having some kind of affair. Maybe Blake even got killed because of it. When the truth was it couldn't have been more innocent.

I try to work out what it means. Tina and Rachel have been chasing wild geese, a mysterious blond, who doesn't exist.

'I'm sorry,' says Detective Carlson. 'Really I am. You girls had us going there. Guess I'm a sucker for a tall story, just like anyone else. But it's like I've been tryin' to tell Tina all along. There is no big mystery here. No secret meeting, no conspiracy.'

I look closer. You can make out Mrs Nelson's made-up face, poking at something on her plate. She's probably mad about missing her favorite waffles. Blake always was a momma's boy, looking for her approval. Guess he never got it.

'If they met up out of town,' I say, 'maybe they didn't want to be overheard.'

'I agree,' says Brewer. 'See there? That looks to me like land documents. I'm guessing Blake was trying to convince mom to ask dad to loan him the deposit for the Homestead. Didn't want anyone who might snitch back to Mr Nelson listening in.'

I look closer, and she's right. Blake has a mess of official-looking papers in front of him. Mrs Nelson has her Book of Mormon, and has it open, like she's begging him to listen to the word of God.

'We also looked into Blake's GPS,' says Carlson. 'Tina had a notion someone coulda used it to track his car,' he adds, seeing my blank expression. 'No one hacked it, and your husband barely even used it. Guess he knew all his work journeys by heart.'

I'm feeling it all slide away. All the intrigue, the investigation. This is real life after all.

Man oh man.

'However,' Carlson leans back a little on his chair. 'We got number-plate recognition all over the state. So we were able to ascertain that Rachel Nelson drove out toward the Homestead about a half-hour ago. Shortly after breaking into a lawyer's office in Vegas, and Blake's locker in the Holy Temple. We've sent cops over to bring her in within the hour.'

An icy feeling edges around my brain.

'My guess is Rachel has been trying to cover up evidence, which fits just fine with me, being as forensics have just confirmed your innocence.'

'*What?*'

'Yup. We got some clever fellas who done some math with your height and the way the victim was hung on that tree. Turns out you couldn't possibly have murdered your husband. So . . . pending a charge of wasting police time and obstruction of justice, you're free to go.'

'No, wait.' I close my eyes. 'You've got it wrong,' I tell him.

'Save it.'

'Just . . . Can I use your computer?' I ask Brewer. 'I need to show you something.'

She looks sorta weary.

'Just, hear me out,' I say. 'If this Aunt Meg did things in that clinic, she could be trying to cover it up, right? I mean, she could be a suspect, even if she wasn't the person who met with Blake for lunch.'

'She could have a motive,' agrees Brewer, glancing at Carlson. 'Problem with your theory is the Prophet's wives all vanished. Just faded away.'

'Uh-uh,' I shake my head. 'Aunt Meg has a blog. I saw it, right before my internet time ran out.'

Carlson and her look at one another. He makes a little head movement. Brewer hesitates, sighs deeply, then turns the laptop toward me.

'Better make it quick.' Carlson checks his watch. 'Won't be long before they bring in Rachel.'

88

Rachel, first wife

The gates are huge – longer than I even remember. White iron posts, swelling in an arc that I guess was someone's idea of homely. Marred only by the spiked tops and stout black sign declaring: NO TRESPASSERS.

I find myself wondering where the gates were purchased. An image of my father, visiting some Vegas store for outsized iron-mongery, swims into my mind.

I raise my hand to the iron posts. The peeling paint is punctuated by shreds of bleached adhesive tape. It looks as though, at one time, they were stuck all over with papers.

I remember, now, the night I left, the sound of them fluttering in the breeze. I had thought them demons – the last warning before I ventured out into hell.

I notice a slip of paper remains and I tear it free. It's so old as to be almost illegible. But I can make out from the darker ink, it's been posted by Salt Lake City Building Services.

From what I can see, it's part of a court order; something about building-safety notices that haven't been submitted.

I guess the Homestead were issued a bunch of these, and ignored 'em.

I put one foot halfway up the iron gates, at the side, where the arc swoops low enough to climb over. Swinging my leg carefully over the spiked tops, I drop back inside. The exact opposite of what I did all those years ago.

The moment my feet hit the sandy earth, the strangest feeling comes over me. As though I've come home. The ghosts of my past are folding me in their arms.

I'm standing on a wide stony road. Directly ahead of me is the guard tower. I had forgotten the guard tower.

It's a squat hexagonal-shaped building, only two stories high, fifty yards or so from the main gate. The upper floor is encircled in panes of glass. The lower part is concrete, with a battered old door. As children, we used to play games, running around it.

Three times anticlockwise and the devil's got ya back!

It never occurred to us to mind that men with rifles stood twenty feet above us. We knew they were there to protect us. To make sure no unrighteous came to tear up our way of life.

There's a searchlight attached to the top. I recall it sweeping at night.

Stay in your bed, Rayne. Don't make a sound!

I approach the watchtower door and try the handle. It opens, releasing a smell of dry dust. I move inside. There's nothing much on the ground floor. A ladder leads up to the sentry posts above. With everything on one level, and Utah's open desert for miles around, I guess there was no need for a tall lookout.

I hoist myself up onto the second story. At one time, it had been lined by windows, but almost all are broken. The floor crunches with ground glass as I walk.

There's a tatty homespun pamphlet at my feet. I pick it up. Stroke dust from the cover.

A large simple font announces it to be *Little Helping Hands Coloring Book.*

This is the kind of self-bound thing we read as children. I never saw a published paperback until I left home. The dog-eared pages are bound with a flimsy plastic spiral. I remember the machine that popped holes for this, in the printing room. My mother operated it, with some of the other wives.

I turn the first page. A rush of memories assails me as I leaf through pictures of smiling young girls, their prairie-dress sleeves rolled up as they help with washing dishes and collecting chicken eggs. Below the images are instructions. 'Keep sweet'. 'Be quick to obey'.

I close it back up and return my attention to my surroundings.

From here, I can see the view over the whole compound. The decaying rooftops look unfamiliar. It's been so long since I was here, my perspective has adjusted to the outside world. The scatter of outsized gingery-wood cabins better resembles a woodland holiday camp than a residential area. They are too large, too far apart, too devoid of variety. As though someone has put a giant mirror right along the center, reflecting everything back on itself.

For all the appearance of space, the wide-open roads and generous buildings are deceptive. Those large internal rooms were packed solid, ringing with the hum of young life and wrung-out mothers. Hungry too, by the end, existing on whatever was left from the community storehouse after the Prophet and his bishops had their pick.

I identify what could have been our family's main living quarters. We shared it with thirty other mothers and their children. Beyond the clutch of family residences, a thick wall made from extra-white cement divides the regular residences from the Prophet's enormous log-cabin house on the far side.

It looks alien, like a place I've never been. I suppose I had been hoping for some sudden epiphany. Instead I feel like an outsider, in a strange place. This makes me feel the loneliest I've ever felt in all my life.

There are silos, dotted all around. I squint into the distance, attempting to match what I remember from my bedroom window. Was I nearer, or further, from the grain storage?

Our tall self-built Temple is right in the middle, a vision in snowy concrete. It is vast – a great turreted castle, with a huge boundary wall topped with white railings, which stretches around the perimeter. Streets radiate out from it in a grid system.

I realize the Homestead layout is based on Salt Lake City. For some reason this feels like another betrayal. Like the adults copied someplace else – someplace better – and never told us.

At the corner of my eye, something is flashing, red, white and blue, out of keeping with the sea of beige and brown buildings and road. When I turn my eyes to the distraction, I see police cars on the highway in the distance.

They're so far away, they look like little blinking beetles in the distance. Even so, the road they're on only leads to one place. In twenty minutes or so, they'll pull up at the Homestead.

Guess they found me.

If I'm really going to do this, go back there, I'm running out of time.

I descend from the guard tower and make my way on foot along the wide dusty road. I look down, remembering how my boots would kick up the stones.

The moment the houses come in plain sight, it's like my feet have a mind of their own. They know where to go.

As I draw toward the first two-story family cabin, I begin noticing details I hadn't realized I still remember. Posts to tether horses, entrances labeled 'husband-only', a water hydrant, flaking to rust. I remember the day this was painted white, along with all the other hydrants and outdoor faucets.

The roads look even broader now there are no cars on them. An occasional upended school desk or abandoned chair are littered on the main track. Tears begin rolling down my face. I wipe them with the back of my hand, but they won't stop. There's no way back now. I'm going to the red graveyard.

89

Tina, sister–wife

After all that time, scared to be alone, I drove back out to the ranch.

Guess God spoke to me after all. Maybe I was hopin' to patch things up with Rachel, but her car's not here.

I pull up, turn off the engine and climb out to the dusty crunch of desert beneath my feet. Not quite sand, but soil enough to confuse a few optimistic cattle farmers before they up and quit. Catch a burning handful and it'll pour right through your fingers, leaving a dirt mark that won't brush off.

I shield my eyes from the sun.

Home sweet home.

Heaped about in no clear order are the agricultural buildings of the old ranch. The corrugated-iron cow shed that Blake used as a workshop. Our big leaky-roofed barn where Rachel canned food. A bunch of mechanical parts are strewn around the ground, along with the weird lifeguard tower Blake rescued from someplace.

Toward the back is the old wooden farmhouse, which at a distance looks a lot like a first-grader's drawing. A triangle on a square, with two windows, a central door, and straight sides sitting right on the dirt – no yard or fence, only a smatter of dollar-bill-color shrubs fighting for a hold.

When you get closer, you see the mix of old and new planks on the front, and the dark patches of roof tile where Blake replaced shingle. Speared through the center is a big brick chimney, as though someone started with high hopes and ran out of good material. A mishmash, but it worked. A little like us, I guess. For a while.

I walk to the front door, which was salvaged from the inside of an old city townhouse – a four-paneled internal door with a round handle that was never designed to lock.

The desert-dust smell hits my nose as I walk inside. That dust blows in everywhere.

Since there's been no one to wipe and sweep, there's already a fine layer on the creaky floor, our little round dining table, and scattered over the big stone hearth. The small battered sofa and Rachel's crochet rug seem to have repelled it somehow, like they know the trick of wild living.

Now I'm back all alone, I'm sorta regretting not goin' downtown. Like someone has left me raw and exposed. I gotta lot of ways of not thinking about things. I think I was sorta expecting to return to the ranch of my memory. Us three girls, circling about the place like moons orbiting a sun, tryin' not to bump each other. Getting' mad with one another. Fucked up for sure, but better than havin' no one. With no one to be frustrated with, there's nothing to disguise all the thoughts in my head.

Truth is, I swapped out drugs for an addiction to something else. Love. Religion. I never really changed what was underneath.

Too painful, right? It's difficult to explain to a regular person, but growing up with a mom who couldn't care less about you . . . It's not actually *that* bad – because to you at least, it's normal.

The problem, the hard part, is *you*. What you become because of it.

It makes you different to other people, and when they don't like you for that fact, well, that's real tough.

That was always the issue with me and Rachel, I think, as I take in the familiar old ranch. That mix of hardness and neediness. Pull me close, push me away. Rachel has it. Emily too. We're like an old T-shirt I saw once. *Same same but different.*

I'm letting all these thoughts pool in my brain, when my stomach growls at me.

I guess if I'm gonna be here alone overnight, I'd better fix my own food. It occurs to me this is the first time I've done that here. I barely know where anything is. I suddenly feel real grateful toward Rachel. It musta been hard work, doing all the shopping and cooking. Growing vegetables, canning things when they were ready. Maybe I didn't like what she put on the table, but I guess I appreciated not having to think about it all.

I start poking around the tiny kitchen. More like a kitchenette really. The kinda thing I remember from my days sleeping in crack dens, though much cleaner, naturally.

There's a propane tank, single-ring burner, a battered old pan. That's about it, besides a little wheeled table, about the size of my forearm, for all the cutting and prepping. I've seen it all before. But I never really *saw* it, in relation to how the hell you get a meal together.

Guess that explains why Rachel wasn't so creative. Now I'm faced with the apparatus, I actually think Rachel was somethin' of a genius in the kitchen.

There's a few packages of noodles and cans of soup in the single cupboard, but I can't face the half-hour it will take to fetch and boil water.

I head for the pantry. Most likely there's something preserved I can spoon right out of the jar. Rachel wouldn't approve, of course. She'd at least want it laid out on one of her plastic plates that showed a view of Salt Lake City Temple at different parts of the day. Rachel always chose dawn. Crazy Emily always pretended to forget, and picked that plate, if Rachel was late to the table with a hot dish. One time, they had this tight-lipped tug-of-war that was so hilarious, but I could see from Blake's face I shouldn't laugh.

Was it you, Rachel? Did you find him jerking off at his fishing spot? Was Emily getting picked that night the final straw? Did you find the sexy underwear he bought me?

I have this image I can't shake, of her swinging a weapon, with this ice-cold look on her face. Slamming it repeatedly between his legs.

It's the kind of thing me and the Vegas block girls would joke about doin' to the Johns who beat on us. Not so much joke, in actual fact. More like fantasy.

I think back to my wedding night. How when I saw Blake without his clothes on, there were some real bad scars that he'd never mentioned, right around his groin. Blake saw me staring. Said he'd had surgery for an STD.

'A youthful indiscretion on my Mexican mission. Don't make a big deal of it.'

Obviously, I was shocked. With all the guys I'd been with, I'd never heard of an STD gettin' so bad you needed *surgery*. I pictured the teenaged Blake, dyin' of shame, prayin' for God to miraculously cure him, until things got so bad he was hospitalized.

When I asked him if it meant he couldn't have kids, Blake had this choked-up expression.

'I thought it was *me* you loved,' he said. 'I didn't realize you saw me as nothing more than a baby-maker. I thought you were different.'

I had looked down at my low-rent honeymoon underwear.

Time to face facts, Tina, said a mean voice in my head. *You're only good for one thing. You want this marriage to work, you'd better deliver.*

'Listen, baby,' I put on a false smile. 'Forget all that. Lie back, c'mon. I'll do you a little dance.'

Blake had huddled back on the bed, slightly pacified. I turned away, allowing him full view of my butt in the thong panties.

'Come over here,' he said, breathing hard. 'How did I get so lucky?' he added. 'My sexy new wife.' He put his arms around me, and kissed me. 'Sit on top of me,' he whispered, fiddling with my panties. 'No, not like that. Turn around.'

That was my wedding night. And when I raised the topic of Blake's scars with Rachel a few days later, she went real quiet, like I'd said somethin' inappropriate. That was when I first realized how much I hated Rachel. She could deny anything if it made her world more comfortable, and screw anyone who got hurt along the way. I was so mad at her for covering it up, it never occurred to me till later that Blake covered it up too.

90

Rachel, first wife

The bizarreness of the deserted Homestead takes my breath away. Every road, every corner, is a memory; forgotten and now found again. The huge doors of the community storehouse stand open. Its vast hangar-like interior is entirely stripped of provisions, empty shelves running into the distance like train tracks.

Our big vegetable patches are entirely given over to desert. The stable blocks no longer hold horses, or even a lingering smell of them. Mildew, dust and neglect is all-pervading.

I pass by the great white outdoor amphitheater, still only half-finished, crumbling construction debris scattered around. Then toward where the ground begins changing color, deepening from tan to yellow. Until up ahead, in the middle distance, is a large outhouse-type building with corrugated-steel walls.

The clinic.

It takes me a good five minutes to hike across the scrubland. The dirt path I remember has long since returned to desert. Thorns and burrs drag at my calves as I pick over the undergrowth. This part always was wild, even before it was abandoned. Remote enough from the main dwellings for night animals to prowl.

Gradually the clinic nears and the ground beneath starts to change. This outer-limits part of the compound is on an old riverbed. Scree rocks are beneath my feet. The scatter of cinder-toffee boulders and amber-dusted sand is burned into my memories.

Desert scrub is more prevalent now. Pale yellow-green clumps climb the sides of the larger boulders. But vegetation hasn't fully grown over what comes next. Little red-sand mounds. Lots of them, only partially hidden under the scrubby grass, within fifty feet of the clinic.

Us kids never understood why we weren't allowed to come here. Now I see it. What it is.

The red graveyard.

Little burial mounds. Maybe thirty. I've stepped on one without even noticing.

This is why they never found it. To an outsider it looks like nothing at all. It's overgrown, and scratchy thorns and pale grasses hide the little stones almost completely. You'd only notice it if you knew exactly where to look.

Toward the center are the oldest graves. These have something approaching headstones. Handmade tablets, fired in the local kiln. At first, you see one, two, then you realize there are tens of them stretching all around.

My eyes drift to the clinic on the horizon.

I'm remembering.

It's dark. I heave myself out of bed and stagger toward the basement door. I'm stumbling, slipping on my own blood and fluids. I crash into a hospital trolley and send several pieces of shiny metal equipment crashing to the floor.

I wait, hunched over a little, praying no one has heard. My eyes fall on the nearest white bed. A girl's eyes glint in the moonlight. She's seen me. Very slowly, she shakes her head, like she won't tell.

A spasm of pain encircles my belly. I grit my teeth, waiting for it to pass. Then turn the handle to the basement. Getting down the stairs is the hardest part. Every step is agony. I grip the banister, praying for strength. At the bottom is a harshly lit room, with a bad smell. Like someone had poured bleach everywhere, but it didn't cover up something worse, glowering underneath. Cool air.

It's a morgue.

There's a metal table, and on it is a line of coffins. Five or so. Small. *Laid out just so in a neat line. At a right angle to them is a metal gurney holding a bunch of medical tools. Birthing things. Forceps, suction cups.*

A bloody pillow.

I'm at the edge of the cemetery now. Newer graves are announced by the kind of metal markers you get with seedling packets. Names have been written with a fingertip before firing. Some just have dates, or tiny handprints, pushed into the clay. Where a gardener might write 'sweet pea', or 'sugar beet', *Ambrosine girl, stillborn* or *Baby boy, 2 months old* is scrawled in the half-formed script of the unschooled.

Babies don't die like this, out in the real world. Not this many, this quickly. Plenty a folk out there might never go to a baby's graveside. It was only when I joined the real world I realized, it's not normal to die young in America.

Inbreeding, I guess. My eyes lift back to the clinic.

Inbreeding and maybe a little help.

I'm at the far edge now, past the burial mounds. There is a tree here. As I reach it, tears fill my eyes. I drop to my haunches, like I used to do as a little girl, desert dust on my prairie-dress hem.

This was where I buried her. Safe and sound, so no one might know what I'd done.

I reach out and put my hand on her grave.

91

Rachel, first wife

I'm outside The Big House.

The sun is setting as I take in the Prophet's enormous residence, a rambling compound of cabins, communal areas and secret passages snaking out in every direction he didn't want people to see.

The front is mazed by wooden steps and balconies, which allow access to numbered family rooms. At the end, it wasn't uncommon to see whole families cleared from their privileged positions in the Prophet's house, and someone else reallocated their premises.

I walk through the door, where a wide hallway is floored in white marble. Only it's all covered in rubble and loose dirt.

It's then I see the statue. Smooth white stone. My father, immortalized in rock. He stands on a high plinth. I'd hoped I was doing the right thing, visiting him in prison. Telling him his followers were starving and he needed to change his edicts. But he always did know how to win. Right when I thought I might have been getting through to him, he went all quiet and said in that singsong melodic voice: 'What if they find that graveyard, Rayne?'

I had frozen in shock. I didn't even think he remembered. I'd forgotten how he did that. Remembered small details to punish you.

For a long moment, I look at his placid face carved in stone. Someone has tried to give him a benevolent expression, but it's not come off right. It takes some effort to drag my eyes away.

Behind the likeness is a white-carpeted staircase, winding upwards.

I follow it up, reaching the grand chapel prayer room at the top, where we were sometimes allowed to pray. It's high-ceilinged, white and gold, in approximation of the beauty of Salt Lake City Temple. Long wooden benches are in disarray; toppled on their backs, moved out of line. This room used to house several hundred people at a time, crammed in, listening to the Prophet's hypnotic monotone for hours on end.

Someone has covered over the entire back wall with brown paper. The kind you wrap old parcels in. I move toward it, re-membering. There are heavenly murals underneath. They were papered over for some community sin. I can see a corner of green fields peeking out.

I walk over, grab the brown paper and rip it. Beneath, the mural spans the whole wall – celestial hills, crystal-clear babbling streams, beaming sunshine, and a benevolent Jesus beckoning. *Come with me. There's no pain here.*

I know, rather than remember, that this is a secret panel. It leads to the celestial bedchamber. One of several ways in.

White beds, white carpet.

Behind this heavenly image, the Prophet conducted lengthy sessions with his underage brides.

I reach out a hand to touch Jesus's smiling face. Just as my fingers connect, I hear a noise from behind the mural. Like someone is banging something in the bedchamber beyond. I picture Aunt Meg, surgical tongs in hand. Then her face morphs to Melissa's and she's lying in a grave, holding a blue shoebox.

My heartbeat picks up. Jesus's sweet smiling face seems to be speaking to me.

Don't be afraid. Nothing in that room can harm you.

My finger moves down all by itself and finds the hole I remember. The hidden hole that makes the handle to the secret door.

The banging starts up again. Loud. Angry. Disjointed.

Bang, bang, bang.

I take a breath. *Brave like Jesus.*

I crook my finger and pull. A portion of the mural peels away. Behind it, a large room is revealed. My throat tightens at the familiar sight.

The walls are wood-paneled and the white carpet is yellowed with age.

It's empty. No one here. My eyes switch to the far window. It's partially broken. Someone has tried to seal it with plastic sheeting and duct tape. As I watch, the wind catches, rippling through the plastic and slamming it back. *Bang bang bang.*

Besides the throws of the sheeting, the room is silent and deserted. Nothing here but memories.

I allow myself to absorb more details now. The bed is gone. Papers are scattered all over the mildewing carpet.

There's another entrance on the far side. At one time it was concealed behind wood paneling, but all is smashed apart and exposed now. This is the way I first entered the room. It connects to a maze of secret passages, one of which arrives at the clinic basement.

In a corner is a broken-open safe, which sits in a sea of type-written documents. I pick a few pages up. Lists of names, dates. None of them make a great deal of sense. Likely they've already been picked over for evidence. The marriage records.

I let the papers flutter to the floor.

Then I notice something on the wall. A bronze plaque, which wasn't there when I was hiding in this room. I walk toward it. The plate commemorates some of the Prophet's wives and children who died in a flash flood.

My fingers trace the names. Four women and two kids were swept away in their car, a little after the Prophet was jailed. No one quite knew how they should be commemorated, so I guess this was a temporary measure. When the Prophet was first imprisoned, it was generally accepted that God would strike down the prison walls fairly soon.

I read the names of the deceased on the plaque, once, then twice. My eyes stick on one name.

Margaret 'Aunt Meg' Ambrosine, first wife to the Prophet.

I can't quite believe it.

Aunt Meg died, almost eight years ago.

92

Emily, sister-wife

I can see by Carlson's expression that he wants me to leave it all alone now. Like he was hoping showing me Kirker's Diner tape would mean I started suspecting Rachel, or maybe even Tina.

I start pushing the keys, and after a moment Carlson asks if I'd rather tell him, and he'll type for me, so we do it that way.

The page I found before flashes up. *A mother's truth*. Aunt Meg's blog.

'There,' I point, after the title rolls up. 'Click that one.'

Carlson does. For a few minutes we both sit there looking at it

It's a badly written page about how Aunt Meg categorically *did not* murder sinners who left the Homestead. Specifically, fifty or so escapees who former Homestead-folk accuse Aunt Meg of 'vanishing'. She also refutes any claims of abuse, or the jurisdiction of any court to convict her husband, since he is a 'living saint on earth'.

The next page is full of this creepy stuff. Like basically saying everyone is a liar, except Aunt Meg and the big-shot men who ran the Homestead.

Carlson clicks on a link marked 'evidence'.

There are pages and pages of typed-out scripture, basically saying the Bible agrees with thirteen-year-old girls being married. Aunt Meg also has this whole section dedicated to crappy pictures of signatures. These are from testimonies Aunt Meg has written out, in loopy writing, worse even than mine, saying the so-called victims of abuse at the Homestead are liars. At the bottom, she has the victim's own *parents* sign it as 'nothing but God's truth'. Then she posts it up.

I kind of stand up when I see that. Like I want to tip the computer screen over. Carlson is sitting, all jaw clenched, fists balled.

'Makes you want to kill someone, don't it?' he says, lifting his eyes to me. 'Sure are some evil people in the world.' He breathes out a sigh. 'Sure you want to carry on looking?'

I make myself sit. I need to do this, for Rachel.

Cagney wouldn't let her emotions get the best of her.

'What about that one?' I point to a link marked 'Clearing my name'.

A bunch of text loads up and Carlson sorta whistles under his breath.

Aunt Meg has listed other things she's been accused of and reasons why she is innocent. In particular, she refers to an accusation by a 'son of perdition' named Jacob Walt.

'What's a son of perdition?' I ask Carlson.

His lips get even thinner. 'It's what they call the young boys who were brave enough to leave,' he says. 'Basically means you're worse than even us gentiles, 'cause you knew the truth and chose to reject it. You're goin' to out-and-out hell. Great many of 'em turn to drugs. Or the construction trade. Not much else they can do. You know those boys got put out to work, aged twelve, for their so-called Prophet? The Homestead undercut every other construction company in the area, 'cause you can't compete with workers who get paid in God's glory, right?'

I read some more. Jacob Walt apparently spoke to a local

newspaper, back when the cult was raided. Aunt Meg has pulled his quote directly.

'A lot of babies born on the Homestead have deformities, meaning they won't survive the year,' Jacob has told a journalist. 'On account of the close relations there. It's more or less normal for a baby to have a cleft palate or a club foot or heart problem, or breathing difficulties. Parents with a great many children hand the ones who aren't gonna make it over to Aunt Meg to take care of. And when I say take care of, I mean *take care of*. As in the baby cemetery got a lot bigger.'

I stab a finger at the screen. Carlson is sitting totally motionless, like he can't quite believe it, reading and re-reading, his lips moving.

'Says right there,' I say, 'if the families couldn't cope, they took the babies that weren't born right to this Aunt Meg person.' I put my fingers into quotes, like I've seen him do. 'To *take care* of them.'

I feel outright nauseous. The idea of those tiny children, struggling to breathe.

'Well,' says Carlson finally, 'I guess that would explain the list of missing names with special baptisms.'

'This would make her a murderer, wouldn't it?' I say. 'What if Blake found something out? I mean, maybe Rachel told him, or spoke in her sleep or something? What if he went out there and took a look around? Discovered a secret cemetery full of baby headstones, and reached a conclusion on his own?'

Carlson nods, then clicks on a few more links. Then he silently taps on the top of the screen.

'Check the date of the last blog post,' he says.

Shoot.

The last entry was eight years ago. Aunt Meg Ambrosine hasn't been active online in almost a decade.

I'm suddenly really tired. Like all my hopes just got snuffed out at once.

'Satisfied?' asks Carlson. 'It's a dead end.'

'What if . . . What if Aunt Meg is hiding out somewhere?' I say.

Carlson just shakes his head. 'I told you already, she straight vanished. We checked her out. She's not at Waynard's Creek. Hasn't visited her "Prophet" husband in years. My guess is she skipped state. Holed up in one of the safe houses and tried to start a regular life. Maybe she did those things they accused her of, maybe she didn't. But she hasn't been in Utah this side of eight years, I can tell you that.'

I process this. 'So you're just gonna send me home?' I swallow.

'We'll be charging you for obstruction of justice, most like, but that doesn't come with a necessity to detain. So yeah, we got an officer who can drive you back in the morning. Unless there's someone who can pick you up now?'

I need to get back, before they question Rachel. I need to get to the ranch.

'Tina . . .' I begin.

He shakes his head. 'Tried her already. Phone's off. Tina's gone dark. We'll keep calling, but . . .'

I process this. Guess Tina didn't manage to stay clean after all.

An idea occurs to me. Someone to give me a ride. Problem is, I really, *really* don't want to call her. I take a breath. Time to swallow my pride.

'How about Blake's mom?' I ask. 'Could you try her?'

93

Rachel, first wife

I sit down. Just right down on the musty-smelling carpet. I can hardly bear it.

Aunt Meg died in that flood? She's dead? All this time, I pictured her as alive. Meeting with Blake. Telling him my secrets. I can't quite get straight in my mind what it all means.

One thing I do know for sure – all those little graves. The basement morgue.

Aunt Meg *got away* with it.

No, Rachel, I tell myself. *She's in hell.*

Hell isn't enough. She was the Prophet's favorite. Lived in luxury whilst the rest of us half-starved.

And what about those children denied proper treatment? How many disabled babies went into that basement and came out in shoeboxes? I think of all those women, sagging under the weight of their huge households, desperate.

A secret cemetery. Little mounds. You helped me before.

The children not born right. Even if they go to heaven, how does that make up for the torment she caused them in life? Despair is so overwhelming, I feel like my heart is going to cave in. All those innocent souls put on earth, to experience nothing but suffering and an early grave.

It's happening right now. Even as I sit here, someone, somewhere is hurting a child.

What kind of God could allow that?

I can't stop thinking this is all Tina's fault. She's the one who made me remember. She's the one who caused me all this pain.

I get up, my legs shaking. It's the darnedest thing. I'm seeing, but I'm not seeing. All I can think is I need to get back out into that grand hallway. I need to get to the statue of the Prophet.

I go down the stairs, into the marble lobby, reach it, and . . . I just *scream*, I guess. Birds outside the open door take flight. I hammer my fists into the white stone, and kick with my feet.

I slap and smash, and then pick up a chunk of rubble from the ground and strike it into the face. I grasp it in both hands and slam it into the nose and the mouth, again and again.

'By the power of Jesus Christ,' I gasp. '*By the power of Jesus Christ! I command you, to leave me alone!*

I push my hands against the statue and heave, but it doesn't move. I try again, sobbing.

All the strength seeps out of me. I fall to my knees, looking up at the familiar face. Its nose is broken.

My nose, I think, despair washing through me, *we have the same nose.*

The rock is still in my hand. Boxes are opening in my head. I start walking back toward the car.

I can't see the police on the road yet, which means they're likely taking the corner around the mountain. Then I pull out, driving for the road out the police don't know about. I need to drive back to the ranch.

I remember now. I remember everything.

94

Rayne Ambrosine, aged fifteen

I'm in the schoolroom, putting the books back when the pains start. I don't know *what* they are, but I have an idea they are *because* of what had happened with cousin Frank.

Put put put.

There is a strange sound. I'm wondering where it's coming from. That's when I realize a steady stream of blood is dripping between my legs onto the lino floor.

I watch as the pool gets so big, the noise changes to like a splattering. I'm frightened now. I've been expecting God to punish me, but I'm not ready to die. I start wailing, and my older cousin Ardeth comes racing in, eight months gone with her second baby and red-faced from running.

'Oh sweet Jesus!' She takes me by the shoulders. 'Rayne, you didn't. Tell me you *didn't*? Your mother's gonna kill you!'

Ardeth was married already. I guess she knows what a miscarriage looks like.

She helps me out back so no one could see, gets me sitting down with a wad of cloth to hold between my legs. Then, even though she's pregnant enough to drop, she sets off at a flat run out the door to get help. That scares me most of all.

Next thing I know, men are showing up, crowding around me. The Prophet is there too. I have never seen him so close by.

'She's not a bad girl,' Ardeth is telling them. 'Please, Uncle Ambrosine.'

'You did the right thing,' he tells her. 'Don't you fret now. We'll take it from here.'

They carry me what feels like a very long way, over bumpy ground, silent and grim-faced.

I watch the ground, black and split open, realizing I'm drifting in and out of consciousness. I wonder if they might just dump me on the wrong side of the perimeter fence, an outcast.

Instead we reach a building I've never seen before. A corrugated-iron kind of thing.

As they near the entrance, the men drop me to stagger forward, a hand under each of my armpits, half dragging me through the door. A great trail of blood follows behind.

'Meg!' the Prophet shouts. He sounds nervous.

A woman emerges who I'd only ever seen a ways off in the Homestead Temple, standing by the Prophet. She has her hair all brushed up in a high crown. Her eyes widen when she sees the puddle I've made.

'Bring her in.' She gestures to a bed. 'You've been a bad girl,' she says, shaking her head as she pulls on green latex gloves. 'You're hemorrhaging,' she adds.

I groan and lean over. The pain is white hot, circling my pelvis.

When the men have gone, she loads up a syringe and pushes it into my arm.

'It'll be over quickly. Better you don't feel it,' she says. 'Lord knows you'll suffer enough when you're married.'

A golden feeling of warmth floods through me. I feel euphoric, light as air. The pain has gone. I smile as my legs are put into stirrups, drifting away. In my dreams, I'm kissing a cute boy I know from the schoolhouse. Then I wake up, something is happening downstairs. That's when I see the Prophet, leaning over me, frowning.

'Why is she making noises like that?' he asks Aunt Meg.

I hadn't realized I'd been making noises.

'It's the morphine,' she tells him. 'She doesn't know what she's doing. With miscarriages, it can feel a little like husband-and-wife relations.'

That's when I feel something cold slip free of me. They both sorta boggle, looking at something in between my legs. Aunt Meg recovers first.

'I'll get a box,' she says quietly.

I fall asleep watching her carry away the blue shoebox, toward the door of the basement.

When I wake up again, I'm so hot I think I must be in hell. My sheets are soaked through with sweat.

The bloodstained prairie dress is at eye level.

'You've got an infection,' Aunt Meg tells me. 'Placenta didn't come all the way out. That's why you smell so nasty down there. I'm gonna try extract what's left, but it's gonna hurt. Not much can be done about it. He doesn't want you to have any more morphine. Thinks it's God's will you should suffer for your sins.' She shakes her head, doesn't look at me. 'I'm gonna give you a mix of what pain relief I can,' she says quietly. 'But it'll make your head a little strange. OK?'

I must have passed out, because the next thing I know, I'm lying next to Melissa. She's telling me not to fret. All the girls in the clinic have either miscarried or had stillborn babies, she tells me. The Prophet doesn't want the wider community knowing.

'He's protecting the others,' she tells me, her sea-green eyes wide. 'Doesn't want them to know how some of the babies turn out.'

We both looked across the room. Aunt Meg is leading a girl toward the basement.

'She's one of His wives,' Melissa explains. 'It's one of the Prophet's secret ways. Leads back to the house.'

That's when I realize there is a way out through the basement.

95

Tina, sister-wife

I'm getting' an idea what it must have been like to be Rachel. The first wife. Here at the ranch, barefoot and alone, with nothing but a million miles of desert and a man who comes back at sundown. Maybe I would have tried to get some company too.

I look around the small farmhouse. The tiny couch we all crammed onto, listening to Blake's ideas on scripture. He had a way of talkin' to all of us, where you just felt what he was sayin' was only for you. Like he could see your soul or somethin'.

'Eve was Adam's companion. His helper. His comfort. His friend.'

Tears are running down my cheeks. I climb up the creaky little ladder to what counts as our second story. Like a hayloft with three separate compartments, one larger than the others to fit a double bed, and a narrow walkway connecting them all at the front.

I pull open the door to the master bedroom, which is thicker than the other two – a second-hand find of Blake's after Rachel mentioned the noise. Inside is a double bed, touching the wall on two sides, and a bedside table, where Blake kept my underwear and other private items.

'Eve was the temptress. The fallen. The seduced.'

I look at that bed for a long time. When I go back down the ladder, I have this real peculiar sensation, like I'm one of those

Rubik's cube games and someone has switched my feelings all around into different places.

Eve gave in to her desires. She tasted forbidden fruit. But Adam never gave up on her, though they were cast from paradise. He protected her, and loved her always.

I can see us all, clear as if we were back there. Hanging on to Blake's every word. He had such conviction, I'd always promise myself to do better. Believe deeper. It never quite stuck.

At sunset when we heard his car approach, Rachel would start smoothing down her clothing, ready to greet him at the door. I'd get that butterflies feeling. Emily got twitchy, like she didn't know where to sit. Then he'd come in the door, and the house would just *explode* with this feeling. Like we'd all been filled up.

But there was always something missing too.

I wander to the pantry, open the door. As expected, it's filled with neat and pretty jars. There is sweetcorn and green beans, zucchini and carrots. There's a selection of gray-looking meat. Cheap cuts. Shin and brisket, collar and skirt, all labeled and arranged by type.

I push around at the back, looking for jam and jelly, since I have a sweet tooth, but can't see anything. The lower shelf contains all the large three-gallon jars. These are filled with potatoes and sugar beets. High-calorie choices, and I notice she's arranged them four at a time. One each.

Love for Rachel flushes through me. All this time I was kicking against her being controlling and repressed. The whole while, she was quietly storing enough food for all of us, for when the apocalypse comes. Not complaining, just loving us all in the best way she knew, without asking anything in return.

I grab a jar of sweetcorn. Guess this'll be dinner.

Then I notice something. One of the lower jars is different to the rest. The lid is the old kind that Rachel doesn't like to use anymore. It's tucked behind some other more recently canned foodstuffs, almost as though someone has tried to hide it.

Curious, I squat down, and wrap my hands around a four-gallon jar of potatoes, and pull. At first it doesn't shift. I dig in, wiggling it to and fro, and slowly it begins to edge off the shelf.

The front slides forward suddenly, and I catch it just in time. It's heavy, but I'm able to kinda swing it to the side and place it upright.

The jar behind it looks wrong. Less packed. Something floating inside.

I pull out my cell phone, and turn on the flashlight. The back shelf is lit up, revealing potatoes and beets in every direction but one.

The jar I'm fixed on. It takes me a full few seconds to realize what I'm seeing. When I do, I stagger back, hand over my mouth, flashlight swinging crazily up to the ceiling.

Floating eerily in the jar are three severed fingers.

96

Emily, sister wife

Mrs Nelson showed up within the hour, but you could tell she wasn't too happy about it. That's the thing about Latter-day Saints; we have to do the right thing no matter what. Catholics have a little more leeway.

There wasn't any bail to pay, so we just went right on out to Mr Nelson's car and got inside. Not much conversation. I guess she was too mad. I figure, she's real good at keeping things in, so she's not going to get shouty like my momma would have. Blake once told me the only time he ever heard Mr and Mrs Nelson have a verbal disagreement was when Mrs Nelson was tipped off about a suedette court shoe discounted to half price at Walmart, and Mr Nelson made her wait two days for the weekly store cash-count and it sold out.

I get the impression Mrs Nelson has run out of outfits now. Like there's no established ensemble for driving your son's widow home after she's confessed and then unconfessed to his murder.

She's wearing a pair of white jeans I never saw her in before, a plaid shirt and makeup like she's done it in a hurry. Her blond hair is caught back in a ponytail. Kinda like an aging cowgirl. Maybe Mrs Nelson has just let go of a few things too.

I kinda let myself drift off a little. I had a lot to think about.

'I believe in forgiveness,' Mrs Nelson tells me, as we get out onto the desert road. 'I'm not sayin' it will be easy, Emily. But I want you to know Mr Nelson and I plan to work real hard on it.'

I try to thank her, but it comes out wrong.

Truth is, I hadn't really thought through the effect of my actions on her. I feel selfish now. Kinda wish I'd just waited for Brewer to drive me in the morning.

We're out on the highway, road rushing by. I've gotten myself ready for a long silence, when all of a sudden Mrs Nelson glances across at me.

'You were trying to protect Rachel, weren't you? Mislead the police. Keep her out of their questioning. What I don't understand is *why*.'

I look out of the window. She never will understand either. I already lost one mother. That's about the worst sin in the world. If I'd have died saving Rachel, God would have cleared my balance sheet. Least that's how I figure it. But it looks like it's not going to work out that way.

Real shame too, because I happen to know the state of Utah allocates twenty-five dollars for the last meal of death-row prisoners, and that can be spent on anything, including Domino's Pizza and full-size Coke.

'That woman always did have a hold over people I could never understand,' says Mrs Nelson.

I don't answer that, since it doesn't seem aimed in my direction, and she sounds mad about it.

Mrs Nelson starts looking real sick the further out into the wilderness we go though. Guess she's only just coming to terms with it all.

'So this is where you all hid yourselves away,' she mutters to herself. 'Beautiful, I suppose.'

I contemplate telling her we are driving along an old riverbed, since I remember Blake being oddly proud of this fact, but decide against it. We never saw eye-to-eye on scenery. He once took me to Canyonlands National Park shortly after we were married, and I was disappointed because I thought we were visiting a Wild West place with the banks and saloons. Instead we walked about a million miles to this big twisted arch of rock, and Blake pointed out the craters below, and talked about how it looked like the surface of another planet. I said it reminded me of a giant tiramisu where someone had dragged a big spoon to carve out the layers. This was a not too subtle hint that I was hungry and hoping we'd visit the pizza restaurant on the road out, and Blake got mad for some reason, so we left.

Mrs Nelson is still talking.

'Blake always did love mountains, nature . . . There was a little songbird used to come to the yard and he . . .' she gets all choked. Starts crying softly to herself.

I feel like I'm intruding on her grief. Like we shouldn't be sitting so close. I just look straight ahead, twisting up the hem of my shirt.

I sneak a glance across at Mrs Nelson. She isn't making crying noises, but tears are pouring down her face.

'Mrs Nelson,' I say quietly, 'you can just drop me at the edge of the compound. You don't need to come all the way to the door.'

She nods, not taking her eyes from the road. 'Thank you,' she adds. 'I don't think I'm ready to see it yet.' She takes a deep breath as we approach and her eyes fill with tears. 'I never gave up on him,' she tells me in a whispery sad voice. 'I knew he wasn't happy. Not since Mexico. Couldn't concentrate on his studies well enough to graduate. That sales job was making him crazy. I knew. I tried to help him. My husband said you have to leave men to make their own mistakes. But if we had just lent him the money to finish college . . .' her voice cracks.

I don't reply, because I don't think that would have helped.

I have a memory of Blake talking about going back to finish his accounting degree after he married Tina. Rachel didn't approve at all, and she and Tina had this battle about who was holding Blake back, who knew him best. Then Rachel took out an accountancy book from Salt Lake City library and looking at all those numbers kinda made Blake's head swim, I think. He had one of his black episodes and Tina never mentioned it again.

'I think Blake meant well, Mrs Nelson,' I tell her. 'He just found some things too hard.'

She nods and there's an expression in her eyes like she so badly wants to believe her son was good.

By the time we get to the fence marking out our property, Mrs Nelson's hands are shaking on the steering wheel.

'Are you OK, Mrs Nelson?' I ask her. 'Do you want me to fetch you a glass of water or something?'

She shakes her head real quick, tears flying from her eyes.

'I need to get on the road,' she says. 'It's already getting dark.'

I move to open the car door.

'Will they arrest Rachel?' she blurts.

I hesitate.

'I think they intend to, Mrs Nelson,' I tell her. 'The police are going out to the Homestead to pick her up.' I take a breath. 'Mrs Nelson, I'm real sorry for what I did. For everything.'

She gives this tight little nod, like she forgives a little but not the whole way. Then all of a sudden she speaks.

'You know, when Blake first told me about you, I actually considered he might have had a revelation,' she says. 'At the very least, I thought you might bring something to the household. Temper Rachel's control over Blake. Then I met you, all big-eyed and teenage, without a sane thought in your silly head, and I realized.' She shakes her head in disgust. 'Blake was just greedy.' She turns to face forward again, hands on the steering wheel, very straight-backed and sad.

I don't think that is very nice at all of Mrs Nelson. But if there's one thing I've learned about living with other women, is sometimes when people are real mad, just leave them be.

I get out of the car. Mrs Nelson pulls away without a word, leaving me standing in the quiet desert evening.

Good thing too, 'cause I got things to do up here I don't want anyone to see.

97

Tina, sister-wife

I couldn't tell ya how long I sat looking at those goddamn severed fingers. All I know is it's gotten real dark outside. Somehow I've been glued to the spot. Just no idea what to do with the information, I guess.

Oh shit.

I close my eyes, tryin' to process what in the hell this means. It all comes down to one thing.

It was her. Rachel.

The fingers float in a cloudy brine. Shreds of ghostly pale, ragged flesh drift where they've been hacked at the joint. A tuft of reddish hair can be seen right above the knuckle of one. Below is circled by a familiar ring.

Blake's wedding band.

Did she even know what she was doing? It's coming together in my head. Rachel was canning the morning Blake was found.

That means . . . I close my eyes tryin' to think.

Rachel loved Blake. I'm sure of it. None of her killin' him makes sense, unless . . .

Blood atonement.

The thought sorta rushes into my brain. What if Rachel did love Blake, but thought him guilty of some sin bad enough to keep him out of heaven? Something which could only be purged by Blake's blood falling to the ground as he died?

I'm tryin' to figure it out. If Rachel really coulda done it.

What sin might Blake have committed? I rattle through my brain, but my Bible studies aren't good enough. There are three unforgivable sins. One is murder of an innocent. I can't call to mind the others. Adultery?

I hear the rumble of a car engine. That can only mean one thing. Rachel is home. When I think how I would wait for that sound. It was the best part of my day. Now I'm frickin' terrified. I hop to my feet, go to the front window, but it's too late. She's parked. I can't sneak out without her seeing me.

Oh shit, oh shit, oh shit.

No. She didn't do it. Rachel never woulda killed Blake.

Pretend she did, whispers a voice. *How would she have done it?*

I track through, assuring myself.

She *was* gone for long enough to get down to the stream and back. She would have to have had a spare set of clothes in her storehouse. Changed for dinner, gone back later at night to wash her bloody dress in the canning machine, when no one was around.

She must have nerves of steel. I kinda shudder. I been living with her. At any point, she could have decided I knew too much.

The car door slams and I hear Rachel's footsteps, but she doesn't call out like she usually does. A slow fear pounds at me as the full reality of my situation dawns. I'm trapped out alone in the desert. No phone signal, no people for miles around.

Panic. Panic.

I try to get myself together.

You grew up in a meth den, with a bunch a pimps, I tell myself. *You can look after yourself. You're a fighter.*

But, actually, all I feel is fear. My legs are weak with it, my arms feel watery and limp. I can't think of a single advantage I have out here over Rachel. I got nothing.

Yes you do. You can lie. She can't.

Pretend you don't know. Hope her repression holds.

I glance around the room, then deposit myself on the couch where I might usually be. I pick up the Bible we always have lying around and open it at random. The words blur.

What would Rachel have done if Emily hadn't confessed? *Set me up, most likely.* Something else burns at me. Rage. All my life, people have let me down.

I trusted Rachel. For a moment, I goddamn trusted her.

All I can think is, I learned how not to feel. How to close myself off, to get through it all. Then I tried . . . With Blake, I opened my heart. But it's too painful. It's too freakin' painful.

I want to go back to how I was. Back to not feelin'.

The door handle turns and in comes Rachel. Even if I hadn't just found what I found, her expression would put me on edge. She looks *real* peculiar. Like she is *not* herself. At all.

'Hey!' my mouth is dry, but I think it comes out OK.

That's when I remember. I didn't put the jars back right.

Fuck.

Without a word, Rachel turns toward the little kitchen.

'Did you open the pantry?' she asks in this weird dull voice.

I stand up quicker than I mean to. The skinny door is ajar, how I left it, keepin' the finger jar just out of sight. All Rachel needs to do is take another step into the kitchen and she'll see it.

'About that. I got some bad news,' I say quickly.

Rachel spins around, pin-eyed and agitated-looking. It's as much as I can do not to take a step back. If she was anyone else, I'd know they'd just shot up somethin' pretty strong. Only Rachel doesn't do drugs. So what in the world has happened to her?

'Um. I think the police busted up your storehouse,' I say. 'I don't know how much is salvageable.'

I swallow. Rachel waits a long moment. Her eyes glide to the pantry. Then she turns away and steps back toward the front door.

'I'll go take a look,' she says, in the same dead tone, and just like that walks straight out of the front door again.

She doesn't close it behind her, and I watch as Rachel walks out toward the big store.

What the fuck do I do now?

A thought grabs at me like an instinct.

Hide.

Hide and hope to God Rachel will think I've gone out for a walk or somethin'. Maybe she'll leave long enough for me to get to the car.

I put a rough plan together in my head. Hide. Run. Drive.

Then I remember. The Chevy has a gun. A hunting rifle.

98

Emily, sister-wife

I go down to the river where Blake used to fish. The water is fast-flowing here, which I guess is why he picked it, since in my opinion it's not very pretty. The big brown rock face opposite oozes water in slimy rivulets, like it's crying black tears. And the juniper tree he sat under is all twisted and parched. I stop for a moment, looking at that tree.

Nothing hanging from it now. Either desert animals or the police had tidied away all the blood splatters. Maybe the branch he was fixed to is bowed lower, but it's hard to tell.

I turn to the water, which swirls past in a lot of little curls and 's' shapes.

There's a part of the rocky water's edge a few feet down, where the stones get flatter, and a gnarled-up shrubby thing is growing out of the bank. I squat down, reach down, pulling my sleeve over my hand. I grope around the underwater bank.

The bush here hangs low, disguising a whole tangle of roots that fix into the bank like netting. Blake showed me that once. Nature's own hidey-holes. Apparently, muskrats use them for nests.

It takes me a good few minutes, pushing deep into the hard roots. For a moment I think what I'm looking for has been swept free. Then I catch hold of something hard and smooth.

Pushed into the roots of the shrub is a little gardening axe. Carefully I work it free, keeping my sleeve so as not to leave fingerprints.

Police look for evidence in good hiding places, not dumb ones.

I saw this trick on an episode of *Cagney and Lacey* where the murder weapon went missing. People dredge the bottom of rivers and such, if they suspect something has been tossed downstream, but I was fairly certain they don't comb the banks. And like Cagney said, what kind of dumbass would hide a murder weapon right by the victim?

I can't help but feel a little pleased with myself for outsmarting all of them.

I look at the sharp edge. The blood has washed away. I don't know if that means there'll be no DNA.

I think back to my last conversation with Carlson.

'If Aunt Meg just vanished, and she really did put babies to sleep,' I asked him, 'does that mean she escaped justice?'

'Probably. Real life, kid. Not like on TV.'

I blew out through my nose. 'But, I mean, what she did was worse than the Prophet, right? And he's in jail for life.'

'We'd better hope there really is a God, and she gets what's comin' to her,' Carlson said. 'But maybe she already had. From what the records say, Margaret Ambrosine was originally married to the Prophet's eighty-year-old father. At the tender age of fifteen.' He glanced at me. 'When the old man died, little Margaret got reassigned to his son, who then became the Prophet. From what we can see, Aunt Meg was a mother herself, if you can believe it. Just the one child, though. Nothing to indicate why that was, we can only speculate.'

'I don't think birthing a child,' I told him, 'automatically makes you a mother. I mean, not everyone is wired that way.'

Carlson was looking at my hands. I realized I had twisted up the belt on my prison boiler suit.

'No,' he said. 'Guess not.'

'It's like what the therapist lady said to me,' I had told Carlson. 'The mothers believe so hard, their children become objects to them. Something to take along to the afterlife. Like those old pharaohs who got buried with their slaves.'

I'm thinking this over, the axe still in my hand. That's when I have it. An honest-to-God real-life revelation. I've been wanting to have one ever since I was a little girl, and here it is. I start to stand up, eyes wide, mouth open. I know who killed Blake.

That's when I feel a solid shove from behind. I tumble head over heels, right into the river.

99

Rachel, first wife

Praise the lord, the police have been kind to my storehouse. I close my eyes in relief. This place sort of grounds me. All the food, neatly packaged. I like to run the older supplies through our pantry inside. But out here is enough for three straight years, give or take.

I got sacks of grain and corn, flour, rice, pasta. Gallon jars of meats and pickles. A few of Blake's Survive Well products also, since they started out their own line in survival foods.

I take a breath, trying to slot what I remember into everything that happened.

The shoebox. My box. In the basement.

Whatever pain relief Aunt Meg gave me is making me see shapes and patterns that aren't there. Don't seem to help much with the cramps either. I have one hand pushed on my pelvis to keep from exploding with pain. The morgue feels unnaturally cold and the sharp smell of bleach is strong enough to make me dizzy. I don't quite understand what I'm seeing. I'd expected to find a secret way out down here, instead I see lots of tiny boxes.

I breathe out and walk one step at a time until I'm standing over it. The blue shoebox. It has my name scrawled on the side in jerky ill-formed writing.

I hesitate. Lift the lid.

My eyes fill with tears.

There is the most perfect little creature inside. She isn't what you'd call a baby. She doesn't have all her parts. She is curled over, her black eyes shining in the light. Her body is tufted with downy hair.

I smile at her. Put out a hand to touch her.

'It doesn't matter you're cold,' I whisper. 'I'm too hot. We balance each other out.'

That's when I make the connection. Melissa told me about the red graveyard, in the scrubland where the dirt was blood-copper-color. The secret place where they bury babies that came too early, or aren't born right, because they don't want outsiders knowing how often that happens here. If I leave her here, that would be her fate. Buried in the graveyard no one is allowed to visit. Unmarked, unloved. A lump rises in my throat. I lift the box.

A light flickers on upstairs in the clinic.

I panic. Then I see another exit at the back, just like Melissa said there would be. I make for it, box tight under my arm. All I can think is I need to hide her. Bury her somewhere only I know about. Or she'll be lost in the secret graveyard. I'll never find her again.

I limp along a series of tunnels, holding the box tight. It's hard to walk and I'm dizzy enough to stagger. The pain is so bad I have to stop a couple of times, leaning against a wall, vomit rising.

I emerge out in a white bedroom, and am halfway toward the door – almost safe – when the Prophet and his wives come in.

I hide, terrified, behind a curtain, praying no one will see me. I have to protect my box.

I'm sweating with fever. It makes it hard to think straight. The pain is indescribable now, a pulsing, sickening thing with a life of its own.

I watch the Prophet come in. How his wives line up and take their clothes off. It all seems to go on forever, the moans, the writhing limbs. Girl after girl. It's all so awful, I can hardly stand it. Aunt Meg is there too, which seems especially indecent, since a few of the girls are young enough to be her daughters. Her low breasts and mottled skin, the wide spreading patch of wiry pubic hair. It all seems more horrible in contrast.

Then Aunt Meg sees me. I hear her whisper to the Prophet that I shouldn't be there.

He turns, perplexed, only half understanding.

'Don't be long,' he tells her, letting her up and beckoning another girl. His eyes linger on the box in my hand for a moment. Then he goes right back to the next wife in line.

Aunt Meg throws on her dress and leads me, grim-faced, back down the secret passage. Back to the clinic.

'You're not going to run away again, are you, Rayne?' she asks. 'I can't help you if you do.'

I just stare at her, the fever making everything seem unreal. I'm holding the box tight.

She looks at it for a long moment, then at me.

'There's a shovel out back,' whispers Aunt Meg, leaning close. 'I won't follow you. Do what you need to do and come right back here. I won't tell him. It'll be our secret.'

I nod, barely able to believe it, stagger to my feet and somehow make it outside. I find a place by a tree and dig a hole.

That's when I hear a noise. Footsteps approaching the clinic. A man's voice. The Prophet. He's looking for it, I'm certain. Looking for me and my box.

I clasp my hands together, pray the hardest I've ever prayed in my life.

'By the power of Jesus Christ,' I whisper. 'By the power of Jesus Christ, I command you to leave me alone.'

I wait, burning up, shovel in hand.

After a moment I hear footsteps headed away. I let out a breath. God had heard my prayer. Flushed with fever and sick with pain, I slam the shovel down, dig out a scoop of amber soil.

I don't remember digging the rest. Maybe Aunt Meg even helped me. All I know is at one point the grave got deep enough for me to lay my little box in the ground. I say a prayer, looking over my shoulder, before tossing dirt quickly back onto the blue lid.

I take a shuddery breath, lift a sack of peas that's been replaced on the wrong shelf. I'd committed a crime, no two ways about it. I mean to say, you can't just *bury* human remains. If anyone finds out, they'll move her, or worse. Dig her up and cut her into pieces, trying to figure out what went on out at the Homestead. What led to that graveyard.

I push the pea sack back into its rightful place. I just want to leave her there. Under that tree. Sleeping. Why can't they let me do that? Gentiles don't always understand.

I hear footsteps outside the storehouse and turn around. A shadow in the desert. My heart beats a little faster. Tina? Why would she creep about out there?

That's when I see a light. One of our kerosene lamps. It bobs outside, then sails toward me like someone's tossed it through the open door. I start back in panic. The lamp smashes against a sack of flour, throwing up a splash of kerosene and fire with it. With a crackle and pop, the hessian sack catches alight.

With my eyes glued to the flame, I hear, but don't see, the big barn doors shut. The click of a padlock in place. It takes a full few moments for the fear to set in.

Tina has locked me in here.

The grain sacks are ablaze now, smoke pouring up.

I'm trapped in here. She's burning me alive.

100

Tina, sister-wife

Someone is firing a gun outside the ranch. Quickly and quietly as I can, I move upstairs. There's nothing much up here but our three beds, roughly partitioned.

From here, there's a little window, looking out onto the wide desert. I risk a glance. That's when I hear a whoompfh! Flame shooting upwards.

My only thought is *Rachel*. She's cutting off any means of escape.

The two cars are on fire. I guess she musta shot out the gas tank and set light to the gas.

I flatten myself back against the wall. Then I drop to the ground and slide under the largest of the three beds. The bed Blake and I shared, when we stayed here.

Almost as soon as I'm out of sight, I hear more noises from outside. Smashing, fire crackling.

I'm weighing up my chances of somehow getting out and past her, when I hear the door slam open. I lie, not daring to breathe, listening to feet stalk around the tiny downstairs.

There are more breaking noises. Rachel must be in the pantry, below me. I hear cannery jars crashing to the floor. The sound of violent destruction. I turn my head slightly. There are cracks between the single floorboard construction of the loft.

I can see utter devastation. Lids and broken glass and pickles and vegetables and briny water, spread all over. A rifle butt swings, taking out another shelf.

Then the breaking stops. The gun barrel dips out of sight. Footsteps begin padding across the house. There's a click of cartridges being loaded.

I squeeze my eyes shut tight. I never believed more fully in God than I do at this point. I have never sent a more fervent prayer than at this moment.

There's a creak on the stairs. The banister taking weight. She's ascending.

I can hear little explosions outside, smashing glass, like the storehouse is on fire. I picture jars of pickles boiling up, popping their lids.

What does it mean, what does it mean?

Rachel's storehouse is *sacred* to her. Guess she's completely lost it.

I'm about ready to come out, and put up some kind of a fight, when I see two heavy boots draw in line with my face.

'Come out, come out, wherever you are.' It's a woman's voice, speaking in a singsong whisper. 'I know you're here. I saw the car.'

It isn't Rachel's voice.

I know the voice. *I know it.* Though I can't place it.

Suddenly, a crazed face is hanging level with mine. The bloodshot eyes are wide, manic, a bristle of hair on the chin catches the light. Her skin, at this upside-down angle, hangs ghoulishly slack, like a sagging mask. A gun is aimed square at my head.

I'm not looking into the barrel though. I'm looking at the face I recognize.

It's Blake's mother.

Adelaide Nelson.

101

Emily, sister-wife

The river has a current, and I'm being swept downstream. I never did learn to swim. It feels like the cold water and realization are hitting me so hard I can't tell the difference.

Right before I went into the water, I kinda had a holy sign. Like God was telling me something about *mothers*. That was when I realized. I'd never told Mrs Nelson the way back to the ranch. She knew it already. Like she'd been out here before. Guess she must have the land purchase documents, since she and Mr Nelson were Blake's guarantors. Easy enough to pull the location coordinates.

I remembered something else, from the security footage of Blake and Adelaide Nelson at Kirker's Diner. I swear it came to me in a shining golden light, like direct from God.

There were papers on the table. Looked official, like maybe land papers. I'll bet Blake told his mom he planned to buy that Homestead property at the lunch. Even though Bishop Young had threatened Blake with excommunication if he bought it. I tried to imagine how that would feel. What if you'd given up your *whole life*, to get to heaven, obeyed your husband in everything, and made darn sure your children would be at your side . . . Then your favorite oldest son just *throws it all away*. Makes some bonehead plan to get kicked right out of the Church. Isn't that something you'd kill to protect? I mean, we're talking about *all eternity.*

There was a Bible on the table at Kirker's Diner too. Maybe Adelaide had brought it along to try and talk Blake out of his decision with scripture. Easy enough for Blake to pick it up by mistake, take it back to the ranch and forget about it. Which would explain why the police found a Book of Mormon at the ranch, with the passages underlined, about javelins and adulterers and whatnot. Blood atonement. Adelaide likely had it on her mind for a while.

If Blake died with his blood spilt on the ground, he'd be saved excommunication *and* forgiven for any sin. Even an unforgivable one like adultery. Blood atonement absolves *everything.* It's like a golden ticket straight to heaven.

That's maybe why Mrs Nelson pushed me into the water. No blood.

My head goes under and I choke. I'm flailing about, but the water is too deep, I'm getting tired. The water is sweeping me away. I stretch out my arms like Saint John of Nepomuk, the drowned saint. Figure I might as well go peaceably. It's hard to keep my face serene though. Water keeps splashing in my eyes.

That's when I feel my arm tug, like it's being pulled out of its socket. The gardening axe. I was holding it when I went into the water. Must have kept a tight grip without realizing. Only now it's lodged itself in the riverbank.

Grabbing it with both hands, I manage to pull myself to the side and catch hold of a desert scrub. Luckily, it's rooted deep enough so I can pull myself right back onto the red earth.

I lie there for a minute, breathing hard, laughing. Then reality sets in. I get to my feet, deciding my best option.

I look out onto the desert, shielding my eyes from the sun. I can make out the ranch, with the old lifeguard tower and out-buildings. Guess I didn't get swept too far.

But I don't know if Adelaide doubled back or drove straight home. Better not take the risk.

Rachel will be in custody by now. Tina is likely in some drugs den downtown.

I breathe out. It's a long walk to civilization. Might take me a day or so, keeping out of sight of the highway. If I'm lucky, I'll catch a ride on the outskirts of Salt Lake City.

Better get away from the river, I decide, in case Adelaide comes looking. Shivering with cold, I start walking.

102

Tina, sister-wife

'There you are,' says Adelaide Nelson, with a lipsticked smile. 'Come out. No need to hide under there.'

She drops the gun level with my face.

'Now,' she says.

I edge out, the rifle inches from my eyes.

Oh God. Blake's death has sent poor Mrs Nelson plumb crazy.

'Mrs Nelson,' I say carefully, 'there's no need for the gun.'

She looks at it. Then raises the muzzle.

I put my hands up.

'I *saw* what you did to my son,' she says. 'You think a mother doesn't keep tabs? Check her son's email? Watch his nasty video uploads?'

For a moment, I'm completely taken aback.

'You think I killed Blake?'

'I saw what you *did* to him. I saw those dirty things. I saw *everything*.'

Oh shit. My first thought is, the state she's in, she could go right ahead and pull that trigger.

'Mrs Nelson. What you saw . . . That wasn't real, OK? It was . . . like play pretend.'

'You are *disgusting*.' Her whole face compacts. 'There aren't even *words* for women like you. You take our men . . . our good

430

men . . .' She's kinda heavy breathing. The gun trembles in her hands.

For a moment I think she's gonna lose it and blow me away, but she collects herself.

'*I* raised him,' she hisses. 'To be *mine*. I spent my whole life *suffering, enduring.* And you think you can come along and *take him away?*'

I shake my head. Nothing else to do, really, with a gun in your face.

She glares at me.

'You think *I* didn't want wives, to help me? Take off the load?' she demands. 'I gave that life up, because I knew it was *right*. I did what my husband and the Church told me.'

She's twisting the wedding ring on her finger. The gun is pointed away from me at an angle. This would be the time to make a grab for it. I decide to take one more chance to reason with her.

'I didn't kill your son, Mrs Nelson,' I say. 'I loved him.'

She blinks real fast, and then a crazed look emerges.

'Of course you didn't love him,' she says. 'Not like I did. Not enough to help him. Not enough to . . . do what I had to do.'

A suspicion is opening up in my head. Something I never thought of before.

'You *know*,' she says, in a sewing circle conspirator's voice, '*I* used to say those things to him. That he was bad. A sinner. Those things he did with you were a cry for help. Blake needed *me* to punish him for his bad ways. To set him back on the path of righteousness.'

I swallow hard. My eyes are on the gun, but they are filled with tears.

A mother will do anything for her son.

Blood on the ground. Blood atonement. The only way for an unforgivable sinner to get to the celestial heaven.

'It was you,' I whisper. 'You murdered Blake.'

103

Rachel, first wife

The smoke makes it hard to breathe. I look around for water, and my eyes land on my carefully packed preserves. Shaking my head, I unscrew a jar of pickles and soak my sleeve in the brine. Holding it over my mouth makes it a little easier to think. Tina's betrayal is the most paralyzing thing of all. The realization is debilitating enough that, just for a moment, I consider walking straight into the flames.

You can never trust anyone, Rayne.

The heat is enough to make me change my mind. I try to think practically. The door is thick, padlocked on the outside. Walls are solid wood. Water. There's no water source out here.

My eyes land on the Survive Well 5000. The big old canning system is half my height and holds ten gallons of water. I start unscrewing the various heavy pressure fixings. About a third of the way through, a better idea occurs to me.

Blake's half-baked fix of the faulty circuitry. *'You always make sure to let the pressure out of that canner, Rachel. Get the settings wrong and it will explode like a bomb.'*

Maybe a bomb is exactly what I need. I stretch my arms out wide, enfolding the stainless-steel body in an ungainly embrace. Then I drag it, gritting my teeth with effort, to sit against the nearest wall. The distance is less than a foot, but the machine is so heavy I'm out of breath and sore by the time it's in place, and there are two deep grooves in the wooden floor, where the base has cut tracks. I flick on the canner. Almost immediately the water inside begins to gurgle.

Quickly, I start turning down the fastenings, much too tight.

The fire is all up one side of the barn when I finish, but the canner is already making an unholy racket, shaking and rattling fit to burst, with angry jets of steam shooting from the rim.

The pressure gauge needle is trembling, well past the safety range Blake told me to keep it within. Any escaping steam means I'm losing valuable pressure, so I try tightening the screws even harder, burning my hand in the process and yelping in pain.

I don't know how long it takes for the canner to go beyond maximum pressure. The solid steel container doesn't look like it would give under any circumstances.

'If you're up there,' I tell Blake, 'you'd better hope you were right with all those warnings. Else I'm coming to get you, and it's not gonna be pretty.'

Heat is melting things now, thickening the air, making it hard to think. It feels as though my eyes are burning. My sleeve has dried out. I stagger, coughing, to a stack of gallon pickle jars, and start hurling them into the flames. It's heartbreaking, destroying my own preserves. Neatly cut rounds of carrots and zucchini splatter into the fire. But it isn't enough. I turn to the canning machine. It's wailing loudly now, like a screaming child.

The floor has caught. I see flames roll under the floorboards, smoke coming up between them. Too late for the canning machine, I decide, casting one last look. Best just make for the door.

I'm hoping the flames have caused enough damage to weaken it. I'm down to the last of the pickles, as I douse myself in vinegar-brine from the sugar beets. Now or never. I run to the door, using my wet sleeve to cover my face.

The heat hits me like a wall as I thud uselessly against the door. I'm flung back into the center of the barn, skin burning, choking.

Flames have risen between me and the pressure canner, cutting off that route. It was a bad idea anyway, I think. Blake always was dramatic. Boiling water is never gonna explode the quarter inch of steel wall of a pressure canner. I feel wisps of hair begin to burn. Then I hear a shrieking noise, like fingers down a chalkboard.

I'm hit by a cloud of steam. It sears the left half of my head, and I feel my cheek and neck puff in blisters. As I twist away in pain, a deafening roar erupts on the far side of the barn. Something hits my face. I put a hand up and feel a nickel-sized piece of metal lodged in my cheek. Blood is running down.

I turn to see the Survive Well has blown a hole in the far side of the barn, soaking it with boiling water.

104

Tina, sister-wife

I try not to focus on the gun Mrs Nelson has trained on my chest.

'You killed Blake,' I say, and I can't keep the sadness from my voice. 'You killed your own son, 'cause you thought blood atonement was the only way to get him into heaven.'

'Blake wouldn't let up on the idea of buying that land,' says Adelaide. 'Bishop Young was going to excommunicate him. But Blake went right ahead, doing deals with that shady realtor firm. Borrowing the down payment from them. I had to make Blake see,' continues Adelaide. 'He was risking his place at my side in heaven. I only came to talk to him. Just to talk. I knew he'd be out fishing on a Friday. I thought I could make him see reason,' she says, shaking her head. 'But God had other plans. God showed me the axe, just lying on the ground, like it was waiting for me.'

I'm struck with a sudden picture. Blake, his last moments alive, staring out onto that lake, fishing rod in his hand. Was he thinking how much he loved us? How to fix our money problems? Was he imagining our new life, on the Homestead land?

Adelaide parking up a little distance. Taking the path down to the river, whilst Rachel's canning machine whirred loudly. The gardening axe left in one of the vegetable beds.

Tears fill my eyes. 'How could you?' I whisper.

'Ye shall defend your families even unto bloodshed,' says Mrs Nelson. 'That's what the Book says.'

This is bad. Mrs Nelson thinks she's some warrior angel or something. Defending her family from temptation.

'Let's talk about this,' I say. 'I'm sure it was . . . just an accident, right?'

'I told myself,' says Mrs Nelson, 'all I need is for Blake to listen to me. I'll walk away.' A black look fills her face. 'He told me our way of life was joyless. That he'd found a better path and we couldn't stand it. He turned his back on me, after *everything I'd done for him.*'

Her face sorta falters. Like a computer crashing and reloading. I get the impression she's remembering something she'd rather forget.

I imagine Blake dismissing her, like he used to with us if we disagreed with him. Turning back to the river, with that surety Blake had that he would be obeyed. His mother raising the axe whilst he faced the water.

Mrs Nelson nods to herself. 'We'll all be there,' she says. 'Side by side. In heaven.'

It was an accident, I tell myself. *A fit of anger.*

Then I remember the other wounds on Blake's body. Hacked-away fingers. Damage to the groin. The cops said it was a frenzied attack. Perhaps all her awful life came boiling up outta her. Or perhaps she had a plan all along to frame us wives. The Bible the police found comes to mind. All those passages justifying violence. Like she'd been exonerating herself for Blake's murder days before it happened.

I step forward and make a grab for the gun. She's too fast for me, snaking back, feet planted firmly apart.

'Um. No sense in killin' me though, right?' I point out. 'I

mean to say, you put your boy in heaven. Good for you, an' all. No sense risking your own immortal soul. Murder is an unforgivable sin too, right? Along with adultery.'

'Only the murder of *innocents* is unpardonable,' she says. 'You're all adulterers.'

Mrs Nelson raises the gun again. I back toward the top of the ladder.

'If you shoot me, my blood will atone for my sins.' I'm kinda babbling, trying to convince her. 'I'll be right up there in heaven with you.'

She takes a step closer. I look at her finger on the trigger.

Time to move, I decide. Best risk it all and make a grab for the gun. Mrs Nelson is in her fifties. Likely strong from dragging around boxes for the store. Physically I might have the edge. I might not. What I can bring is the element of surprise, which in a fight is often all you need.

'Blake had to bleed,' she says, in a strange faraway voice. 'There had to be blood on the ground.' Her eyes flick to me. She lowers the gun. 'That's why I can't kill you,' Adelaide says.

Relief washes over me. My muscles relax a little, my plan to grab the weapon suspended.

'I can only let you die,' she concludes. Before I realize what's happening, she jerks the gun toward me. It catches me straight in the stomach, the narrow barrel driving up under my ribs. I double over in pain, and that's when I feel her give me one almighty shove.

I go tumbling right over the edge of the loft.

As I land at the base of the eight-foot ladder, my left leg hits the ground first, taking all my weight and folding painfully under me.

'Fuck!' I writhe on the floor in agony, clutching at it.

Mrs Nelson descends the ladder calmly, and stops, taking a good look.

I breathe out hard. She walks nearer and prods my twisted leg with her gun.

I scream. It has absolutely zero effect on her expression. 'Please . . .' I gasp, 'please, I think it's broken.'

'No blood,' she says with satisfaction. 'Out here I guess you've got three days or so.'

I close my eyes, tears spilling out against the pain. All I can do is sorta moan, and blow out breath like a woman in labor.

'Tell me where Rachel hid the axe,' she adds, 'and I'll leave you a bottle of water.'

For some reason, my mouth is suddenly dry, as though I'm already dying of thirst. I lick my lips.

'What . . . I don't know what you mean,' I manage, huffing out the words through gritted teeth.

'I left Rachel's gardening axe as evidence,' says Mrs Nelson patiently. 'The police didn't find it, so she must have hidden it. The officers are going to be needing the axe, to come to the right decision.'

I'm totally confused. Because Rachel couldn't have hidden that axe, unless she was lying about her whereabouts. Which Rachel doesn't do.

'I don't know what you're talking about,' I tell her. 'Rachel . . . Rachel is innocent. You set her up and you'll go straight to hell.' I sorta shout this last part.

Mrs Nelson shakes her head.

'You gals sure have given me one heck of a problem,' she says. 'But it's nearly over now.' There's a madness in her eyes that I realize I've seen all along. Before, it was shielded, behind a buttoned-down rage. Now it's up front. Wavin' its arms around.

I lie back, gritting my teeth against the pain.

Take it easy, Tina, I tell myself. *Someone will come. Rachel. The cops. Just keep your mouth shut until she leaves.*

'I put my boy in heaven, where he belongs,' says Mrs Nelson. 'We'll all be up there together.' She closes her eyes like she's dreaming. 'One happy family.'

'Do you have any idea how *crazy* you sound?' I can't help myself. 'Talkin' about heaven like it's a first-class lounge at an airport?'

Shut up, Tina. Shut up.

Mrs Nelson walks to the door. Then she stops, like something has occurred to her. She goes to the little stove and turns on the kerosene gas.

Oh God, no.

'Stop!' I shout. 'Please!' I'm so afraid, I'm crying and I hate myself for it.

She's going to goddamn burn me alive.

'God speaks to me,' she says, in a strange, distant voice. 'I wasn't listening. I know what he wants me to do.' She looks at me, collapsed on the floor, then she lights a match. 'No blood,' she says, nodding to herself. 'Better to be sure.' Then she drops the flame.

105

Rachel, first wife

I crawl out of the smoldering side of the barn, cheek stinging from the shrapnel wound. The first thing I do is take a lungful of clean air. I'm alive. I can hardly believe it. The pressure canner really did go off like a bomb. Guess Blake's enthusiasm for dangerous machinery finally paid off.

I get to my feet, wiping soot from my mouth, trying to come to terms with what just happened. Tina must have relapsed, I decide. Gotten hold of some drugs and taken them. Maybe she's out of her mind, crazy high. Or paranoid, thinking I'm trying to kill her. I remember from my missionary days, that happens to addicts sometimes. I feel calmer now. This is all making sense. Truth is, I can't bear to think of another reason Tina might do that to me.

She needs help, I tell myself. *Please God, let us both get out of this unharmed.*

I notice Mr Nelson's car is here, parked a little further out from the ranch.

'Mr Nelson?' I'm a little wary, though I should be relieved. Old instinct, I guess. Never be alone with a man. He's nowhere to be seen. My next thought is if Tina has gone crazy, then Mr Nelson is in danger.

I remember Blake's gun in the Chevy. I take a slow walk toward where I parked it.

Smoke is curling from the wreckage of a burned-out car. Our Chevy has been torched. I move closer. The trunk looks intact. A powerful heat is still throwing out from the chassis. In movies, the gas tank explodes.

I've just nearly burned to death, I decide. No matter what it takes, I'm gonna get that gun. Licking my fingers to guard against the heat, I tap the catch, then press to open. It pops, gray smoke spilling lazily out. The gun is inside, warm but not scorched.

I lift it free, heart beating. I check the barrel and, thank the Lord above, it's loaded. Blake always did promise me he kept it empty, but just for once I don't mind at all he told me a mistruth. Gun slung over my shoulder, I make for Mr Nelson's car. The storehouse is blazing, reducing our food supply to ash. I feel as though someone has torn part of me away.

Then the door of the house opens, and to my surprise, Adelaide Nelson steps out, smoke billowing from behind her. She's carrying Mr Nelson's favorite Winchester rifle, with an ease I never figured her for.

For a moment I'm in complete shock. Like, how in the heck did she get here? Mrs Nelson has never been to the ranch, and it isn't easy to find. Did the police bring her? But there are no other cars. By the natural way she bears the rifle, she either hunts or used to, which doesn't seem to fit with how she likes people to see her.

Mrs Nelson looks surprised to see me and then her face reconfigures.

'Rachel!' she says. 'You need to get back. There's a fire in the ranch.'

I'm trying to take it all in.

'Are you OK?' I manage, staring at the Winchester in the crook of her arm. 'What happened? Where's Tina?'

She half runs and her face crumples. It's such an unexpected expression, I almost take a step backwards. Loud crackling has started up now. The wooden walls of the ranch are catching alight.

'Thank the Lord I made it out in time.' She raises her eyes to the heavens and staggers toward me. Her hard eyes fill with tears. 'Tina had me drive her out here,' she says, her eyes darting around in terror. 'She needed a ride and I couldn't refuse, even though I never wanted to see . . .' her voice breaks. 'I didn't want to come here,' she concludes. 'The place where my boy was murdered.'

She takes a juddering breath, collecting herself, then sees me cast another anxious glance at the Winchester rifle, rested easily at her side.

'Tina had me bring the gun,' she explains, to the unasked question. 'She said wild dogs might have gotten inside, since the house was left unattended.'

This seems incredibly unlikely. I look over her shoulder at the burning ranch.

'Where is Tina now?' I ask.

Panic seizes her features. 'Tina *attacked* me, tried to trap me and burn me in there.' She swallows, fear rippling her face. 'She must be nearby still, we need to get away from here, go to the police.'

I let her pull me away from the burning ranch. A horrible uncertainty is coursing through me. Like someone's pulled the rug out from under my feet. It feels exactly like when I first left home. When I stepped onto that asphalt road, waiting for lightning to strike me down.

Discovering everything you once knew is a lie. There's nothing quite like it. It never quite leaves you.

'I think Tina may be on drugs,' I explain. 'She needs help.'

Adelaide's voice is thick and tear-choked. 'She told me she meant to burn you in the barn too. We need to get away from here, *now*.'

Her features jerk around with emotion, but there's something not quite convincing about it. Like a puppet show.

'There's two of us,' I say, 'Tina is unarmed. We need to be certain she hasn't overdosed or tried to hurt herself. It's the desert. She could dehydrate or get cold pretty quick without shelter.'

Mrs Nelson's face reworks itself from panic into a warm smile. She puts out a hand.

'Sometimes things like this bring families together,' she says. 'Make you realize who the important people are. I know we haven't always gotten along. I know I blamed you for Blake's death. I was wrong.' Her palm closes on mine, warm, assuring. Both of us hold rifles in our free hands; mine gripped in sweaty fingers, hers easy, like an extension of her body. She smiles at me. 'If it took his passing to make us true friends, then that's God's work. We're family. For eternity.'

I've waited seven years to hear Mrs Nelson confirm this fact. Now she's saying it, the words sound somehow hollow. I should feel elated.

'You know, Rachel, there's a polygamous community out toward Texas,' she adds. 'Good people, by all accounts. I've got some relatives there. I'm sure you'd be a welcome wife to some nice family. So long as you worked hard, and did what your husband told you, this whole business would be forgotten in a few years. And you'd have children to care for.'

The ranch blazes and spits behind us. Smoke rolls out in great waves.

'I already have a family, Adelaide,' I say. 'It just looks a little different to how other folk might imagine.'

I catch a flash of it then. The Mrs Nelson I remember. Icy steel under the lacy glove.

'Rachel, Tina is a killer. I can't let you put your life at risk.' Her grip on me tightens. The muzzle of her Winchester rifle twitches, just a little. 'Drive with me to town. We'll call the police.'

'No.' I wrench my arm away. 'I can't leave Tina. I don't think she would hurt me intentionally.'

Suddenly the door of the house busts open. Tina rolls free into the sandy earth. She's crawling, dragging her leg behind her.

'Rachel!' She looks up at me.

I meet her eyes, swallowing. Doubt coils sudden fingers around me. There's a desperate look on Tina's face as she inches closer to us.

'She seduced Braxton,' says Mrs Nelson, 'at the funeral. She put all our immortal souls in danger.'

I don't want to believe it. But I remember Tina went into that back room with Braxton. They were both missing when I was arrested.

I look in Tina's face and know instantly it's true. My heart goes into free-fall.

Everyone you trust will let you down. Outsiders. Gentiles.

Tina drags herself nearer. I let my rifle fall, pointing it in her direction.

'Stop,' I say. 'Tina – stop.'

'She is an *evil* person,' says Mrs Nelson. 'Come with me, Rachel. Come back to God's light.'

'Rayne,' says Tina, 'do you love me?' It comes out as a rasp.

'What?' It's such a strange question, I don't know how to react. My gun is pointed at Tina. Something about Mrs Nelson's proximity is making it hard to think straight.

'You can't *trust* her,' says Mrs Nelson.

'How *can* I trust you?' I ask Tina, tears in my eyes. 'You tell lies.'

Tina coughs. 'I didn't ask if you trusted me,' she manages. 'I asked if you loved me. If you do, Rayne, if you do, pull the trigger.'

Her eyes are on mine, a determined steady gaze.

'Pull the trigger,' she says.

I look into her face, a sob shaking me. I don't know what to do. Mrs Nelson lurches at my rifle.

'Do it!' shouts Tina. 'Now!'

All I can do is have faith. I squeeze my finger tight.

106

Rachel Nelson

The gun blast echoes around the mountains, causing birds to take flight. Tina is thrown back toward the ranch. I drop the gun, my hands flying to my mouth, horrified.

What did I do?

'What have you done?' demands Mrs Nelson.

'I thought she had some plan,' I whisper. 'I didn't . . .'

'Blood atonement,' says Mrs Nelson. 'She wanted to atone for her sins. Get to where Blake was.'

I don't think Tina would hold a lot of faith in blood atonement, but I guess Mrs Nelson imagines everyone thinks like she does. Her eyes land on mind, and there's a whirling fury behind them.

I need to get to Tina. She's not moving. Her body is a broken mess. The ranch burns behind her.

'You've ruined *everything*,' says Mrs Nelson. 'All my good work with Blake.'

Her tongue snakes out and licks her dry lips.

That's when it dawns on me.

Oh my God. She killed Blake.

'You're my child too, Rachel,' she whispers. 'I see that now. I've been blind. God didn't want me to take the easy path.'

Blake's hunting rifle lies useless on the ground, ammunition spent.

Mrs Nelson raises her Winchester, pointing it at me. I set my jaw, readying myself for the impact.

There's a noise like dripping water, and from nowhere comes Emily, soaked to the skin, lunging at Mrs Nelson. I'm so surprised, I step back. By the time I've made sense of what in the heck is happening, I see Mrs Nelson slam tiny Emily with the butt of the rifle, smashing her onto the sandy ground. Mrs Nelson levels the rifle at me again. My eyes move to Emily, lying in the dirt coughing, blood pouring from her mouth.

'Don't be afraid, Rachel,' she says. 'It's a mother's task, to punish her children. This will soon be over.' She swings the gun down to Emily and takes aim.

'You get away from her!' I don't think about anything other than saving Emily. And since the only way is to put myself between Mrs Nelson and my injured sister-wife, that's what I do.

Mrs Nelson's eyes flash up to my face, filled with rage. Her gun is pointed square at my heart now, her finger tightening on the trigger. Emily's eyes widen in amazement. Guess she didn't realize how much I cared for her until this moment. Funny how life is.

That's when I see Blake's hunting rifle slide across the dirt of its own accord, passing in between Mrs Nelson's legs, then stopping.

Her eyes track down confused, and then the long muzzle jerks up hard, slamming her in the groin.

Mrs Nelson folds forward, gasping in pain. Suddenly there is Tina, standing behind her, both hands on the rifle like she's taken an upwards golfing stroke.

Mrs Nelson looks back over her shoulder, still doubled up from the low blow.

'How did you . . .?' she manages.

'You know what they say, Mrs Nelson,' says Tina, leaning awkwardly to one side. 'Good girls go to heaven. Bad girls go everywhere.'

She swings the butt of the gun, making an eye-watering crack as it connects with the base of Adelaide's jaw. Mrs Nelson goes down, hitting the desert floor hard. She's out cold.

'Not to mention, Vegas girls fight dirty,' concludes Tina with satisfaction. Her eyes lift to mine, then drop to Emily. 'You both OK?'

'Just a busted lip,' says Emily, cheerily, sitting up and examining the blood in her hand.

'Tina, are *you* OK?' I'm staring at her, wondering whether to believe my eyes. 'You could barely walk back there.'

I lean down to pull Emily up out of the dirt.

'Yeah well,' says Tina, 'I wanted Mrs Nelson to think I'd broke a leg. You learn pretty quick how to play dead and dyin' when you're workin' the strip in Vegas,' shrugs Tina. 'It's more like a sprain.'

Emily stands. 'Thanks,' she says, wiping blood from her face and staring wide-eyed at Tina. 'I saw Rachel shoot you.'

She lowers her voice.

'Did God stop the bullets?'

Tina laughs. 'Nah. I tampered with Blake's gun back in Vegas. Put in blank bullets. Makes a loud bang, but that's about it.'

'You didn't trust me?' I manage.

'Let's just say I'm not a *moron*. I mean,' she rolls her eyes, 'who goes on a road trip with a *murder suspect* and a loaded weapon?' She peers at Mrs Nelson, unconscious in the dust. 'Lucky I swapped the bullets out though, right?' she adds. 'I figured if Mrs Nelson thought you'd actually shot me, she'd freak out. Give me a chance to sneak up.' She frowns, sweeping hair from her face. 'Kinda surprised it worked,' she admits. 'Didn't think you had it in you.' She pauses, wrinkling her nose. 'You know you stink of vinegar?'

'Pickle brine,' I tell her.

That's when I hear sirens on the horizon.

'I found Aunt Meg,' I tell Tina. 'Or didn't find her. She died. Years ago.' Suddenly it feels as though my heart is breaking. Tears rise up and won't stop. 'I think . . .' I sob, 'I think she was killing babies that weren't born right, but she never got caught.' My chest is heaving. I let my eyes settle on the copper mountains in the distance. 'I don't know . . . I mean, how can there be a God when such awful stuff happens?'

Tina slings an arm around my and Emily's shoulders, pulling us close enough to hurt.

'Of course there's a *God*,' she smiles. 'Else how could you love a couple a freak shows like us?'

107

Five months later

Rachel Ambrosine-Nelson

Turns out, I had it wrong. We were the right wives, with the wrong husband. So, we're going to make it work, Tina, and Emily and I. Marriage is all about communication. Keeping the lines open. We've all talked about that a lot. It's important if you're gonna help other women.

We got the keys to the Homestead gates last month, and boy, you wouldn't recognize the old place since we got to work. It looks *completely* different.

When the three of us first stepped into that deserted compound, I wasn't sure we'd done the right thing. Tina worked actual *miracles* with the state. I mean, I don't even know how she brokered it so quickly, given everything was in Blake's name and had to go through some complicated probate law. I think she pulled the grieving widows card. But the reality of actually owning such a big place only really hit us when we arrived. Then Emily starts *running* through all the rooms, shouting, clapping her hands, singing crazy songs. She said it was all about moving out the bad energy. Wouldn't stop acting the clown until Tina and I were folded over, crying with laughter. Honestly, Emily is an absolute *riot*. Guess she never let that side of herself out before.

She got community service, on account of wasting police time with her confession. By rights, she should have been charged with hiding the murder weapon too, but I've kind of kept that quiet for her. I've learned it's not always so important to follow rules to the letter. Sometimes you can make your own interpretations. Emily found Blake's body early that morning and thought she was covering for me. I've told her since, she should have credited me with more intelligence than to leave my own gardening axe at the scene. In any case, community service has really been the making of Emily. It's given her a confidence she never had before.

I suppose you could call us a refuge now. We thought we had a lot of rooms here, but, shoot, they sure have filled up fast. The best thing is the women. They just get right to work, cleaning and cooking, digging and sorting. As Tina would say, shit just gets done. My folk were bred to it, I suppose, and a lot of people who come here are old Homestead people, sick of life in Waynard's Creek. We get all kinds of women too. Recovering addicts trying to get away from their pimps. Victims of domestic violence. We don't turn anyone away.

I was worried about our reputation, since the media had painted us as husband killers, even after the truth came out. Turns out that was one of the things the women came to us for. They figured if we stood up to our husband, we could teach them how to stand up for themselves.

In any case, we work real good as a team. Tina calls us the three amigos. She takes care of the legal side of things. Making sure our guests are protected. Getting all our paperwork in order. I know a thing or two about construction. Growing up in a badly built house, it seems, teaches you a good deal about how to build things right, so I do a lot of that. Structural things.

I manage our little metal and gem mining business too. Aside from copper, there's topaz here, and a few other pretty stones. Tina was clever with leasing us some equipment to get started, and we get enough out of the ground to make artisan jewelry. Emily found she had a talent for that, and her pieces sell for a pretty penny to city folk down in Salt Lake. She even got wrote up in the *Salt Lake Tribune*, how Emily Martinelli-Nelson makes fairytale things more or less from dirt.

With the sale of extra copper and gemstones, it's enough to give us all a comfortable life. Though we still like to grow and can our own food for the heck of it. Sometimes I run talks up at Brigham Young College too, about our experiences. People seem to like to hear about them.

Emily has ideas about just about everything. But besides jewelry, she is mainly good at cooking. Lately she has been making these spectacular cakes with popping candy, which just put a smile on everyone's face. You need that in a home. Fun. Surprises.

Tina and I are considering the possibility of a husband. Someone who'll fit right in our family. Perhaps a widower, with children already. We've discussed it, and we'd all like to raise children together. Turns out I can have children after all, and Tina is less interested in the pregnancy side of things, so that'll fall to me. Emily isn't interested in marrying again and prefers her independent space. She's happier in a big-sister type role, but she'd like to help out.

In any case, we've a few things to do first. Emily is planning a trip to Italy for us. She's always wanted to learn Italian, and has been attending evening classes, in the city. Tina wants to take us on this crazy road-trip to Vegas. I don't know what in the world might happen, but I've already told her, *no tequila*.

Sometimes I think about Blake. I miss him. Even miss his very certain view on things. The apocalypse, scripture. Now us wives have begun reflecting on ourselves more deeply, I've started to wonder if Blake might have benefitted from some outside help.

The strangest things give me comfort sometimes. Like, I got to thinking, Blake maybe went out to Waynard's Creek, because his conscience was troubling him. Deep down he thought there was something about that graveyard that would help me, if he could find it out. Tina thinks that's crazy. Thinks Blake was covering all his bases, since he likely needed me to sign for the land and I might have refused. Emily isn't sure either way. Guess we'll never know.

Sometimes I go out to the tree where I dug that grave all those years back, and just think about things. People know not to bother me there. It's a little space for myself. Funny thing is, now I *have* that private place, I don't feel so inclined to keep my guard up all the time. It's a slow process, but I'm learning to be more open. Let my wives in more.

What we definitely don't have space for is a husband each. I simply don't know how I would find the time. Looking back to those early days with Blake, all in one another's pocket, it's too much responsibility for one woman. Better to share the load.

It might need a little time for a new husband to fit into our arrangement, but we can train him up. They say a plural marriage is like a wheel. The more spokes you have, the stronger it is, but when you add a new spoke, it takes a while for the wheel to get its groove back.

Well, we've got our groove now, and like Tina says, people better get outta our way.

108

Emily Martinelli–Nelson

It's crazy to think about it now. I said I thought it would make a real good movie and we should contact producers, but I don't think Rachel or Tina took me seriously.

I told Tina about Aunt Meg. What Carlson and Brewer found out. 'Turns out a lot of birth-defect babies were born on the Homestead,' I told her. 'Like, far more than usual. Inbreeding. People who couldn't cope with caring for a badly disabled baby would hand 'em over to Aunt Meg. At that point, those children disappeared from any records.'

Tina had started picking at her nail varnish. 'Rachel said there were at least twenty graves in that cemetery with no names or dates,' she said.

'It's possible Aunt Meg thought she was doing them a kindness,' I pointed out. 'Putting them out of their misery. The birth problems were pretty bad, they likely would have died very young. Maybe Aunt Meg thought she was sending them straight to heaven. Thought that had to be better than living not able to breathe or swallow right.'

We were both real quiet then. I guess it was dawning on us. What actually happened.

'Think they can prove anything?' I asked Tina. By this point, Carlson had managed to find the coroner's report showing

Margaret Ambrosine drowned almost eight years ago. Her car washed all the way downriver and wound up in Arizona. Aunt Meg has been dead a long, long time.

'Maybe they can prove something,' said Tina. 'Maybe not.' Then she told me how Rachel had miscarried in her early teens. That she'd secretly buried the remains and carried a fear she'd broken the law somehow. 'That's the problem with keeping things all to yourself,' Tina had said, shaking her head. 'If Rachel had just told someone outside her loony cult, we coulda let her know. There's no *law* against burying an early miscarriage.'

Soon after that, Rachel took me for a long drive in the car. Told me she had something important to say.

First off she was humming and hawing 'bout what happened with Mrs Nelson. Rachel explained to me how the police had missed Blake's fingers in that jar, 'cause Blake's mom hadn't done the canning process right.

'After she killed Blake, Mrs Nelson must have snuck into my storehouse whilst we were sleeping,' said Rachel. 'Thought she was awful smart, since canning would destroy any DNA she might have left and whatnot, and the evidence would make me the obvious suspect. But if you don't get the seal properly clean, the contents spoil,' Rachel continued, sounding, if I'm honest, more pleased about Mrs Nelson's second-rate canning abilities than was strictly appropriate. 'You get a cloudy brine. Can't see what's in your jar. Eventually the sediment will settle back down, but I guess that hadn't happened when the police searched the ranch. Canning is a little bit of an art form. Not everyone gets along with it.'

She sort of smiled to herself at that. I decided Rachel should be allowed this housekeeping victory over Mrs Nelson after all she's been through.

After telling me all this, Rachel looked real serious, and I figured we were getting to the reason she'd driven us out together.

'You know what,' she frowned. Not a Rachel frown, where she tries to stop her face crinkling halfway through. A proper honest-to-goodness brow-furrow I had never seen on her before. 'I'm sorry. I'm really sorry.'

No 'with God's forgiveness', nothing like that. Just a plain old apology. I hadn't realized Rachel had it in her. I smiled.

She looked across at me from the driver's seat, still frowning. 'I kinda tricked you. I mean, when you first came for that family dinner, with us, I kinda put on a show, pretended everything was great. Truth was, I wasn't ready to share my husband at that point.'

'Don't feel bad,' I say. 'You loved Blake. You wanted to get him what he wanted.'

She pauses.

'It wasn't just that. I really wanted you to join the family.'

'You did?'

'Sure. I mean. Sister-wives, right? What could be greater? And you seemed so *sweet*, and . . . sorta *artistic*. I really admired it.'

'You did?' I was straight amazed to hear that.

She took a big breath, let it out.

'It was much better, with you there,' she concluded. 'Even though we didn't get along so good, it was better. But I should have told you. I should have told you that Blake had some control issues, and debts. That I have a certain way I like to run a household. Can you forgive me?'

'Well sure I do.' I smiled at her. 'On the one condition we go get some ice cream.'

'I know just the place,' she said, 'on Brigham Young Campus. The peanut butter cup is the best thing you'll ever taste. We'll bring a quart tub back for Tina.'

Over ice cream, Rachel told me some things about Blake I'd

never heard her say before. How when they first got married he hadn't been so uptight about becoming self-sufficient and preparing for the end. Like something had misfired in his brain. I don't know if Rachel's right about that. Maybe she was a little bit right. Mainly, I think the stress of three wives just wore him down. Those days he kinda moped around, or laid on the couch not moving, I think it was plain old guilt. Like he'd persuaded us all into this marriage and then couldn't really deliver his side of the bargain. He'd get all riled up, with some crackpot scheme to try and fix things, then just fail all over again. Catholics understand a thing or two about guilt, so I know what I'm talking about.

As we bought more ice cream packed up to go, Rachel told me about the plan to buy the Homestead.

'We can turn it into a sanctuary,' she said. 'A lot of women who fled the Homestead are still locked into abusive marriages, no way out. They got no social security, no ID, no fixed address. Can't earn money, and have to rely on their husbands. We can give them a fresh start. A place to be themselves.'

I told her I liked that idea a lot.

Not long after that, Officer Brewer came by to supervise my community project, and confirmed Rachel had a special claim to the land – some loophole in native land law that made her a settler and entitled to buy it from the state at cost – less than half market price. Also, for compassionate reasons, Vegas Real Estate wouldn't be claiming back the money they loaned to Blake, which left us more or less enough to buy the Homestead outright. I didn't really understand all the details. Between you and me, I think Brewer and Carlson pulled a few strings.

Officer Brewer also filled me in on what happened to Mrs Nelson, after she was dragged away spitting blood and swearing vengeance.

'They're still deciding if she's fit to stand trial,' Brewer told me. 'I don't know if they'll get any sense out of her. They got her in a psych ward out of state. She started out ranting and shouting about how she was doing God's work, and anyone who stood in her way was goin' to hell. But since Mr Nelson refused to confirm her alibi for the night of the murder, she's more or less shut down.' Brewer shook her head. 'Most likely is they'll consign Adelaide to a psychiatric prison for her own safety.'

'Guess not all moms are nice,' I said.

Brewer got a real sad look in her pretty eyes then.

'Guess not,' she said. 'How are things with Rachel nowadays?'

That took me by surprise. 'They're good,' I told Brewer. 'Things are real good.'

109

Tina Keidis-Nelson

I feel like we've all grown three feet taller. Especially Rachel. She even gives little talks nowadays, up at the university. How the abuse she suffered growing up drew her to a controlling kind of husband. I'm real proud of her, since I know how hard it is for Rachel to be open about these things. Seems to have done her good too, 'cause now she speaks about 'em all the time, she's not carrying 'em on her shoulders any longer, hidin' who she is.

Rachel thinks maybe Blake had some mental problems. Bipolar disorder, even. But that's just Rachel. She always thinks of the nice reason why people do shitty things. Me, I've seen too much bad. You want my opinion, Blake just got carried away with his own power. All these women, fighting over him. It went to his head. Got addictive. He wanted more. I don't think he was all bad though. It's like my mom used to say. You wanna know if someone's a bad person? Don't listen to what they say, don't think about how they make you feel. Look at what they *do*.

So I guess that makes my Blakey both good and bad. Like all of us. Only us wives are all going to try to be better, for one another. Rachel's already on my case. She was the one who made sure we bought the nice Mormon boy a new car, since Mrs Nelson burned out his, and gifted it with a box of Milk Duds as a thank you.

460

We're makin' a life for ourselves out here and it's workin' out real well. Rachel's got me hoeing fields and canning food too, would ya believe? You never hear me admit it out loud, but I kinda like the simple life. Even though the copper mine earns us plenty of money.

I'm carryin' a big crate of corn toward the kitchen, when I see Detective Carlson at the gate. Can't help it, right away I'm smilin'.

'Hey you.' I start unbolting the padlock on the gate.

'Hey yourself.' He kinda does a double take. 'Holy hell,' he says, looking me up and down. 'First time I seen you dressed like a farmer's wife.'

I look down at my shirt. 'This? Ah well, when you're out in the sun all day, you burn unless you cover up.' I put a hand to my hair, tied back, 'And you get sweaty, you know, with your hair loose.'

'Suits you,' says Carlson. 'You look like the girl from that movie about horses.'

He waits as I pull away the last padlock and open the big wire gate.

'What's with Fort Knox?' He helps me drag it back.

'We're waiting on a camera and key-code system to be installed. In the meantime we want these women to feel safe, Detective Carlson.'

He grins at me. 'Ah, you can call me Tate. We're friends now, right?'

'Tate?' I turn the name around in my mind as I pull the gate back. 'OK.'

He takes in the compound. The roadways have been cleared, and the cabin homes repainted and smartened up. Still a lotta work to do, but we're gettin' there.

'We call it Heaven,' I say. "'S a little inside joke. Wanna come see the place?'

His eyes track to the far west, where a police line flutters in the breeze. Diggers came out last month and exhumed the cemetery.

'Sure.' He hesitates. 'I actually came to tell you what we dug up.' He looks devastated for a moment. 'Lot of little bodies in there. Dating back to the seventies even.'

A deep sadness washes through me.

'There's plenty of remains to get through,' he continues. 'But it looks like most of 'em suffered from the same set of genetic disorders. A number have swollen skulls, indicating a condition called hydrocephalus. That's water on the brain, to you and me. Very rare, but I guess when you narrow the gene pool like they did here, rare things become common. They also found evidence of problems with heart valves. A couple of bodies had sorta been mummified in the copper sands, so they were able to identify that.'

'Were they euthanized, do you think?'

He lets out a deep sigh.

'That's gonna be hard to say. There's no trauma to those corpses. No sharp injuries. Cause of death for some could be suffocation.' He pauses. 'However, with water on the brain, convulsions and suffocation as a result of breathing defects is not uncommon.'

His eyes meet mine. He has nice eyes, I think.

'Comes down to we can't say for sure,' he says. 'Those remains are too old. Maybe someone put a pillow over their faces. Maybe they died of natural causes. Whoever is responsible is dead in any case, or in jail for the rest of their life.' He lets out a big sigh. 'Like I told you, there were no happy endings on the Homestead.'

We've reached the main house now. The door is wide open and women are coming in and out of the big door, smiling, talking.

There's a big kitchen out back and cooking smells are wafting free. Nearly time for lunch.

'You sure about that?' I smile at him. 'These women look pretty happy to me. Especially the ones who were raised with Rachel. You know what a lot of those ex-Homestead people say? They say: "There is a hell – I've lived it, now I'm in Heaven."'

Carlson smiles. 'I take your point. I think you're doing a real good thing here. Maybe if we'd have approached things different, change woulda been faster. Gotten people to leave of their own accord, rather than gone in guns blazing. But we did what we did to protect those kids.'

'You did the right thing.' I put a hand on his arm. 'Lot more girls woulda been hurt if you hadn't acted fast.'

Carlson gives a half-smile. 'Thanks. Hey,' he adds. 'I heard Mr Nelson came by.'

'How d'ya hear that?'

He just taps his nose. 'So . . . How much money did he give you?'

I blow out my cheeks, remembering the weird account from Rachel. How Mr Nelson appeared at the gate, all awkward, like a crab out of his shell, and pushed a check into her hands, mumbling something about God's work. Rachel was so busy goggling at the amount it was written out for, she barely had time to yell 'thank you' before Mr Nelson's truck was hightailing it out in a cloud of dust.

'Mr Nelson donated enough money to do a few important things,' I tell Carlson. 'You should stay for lunch,' I add. 'See what we've done with the place. It's real different.'

He shuffles his feet. Sorta peeks up at me. He looks so cute when he does that.

'You know,' he says, rubbing the back of his neck, 'I thought maybe I could take you out to dinner sometime.'

I've been waiting *forever* for him to ask.

'Like a date?' I grin at him.

He looks at the sandy dirt. 'It could be . . . I mean, whatever you're comfortable with.'

'Dinner sounds fun.' I smile at him, then pretend to frown. 'You're not secretly married, are you?'

He grins at me. 'No, Ma'am.'

'How would you feel about a plural situation? One man all to myself is a heavy order right now.'

He holds his hands up in mock surrender. 'Presently I'm only comfortable disappointing one woman at a time.'

I laugh. 'Maybe we'll learn ya.'

Acknowledgements

And so, to the 'thank-you's. Where can I start? Books are absolutely a team effort, and I've been so lucky to have the best team the whole way. My agent and friend Piers Blofeld, who has championed me, defended me, offered great feedback and generally been the agent every writer wants on their side. The whole team at Sheil Land also get my heartfelt thanks.

In the UK, King of Editors Emad Akhtar, who has astounded me with his capacity for hard work, very very good edits, and for being such a cheery and likable individual. Lucy Frederick deserves the same compliment, and I am so very grateful to have incorporated her many excellent ideas into the book.

I've been completely spoiled to have benefitted from not just one set of great editors, but two. In the US, Shana Drehs blew me away with her enthusiasm, reading and offering on the book in twenty-four hours – such a ringing endorsement is what every writer dreams of, so thanks for making that particular wish come true. And, of course, the extra spot-on edits which made the book shine.

On both sides of the pond, eagle-eyed copyeditors Francine Brody in the UK and Diane Dannenfeldt in the US deserve thanks for bringing order to chaos.

Thanks to the lovely, lovely, people at Inflatable Islanders

Bookgroup, who have completely upped my reading game. I didn't really understand about hardcover books before I met you all. And don't get me started on chip-and-dip platters. Particular thanks to Alys Brooker who was the first reader of this book.

Finally to my friends and family. My sister (bestselling author) Susannah Quinn, who is one of those great (and underappreciated) people who always tells the truth, and makes all my books a million times better, in ways I don't foresee. My partner Simon Avery, for being generally awesome and one of my favourite people on the planet, in addition, of course, to my incredible children, Natalie and Ben, who will actually run the planet someday.

Credits

Cate Quinn and Orion Fiction would like to thank everyone at Orion who worked on the publication of *Black Widows* in the UK.

Editorial
Emad Akhtar
Lucy Frederick

Copy editor
Francine Brody

Proof reader
Jade Craddock

Audio
Paul Stark
Amber Bates

Contracts
Anne Goddard
Paul Bulos
Jake Alderson

Design
Rabab Adams
Joanna Ridley
Nick May

Editorial Management
Charlie Panayiotou
Jane Hughes
Alice Davis

Finance
Jasdip Nandra
Afeera Ahmed
Elizabeth Beaumont
Sue Baker

Publicity
Leanne Oliver

Marketing
Katie Moss
Jennifer Hope

Production
Ruth Sharvell

Operations
Jo Jacobs
Sharon Willis
Lisa Pryde
Lucy Brem

Sales
Laura Fletcher
Esther Waters
Victoria Laws
Rachael Hum
Ellie Kyrke-Smith
Frances Doyle
Georgina Cutler

Truth is stranger than fiction

Wondering how much of *Black Widows* is based on fact?
Cate Quinn has written a research history
to accompany the book.

To find out more, go to
www.catherinequinn.com/blackwidows